NEVER GO
TO THE POST OFFICE
ALONE

STELIOS KOULOGLOU

NEVER GO TO THE POST OFFICE ALONE

Translated by
Joshua Barley

AIORA

Joshua Barley is a translator of modern Greek literature and writer. He read Classics at Oxford and modern Greek at King's College, London. His translations of Ilias Venezis' *Serenity* and Makis Tsitas' *God Is My Witness* are published by Aiora Press. *A Greek Ballad*, selected poems of Michális Ganás (translated with David Connolly), is published by Yale University Press.

We are grateful to Nestor Tyrovouzis, Head of Public Diplomacy Office of the Greek Embassy in Moscow, for his help in obtaining permission to reproduce the cover artwork.

Original title: *Μην πας ποτέ μόνος στο Ταχυδρομείο*

© Aiora Press 2021

All rights reserved. No part of this publication may be reproduced, stored in a retrieval system, or transmitted, in any form or by any means, whether electronic, mechanical, photocopying, recording or otherwise, without written permission of the publishers.

ISBN: 978-618-5369-40-8

First edition June 2021

AIORA PRESS
11 Mavromichali St.
Athens 10679, Greece
www.aiorabooks.com

CONTENTS

PART I:
Ticket out of Hell 11

PART II:
Russian Roulette 101

PART III:
Juliet 207

PART IV:
The Red Sketch Pad 285

EPILOGUE 373

Every kind of passionate love acts at the expense of love for the Father of Peoples
>	A. TVARDOVSKY
>	By Right of Memory

Politics is the sworn enemy of love
>	OCTAVIO PAZ
>	The Double Flame: Love and Eroticism

PART ONE

Ticket out of Hell

'I don't need palaces,' says Christina, a young woman, sadly. 'I don't need soft armchairs or paintings. I don't need anything.'

'Why not?'

'I'm a young woman.'

'So what do you need?'

'Don't you know? I'm embarrassed to speak in front of everyone.'

'A man!' interrupts a middle-aged kolkhoz woman. 'It's hard for her to sleep without a living body beside her.'

Alexander Dovzhenko
Poem of the Sea

[Early December 1989, roughly four weeks
after the fall of the Berlin Wall]

'Mr Danaher, would you hand me the video from Red Square?'

I took the tape out of my bag and gave it to Yul Hardman, the head of the FBI team. Of the three agents, only he was asking questions. His two colleagues were silently taking notes—they were about thirty-five or forty. We could have been classmates. It was a matter of hours since I had returned from the Soviet Union and I was still jet-lagged. I insisted that my 'special briefing'—as the interrogation was euphemistically called—should take place in the newspaper's offices in New York, with the big boss Humphrey Weber present. I felt better on my own turf, in the editors' meeting room on the fifteenth floor of the West Broadway building. It was a cloudy day, yet one of the agents pulled down the blinds to make the television image clearer. Hardman motioned to him to put the tape into the video player. It was of the October Revolution Parade. The Soviets follow the old calendar of the Russian Orthodox Church, so the parade took place on 17 November. The images I had shot myself appeared on the screen.

Two men of the guard of honour were goose-stepping in front of the terracotta-coloured facade of

Lenin's Mausoleum, while the megaphones of Red Square played military marches and revolutionary songs. Then the camera turned towards the side where I was, the officials' platform opposite the Mausoleum. Several citizens were holding red flags, waiting for the parade to begin. They had their backs to the empty shop windows of GUM, the great state department store. The next shot was of the platform that had been erected for the occasion. Suit-wearing diplomats and journalists were sitting on its wooden tiers. Erich, seated beside me, now occupied the screen.

The image froze as Hardman took the remote control.

'Is that the child?' he asked me.

I nodded. The video allowed me to think back to those moments, which had taken place over just a few days and had changed my life forever.

Erich had a large red sketch pad on his knees and was engrossed in his drawing. When he realized that the camera was on him, he turned and grinned. Then I began to shoot the first military divisions. Having come from the direction of the river, they were waiting just before St Basil's Cathedral for the signal to march. Erich nudged me and the image wobbled.

A child's voice could be heard: 'Look, Kevin—Gorbachev!'

The camera turned clumsily to the Politburo's podium atop the Mausoleum. Mikhail Gorbachev had appeared alongside his rival, the conservative leader Yegor Ligachyov, as well as the chairman of the KGB, Oleg Yelin, and the whole Soviet leadership. When the rows of missiles and the infantry had passed, the day's unprecedented events began to unfold. For the first time in Soviet history it was permitted for the recently formed independent movements to follow the military forces in the parade. As various unofficial organizations marched past Gorbachev—such as the Committee in Support of Glasnost, i.e. of transparency in public life, and Memorial, an organization for the rehabilitation of victims of Stalinism—many of the demonstrators halted and shouted towards the Politburo, 'Freedom for the Baltic nations!', 'Democracy!', 'Down with Communism!'. Some waved banners seeking free elections and an end to the Communist Party monopoly. The camera wasn't steady; my hands were shaking. I was shooting a historic moment: never before in the Soviet Union, nor in pre-Revolution Russia, had the people dared to question the tsar to his face. The events developed at cinematic pace. As Gorbachev left the podium, conspicuously annoyed, he was heckled by the demonstrators. The whole of the Politburo and the president followed, generating even more heckling. A clamour, fear mixed with surprise, rang through Red Square. Every time I watch the events of that day, it gives me goosebumps.

On the screen Erich was talking to some people at the edge of the platform. They were dressed like Eastern diplomats, with grey suits and old-fashioned ties.

The image froze again.

'Is one of those Müller?'

I pointed to the screen.

'The blond one talking to the child. With the angular face.'

'Was this the first time you saw him?'

'Yes. And I didn't even notice him then.'

Hardman turned to me. He was fifty-something, with a double chin, thinning grey hair and blue feline eyes.

'His face immediately grabs your attention,' he observed, pressing 'play' again.

The special forces of the Ministry of Internal Affairs, stationed close to the Rossiya Hotel, left of St Basil's, began to fan out towards the square. A squadron of mounted police officers made a circling manoeuvre aimed at the demonstrators, who were still chanting slogans. Quickly, however, most of the demonstrators backed off. On the opposite pavement, outside GUM, small groups of people were discussing what had happened. The camera turned back to the platform, which had almost emptied. Then the tape stopped. One of the FBI men got up from his chair and, instead of pulling up the blinds, turned on the lights.

'I want you to describe exactly what happened that day,' Hardman said.

'I had arranged to meet Erich and his mother that morning at nine in Manege Square, just off Red Square. We met outside the Moscow Hotel. A huge black-and-white banner of Lenin was hanging over almost the entire building. He seemed to be looking down disapprovingly on the manoeuvrings of perestroika. Erich was holding a large red sketch pad and wearing a blue anorak and white woolly hat, his mother a grey coat and short brown Soviet-style fur-lined boots. We arranged to meet again at twelve noon in the same place. Before she left she bent down to kiss Erich, who pushed her away impatiently. Then she turned to me and mouthed the words 'I love you'. As we walked towards Red Square, I stroked Erich's head and clasped his neck protectively.

'Do you like drawing?' I said.

"My grandpa gave me this pad,' he answered, without looking up.

'What do you like drawing?'

'My grandpa, my mother…'

'Do you love your mother a lot?'

'I love my grandpa more,' he said curtly.

'We went past the three checkpoints, showing our special permit, and sat among a group of African diplomats on the platform. I wanted to avoid indiscreet questions from any early-rising colleagues of mine, and from the American diplomats, most of whom I knew pretty well. I didn't leave that spot, nor did I speak to anyone. Then I began to shoot what you've just seen.'

'Then?' asked Hardman. His voice was neutral. I couldn't tell if he believed me.

'When I put down the camera and looked around, most of the diplomats and journalists had already left. Only then did I realize that Erich wasn't there. I hurried off the platform and searched for him in the receding crowd. Despite my best efforts I couldn't find him anywhere. As the crowd thinned further, I felt weak at the knees. I wanted the ground to swallow me up. They say there's no greater nightmare than losing your child in a crowd, but that's not true: the worst thing is losing someone else's child, whom they have entrusted to you. It was after twelve noon now and Red Square was empty. Only some elderly street sweepers were left, wearing torn clothes and brightly coloured headscarves sweeping up. I took a deep breath and headed towards the meeting point, hoping that the child had gotten caught up in the commotion and we would find him soon. I can't explain it any other way than to say that he had suddenly disappeared from my side.'

'And you hadn't even suspected the boy's true identity?' asked Hardman. In his voice I detected a whisper of irony. I didn't know if he took me for a liar or a fool.

'They hid it from me. I'm not in the FBI, after all.'

'Well, you'd better tell us everything from the start,' said Hardman, seeking approval in Weber's indifferent gaze.

[Moscow, late October 1989]

It all began about three weeks before the parade, prompted by a piece I wanted to write on the Society for the Development of Soviet–American Human Relations. Their offices were on Kuznetsky Most, opposite Tsum, the department store in central Moscow. The building was an old aristocratic mansion with plaster sculptures on every landing and a mosaic ceiling. When I reached the second floor, one of the young 'pioneers' stopped me.

'Kevin Danaher, American journalist. I have a meeting with Mr Tamurian.'

The boy nodded, as if expecting me. He pointed towards the end of the corridor, where a middle-aged, rather stout woman appeared. She was dragging her feet wearily, like all Soviet women of her age who have worked as public servants. We went into a large oblong hall with a wooden floor. It must have been a ballroom once; now it was a kind of small theatre. At one end was a stage, backed with a cheap mustard-yellow curtain. A handmade poster was pinned onto the curtain and bore the slogan 'Amerikan boi, Amerikan boi, ouyedu s' toboi.' Underneath was the English translation: 'American boy, American boy, I'm coming with you today.' Two metres from the stage began rows of red cinema seats. About a hundred women were sitting there, all made up in the Soviet fashion, with lipstick redder than the flags of the Revolution. Most wore skirts just above the knee; jeans were always hard to find and expensive. Though badly dressed, most of them, true to form, were Russian beauties. The youngest seemed about seventeen; the oldest can't have been more than thirty-five. My guide motioned to me to sit in an empty seat in the last row. I took out a pad and began making notes on the auditions.

Each of the women walked onto the stage in turn and presented herself in broken English. Those who knew a few extra words explained why they wanted to meet an American man and go with him to the US. The others just managed a 'Hello, America!', which sounded ridiculous in a Russian accent. A video camera had been set up in the front row to record the auditions, and a photographer was snapping constantly. I spotted Sergei Tamurian. Nicknamed 'Pioneer' in the Moscow underworld, he is the president of the Society for the Development of Soviet–American Human Relations. Pudgy, with a friendly round face and a gleaming bald head, he was getting on for sixty—but looked about ten years younger—and was always busy. Now and then he interrupted the girls to give directions on their manner and behaviour.

'Many of our customers in America choose their bride before they've even set foot in Moscow, just from the videos and photographs we send them,' he interjected at one point. 'They judge you from your appearance, your clothes, your smile... Let me remind you that most American men have an image of Soviet women as tractor drivers, like those on the Communist propaganda leaflets. Show your femininity!'

The show lasted more than two hours. It was a dress rehearsal, as a dozen prospective husbands were coming to Moscow from the US in a few days. Pioneer was giving endless instructions. He reminded the girls that their conversations with the bachelors—who he called the 'boys'—had to be politically correct.

'I know that most of you are struggling in your daily lives and aren't happy with the Party's politics. But you must keep in mind that in the West they love our general secretary more than we do. Perestroika is one of the first topics the boys will bring up. For God's sake, don't tell them that you don't like Gorbachev or that you're not interested in democratization. No one wants to marry some moustache-less Stalin.'

On one side of the hall I noticed a door leading to a kind of foyer. There was a counter laid out with apple juice from a Georgian sovkhoz and sandwiches with fatty salami. The girls went there once they had made their pitch satisfactorily. They nervously lit cigarettes and dived into the buffet. I followed one of them. She had come with her mother, and caught my attention as she was somewhat inferior to the others: short, with glasses perched on a crooked nose. Considering the merciless capitalist law of supply and demand, she had little chance of finding the man of her dreams.

One of the good things about communism is that it managed to make the Soviets optimistic. Sometime in the early sixties, Khrushchev had predicted that twenty years later communism would surpass capitalism and everyone would be eating off golden spoons. Food would be so plentiful you wouldn't need to buy it—nor bus or metro tickets or tickets for public shows. A whole generation of Soviets grew up believing that it was simply a matter of time before they entered this earthly paradise. But the decades went by without the prophecy coming true, and belief in Marxism's miraculous powers gradually gave way to the supernatural expectation of some imminent miracle. The young woman believed that she would find in the West what had failed to materialize— despite Khrushchev's predictions—in the East. Her mother had come in solidarity; at heart she remained hopeful that God is great and loves all equally. The girl explained to me why she preferred American men to Russians.

'Our men are always drunk. They don't look after their women and they want everything on a plate. But you in America…'

She seemed ready to propose marriage on the spot. Thankfully Pioneer, appearing in the foyer, rescued me from the situation.

'I'm all yours,' he said, extending a hand.

'Is what you're doing a kind of legal prostitution?'

Pioneer looked at me coolly, then turned towards the dome of St Basil's.

We had moved to his suite at the Rossiya Hotel in Red Square, opposite the Kremlin. His driver had been waiting for us outside the Society's building in his white 'Be-Em-Ve', a trademark of the Russian nouveau riche. I sat with Pioneer in the back seat. In the passenger seat was a large neck on legs. We reached the hotel in five minutes and went up to his suite on the top floor. Two more 'gorillas' were guarding the door, revolvers bulging out of their tight jackets. They were typical 'Afghani'—veterans of the Soviet–Afghan War, about thirty years old. Their faces showed no trace of the docility of the rosy-cheeked Soviet citizen beloved of history.

Still looking at the Kremlin, Pioneer pressed a button and one of his men entered the suite. Perhaps I had gone too far with my question on legal prostitution and the interview would be over before it had begun. I had discovered that if a prospective American husband expresses interest in a girl's photo, the Society offers him a ten-day trip to the Soviet Union. For three and a half thousand dollars, the package includes a tour of Moscow and Leningrad, and a guide, translator and personal apartment to boot. For the prospective brides there were almost no costs: they paid fifty roubles (five dollars at black-market rates) to submit their application, accompanied by photographs—or twenty-five roubles if they were under twenty. The Society earned a further three thousand dollars if the match resulted in marriage.

'Tell Alexei to come and bring the statistics,' Pioneer ordered the Afghani.

A moment of awkwardness ensued. Pioneer rapped his fingers irritably on the table between us. I pretended to jot something down. He lit a Marlboro without offering me one.

'Don't try to make me out as a pimp. Our Society offers a social service; we receive thousands of applications every day from all corners of the Soviet Union. Hundreds of mothers call me, begging me to accept their daughters as prospective brides. I have a letter from a forty-year-old divorcee, asking us to find a husband for her or her twenty-year-old daughter. I could show you hundreds of such letters: "I'll marry anyone. White, black, gay, Christian, Jew..." Of course, I can't satisfy them all, but at least I provide hope. And, for those who find a husband, a ticket out of hell. A way out, mind, not a ticket to paradise.'

A lanky Russian walked into the suite without knocking. He was about forty and held a black folder.

'May I introduce you to Alexei Kariokin, my business partner,' said Pioneer. 'He manages the Society's database. Every prospective young woman completes a detailed questionnaire. At any moment we can meet the demands of even our most whimsical American client. Alexei is also a nuclear physicist. He works in a research institute outside Moscow.'

The cultivated and soft-spoken Kariokin, therefore, did the same as every self-respecting Soviet: he had another job alongside his role as a scientist.

'If only I could focus my energies on nuclear physics,' he lamented. 'But you can't get by on twenty dollars a month. I imagine you know our saying: "They pretend to pay us and we pretend to work."'

'I know another one: "How does a Soviet citizen live on a hundred and fifty roubles a month?" There's no answer, because you literally cannot live on so little!'

They exchanged glances, as if saying, 'This feller isn't entirely ignorant.' I'd scored a point.

Alexei added with pride, 'When we started our Society two years ago—in 1987, with the leniency of perestroika—we saved the data on the computer at the Institute of Nuclear Physics. Now we've bought two machines of our own.'

Pioneer took the folder impatiently from Kariokin and flicked through it.

'I'm sure you know the Literaturnaya Gazeta. It's one of the most highly regarded Soviet newspapers. It recently organized a poll of high-school girls: sixty-five per cent said they would become prostitutes just to be paid in foreign currency. Of course, I would prefer everyone to get married for love, but under these conditions we provide the most honourable solution. Do you know what the authorities did? They didn't allow the research to be published, so as not to fuel anti-communist propaganda.'

He pushed the papers towards me, as if giving them to me, but then pulled them back.

'There's another study that has riled the Politburo,' he continued, looking through the file. 'It was done a few months ago for Moskofskij Komsomolets, the paper of the Communist Youth. The question was which professions were considered to be prestigious by school girls. Prostitution ranked ninth, behind various professions dealing with travel and contact with the West: air hostess, guide, official translator etc. Needless to say, journalism ranked behind prostitution,' Pioneer jibed, handing me the file.

I reached out to take it.

'Perhaps they're right, in a way.'

Pioneer grinned. I think he had warmed to me.

'One more question. Is it true that you're called Pioneer because you started the illegal mafia activity in Moscow?'

This time Sergei Tamurian really was irked. He got up and paced the room, then pointed at the Kremlin.

'That's where you'll find the real mafia of this country. Lenin is its founder, not me. Do you want to know what I do?'

'That's why I'm here.'

'I thought you were interested in the Society for the Development of Soviet–American Human Relations, but no matter. I started in the clothes business. Moscow didn't make coats, so I struck an agreement with a state factory in Kazakhstan. They sent me the coats and I sold them to shops here. What do you call that in your country?'

'Trade.'

'That's what it's called everywhere, apart from here, where trade is forbidden. The official plan set out that one million coats would be produced every year here— so the bureaucrats of Moscow had decided, even though we needed ten million. The same happened with potatoes, meat, almost all products; people traded to cover the deficit. All these activities, which are considered normal in other countries, are here classed as mafia dealings by the official propaganda.

He turned to the table, took another Marlboro and lit it, agitated. He made to sit down but changed his mind.

'And the maddening thing is that if you want to do anything business related, you have to pay the party mafia. No truck of ours comes into Moscow without paying off an army of corrupt officials. I had to grease the palms of party officers, heads of businesses and shops, the party secretary of Kazakhstan, the chief of the railways, the sergeant-at-arms of Moscow. When my business grew, I ended up with one hundred and sixty people on my payroll. I paid them like employees, every month. Most were Party or government officials.'

He paused for a moment, before adding, 'Do you want me to tell you something else? But don't be afraid. Write it down.'

It was my turn to smile.

'There were many on my payroll who now claim to have inspired perestroika.'

My next question would later give me considerable cause for regret.

'Like who?'

Pioneer exchanged a glance with his partner, who remained expressionless, then forcefully stubbed out his cigarette in the ashtray, as if he were squashing someone.

'Like Oleg Yelin, the chairman of the KGB. He controls the operation. Gorbachev really does believe in the reforms, but is desperately alone. The mafia still governs the Kremlin.'

We both instinctively looked out of the window at the red star high up on the wall of the Kremlin. I had found out much more than I expected.

Shaking his hand, I said, 'You didn't tell me why they call you Pioneer.'

'Next time', Tamurian replied. 'These days I'm spending my evenings at the new casino, in the Leningradsky Hotel. Have you written about the first casino in the history of the USSR?'

'With all these developments, I don't know where to begin. It's not a bad idea, though.'

'Come for a drink sometime. And if you ever need help, let me know.'

He assumed the manner of someone who has the whole world in his pocket. As I left the suite, it didn't cross my mind that I would need Pioneer's help—and very soon.

In some ways I was also a victim of the fall of the Soviet Empire. From early 1989 there was a growing lack of essential items, the mines stopped working all summer because of the first official strike in Soviet history, and the Communist Party and Komsomol had major internal problems. In the summer, Poland swore in a prime minister who was adviser to the anti-communist Solidarity union, and there was turmoil—protests and revolts—in all the 'sister' countries. In the autumn, even the bribery system seemed to be faltering. Despite my secretary Natasha's promises of a sizeable fifty-dollar kickback, the employees of the telephone company insisted that they couldn't fix our newspaper's international line for at least two days.

To call abroad from the Soviet Union, you usually need to go through a switchboard, which can take twenty-four hours. Just a few months ago we were granted a direct international line. We connected a fax machine to it too. But the line had gone dead and I couldn't send my article on the interview with Pioneer and the surveys of schoolgirls.

'What was that saying you told me?' I called to Natasha, who was at her desk in the room next door. 'That in the Soviet Union, only cars run on petrol—everything else works on a greased palm. Well, it seems even that state of affairs is over. Nothing works in this country anymore.'

Fortunately—or unfortunately—we could still receive calls on the old line. I picked up the receiver and heard the grumbling voice of Bruce Whitesmith, editor-in-chief of the Sunday edition.

'It's Friday morning and I still haven't received Sunday's topic. You'll appreciate that we've had to move it to next week.'

'Are you mad? What if someone else publishes it? Do you realize what we have in our hands? That sixty-five per cent of schoolgirls say they would become currency prostitutes! It's a shattering revelation of the crisis in the Soviet—'

'... and I have to hand in sixty-five per cent of Sunday's material by six o'clock this evening. If I don't, it'll be a shattering revelation of the crisis in our newspaper, since we won't be able to publish it. But with all the demand for wives among Western men, where's the time for informing American public opinion?!'

Whitesmith was in a good mood; he didn't even let me explain.

'Next week I'd like you to write a piece on how a Westerner feels now about the mess of real socialism; just a few years ago, instead of studying he was pontificating in lecture halls on its wonders and wanted to make the United States a Soviet country.'

I was never in favour of Soviet socialism, but Bruce considered all those who took part in the American student movement of the early seventies to be paid Russian agents. I considered his politics to be slightly left of Genghis Khan.

'If we had won, you would now be editor-in-chief of a newspaper in a gulag,' I joked. 'Incidentally, I don't see myself staying here forever. When is another position opening up?'

Moscow was my first posting as a reporter, though I had previously been sent on short-term assignments to Vietnam and Eastern Europe. I had entered journalism ten years before, covering the Nicaraguan revolution for a left-wing American paper, a point that Whitesmith couldn't easily forgive.

'So instead of the capital of the global revolution, you'd prefer to live in some capitalist hellhole—New York, Paris, Milan…?'

'Here I identify entirely with the average Soviet citizen. I've been here since 1985; I arrived on the scene at pretty much the same time as Mikhail Sergeyevich Gorbachev. I've almost seen out the current five-year plan for constructing socialism in the USSR, even though I think it may well be the last. I want to see how the perestroika experiment pans out, then go to the West like everyone else. We used to want to change the world; now we just want to move to the other world!'

'That sounds like a good headline,' said Whitesmith. 'But back to business. When will I have Sunday's article?'

'It's ready, but the fax is down. I could send it from a colleague's office, but the information I have on the surveys of the girls is a scoop, never mind the stuff on Oleg Yelin, head of the KGB and member of the Politburo—'

'Is there no other public service with a fax?'

'At the Central Post Office.'

Like most people in the West, my editor-in-chief didn't understand the concept of a Soviet public service.

'Great. Send it from there. It'll be a chance to see how the average citizen is treated. Didn't you lefties say that we shouldn't cut ourselves off from the people?'

I was minded to make some jibe about the Ku Klux Klan, but in the end I just promised to send the article in the next few hours and put down the phone. Natasha could have gone, but I was in the mood for a walk in the centre of Moscow. I went to the next room and said, 'I'm heading to the Central Post Office on Gorky Street to send the fax. Or do you want to go?'

Natasha looked lovingly at the Swedish furniture: our office had been refurbished a few weeks before. There were new carpets and modern, grey office furniture, bookcases and filing cabinets in white Formica, a sofa of black synthetic leather, computers, a fax machine, two video players to record news from the major channels, new telephones and grey metal blinds.

It was a stark contrast to the rest of the grubby block on Taganka Square that housed our offices.

She pointed to the furniture.

'Since the refurbishment I don't want to set foot outside.'

She was the most beautiful woman I had seen in all my time in Moscow. She had very pale skin, large and narrow green eyes and long dark hair. At first she annoyed me by jumping the enormous line and going straight to the counter for the fax service. She said something forcefully, practically shaking her fist at the rosy-cheeked woman at the counter. I couldn't hear what she said as I was in the middle of the line. In front and behind me were low-ranking Russian employees of Western companies that had recently set up in the Soviet Union. I could just glimpse her long legs and aristocratic presence, not lessened in the slightest by her cheap clothing—a long grey trench coat with a khaki knee-length dress underneath.

The Central Post Office is a grey-yellow Stalinist building at the end of Maxim Gorky Street, just off Red Square. The ground floor is a great hall with cheaply painted wooden booths. In front of each of these, one of which is the newfangled fax service, was an endless line of patient citizens. At the back of the hall is a bust of Lenin, with a quote on its pedestal: 'Socialism without telecommunications is an empty word—Vladimir Ilyich Lenin'.

I observed the heated discussion. Then she gave a document to the clerk, who looked at it indifferently and began talking on the telephone. When my turn came after about twenty minutes, I felt a kind of revenge: the impatient, beautiful woman was still waiting. To this day I can't remember if I initiated conversation, or if she began the hostilities. As I reached the counter, I remember her piercing me with that look which, as I found out later, no man can withstand. She was even more beautiful up close; her thick eyebrows almost met in the middle, giving her face a wild, exotic look. From the small wrinkles around her eyes, I guessed she was about thirty.

The clerk was telling her that it was impossible to send the fax to East Berlin, but she insisted it was urgent. Later she would emerge as the most persistent, obstinate person I had ever met. I gave my article to the clerk and turned towards her with a smile, which she immediately reciprocated.

'Are you from East Germany?'

'Yes ... but I've become used to living in this country. And you? Italian?'

'American.'

'And what are you doing in Moscow? Business?'

'I'm a correspondent for a New York newspaper.'

Only then did I twig the usefulness of these socialist lines: you meet people.

'You seem to be in quite a rush to send your fax. You jumped the line.'

'It was rude, yes, but it's an urgent matter.'

She smiled wickedly, like someone who decides to tell you a secret because you inspire their trust.

'I'm in a lawsuit with my country's authorities.'

'With the communist party?'

She glanced around, as if to be sure no one was listening.

'If you're looking for a scoop, don't waste your time. I study movie directing in Moscow and I'm shooting a short film; I need to, for my degree. The East German Ministry of Culture had promised to fund it; we even signed a contract. Now they say they can't, because of the political situation. I'm trying to get in touch, but there are problems with the telephone lines—whether in Moscow or Berlin, no one knows.'

I pointed to the slogan at the back of the hall.

'As Lenin says, socialism without telecommunications…'

She laughed heartily.

'What's your name?'

'Marlene. Marlene Hoppe.'

A few awkward seconds intervened. I had to find something to continue the conversation. She seemed to be thinking the same. I got there first: 'Do you think Erich Bauer will fall? There are protests all over East Germany.'

She laughed.

'That's the first time I've been asked that in the line!'

I felt like an amateur. It was true: the only thing that wasn't discussed in these lines was the political situation.

'Aren't you interested in politics?'

She assumed an air of mystery.

'Only in as much as it affects the funding of my film.'

At some point the fax clerk woke from her lethargy, got off her chair and shouted at those in the line, 'Comrades, pereriv! We will continue after three o'clock.'

She threw our documents in our faces and slammed the window of the booth. It was precisely two o'clock—time for a pereriv, a break. From two to three, all work in the USSR stopped. I imagine that even missile launches are not programmed for that time. It's the only government measure that was implemented with complete success in the Soviet Union.

When she looked at her watch I noticed her long and slender hands.

'I have to go to Mosfilm to edit the pilot of my film. There's a fax machine at the studio—shall we try to send our documents from there?'

It was a rare sunny day in Moscow. We left the Central Post Office and went towards my car. She was becoming less formal.

'What do you want to send?'

'A report on a secret survey: sixty-five per cent of girls in the Soviet Union dream of becoming currency prostitutes.'

'Only sixty-five per cent?' she asked archly.

'Just a moment,' Hardman said. 'Before you continue, I want you to remember if it was you or her that initiated the conversation.'

'I'm racking my brains. I just can't remember. Is it relevant?'

'Everything's relevant,' Hardman replied. 'Continue.'

We arrived at the buildings of Mosfilm, the state movie company, at around two thirty. The guard asked for my entrance pass and didn't let me in. Moscow's studios, as well as all of its public services, institutes, universities and libraries are like the headquarters of the KGB: no one goes in without a special permit. Marlene tried without success to make the guard turn a blind eye.

She turned to me. 'I'll try to send your document too. Wait here.'

She practically grabbed the pages out of my hands and went inside. I looked idly at two girls of about eighteen, who were sitting on a bench outside the entrance to Mosfilm waiting for the bus or perhaps their favourite actor. I asked the guard if I could use the telephone in the porter's lodge to call my office. She had no objection; there was no rule against it. I was reflecting that the Soviets are fundamentally good people brought down by the system when I heard Natasha's voice at the other end of the line.

'Kevin, thank God you called. Fabio is back; we just spoke on the telephone.'

Fabio Ceruti, correspondent for the Corriere della Sera, is one of my best friends in Moscow, the only one I could trust to send a fax from his office without fear of him intercepting the story. But he had been away with his secretary on a trip to Lithuania and, though he had another secretary, with her boss away she had gone out shopping that morning and closed the office.

'I may not have to go to the Corriere office. Someone is trying to send the document for me. I'm not with them so I don't know if it's gone.'

'You mean you gave your article, with all that information in, to someone else?!'

I reassured her. Marlene appeared shortly afterwards, smiling broadly.

'The office with the fax machine in is locked, and the man with the keys won't be here until tomorrow.'

'Don't worry; I've found a fax machine. Let's go there.'

'I can't. I must do the editing. If I miss my turn I'll have to wait another two months.'

It was the perfect opportunity to get her to call me.

'OK, give me your document and I'll send it. Call me later.'

She hesitated, muttering something about my 'precious time'. I told her that the office secretary would handle it. We arranged for her to call me in the evening, after the editing. An hour later I was waxing lyrical about the post office to Fabio, when his secretary Elena came into the office to say that the documents had been sent to New York and East Berlin without any trouble. Elena, who knew both German and our personal lives, had a mischievous look on her face.

'The girl you met works in film, eh?'

'Elena, you could be a reporter. Why don't you leave the Italians and come and work for an American paper? I'll pay you more.'

'The fax was about actors and movies,' she explained.

'You shouldn't read other people's faxes,' Fabio said, with mock severity.

Hardman interrupted me with a sweeping gesture.

'Didn't you even look once at the fax?'

'It didn't cross my mind. Anyway, I don't speak a word of German.'

He exchanged a glance with Weber and gestured for me to continue.

'Can I light a cigarette?' I asked, searching in my pockets.

'I thought that smoking was forbidden in your offices,' Hardman said to Weber.

'Almost everyone has given up, but this guy isn't like the others,' the boss said, shaking his head sadly. 'He was born in Ireland, you know. They're hotter-headed there, I reckon. But what's inside the head… Well, I'd better not comment. Before he went to Moscow, I was set to make him political editor of the paper, a position that any journalist would die for. But he was desperate to go to the Soviet Union. It's like I knew he would destroy his career. Well, let him destroy his health too, if that's what he wants.'

I took a long drag and carried on telling the agents my woes.

Two days later I was waiting for her at 9 p.m. at the entrance to the compound on Kutuzovsky Prospekt. My house is—and I'm saying 'is' because I still think of myself as a legal resident of Moscow, despite my recent troubles with the Soviet Union—in the best compound of the Soviet capital. It resembles the large complexes of prefabricated apartment blocks that serve as low-rent homes in the West, but in Moscow are considered luxurious. It is surrounded by walls and high barbed wire. The apartment blocks are built on three sides of a rectangular parking lot. Its entrance, like those of all the compounds, is guarded by special forces from the KGB and access is permitted only to foreigners with residence permits, diplomats, journalists and business people. Lowly Soviet mortals must be accompanied by Westerners unless equipped with special permits. Officially, all of these measures are for our protection, but you don't need to be Sherlock Holmes to realize that the system impedes contact between 'innocent' Soviet citizens and Westerners 'contaminated' by capitalist ideas.

I developed a giving relationship based on alcohol with most of the KGB 'boys' who guarded the entrance. They like me or, rather, they like the fact that there's always a drink to be had in my apartment. We don't drink together, because Soviet livers are larger than our American ones, but every now and then I give them a bottle to overcome the cold and the boredom of an eight-hour shift in their wooden cubicle. They don't mind if it's vodka, whisky or wine and I guess they would even drink methylated spirits if I offered it. That evening I promised them their favourite tipple—a bottle of Metaxa brandy. My other great friend in Moscow, Vassilis Pappas, press attaché at the Greek embassy, supplied me every so often with a crate. I wanted the boys at the entrance to associate the pleasure of Metaxa with Marlene's face, so I wouldn't have to go down to the entrance to collect her every time she visited—something told me that she would be calling in again. As we walked to my place I explained to Marlene that the KGB officer following us wasn't invited to dinner; he would just take a bottle and go.

'With a crate of vodka you can get right into Gorbachev's bedroom,' she smirked. 'But I expected the KGB at least to keep up some appearances.'

'No one does anymore. We can't go out in the evening, because the cops play the syringe trick. As soon as they see a Western car with special number plates they stop us and threaten us with an alcotest.

'Our cars have distinct yellow licence plates that start with a number indicating country and a letter indicating profession: K for 'korespondent', D for diplomat and so on. A couple of years ago a Soviet citizen would get a visit from the KGB if there had been a car with yellow licence plates in their drive the previous day. Thanks to perestroika the locals don't have such problems anymore, but we do. We give the cops a few roubles to get rid of them, but the tariff keeps going up: it was five at the start, now it's fifty!'

'You shouldn't pay them.'

'Do you know how the alcotest works here? With a multi-use syringe. Plus you have to wait all night in the police station for the results.'

'Take the metro then,' Marlene smiled. 'It's the only thing in the USSR that runs on time.'

Most of my dinner guests had already arrived. There was Ellen Forsythe, who works for an American television network; Leonard Darrell, the American consul in Moscow, with his wife; and Yuri Lubimov, one of my latest journalistic discoveries. Yuri had spent forty of his roughly sixty years as a Soviet spy in the West. He was an affable character with perfect English and good manners, but a split personality. Having lived for years in Great Britain, where he operated under the guise of a Western businessman, he realized that the current form of socialism had no future and that Gorbachev's reforms were imperative. But, with the cuts to spy numbers in the defrosting of the Cold War, he was recalled to Moscow, where he landed with a bump into the harsh Soviet reality.

When Marlene and I entered the living room he was talking nostalgically of the good old days when he was chauffeured around in a Cadillac. Now he was forced to roam Moscow to find spare parts for his Lada. For some time, the Soviets had been taking their windscreen wipers into their homes every evening because of a market shortage.

'Life plays strange games,' Lubimov was saying. 'Sometimes my wife and I would yearn so much for our country that we would shut ourselves in a room and drink vodka and eat blinis—making sure, of course, that the door was locked. I thought I would be happy to come back, but after forty years of life in another community it's hard to adjust.'

The consul was strutting around self-importantly, as though he had fought on the front line in the battle against the evil empire. Marlene was impressed by my apartment. Like every self-respecting foreigner, I had long joined in the favourite sport of the perestroika era: buying beautiful old furniture and other antiques at knock-down prices. The auctions had begun with Gorbachev's liberalizing of the economy. My apartment had been turned into a small museum: two harps, a grand piano, a long oak dining table and twelve chairs with hand-carved metal arms, as well as nineteenth-century rocking chairs, art deco bookcases and cupboards, silver trays and candlesticks, engraved porcelain vases, Chinese screens, old cameras and Soviet radios from the 1950s that I had put in special wooden cases, two large pre-Revolution couches, socialist realist paintings and dozens of rugs from Kazakhstan, Azerbaijan and Dagestan that didn't fit in the loft—I had laid them on the floor, one on top of the other.

It was no surprise that Giuseppe and Fabio, with his obligatory Russian woman in tow, arrived late. I had long accepted that, in Sicily, time moved at a different pace. Giuseppe is Fabio's older brother, about forty and with a paunch, a moustache and gleaming eyes. A lawyer by trade, he is a last-of-the-Mohicans Marxist–Leninist, belonging to the hard-line wing of the Italian communist party. At that time he was visiting Moscow as the head of a delegation of communist lawyers, commissioned to study the institutional innovations of the Soviet constitution and the possibility of implementing them in Italy.

He had visited Moscow many times as an official guest of the Soviet government, particularly because of his gutsy stance at the time of the 1986 Chernobyl disaster. Sincerely believing the official statements, which played down the scale of the disaster, he publicly drank milk from Ukrainian cows in the centre of Palermo. It was a symbolic gesture to expose imperialist propaganda, which was attempting to exploit an insignificant nuclear episode to slander the entire socialist system. A few days later Gorbachev revealed the true dimensions of the catastrophe, and the Ukrainian milk proved to be radioactive. But neither Giuseppe's health nor his faith were shaken in the slightest. Realizing, therefore, that not even nuclear war could shatter his convictions, our mockery was limited to telling him that he was glowing from the overdose of radioactivity he had consumed in the milk. This riled him, but he didn't hold it against us. In any case, he is devoted to Fabio and, therefore, by extension considers me part of their big Sicilian family. A broad smile spread across his face whenever he met Soviet citizens; he considered them all comrades, or at least fellow passengers on the boat of happiness. He didn't know Lubimov, but couldn't hide his joy when he saw a representative of the socialist homeland at a meeting of fallen Westerners.

'Giuseppe—or, if you prefer, Joseph. Like Stalin.'

He reached out his hand in greeting. The consul's smile disappeared, while Lubimov's hand remained hanging for a few seconds. But the experienced former spy rallied quickly and smiled.

'My name is Yuri. Unfortunately, that's my only connection to Yuri Gagarin.'

'Oh, well I wasn't named Joseph by chance,' persisted Giuseppe. 'Our father was one of the leaders of the Communist Party in Palermo. I was named in honour of Stalin.'

'I thought that only happened in the Soviet Union,' Lubimov said. 'The Party encouraged parents to give their children names unrelated to their grandparents to get rid of religious or family ties. A catalogue was produced: Viomichania, Smaragdi, Diania, Oktovrina, Rem—which comes from the Russian initials for revolution, energy, peace—Ninel…'

'Ninel?' asked Giuseppe, like a good schoolboy who wants to study even through recess.

'It's "Lenin" backwards.'

'Ingenious,' said Giuseppe, glowing with pride at the resourcefulness of his Soviet comrades.

I decided to butt in.

'With all these name games, you've forgotten to introduce us to the young lady.'

Our eyes turned to Fabio's latest conquest, a leggy twenty-something with short strawberry-blonde hair, a charming upturned nose and cunning blue eyes. She was wearing a poorly made green suit, and perched shyly on a chair. I thought there was something provincial or awkward in her appearance, and I was right.

'This is Larissa,' Fabio said, introducing her.

'I've seen you somewhere before,' Lubimov said thoughtfully.

'You might have seen her in the paper or on TV,' Giuseppe explained with revolutionary pride, as if introducing the head of a model agro-industrial sovkhoz. 'She is Miss KGB.'

Fabio had struck again. The notorious secret service, to show that it had really modernized, had started organizing beauty contests among its female employees. The fact was widely broadcast by the Soviet media, and the Western correspondents had rushed to interview the first 'Miss' in the history of international espionage. Fabio was in no doubt that it was a well-planned propaganda exercise. In fact, he told me that Larissa's boss was present when he interviewed her and didn't hesitate to answer difficult questions on her behalf, or even correct his subordinate. But, like a good journalist, Fabio had actively confirmed the KGB's softening.

The consul formally shook Larissa's hand, then turned to me and said mysteriously, 'A marvellous opportunity to redeem your relationship with the KGB.'

We all looked at him, expecting more. He was around forty, with a freckled round face, small eyes and gold-rimmed glasses. His thinning hair was cleverly flattened with brilliantine to cover his whole head, and his fingers were long and thin like a pianist's. He came from an aristocratic Boston family, rich in diplomatic history; his father and grandfather were considered among the best to have passed through the State Department. Leonard had assimilated the family tradition: his humour was more cultivated than slapstick, and his manners flawless, concealing his emotions. We had known each other for some time and had a good working relationship. But I could never pinpoint his feelings towards me. He was good company in a Moscow where, were it not for the stormy political developments, we would be bored to death. I had decided, however, that we wouldn't be close friends. He was usually measured in his words, hence my surprise at his mentioning my relationship with the KGB.

He took a deep drag on his cigar.

'I'll explain, as it's no secret. A short while ago the Soviet government filed a complaint at the embassy about one of Kevin's interviews. Sergei Tamurian, one of the godfathers of the Moscow mafia, maintains that he had Yelin on his payroll. The head of the KGB is furious with you,' he added, turning towards me.

There followed a few seconds of silence.

'Your boss is right,' Giuseppe said protectively to Larissa. 'Kevin and my brother never miss an opportunity to criticize the Soviet Union. At first they didn't like the system and now, with the reforms that they wanted in place, they're still not happy.'

'I'm afraid that I can't do anything,' Larissa replied earnestly. 'I've only seen comrade Yelin in photographs. He didn't even come to the beauty contest.'

'Don't worry, Larissa, the consul is joking,' I reassured her. 'I did nothing other than write down what Pioneer told me. Anyway, the interview brought good luck.'

I turned to look at Marlene. Then I told the story of the broken telephone line and how I had met her at the post office.

'Why didn't you just go to another newspaper's office to send the fax?' asked the consul's wife.

'Because the bastard didn't want us to steal his scoop,' interjected Forsythe, before murmuring to Marlene, 'You've met one of the best journalists in town.'

'I knew that from the start,' she said, her eyes shining. I was sure I had charmed her.

'Larissa—a lovely name. It reminds me of Pasternak's heroine in Doctor Zhivago.'

We had sat down for dinner around the large candle-lit table. I wanted to avoid the usual political journalistic discussion, particularly in the presence of the KGB—even in its most beautiful version—so I attempted a literary opening.

'I've only just read it, though I studied literature at university,' said Larissa. 'It was banned until recently.'

'Oh, wonderful, now we've got onto dissident literature,' Giuseppe grumbled.

'It's one of the great romantic novels,' said Marlene.

'Not only romantic,' I added. 'It's the story of two lovers in different camps during the Russian Civil War. They are shut in a cottage on the steppes, while outside people are killing each other. Their love manages to overcome the hatred sown by ideology.'

'Are you not overly conflating love with politics?'

Marlene phrased this comment as a question, but in reality she disagreed with me.

'But the greatest love stories of literature are meaningless outside their social context. Romeo and Juliet's love takes its drama from the fact that relationships between offspring of rival families were forbidden. The love story of Larissa and Doctor Zhivago would be straightforward if it didn't happen during the October Revolution.'

Fabio was a good wingman.

'He's influenced by his new book.'

Marlene put on her charm again: 'You write books, too?'

'He's already written three,' Fabio replied in my place. We stuck up for each other fanatically throughout our time in Moscow.

'This time I'm writing a political thriller. But really I'm looking at whether communism destroys romance.'

'I warned you, didn't I!' Giuseppe guffawed triumphantly. 'The theory is simple: the communists are to blame for everything, even desire.'

'All totalitarian regimes try to control romantic relationships,' I persevered. 'The Nazis forbade Germans from having sexual relationships with non-Aryans for the sake of racial purity; the communists were the same with class. At the time of the Revolution it was a serious problem to be connected to a member of the old aristocracy, the "exploiting class". Before perestroika, Soviet citizens had no right to have romantic relationships with Westerners. It was strictly prohibited.'

'A few years ago it wouldn't have crossed my mind to live permanently in Moscow,' Fabio cut in, giving Larissa a smacker to redress the balance.

Giuseppe was in the mood for ideological sparring. He looked patronizingly at Fabio, as if his little brother were crawling on all fours and spouting charming gibberish. Then he turned to the others: 'Well, we've really cut to the chase now. In the West, of course, everyone gets married from pure romantic love. In Italy, politicians' daughters marry famous journalists and, entirely coincidentally, the offspring of large and wealthy families marry each other. They're called strategic marriages: two families increasing their wealth and power so as not to share it with the poor. According to Kevin, then, economic expediency is called romance.'

The consul looked disparagingly at this traitor of Western values, but the fact he was Sicilian somewhat placated his racist disposition.

Giuseppe moved on in his counter-attack: 'Romance is forbidden! There is Communism here!' he said, parodying Western stereotypes. 'Well, go to the parks and count the couples.'

'That wasn't allowed until recently,' Larissa interrupted, sounding like a specialist.

'One of the things that made a big impression on me when I went to the West was that young couples walk hand in hand and kiss in the street,' said Lubimov, who had remained silent until then. 'Here, if a couple were seen kissing in the street or on a bench, the passers-by themselves would intervene. I have been there myself at such occasions and the most usual observation was, "Will you stop behaving like Americans!" We're a puritanical society.'

'Then how do you explain the fact that my brother has been through half of Moscow?' exclaimed Giuseppe. He realized his gaff immediately, for he looked sideways at Fabio and bit his lip.

There was a nervous hush. Larissa looked down and Fabio stroked her hand under the table. To break the ice, I thought of joking that Miss KGB would arrest

Fabio right after the meal, but that would have been a little crude. In the end Lubimov broke the silence: 'There's a double standard in our society. The leadership encourages common citizens to be moderate and avoid extramarital relationships, but neither the leadership nor the citizens keep these rules. In the end, anything goes.'

'At university we made up a saying based on the well-known one about work,' added Larissa: 'They pretend they're priests; we pretend we're nuns.'

Giuseppe looked at her askance, like a right-wing reactionary.

'Were you not a Komsomol member at university?'

'We all had to join Komsomol. But despite the official guidelines, there was a certain... romantic atmosphere.'

'Might I clear something up?' I said. 'There are two things here. Sexual attraction is quite different from romantic love. Sexual attraction is a purely bodily attraction to one or more people. Romantic love is the attraction of the body and soul to a unique individual.'

'He's studied the topic even more than me!' Fabio observed, his spirits up again.

'I don't quite get your theory,' said Marlene, with an air of indignation. 'You mean that we in the East are condemned never to fall in love?'

'Of course people fall in love, but a totalitarian system doesn't allow them to enjoy that love; it tries to destroy it. That's what interests me: is there a love great enough to defeat the system?'

'Well, the bed is the final bastion against the regime. No one can conquer it,' insisted Marlene.

'I'm not entirely sure,' Lubimov rebuffed. 'They often have gone right into the bedroom. If the party organization in a workplace discovered that someone was having an affair with a married comrade, they could hold a special meeting to put the lovers back in line. If the head of a provincial hotel realized that the woman with you was not your legal spouse, they could refuse you a room or inform your party. We used to tell a joke: Why are beds so big in the Soviet Union? So that all three can fit in—husband, wife and Lenin!'

Then the former spy added something that I would remember several days later, when things had gone seriously awry.

'A romantic relationship presupposes a private life, but here they try to monitor everyone and everything. If microphones were placed in this apartment, they would be recording pillow talk too.'

'Let's not exaggerate,' I said as I went to the kitchen to fetch a bottle of wine. 'There are twenty thousand foreigners in Moscow. They would have to employ tens of thousands of people just to hear what we're saying.'

'Thank you, Svetlana, the food was wonderful.'

Svetlana, my recently appointed housekeeper, had cooked her first dinner for me. It was the first time I had employed someone who didn't belong to the UPDK, the public service that equipped us with everything from wall paint to maids. Until a few months ago, it was strictly forbidden to hire people from outside the UPDK, but in the general collapse the system had relaxed. She received a hundred and fifty dollars a month, like her predecessors. We suspected, however, that the latter—even if they didn't belong to the KGB—were prepared to snitch on us to keep the privilege of earning hard currency. Only those who worked with foreigners were paid in dollars. Svetlana was about sixty and her large innocent eyes had made me trust her from the get-go. That evening, I found out she had a daughter of marriageable age.

'May I ask you a favour? My daughter Masha is a student at the university. She has a relationship with an American businessman and wants to go and see him, but she can't get a visa from the American consulate.'

I promised that I would arrange the matter with the consul and returned to the party. Larissa and Marlene were discussing Berlin.

'I was there last week,' Miss KGB was saying. 'I like it so much; I go whenever I can.'

'There's nowhere like it,' Marlene replied, half joking. 'What other city has a wall down the middle?'

She had certainly charmed the group. Her table manners were impeccable and her political commentary more advanced than she had let show in our meeting at the post office. When the consul asked her if Bauer's regime in East Germany would collapse, she replied that there was no doubt about it. The question was if it meant real change to the system or simply a facelift for the regime.

Every so often she looked at me, as if confirming that I was noticing her. At some point she whispered, 'When will you show me your latest book?'

'Today, perhaps. You can stay when the others have gone.'

She seemed to be expecting this proposal. As I led the other guests to the door, Fabio passed final judgement: 'Bingo! She's without a doubt the sassiest woman in Moscow.'

[Prague, 1983]

'No, it isn't a mummified Brek, it's his lookalike,' laughed the guide at the Prague Museum of National Security and Police. She looked good when she laughed, Patrick thought. She had blue eyes, smooth skin and long curly red hair. This beauty was guiding a group of Western journalists around the most nightmarish museum in the world.

When the head of the Voice of Lyon had mentioned the invitation from the Czechoslovakian embassy in Paris, Patrick had jumped for joy. Fifteen years after the Soviet invasion of 1968, the Czechoslovak communists felt so secure that they invited Western journalists to demonstrate the success of 'normalization', as they called the heavy winter after the Prague Spring. Apparently, none of the major newspapers had accepted the invitation, so they contacted regional ones too. Patrick realized it was a barefaced propaganda mission, but he was hardly interested in politics. It was an opportunity to visit Prague. An Italian friend of his, who had been there the year before, had told him that it was one of the most beautiful cities in Europe, quite apart from the fact that its women couldn't wait to meet Western men. Besides, for a French journalist this official trip provided a unique opportunity to speak to government officials in Czechoslovakia. The alternative solution—travelling to Prague on a tourist visa—would confine him to recording impressions of the city's grey atmosphere and the melancholy of a few dissident intellectuals who were in and out of prison. It didn't take much to persuade him—he was about thirty and was just beginning his career as a journalist. The editor's promise to publish his work was enough.

That was how he ended up at the police museum, surrounded by European journalists of the communist press, all listening to the beautiful guide eulogizing Brek, the dog-hero of socialism.

Brek had been a trained police German shepherd. In his twelve years of service for the Special Forces as a border guard, he had located sixty people trying to escape to Austria. He had been injured many times during his career. In recognition of his valuable services, the authorities gave him the right to see out his life in the cosseted environment of the central police offices. He was then mummified and displayed in the museum. But, since poor Brek's hair couldn't stand the visitors' constant petting, the museum's directors decided to take the embalmed body of the brave but now threadbare dog away and put another mummified

German shepherd in his place. Brek's lookalike held prime position in the wing of the museum dedicated to failed attempts to escape the country. There was also a dog—no one could ascertain if it was Brek or his lookalike—posing on one of the postcards for sale at the entrance to the museum. The caption read, 'Defending the borders of the Socialist Democracy of Czechoslovakia is the honourable duty of every citizen.'

In glass cabinets beside Brek's lookalike were other exhibits testifying to the need for revolutionary vigilance. Every cabinet concerned a failed escape attempt and contained confiscated apparatus: a makeshift hot-air balloon used by two counter-revolutionaries to cross the border, before the wind ruined their plans by suddenly blowing them east; two green frog-suits for swimming across the river, with dissident pamphlets in their folds.

The neighbouring hall was dedicated to failed attempts by imperialists to sabotage socialism. An entire cabinet was full of banknotes from the wealthiest Western countries, proof that international capital was not skimped if it meant bringing down the proletariat. The next cabinet contained Trotsky's three-volume History of the Russian Revolution, along with dozens of other anti-revolution books confiscated at the borders, thankfully before they polluted the pure citizens of Czechoslovakia with their malignant content. In the third cabinet there was James Bond–style spy equipment: lighters-cum-cameras, pen-pistols, poison-scattering gloves.

The third hall was dedicated to the Prague Spring.

On a newspaper displayed on the wall, underlined in red marker pen, were the names of Vaclav Havel, Alexander Dub ek and dozens of other 'revisionists' who hid their anti-Leninist theories under the guise of 'socialism with a human face'. The counter-revolutionaries, it seemed, had penetrated everywhere; they had occupied the Party, the government, the trade unions, the Society of Authors. As the documents demonstrated, they had organized an unchecked White Terror until 1969, when the process of normalization began and comrade Gustav Husak took control. Patrick noticed that the Soviet tanks of the 1968 invasion were nowhere mentioned, but decided not to remark on it to his companions. It was as though no invasion had taken place.

His attention turned to the red-headed guide who, at some point, had left the journalists to digest the works and days of the counter-revolution and headed for the museum exit. He waited for her in the hall with Brek's lookalike, pretending to be dumbfounded by the achievements of the first dog in the history of humanity to assimilate Marxist–Leninist dogma. When she approached, he asked if this was the real Brek before him. She laughed.

'No, it isn't a mummified Brek. It's his lookalike. So, do you like the museum?'

He tried to discern what answer would please her.

'I see it's not easy to escape from a socialist–populist democracy.'

She laughed again.

'I've been working here since 1975, when the museum opened. That's the most diplomatic answer I have ever heard.'

He decided to play all in. He took a depth breath and said, 'I'm wondering... since your society is so wonderful, why do people want to leave?'

'I'm afraid you're asking the wrong person. My expertise is limited to the museum's exhibits.'

'Now that is a diplomatic response.'

'One all, then. Is this your first time in Prague?'

'Yes, I arrived just yesterday. I suppose that there are other, more... remarkable sights in Prague.'

'You said it, not me.'

'What do you mean?'

'There's a joke going around. Some Russian tourists steal a Swiss watch belonging to a resident of Prague. He goes to the police and makes the following accusation: "Some Swiss tourists stole my Russian watch." The officer asks twice him to repeat the accusation, before asking, "Do you mean that some Russian tourists stole your Swiss watch?" "You said it, not me!" the citizen replies.'

He laughed so hard that the journalists in the other room turned and began walking over. He didn't have much time left.

'I know a few good jokes too. Can we meet somewhere else?'

She hesitated, but Patrick persisted.

'Will you come for dinner this evening?'

'Eight o'clock. At the museum entrance.'

'I didn't catch your name this afternoon?'

'Anna.'

'Anna. Nice name. I'm Patrick. Patrick Ventura.'

They walked to U Mecenáše, a restaurant on the side of the Lesser Town and one of the few places that, with some luck and a greased palm, you could get a table. At the others you had to book days in advance. When they arrived at the entrance, Anna opened her bag, took out a few Czech banknotes and, before Patrick could protest, gave them to the porter. His face lost its surly expression and he waved them past.

As they left their coats in the cloakroom, Patrick saw that she was wearing a tight red dress that accentuated her legs. The waiter led them to a table for two and lit the candle. Her big eyes glowed even more.

'Your turn to tell a joke.'

'I don't know any; I just said that so you'd come. You're so beautiful.'

'You disappoint me. I thought that you'd have some fresh joke from the West.'

'I know one about Czechoslovakia—a friend told it to me when he found out I was coming here. A Czechoslovak lets the genie out of the bottle. In return the genie promises to fulfil three wishes. The Czechoslovak asks three times for the Chinese to try to invade Czechoslovakia but to be driven back. "OK, I'll do it," the genie says. "But why are you missing this chance of sorting your life out? I don't see why you're asking for the same thing three times." The Czechoslovak says, "So they'll run over the Soviet Union six times."'

Anna smiled.

'I knew it.'

'You probably didn't like it. Sorry, I didn't want to put you in a difficult position or offend your convictions. I'm not interested in polit—'

'No, it's not what you think. It's just I've heard it so many times.'

She remained thoughtful and then said, 'I must admit that I'm embarrassed to work at the museum.'

'I can understand that.'

'No, you can't. I have nowhere else to work—and, as you know, everything here belongs to the state. I graduated from the School of Translators and worked for five years as an English translator in the Ministry of Foreign Affairs. Then I was sent to the police museum. Despite my best efforts they won't give me a transfer. It's a kind of ideological re-education.'

He made a questioning gesture, as if asking, 'Did you get into trouble?'

'No, not me. My ex-husband. He was a diplomat but was expelled from the Party in 1970 during normalization. They accused him of being sympathetic towards the Prague Spring and kicked him out of the diplomatic corps. We split up shortly afterwards, but nonetheless, I, as family, felt the repercussions. Why am I telling you all this? I don't know. I feel I can trust you.'

He leant towards her and took her hand, then stroked her hair. Anna turned her head and kissed his hand. And it's not even my second day, Patrick thought. His trip to Prague had started very well indeed.

'Dinner must have cost a fortune,' said Anna, indicating the bill that Patrick was holding. 'U Mecenáše is one of the most expensive restaurants in town. In Czech it means "Chez Maecenas".'

'It's very cheap,' Patrick replied, taking a fistful of korunas from his pocket. 'Only twenty-five dollars on the black market.'

'So, an average month's wages.'

'How do people get by here?' asked Patrick, eager to find out about the place.

'Don't imagine that the average citizen comes here. Their restaurants are very cheap. Besides, life is organized differently from in the West. Here, the rents, electricity and phone bills are almost nothing and food—if you can find it—is very cheap. Even if you have money, you won't find more things to buy, so the twenty-five dollars that we get in korunas is like pocket money—for street food, or the cinema.'

'Pocket money,' Patrick mused. 'Not a bad idea. I worry how I'll pay my rent every month, my bills, my credit cards. It's like you have a father figure looking after you.'

'We must go,' Anna interrupted, pointing to the waiters, who had cleaned the neighbouring tables and were lingering around theirs. Patrick noticed that the other customers had left. He poured the remnants of the second bottle of red wine into his glass.

'Our night is just beginning,' he said cheerily. 'I've heard there are some good jazz clubs here.'

'I'm afraid they've been closed. There was a decision made recently by the Central Committee on the moral education of youth. Life stops at 11 p.m. Nowhere is open.'

Patrick thought that Prague was the ideal city for intimate encounters. He feigned disappointment.

'Not even one? Why?'

'Daddy puts us to bed early,' Anna said sarcastically.

Patrick hesitated. Then he took her hand and stroked her hair again. When he saw that she responded, he suggested, 'Shall we go to the house I'm staying in? I've brought a good French red wine.'

He took from his pocket a piece of paper with the address. The invitation from the Czechoslovak government did not include a hotel, so Patrick had chosen to stay at the house of a fellow journalist's mother. The daughter had left her country to work in Paris, on the Eastern Europe desk of Radio France International. A common friend had put them in touch. Officially he was being hosted, as it was strictly forbidden for individuals to let rooms, but he paid half the price of a good hotel to help the journalist's mother. It was a big house and, as Patrick's friend had explained, the mother would be happy just to see someone who was from the place where her daughter lived.

It was snowing on Charles Bridge, the angel statues were cloaked in snow and the river at their feet had frozen. They stood for a moment and turned to look at the castle. Floodlit and covered in white, the imposing palace on the hill looked as though it belonged to the wicked witch in a fairy tale. In the middle of the bridge Patrick took her in his arms and kissed her on the mouth. She gave herself to him.

By the time they reached the house, at about one o'clock, they were freezing; you could have counted the taxis on the fingers of one hand. They took off their sodden boots and left them in the hall. All the lights were off: clearly the lady kept to the state timetable. They tiptoed up the wooden spiral staircase and went into Patrick's room. He went down to the kitchen to fetch two glasses. When he turned on the light he thought he heard a noise, but didn't pay any attention. By the time they had drunk the wine, kissed again, undressed and got into bed, it was after two.

In bed with the guide of the police museum, Patrick thought. He hadn't yet managed to avenge the Soviet invasion and crushing of the Prague Spring when the door to his room opened. In the half-light created by the lamp in the passageway he made out the silhouette of the lady of the house in her nightdress. She started shrieking in Czech.

Patrick just managed to cover himself before asking Anna, 'What the hell does she want?'

'She's saying I have to get up and leave the house at once. She thinks I'm a prostitute, one of those who sell themselves to Western tourists.'

The woman had left the room, but they could see her pacing up and down the passage.

Patrick wriggled into his trousers and a jumper, while Anna sat on the edge of the bed, already dressed. He begged her to explain to the woman, who spoke no foreign language, that she was a guide, not a prostitute. Anna hesitated.

'She won't understand.'

'Tell her.'

She went to the half-open door and said something loudly in Czech. The woman's reply was abrupt and just as loud.

'She says that those who go with foreigners are in the pay of the secret police and I must leave at once.'

'Then we'll go together,' Patrick said decisively. 'Let's find a hotel.'

'Your visa, please. And the lady's passport and visa.'

Patrick instinctively looked in his pocket, before remembering that he had given the visa document to his landlady the previous day. According to Czechoslovak law, every visitor had to declare where they were staying at the nearest police station within twenty-four hours of arrival. The landlady had explained—via a neighbour who spoke French and looked like an old aristocrat—that she could arrange it herself as she knew an officer at the police station. Now he took out his passport, slipped a twenty-dollar bill into one of the first pages and gave it to the clerk of the Intercontinental.

'We were staying in a guesthouse but didn't like it so we came here. Our visas are with our bags at the guesthouse.'

The man took the money and said with a smile, 'Very well, you'll bring it to me tomorrow. The lady's passport?'

'I don't have one. I'm Czechoslovak,' Anna said in English.

The clerk put the twenty-dollar bill back in the passport and returned it to Patrick.

'Sorry, I thought the lady was foreign. It's strictly forbidden for Czechoslovak citizens to stay in the hotel.'

Patrick rummaged in his pocket, but the clerk cut him short.

'It's not a question of money. There are strict rules.'

'I'd like to know why.'

The man shrugged his shoulders and sat back in his chair. It was as though he had been asked why mankind's exploitation of other humans had not been abolished. He yawned widely and picked up the paper he was reading before these unexpected night-time customers had interrupted him. Patrick looked at his watch as he walked to the door. It was three thirty.

'I repeat my suggestion,' said Anna. 'Let's go to my place.'

'And I'll repeat that's impossible,' Patrick replied. 'I don't feel comfortable in the same house as your ex-husband.'

'But it's completely normal,' Anna insisted, almost desperately. 'The lack of apartments means that couples who split up often have to live in the same place. Many people live with their old and new partners in the same apartment.'

'That's what we call a ménage à trois,' said Patrick obstinately. 'A nice system: on the one hand, Czechoslovaks are forbidden from staying in a hotel and, on the other, foursomes are encouraged.'

Anna looked to the sky in exasperation. It had stopped snowing, but was excruciatingly cold.

'I have an idea,' she said. 'A friend of mine, a student, usually stays near here at her boyfriend's place. I think her own room in the student halls is empty. We can go and get the key.'

They walked through the old Jewish quarter and then by the river. Anna nestled into his arm.

'It's blatantly obvious that you're travelling in a socialist country for the first time.'

'Why?'

'You don't know a thing about our lives. Here almost everyone has married and divorced at least once. The only way a young person can get out of their family home and find a flat is by marrying, since the state gives priority to married couples. That's why everyone splits up.'

The entrance hall of the dark apartment block reeked of socialist cockroach poison. Anna gestured to him to wait and began to climb a wooden spiral staircase that creaked ceaselessly. Patrick lit another cigarette— that evening alone he must have smoked more than a packet. Shortly Anna came down, holding a key in her hand.

'My friend has no problem at all. But there's a porter in the student halls who might not let us in if he sees us.'

'It sounds like a farce.'

The halls were three-quarters of an hour from the centre, and dawn was breaking before they found a cab. During the ride they remained silent, apart from one moment when Anna leant over and whispered, 'I remembered a joke. Socialism is like the horizon: as you approach it, it gets further away.'

'The same goes for sex under socialism. The closer you think you are to it, the more impossible it seems,' Patrick remarked, laughing.

Despite Anna's entreaties and arguments, the porter—a fat lady dressed in black—was unbending. It was strictly forbidden for men to go into the girls' halls. Nor did she accept Anna's generous offer of korunas.

'She's like the porter who didn't let us into Mosfilm on the day we met,' Marlene said, drawing back from the computer screen.

I was sitting next to her with a drink in my hand. I had taken the opportunity to reread my novel.

'Come on, aren't you bored? You can continue reading tomorrow,' I said.

'No. Please, a bit more. It's interesting.'

'Then I'll go to my room. When you've finished—'

'No, don't leave me alone with this ghastly machine. I don't know how it works at all.'

'Come on. Don't worry. I'm learning a lot from you. Yesterday at the museum I learnt that it's difficult to escape. This evening, that it's difficult to live here.'

Patrick was trying to console her. They had ended up drinking vodka in a basement café in the city centre—one of those that the proletariat visit for a drink before going to work in the factories. Dawn had broken, but it was murky and drizzling—ideal weather for Prague melancholia. There was traffic on the road and from the café window Patrick could see the red trams plying their way loudly through the snowy roads. Anna was crying silently and, when Patrick took her hand under the table, she said faintly, 'I can't live in this country anymore.'

'Don't be sad. I'll help you leave. We'll leave together.'

She looked at him beseechingly.

'It's very difficult. They don't let anyone leave.'

Suddenly the café door opened and four bulky men walked in. The patrons' conversations stopped abruptly and complete silence fell over the room. Patrick tried to work out what was happening: the new arrivals weren't wearing uniform, nor did they look like secret police. But they did have red armbands, like the students of the security teams in May 1968 France. Patrick glanced at Anna. Her face was pale and her hands had frozen on her glass. Having looked closely around the room, the four men went to various tables, asking for identity cards, looking at them and handing them back. A couple of times they asked a few questions and took notes. They walked past Patrick and Anna's table without stopping and investigated another at the back of the café. Then they opened the door and left. The chatter returned, the waiter began to go between tables and Anna's hands moved again at last. Patrick's curiosity was piqued.

'Who were those guys?'

'Militia. After the last decision of the Central Committee on increasing productivity and fighting parasitism, voluntary militia groups were formed throughout the country. During working hours they check cafés, cinemas, public baths, even parks, to see if people are dodging their work. They send notes to your workplace if they consider you suspicious or if you can't explain why you aren't at work. If the bosses judge that you were unaccountably absent, they will do anything from cutting a month's salary to firing you.'

'I think my grandmother told me about a corps like this who would catch children playing truant,' said Patrick thoughtfully. 'What were they called now…? Not policemen… children's surveillants. But why were you scared? The museum is closed at the moment.'

She shrugged her shoulders, then looked down. Finally she said, 'I don't know. We're just afraid. No reason. I knew I was innocent, but to them I was suspicious.'

He took her hand tenderly and advised her to sleep for a few hours before she started work at the museum again. He wouldn't be able to rest: official visits had been planned to the Škoda factory and, in the afternoon, to the offices of Rudé právo, the daily newspaper of the Communist Party. In the evening he was invited to the French embassy along with the other French journalists. It would be a good opportunity to discuss Anna's problem with a diplomat. If possible he would also ask Gustav, the journalists' official escort, who had expressed his willingness to help with any problem. He told Anna that he would pick her up from the museum the next day at six.

At the reception at the French embassy that evening, Patrick cornered the second secretary. His reply was categorical: 'Forget it. Permission to migrate to the West is given in exceptional circumstances. I'm amazed at your friend's boldness in even going out with you. Don't forget that we are all potential spies.'

'What if I marry her?'

'Do you love her that much?'

'She's a charming woman, but I hardly know her. I don't know if I'm in love with her. But I don't like it when people who are suffocating and want to leave are kept against their will.'

'I imagine that you don't want to discuss the pros and cons of the socialist system now.'

'I know very little about socialism, and politics interests me even less.'

'So, you're interested in women. Well, we have precisely the same interests. But if you want to have fun, the best I can advise is to find a girl contracted to a hotel. She may not be of the same moral standing, but your practical problems will be sorted out.'

'Don't be shocked,' he continued, before Patrick could reply. 'Your landlady was right when she said that all these women work with the secret police. They give information in exchange for a work permit. The poor dear thought that you had met the girl in a hotel: she couldn't imagine that she works at the police museum and knows English because she's a guide.

Unfortunately, the Czechoslovaks have a warped picture of us French. They think that we incline towards the easy.'

'And marriage? I would happily have a sham marriage.'

'Marriage doesn't always result in an immediate emigration permit. Sometimes it takes four or five years.'

'Strange. Our official Czechoslovak escort seemed more positive than you.'

The French diplomat made a face as if to say, 'As gullible as the rest.'

Patrick told him of his discussion with Gustav that afternoon, when the small coach was transferring them from the Škoda factory to Rudé právo. Gustav had been so interested that he took down Anna's name and profession and promised Patrick that he would hand on his request to higher powers and get a reply in the next few days. Contrary to the French diplomat, he had been led to believe that emigration permits were given without much trouble in the majority of cases.

'Did you tell him it was a whirlwind romance?'

Patrick nodded.

'Ah, well, that changes everything,' the second secretary said sarcastically. 'Socialism has great respect for romance.'

'You too must have observed the concerted efforts at slandering socialist Czechoslovakia.'

Patrick's request had been swiftly transferred to Gustav's superiors. Without really understanding what was happening, the next day he was in the office of Ivan Plita, the undersecretary of internal affairs on matters of national security. After the initial formalities, Plita had cut to the chase. He was trying to pin down Patrick's political persuasion or elicit a declaration from him on 'the concerted efforts at slandering socialism'.

Patrick laughed almost impetuously.

'I only recently began my career in journalism, covering a few cases in Lyon's court of appeal. Your embassy's kind invitation provided an opportunity for me to visit Czechoslovakia, but it's my first trip to a socialist country and I know hardly anything of the situation. It may seem strange to you, but I'm not interested in politics.'

'But you'll have noticed the attempts at slander that I'm talking about.'

'Well, I will take your word for it. You certainly know more than I do.'

Plita hummed and hawed contentedly. He was short and weedy, about fifty. His flimsy hands played constantly with a Czechoslovak military medal.

'Let me give you one more example. I don't know if you've heard of the case of citizen A.K.?'

'No.'

'Strange—it caused quite a stir in the West. He was a Czechoslovak citizen who wanted to stand for the presidency of the Democracy. He printed a pamphlet of his views and published it at his own expense.'

The undersecretary paused, as if waiting for Patrick to comment.

'And the pamphlet contained... anti-socialist views?'

'Not exactly. He merely stated that the decision-making process of the UN should change, and suggested ways of ridding Czechoslovakia of bureaucracy. The recent National Party conference had already made almost the same suggestions. He also borrowed some statements on the need for greater participation of citizens in designing and applying party decisions.'

Patrick's face must have worn a strange expression, for Plita smiled. He threw the medal onto his desk, stood up and paced the room.

'The problem is that he made political suggestions and wanted to stand for presidency. Don't ask me if that's forbidden by the constitution, as a prejudiced colleague of yours asked me recently. No, in theory such activities are not forbidden, since they obviously aren't trying to overturn the constitution, nor reinstate capitalism. But everyone in the country knows that these things are up to the Party.'

'You mean it's better for people not to be interested in politics, like me.'

The undersecretary looked at him closely, as if he was wondering if Patrick were an agent provocateur or simply naïve.

In the end he continued. 'Our psychiatrists examined this patient and concluded that he was suffering from reformist psychosis, the paranoia that one can change the world. The case of patient A.K. was published in the Journal of Criminology, an official publication of the Czechoslovak Ministry of Internal Affairs, precisely to stress the need for party organizations and the socialist health system to remain vigilant. Despite the fact that we ourselves published this case, it was translated in the West and used to depict Czechoslovakia as a kind of Orwellian society.'

'Well... that's an exaggeration,' Patrick managed to say.

The undersecretary seemed relieved. He offered Patrick a cigarette and lit one for himself.

After a couple of pleasurable puffs, he said, 'We want you to write that this man really had psychological problems. Then you'll be able to take your beloved and go wherever you want.'

Patrick was left speechless. Plita continued, 'Otherwise it will be very difficult for me to persuade the ministry to give her a permit. You will certainly be aware that comrade Anna Linova married a diplomat, a man who knew many state secrets. She belongs to category B, which means it's almost impossible for her to leave the country.'

At that moment Patrick decided to take Anna out of Czechoslovakia at all costs. All he could do now was pretend.

'I'll need some time to consider your proposal,' he said, before adding mischievously, 'Of course, there was a revolution here and perhaps reforms aren't necessary. But don't forget that in the West many are against revolutions, but few are against reforms.'

'When does your official visit end?' asked Plita, ignoring his sarcasm.

'This evening. I'm leaving tomorrow for Budapest.'

'I will inform the embassy in Paris so that, if you wish, you may return,' he said, breathing a sigh. 'I can also arrange an interview with the psychiatrist who is looking after A.K. His therapy is progressing well.'

They left around eight on the Prague–Budapest train and made love almost without stopping until dawn, when they reached the border. With a few extra korunas they had secured a compartment in first class with four bunks. They celebrated their sexual freedom by testing all four of them, drinking endless quantities of cheap Russian fizz.

Hardman stood up suddenly and his two assistants stopped taking notes. Weber had his elbow on the table and was leaning his head on his palm.

'Is it really necessary for you to read us your novel, too?' the FBI team leader asked irritably.

'You won't be able to understand the rest of the story otherwise.'

'OK, keep going,' he said, without sitting down.

In the first break from their frenzy of passion, before they were drunk, Patrick took several close-ups of Anna with the compartment's red curtain for background, framing the shot like a passport photo. Throughout the evening he promised her several times that he would get her out of the country—besides, he had started to fall in love with her. To be precise, he felt very much in love with her. They both agreed that they hadn't made such passionate love in years. Anna insisted that he shouldn't write anything to jeopardize his career and so, despite her fears, she saw no solution other than an illicit escape. Just before she got off the train at the last Czechoslovak border city, she kissed him and told him to take care. For many days afterwards he smelt the scent of her body on his hands.

'Come on, Kevin, please show me the rest!'

'I wish I'd written it. Unfortunately I still have several chapters to go. I need to be quick, because my contract stipulates that I have to hand in the whole book in two weeks from today.'

'What inspired the story? Don't tell me it's your own.'

'It's the story of a French journalist that was told to me in Paris. It's true, however, that in 1983, the year the book is set, I went to Czechoslovakia for the first time and that helped me describe the atmosphere.'

'Why did you come to Moscow? Did the paper ask you to?'

'I insisted. The Soviet Union was a mystery, which perestroika was transforming into an exciting adventure... with an end that no one can predict. Just like a good novel.'

'Perhaps it's you that's looking for ideal love. Perhaps all this theory of yours about love under socialism is nothing but your search for it.'

She had nestled into an armchair next to the desk. Something was preoccupying her.

'Is that your wife in the photograph?'

'Yes. And next to her is Howard, my son. Cynthia is an architect. They came here for a time, but she wanted to continue her career in America, and Moscow was a difficult place for our son. They both went back, but they come every now and then to see me. I miss Howard: he's four years old and I've hardly lived with him.'

'I miss my son too—Erich. He's nine years old and lives with his grandpa in Berlin. I miss him more than anything in the world.'

'I didn't know you were married.'

'Like everyone under socialism, I married young and divorced quickly. Just like in your novel.'

'I know almost nothing about you. I remember what you said when I met you at the post office and asked you about East Germany: "I've become used to living in this country." You don't seem to hold a particular fondness for your homeland.'

She looked at the ceiling.

'I love Germany, but I don't like the Germans much. They stick so rigidly to duty. After six years in the Soviet Union I feel more Russian than German. The Russians might be disorganized, but they have enthusiasm and dreams. I like the Slavic spirit.'

I went over to her, kissed her tenderly then took her hand and led her to the bedroom. I undressed her slowly, looking at her beautiful naked back in the old mirror that spanned the entire wall. We made love silently, but it was as though I had known her body for years.

When we had finished, she lit a cigarette and asked me, 'Does communism manage to destroy the love of your characters in the novel?'

'I won't give away the end. Anyway, I haven't written it yet.'

She looked at me knowingly.

'Tell me then, since you're one for theories, does passionate love exist under socialism?'

'Of course. Why do you ask?'

We looked at each other and I think both of us knew very well why she asked.

We stayed together for about a week, hardly separating for a moment. They were the best days in all my five years in Moscow. As international attention had turned from the Soviet Union to East Germany, Hungary and the other Eastern European countries, I had enough free time to devote myself to the person I considered the great love of my life. Marlene abandoned her student residence and came to live with me. When we went out in the evening she liked going to the first non-state restaurant in the Soviet Union, on Kropotkinskaya Street. It was the only place in Moscow where they didn't just throw a plate of food in your face and where the waiters didn't knock into you as they were lighting the candles. She usually wore an expensive pearl necklace, which glowed in the candlelight and made her pale neck even more attractive. It was the only thing that remained from her marriage, she told me. I had realized that she had hardly any money, yet she wouldn't let me pay even her taxi fare on the couple of occasions when she went to her room for various chores.

I only spoke to Fabio on the phone; he was smitten with Larissa and they were seeing each other regularly. Two weeks with the same woman must have been a record for him in Moscow. Even when Larissa was away in Berlin, he stayed at home or went out only with the third member of our group, Vassilis Pappas. We joked that Miss KGB had forbidden Fabio from seeing other women while she was away, or she would send him to a gulag for ideological re-education. Vassilis, as a true Greek, would repeat that Aristotle considered friendship 'the most necessary thing in life', more important even than eros—romantic love. But contrary to friendship, which is a conscious choice and tested by time, eros is a mystical passion.

It was a mild autumn and in the evenings we went for walks in Moscow. One night, on the full moon, we ended up at Patriarch's Ponds, the place where Bulgakov's The Master and Margarita begins. From the very first days of our acquaintance we had agreed that he was one of the greatest Russian authors of the twentieth century. We walked arm in arm on the banks of the little lake. Couples were kissing on the benches under the trees, waiting for dawn. Around one bench was a large group of young people. Someone was playing the guitar and the rest were singing romantic Russian songs. Marlene knew most of them and we started singing along, drinking homemade vodka from the shared bottle.

She seemed happy. At one point she leant down to kiss me.

'I feel like the luckiest woman in Moscow. You've completely changed my life.'

'But—'

'I can't live like this anymore. I mean I can't live in Moscow or in Berlin anymore. I want to take my son far away; whatever happens with these regimes, I'm worried that it'll take years for them to get back on their feet. I feel like I'm wasting the best years of my life.'

'You mean that you're planning on leaving me?'

I said it as a joke, but I felt a frog in my throat.

'I want to stay with you forever, but I can't see our future together. You're still attached.'

It was the first time she had mentioned this subject.

'Marlene, I haven't felt like this in years. I don't feel I can go on with Cynthia, but I need a little time. Besides, the political situation changes so quickly that I'm afraid I'll need to stay here a little longer.'

'Don't worry; I'll be with you forever,' she said, as if a load had been taken off her.

'Come on, play something,' she continued cheerfully. 'You told me you play guitar.'

I could never deny her. So I started scratching away at the guitar, singing a Beatles song. Suddenly she tugged at my sleeve.

'Quick, let's go.'

There was a note of desperation in her voice. I glanced around and noticed a male figure some way off. He was wearing a trench coat, but I couldn't make out the features of his face. He looked like a passer-by who had stopped to listen to our little show.

'Why? What's wrong?'

She took my arm and we left quickly. Marlene turned around every so often to see if he was following us. A shadow came over her face. I felt I was discovering another side to her that I didn't know. We got into the car and didn't say a word until we reached Gertsena Street. I parked by the kerb and turned off the engine.

'Perhaps you should tell me the meaning of all this?'

'It's nothing.'

'We ran away like hunted animals.'

'I'm afraid. Nothing more. We're afraid even of our shadow here. Wherever I go in my life I'll be afraid. It's a Kafkaesque fear; there's no cause. Perhaps I'm afraid because we get on so well.'

'You've come to Moscow to study. You're making a film. Is there something I don't know?'

'No. I've told you everything.'

'Then tell me what the hell you're afraid of. Who was that man looking at us? An old flame?'

'Kevin, believe me. I told you that I've been on my own all this time in Moscow. I only had one platonic relationship with a Russian filmmaker. All I care about is getting back to Berlin and seeing Erich. He's the only man in my life—apart from you.'

We went home without another word. The next morning I had to leave early for an emergency assignment in Nagorno-Karabakh. I rose at dawn. She carried on sleeping. Before I left the flat I kissed her tenderly. When I returned to Moscow two days later she had disappeared.

[Moscow, 10 November]

'Kevin, New York wants you again.'

The teleprinter was ringing ceaselessly, piercing my ear as stories from Reuters and TASS were churned out, and the office television was constantly on, relaying the latest developments. The previous evening, 9 November, the Berlin Wall had fallen. The editors of the paper hadn't stopped ringing, asking for more and more: the reactions of Gorbachev or some other Politburo member, the geopolitical plans of the Red Army after the apparent loss of East Germany, the likely conspiratorial moves of the Party hardcore, looming developments in the other Soviet satellites, from Czechoslovakia to Romania.

I picked up the phone and heard Whitesmith seeking an urgent answer to whether Gorbachev had pushed Erich Bauer off his seat, or if the East German dictator had fallen under the weight of the events within Germany. Needles in haystacks. Questions on the course of the twentieth century that I had to answer in a few hours.

I promised that I would do what I could, and took another aspirin. I had a splitting headache from two days and nights without sleep since I returned to Moscow. Svetlana had told me that Marlene had gathered her things and left a few hours after my departure. Since then she had shown no sign of life.

When significant events were taking place, the American consul and I would speak on the phone or go out to lunch to exchange opinions. The fruit of such meetings would emerge in his diplomatic telegrams to the State Department as 'Well-informed sources in the Soviet capital consider...' or in my reports as 'A senior diplomat who preferred to remain anonymous revealed that...'. The third time we spoke that day, the consul had a bright idea: he suggested we go that afternoon to the opening of the exhibition on Soviet technology. Someone from the Politburo or the government would certainly be there, so we could kill two birds with one stone: atmosphere and official response.

The last person I wanted to see at the exhibition centre opposite Gorky Park was Oleg Yelin. He had complained to the embassy about my interview with Pioneer and was clearly looking for a chance to reprimand me. On the other hand, for a Western journalist there was no one more suitable that day than the head of the KGB.

A dozen colleagues had made a ring around him, and when I approached they were asking him about the role of the Soviet Union in Bauer's demise. Predictably he was denying any involvement. He recognized me immediately: we had once conversed for some time at a reception at the American embassy. As part of perestroika, a group of CIA agents had come to Moscow to meet their KGB counterparts. Perhaps it was a mistake for me to ask, 'Several weeks ago Gorbachev publicly stated to Bauer that those who are slow to adapt to developments are overtaken by life. It seems that his fate was decided from then?'

He looked at me with venom.

'I have no inclination to answer your questions, Mr Danaher.'

'Why this special honour?'

'Because between the leadership of the Party and that of the mafia you prefer the latter.'

'I simply published my interview with Mr Tamurian. You could rebut it.'

'I don't tend to bother rebutting mafiosi.'

Then he asked angrily, 'Are you one of those in the West who consider media to be the fourth power?'

'If that helps the conversation...'

'Well then, be careful not to use your power. For there are others with powers, and they might use them.'

'Is that a threat?' I asked, as the consul pulled me discreetly away.

He looked at me menacingly. 'Anything but. Simply advice.'

He turned his back and went away, drawing with him the other journalists and his minions. I remained alone with the consul. He murmured, 'Doesn't sound good.'

'They have so many problems; there's no way Yelin's going to bother with me.'

We began walking towards the back of the exhibition. The consul changed topic.

'What happened to that ethereal being you introduced us to?'

I told him my sorrow and felt better. Heartbreak provokes the same reactions as bereavement: you tell every detail of the final moments to rid yourself of the unbearable weight of their memory.

'Yet she seemed enchanted by you.'

'She probably couldn't handle the charm.'

'Perhaps it's for the best. Don't forget that there's Cynthia, too.'

'I was seriously considering separation.'

'You're outrageous! Have you told Marlene?'

'More or less.'

'That makes her disappearance even more mysterious. You would expect her to be permanently attached to you.'

'She's not your average woman, believe me.'

'Come on, Kevin. We all say that.'

I took another aspirin for my headache. Leonard, like a good diplomat, offered consolation.

'Focus on your work and you'll forget about it. Historic events are taking place!'

'That's the worst thing. I can't concentrate.'

We had reached the end of the exhibition. The consul changed topic again, pointing at a bench.

'Look at this new Soviet invention. A telephone with a special display that tells you the number that's calling. If you want you pick it up; if you don't, you don't. Ideal for Don Juan.'

'That's just what I need. Every day I'm hovering over the telephone hoping that when it rings it'll be her, but it's always Whitesmith.'

The device cost just ten dollars. I bought one for me and one as a present for Fabio, then I returned to the office to write my piece. 'The chairman of the KGB denies any Soviet involvement in the fall of Bauer and the "wall of shame"'.

When two days later Marlene reappeared, I was playing in my living room with Howard. We were kneeling on the carpet around a 'made in the USSR' electric car track, but the cars were constantly derailing. Cynthia was in the office, bent over some architectural plans. She picked up the phone and called for me. I was visibly shaken when I heard Marlene at the other end of the line asking to meet immediately. From that moment, I think, Cynthia started to suspect that another woman had come between us. I tried unsuccessfully to sound formal, took my trench coat and left with a muttered excuse.

She would be waiting at Pushkin Square, outside the newly opened McDonald's. The appearance of the famous fast-food chain in Moscow had caused a sociopolitical shock. A few hours after its opening, the line was longer than the one outside Lenin's Mausoleum. A famous television presenter had identified the opening of the McDonald's with the dawn of democracy in the Soviet Union. The far-right, anti-Semitic group Pamyat had organized a protest, since Coca Cola and other products of the corrupt West were being flaunted in the square of the great Russian poet.

I arrived about six o'clock. Despite the light snow, the line snaked around the square and was already spreading towards Gorky Street. You had to wait at least two hours to be served. As happened with any Western import—ideas or products—Russia had managed to make it its own, effecting a complete transformation: fast food had become its opposite. The same seems to have happened with Marxism, but that's another story.

I found her shivering in the middle of the line. Then I saw Erich for the first time. He looked a little older than nine, and I realized immediately that he was her son: he had the same beauty. Marlene kissed me on the cheek, but I felt that her lips were burning.

'Kevin, this is Erich. Erich, let me introduce you to Kevin.'

She had a cunning look about her, as if introducing two men competing for the same woman. From her smile I felt that she was enjoying herself, that she liked playing the contested woman. The child muttered something in Russo-German. When I suggested we go to one of the good restaurants in Moscow, he scowled and looked imploringly at his mother.

'I promised him that as soon as we got to Moscow we would go to McDonald's. There isn't one in East Berlin and what with all the crowds after the Wall came down, we couldn't visit West Berlin.'

I hadn't seen her for six days, but it seemed like several centuries.

'When did you arrive?'

'This morning, on the plane.'

Thankfully the free Soviet black market solved the problem of the line on Pushkin Square. Organized groups of queuers were formed a few days after the opening of McDonald's. Instead of waiting for hours, you could order from a group that had people in the line. Those taking the order would inform the person at the front and the hamburgers would arrive in five minutes. They charged fifty per cent extra—next to nothing, if you consider that in the Soviet Union a main meal costs less than a dollar on the black market. We ended up eating our hamburgers and fries in my Volvo station wagon. On the back seat, the child was having his first taste of Western haute cuisine and inspecting the electric windows. I gave him another Coca Cola to play with and then turned to Marlene. My face must have been full of questions.

'The boy's grandfather was suddenly taken ill and I had to go to collect him,' she said in a completely natural tone. 'I left in such a panic for the airport that I didn't even manage to leave a note. I planned to call you from Berlin, but then the Wall fell and in all that confusion... Are you angry with me?'

I was just happy to see her again. I stroked her hand gently, trying not to let the boy see.

'Was it your wife who picked up the phone?'

'She came with Howard yesterday. I'm afraid we'll have some practical difficulties.'

Erich said something in German to his mother.

She turned to me and said with a smile, 'He's pestering me... He wants to ask you a favour.'

I looked at him. He looked down bashfully and said something in German again. Clearly he was asking his mother to say it.

'He's wondering if you have permission to sit on the platform during the parades in Red Square,' Marlene explained.

'I have an invitation for this year's parade. Does he want me to shoot Yelin?'

I remember Marlene recoiling slightly at Yelin's name, but I didn't pay any attention then.

'He wants you to take him to the parade for the anniversary of the Revolution. He loves all that—the missiles, the tanks, the atmosphere.'

I have found parades unbearably tedious ever since childhood, but that moment I saw Erich smile for the first time. His mother smiled at me too. Well, this is what happens if you always give children what they want—and more to the point, women...

I saw Marlene every day after that. It's true that my contract with the newspaper didn't account for the use of the office as a studio flat, but nor did it forbid it. She would come to my office around ten in the evening, after I had sent Natasha home. We would stay until one, making love against the backdrop of the teleprinter, the newspaper archive and the fax machine, the symbol of our meeting. If I ever split up with Cynthia and married

Marlene I would make the fax machine our coat of arms. The Taganka compound might have been ugly, but Moscow by night was magnificent from the tenth floor—especially when Marlene was lying naked on my desk, looking out at the lit streets, and I was behind her, biting her neck and stroking her thighs. I was living a fairy tale—the incident at the pond and her sudden disappearance hardly concerned me. I was madly in love with her and it seemed reciprocal. I had started doubting my theory on the ruin of romance under communism.

Cynthia's presence seemed to concern me more than Marlene—on the surface, at least. She had led me to believe that she was jealous, but able to control her emotions. Her short film would be completed in a few days and she wanted to leave Moscow soon, though she hadn't decided if she would return to Germany. In any case, she would wait and see how things developed, whether this would be the final fall of communism. At some point, when I asked her if she would like to live with me in New York, I saw a spark flash across her eyes. She replied that she would love to, and that after a short period of adjustment she would be able to handle her own expenses—and Erich's too. But she added that I would have to decide about all that.

I was still in a quandary, mainly because of Howard. But every day I realized more that my relationship with Cynthia couldn't last. If there were problems before, now I was completely devoted to Marlene, in mind and body. I loved Cynthia and didn't want to hurt her by revealing the other woman in my life, but I watched our relationship deteriorating as time went by. In the end the usual happened—someone else decided for us.

Given the incident that occurred on the evening before the parade, I should have realized that something was going to happen. I had capitalized on a day off from my insatiable relationship with Marlene and gone home early. Howard immediately called me over for a game of tanks. We each had a tank and were bombarding one another. The television, meanwhile, was bombarding us with the evening news, which was solely about the preparations for the big parade the next day.

Howard turned to me and asked sweetly, 'Dad, can I ask you a favour?'

'Go ahead,' I said calmly, hoping that he wouldn't ask the one thing I couldn't fulfil.

'Will you take me tomorrow to the parade on Red Square?'

I could have pretended that I wasn't allowed to take anyone with me, but I wasn't thinking straight.

'I'm not going.'

'But you just said to Natasha on the phone that you're going, didn't you?'

I felt Cynthia's eyes pinned on me.

'I've changed my mind. I'm not going.'

Children have a rare instinct for whether you're telling the truth. Howard ran into Cynthia's arms, crying. 'Mom, Dad won't take me to the parade. I hate Moscow. I want to go back to New York.'

It was almost twelve thirty when I finished my fruitless search of Red Square. It was one of the most awful moments of my life: I now had to go and tell a mother that I had lost the child she had placed in my trust for a few hours. As I walked towards our meeting point, late, I starting thinking of logical arguments to calm her. In reality I was trying to calm myself. There's no way we wouldn't find him... We would go to the police... I would explain that I was a foreign correspondent and they had to mobilize all their forces. I might even call the consul for help. Or grease the palm of the Moscow police chief.

I waited more than half an hour for Marlene at the old stables. In the end I was feeling relieved—I decided that the child, when he lost me, had probably gone by himself to the meeting point and found his mother before I arrived. I took my car, which I had parked on Kalinin Prospekt, just beyond the Lenin Library, and arrived in Taganka Square via the ring road about one thirty. The office was closed, as I had given Natasha a day off. She would be celebrating the anniversary of the Revolution at her dacha outside Moscow. The telephone was ringing madly as I opened the locks of the new iron-barred door one by one. Similar doors had been installed throughout the compound following a recent spate of break-ins. I managed to grab the phone. It was Whitesmith, from New York.

'Kevin! Where the hell have you been? We've been looking for you for ages. What's happened? A new revolution?'

His voice was triumphant. Any shake-up in the

Soviet Union would prove he was right to have supported Pinochet and the dictatorship in Chile. As I was muttering some excuse, the doorbell rang. I told him to wait while I opened it. It was Marlene, smiling.

'Sorry I'm late. I imagined you'd have come here.'

When I realized she didn't have Erich with her, I spluttered something like, 'Erich isn't with me. I lost him in the parade.'

Before she could reply I returned to the phone, told Whitesmith I would call him back, and put it down without listening to his protests.

Marlene went pale and flopped onto the leather sofa. I described to her what had happened and then picked up the telephone receiver.

'I'll call the police.'

She gestured that it would be futile.

'Didn't you notice any movement around you?'

I connected my camcorder to the television and, as calmly as I could manage, began to look for the scene with Erich and the foreign diplomats.

Erich was speaking to one man, while two others around him were following the conversation. He didn't seem annoyed or afraid; he even laughed at one point. Then the camera turned back to the scenes in the square.

Marlene groaned. 'They've kidnapped him. That's Müller, officially the first secretary of the German Democratic Republic, but in reality the Moscow "stationmaster" of the Stasi, the East German secret service.'

'How do you know him?'

She lit a cigarette.

'I'll explain.'

'Perhaps you should have done that some time ago.'

At that moment the telephone rang. I prayed it was the kidnappers. If they wanted a ransom I'd give it without a second thought. This time it wasn't Whitesmith, but Weber himself.

'Kevin, I don't get it. Historic developments are taking place over there, we're thinking of bringing out a special edition and you disappear and then put the phone down on Whitesmith.'

'Something serious has happened,' I replied.

'Have you got a scoop?' his voice was suddenly excited.

'It's a private matter.'

'Has something happened? Cynthia and Howard are fine. We called earlier, but they had no idea where you were.'

'It's something else. I can't tell you.'

'Kevin, you're out of your mind!' he fumed. 'We didn't send you to Moscow to get caught up in private matters or whatever other matters these are. We won't manage to put out a special edition now, but for tomorrow's issue I want a full report of what happened in Red Square. Were you even there?'

'I recorded it all on my camcorder.'

'Well, maybe you should find a job in TV!' exploded Weber, slamming the phone down.

Hardman interrupted me again with a gesture. I had the impression that if I went on much longer he would want to put a sock in my mouth.

'Is that what happened, Mr Weber?' he asked the boss of the paper.

'Generally speaking, yes. But I don't remember the details of the conversation.'

The FBI chief eyed us both suspiciously, then said, 'Continue, Mr Danaher.'

I paid less attention to Weber's threat than I would have under other circumstances. I turned impatiently to Marlene. She lit another cigarette, while the previous one still smouldered in the ashtray. Her lovely green eyes were teary.

'About ten years ago I married Wolf Bauer, the son of the general secretary of the communist party and president of East Germany. One year later I had Erich, who took his grandfather's name. When he was two years old, I decided we would separate. Wolf was an alcoholic, incapable of working and emotionally emasculated. He was a spoilt prince who had everything and never had to worry. He felt sidelined within his own family, particularly after the death of his mother, before I knew him. The dictator had a great weakness for his daughter Eva, who was interested in politics. Wolf was a weak character, who got married in a final attempt to stand on his own two feet. When he realized that no woman could replace his mother, he devoted himself entirely to alcohol. He didn't care about our child and he became more and more violent towards me.

'Erich Bauer was uncompromising when I announced my decision to separate from his son. Two months earlier, in early 1982, his daughter Eva had died of a heart attack. That thickened his skin. He told me that he understood my problems with his wayward and incapable son, but the Bauer family honour and image in the country came first. He advised me to be patient for the sake of my son to whom, it's fair to say, he was devoted. He told me that he would give all his property to the child.

'One day I decided that I couldn't live like that anymore. I was suffocating. I took a small suitcase with a few possessions, went outside and started running down the street, until the official residence of the general secretary, where we lived, had disappeared. I planned to find a job and then go back to collect Erich. The dictator behaved like a mafia boss to a treacherous, defecting member of the "family". Perhaps he was afraid that I would publish what I knew about the opulent way of life in the palace. Two weeks later, Bauer forbade me from seeing my child. I went to find him, fell on my knees and pleaded to be able to see him just once a month. He told me it was too late, and after that he refused to see me or speak to me on the telephone.

'When Erich started to ask for me, Bauer ordered the rewriting of all the books at the special school where children of the nomenklatura went. They erased the word "mother" from all texts and gave strict instruction to the child's governesses: when he asked for his mother, they would deny the concept of a mother and deny that he had one. Two of the governesses couldn't handle the psychological pressure and resigned, one after a nervous breakdown.

'Since the child kept asking for me, they decided to change tactics. They would slander me to the point that he would hate me. Then I too, in my desperation, made a mistake. Six months had passed and I hadn't held him once. I would stand outside his school and try to see him from afar, without being noticed. I had the misguided inspiration of finding a lawyer to pursue my rights as a mother through the courts, since our laws were supposed to be much more progressive than capitalist ones. The lawyer was considered a supporter of dissenters and unjustly treated people, but in reality he was collaborating with the secret police. Since he had contacts in the West and went to West Berlin almost every day, I asked him to disclose the case to a newspaper. It was the excuse Bauer was looking for.

'To make ends meet I was working in a state gallery in the centre of Berlin, being a fine arts graduate. First they ordered the director to sack me, and a few days later they arrested me and took me to a remote villa, half an hour from Berlin. They accused me of collaborating with the CIA in an attempt to escape the country with my child, thereby intending to bring the socialist system, the general secretary and the party into disrepute. I was supposedly preparing the ground through publications in the Western press. Their only evidence was the lawyer's testimony and a photograph of me posing in the gallery with an American painter whom we had invited to exhibit.

'The inquest was completely Stalinist: they tried to make me confess to something that we all knew was absurd. In this kind of omnipotent regime you feel desperately alone. I hadn't seen any relation for two months. No one in my family knew that I had been arrested; they thought I had disappeared or done a runner. Your only hope is to confess to guilt, to put an end to the isolation and psychological torture.

'Meanwhile they were telling my son that I was planning on kidnapping him in a helicopter of the "evil" Americans and taking him far away from his grandfather and father. When he asked where I was, they replied that I had abandoned him and was going around with other men to make his father ill. Erich is used to getting what he wants—toys, computers, his own room to watch movies with his friends. Bauer had promised him that when he grew up he would buy him a Ferrari, even a private jet. They told him I wanted to take him to poor capitalist countries, where he would be unhappy.

'I was stubborn and refused to sign the confession. I was so desperate—not being able to see my child—that life didn't interest me anymore. In the end I was saved by Indira Gandhi. The Indian prime minister had taken a liking to me when we had visited India as a family, before my troubles started. She was on good terms with my father-in-law, since she was considered leader of the Non-Aligned Movement and an ally of the Soviets.

'Shortly before her assassination she officially visited Berlin. I heard about her visit by chance, on my guard's radio. I had realized that my doctor was in love with me—he was the same one I had in the palace, as they didn't trust any others. I pretended that I liked him, and I gave him a note for Gandhi.'

'You mean that you got involved with the doctor?'

She hung her head sadly.

'I had no other choice. I was fortunate that the note didn't fall into their hands when I was writing it. I twice escaped by a whisker—they would have accused me of inviting foreigners to interfere in the country's internal matters. In the note I made just one request: that they let me see Erich for a short time.

'Bauer didn't agree to let me see him, but he allowed Gandhi to visit me. She could hardly recognize me; I had lost almost fifteen kilos. She told me that the only thing she could do was ask them to send me to Moscow using my studies as a pretext. Don't imagine things were like now, with perestroika. Back then Moscow was considered luxury exile. So I ended up here for six whole years, without the right to return to my country, not even to visit.

'I hadn't seen Erich since then. It was the thought of him that kept me going, nothing else... I didn't dream of anyone else all those years. When Bauer fell, along with the Wall, I realized that all the commotion provided a unique opportunity. I went to Berlin and waited outside his school. Even though he hadn't seen me for such a long time, he recognized me at once and we fell into each other's arms. His bodyguards knew the whole story, but those days they were at sea; they were afraid for their own fate. The dictator and his son had been put under house arrest. I told the guards that I would go for a walk with Erich and then take him to his grandfather's villa, but of course I would prefer to die than lose him again. My one-time father-in-law was furious with the bodyguards and I found out that he swore to get the child back.

'He might have been downgraded from general secretary, but he still lurks in the background, pulling strings. His successor to the party leadership is one he groomed and who considered him his spiritual father. The communists are still in power; they control the army and the police, the secret service, the big companies, foreign affairs... the whole state mechanism. I knew that they would want to get the child back as soon as they had reformed, but I didn't have the money or a visa to go to another country. I got him a passport quickly and we fled to Moscow.'

'You hid your whole life from me.'

She was whimpering.

'I tried to tell you many times, but changed my mind at the last moment. The first days that we met I had no reason to reveal my past. When I fell in love with you I was afraid that, if I told you the truth, you would accuse me of hiding all this from you. Then I wanted to forget the past, to begin a new life with you. How could I imagine that they would kidnap Erich?'

'And that night at Patriarch's Ponds, was that...?'

'Yes, even here in my unhappiness they didn't leave me in peace. Kevin, if I lose the child again I can't go on. I can't endure more of the torture I've been through these last years—not one minute.'

'Don't worry; we'll get him back,' I said, wiping away her tears.

PART TWO

Russian Roulette

Olga didn't say a word.

'Hey!' Vladimir cried. 'Why don't you love me like I love you?'

'I love my country,' she replied.

'But so do I!' Vladimir exclaimed.

'And I also love…' Olga continued, detaching herself from the young man's embrace.

'What?'

Olga raised her clear blue eyes to him. Her reply was terse.

'The Party.'

SERGEI ANTONOV
The Great Heart, 1957

That afternoon I knew I would find the American consul at the old furniture auction near Lenin Stadium, beside the river. We met at that place almost every week. I sat next to him in the front row and he immediately proposed a deal: if I withdrew my interest in the nineteenth-century escritoire, which we had both had our eye on for a while, he would withdraw his from the screen with the hand-carved engravings.

'I'll give them both to you. I just want one favour.'

I told him about the kidnapping. The auction had begun and Darrell raised his number. Having won a wooden hatbox, he turned and asked me exactly what I wanted.

'To find out where the child is now.'

'Come on, Kevin, you know that's not the embassy's job.'

'But I know there is a unit in the embassy that does exactly that kind of job. They must have some informer among the East Germans.'

He looked at me thoughtfully. The escritoire would shortly be sold without him noticing.

'You know that I find Marlene beautiful and charming, I told you that from the start. But I think you need to put a stop to this, and fast. An entire world is crumbling. You can't abandon everything just to try to free this child.'

'Fine, but I'm to blame for his kidnapping.'

He paused to consider whether he would bid for an old mirror.

'No, you're not. She's to blame for not telling you who she was. She didn't warn you about her son. Don't you see that you're unwittingly getting into serious trouble? You have Cynthia and your son, your career…'

'Career isn't everything.'

'Bullshit, Kevin! Bullshit! If it weren't for your career, you wouldn't be in Moscow. You'd be planting potatoes in Connecticut.'

'I love her, Leonard. I'm in love with her.'

'You're mad, Kevin. You can't fight Müller. He controls everything. The Stasi has the biggest network of any secret service on the planet. It's better organized than the CIA. After the Second World War it was reorganized by the Soviet secret service, but the students quickly overtook the teacher. You know what the Germans are like: much more methodical and faithful to their duty. They have the Prussian tradition behind them, while the Russians have nothing to show but the disorganization and dissolution of the Tsarist state —all the chaos that led to the Bolshevik Revolution. You can do business with the Soviets with a little vodka and a few thousand dollars. The East Germans are trickier; they're not worn down by alcohol. They believed that their socialism was superior to the Soviet brand, and they don't hide their scorn for the Russians.

'Apart from being stationmaster, Müller is also first secretary of the most important embassy in Moscow. Without us, the Soviets can survive—we were essentially enemies until a short while ago. Perhaps we still are. But without East Germany, the whole Soviet Empire will collapse and the division of Europe will be meaningless. Marlene is right when she tells you that Bauer and his henchmen are still governing her country. And if you want some extra information, the conservatives are gaining ground here too. The Soviet regime realizes that perestroika puts everything at risk. Gorbachev will probably fall into line with them, and I'm afraid that today's episodes in Red Square will likely be a catalyst. Some of our informers claimed that they were organized by the KGB.'

'Can I publish that?'

In all the chaos, I still had to find something interesting to write about the day's events.

'Sure, just don't attribute it to me. It's a known secret that in this country even the opposition organizations are infiltrated by the secret service. After today's fiasco, the conservatives expect Gorbachev to fall into their arms. When his own people—the organizations that were born because of his very reforms—jeer at him, he has no choice but to turn to the conservatives. They've been telling him for ages that this perestroika lark had better stop. He can't remain friendless, shut inside the walls of the Kremlin. The General Staff of the Red Army are furious about the fall of the Wall and from their point of view they're right: if they lose East Germany and Poland, they lose their buffers, their protection against attack. It seems cynical, but that's our world. Cynical.'

'Yes, but Gorbachev doesn't get on with Bauer.'

'Don't be naïve. They might have disagreements about which is the fastest route to communism, but Gorbachev didn't want Bauer to fall and Bauer doesn't want that for Gorbachev. They belong to the same camp, they're comrades at arms and they've known each other a long time. They're peas in a pod. And you're going to fight them all and free the child yourself? I think you've been watching too many movies.'

'I see that, for a diplomat, love means nothing in the face of power relations and geopolitical interests.'

I got up angrily to leave, but the consul grabbed my arm and sat me down. Staring ahead at the Russian auctioneer, he said sarcastically, 'Do you know Lenin's famous saying, that all paid work is prostitution?'

'What's that supposed to mean? Self-criticism?'

'News on the daughter of your maid. You know, the student in love with one of our countrymen and wanting a visa… Well, we asked the Soviet police—it's a process we follow in all visa applications to see if they have a clean criminal record.'

'And what was the result of this… creative partnership?'

'Interdyevouska… The word comes from the Communist International's Internationale. An international girl—a currency whore. She's been arrested three times by the Department of Morality for selling herself to foreigners in the expensive hotels. I'm afraid that the system has corrupted us all.'

'You're right. Every single one of us.'

A satirical Soviet newspaper had written that Moscow's Leningradsky Hotel would someday take its place in history beside the first Soviet worker-peasant-soldiers of St Petersburg: it was here that the first casino in Soviet history opened. The Leningradsky is between the ring road and the railway station of the same name. It is one of the seven wedding-cake buildings that decorate the Moscow skyline. The tallest is 240 metres high, including its cherry-on-the-top tower. Building work began in 1947 and mainly relied on the forced labour of political detainees. Stalin himself supervised the architectural plans, ensuring that Moscow's buildings were taller than New York's skyscrapers. An eighth similar structure was to be built next to Red Square, where the Rossiya Hotel stands today, but it was called off because the Kremlin would have looked like a provincial hovel next to it. Three of the buildings are today either occupied by public services or are residences reserved for the favoured artists of the regime. Another is the Ministry of External Affairs, another the university, and the final two are hotels. Soviet citizens who worked voluntarily on Saturdays, Subbotnik days, to complete these cathedrals of socialism could never have imagined that one of these buildings would eventually be turned into a temple of vice.

Entry to the casino cost ten dollars with proof of the lawful provenance of the currency—or fifteen without proof, with the extra five dollars for the porter's pocket. Most of the hotel's customers were Soviet party officials and mafiosi, and they simply moved to the ground floor when the casino opened. The main hall had two roulette tables, five or six tables for blackjack and a bar at the back. A few months after its opening, a trivial altercation between two customers ended up in a shoot-out, with two dead and several wounded.

The evening that I went to look for Pioneer I found the Leningradsky casino packed and smoky. Most customers were Russian, with some Azeri or Georgian and some Kazakh. Pioneer was there—I noticed the familiar Afghani first; he was keeping a close eye on the punters. Pioneer was sitting at the roulette wheel with a mountain of chips in front of him, but had abandoned the game of chance for a Latvian beauty. There he was playing with certainty.

He was pleased to see a Westerner with whom he could put the world to rights. He shoved the girl off his lap and motioned that I should sit beside him. A waiter was summoned and rushed over with a broad smile plastered across his face. After I had ordered a Russkaya and tonic, Pioneer asked me what good fortune had brought me to this lair of his. I requested to talk privately and he dismissed the other girls loitering around him with the air of someone who can call them back whenever he wants.

I took a few sips of the vodka, then gave him the gist of the story, asking him to help locate the child.

He lit a cigarette and blew the smoke in the face of an indiscreet leggy woman in a miniskirt, who was approaching. He cast an eye around before saying, 'I think you're in luck. Wait a moment.'

He went over to a blackjack table, where he watched the game for a minute or two before whispering something in the ear of a player with greased-back hair and long sideburns. He put his arm over his shoulder and they walked towards the exit. He returned shortly, looking thoughtful.

'I'm afraid you're out of luck. The ball landed on zero.'

'I haven't played roulette in a while. What do you mean?'

'If they're holding the boy in the East German embassy, you're in trouble. The place is controlled by another "family". The guy I just spoke to is one of the key players there. He told me you'll need half the Red Army to get in. It's like a fortress: none of the offices look outwards, so spying is impossible. There's no telephone in any office—they're all in passageways—so there's no way of tapping the phones, even with the latest technology that can listen from across the street. They have a well in the garden too, so they'll have water if there's a war.'

He looked at me sadly.

'How did you get mixed up in all this?' he said. Then, pointing at the girls who were kicking their heels, he added coyly, '... with so many women in the city.'

'How could I know? The day we met, you drowned me in statistics.'

'I heard that you had trouble with Yelin after my interview. Do you have anyone to help you?'

I shook my head, but my mind went to Yuri Lubimov, the former spy who had come to dinner.

He looked at me like a doctor who'd handed me a cancer diagnosis.

'You'd better give up. Stay here with me and play American, not Russian, roulette.'

'I can't abandon a child.'

I must have struck a chord, because he slapped me heartily on the back.

'You're a great guy. I'll let you know when I have news.'

I downed the rest of my vodka.

'Want another one? Relax here with us for a bit.'

He pointed to the girls, before introducing me to a Kazakh with long, narrow eyes.

'She's all yours.'

She bared her cleavage in affirmation. Just my luck! After so many years in the Soviet Union I had found the first person who really believed in common ownership, but I wasn't in a position to take advantage. As I left I discerned a mixture of confusion and sadness in the eyes of Pioneer's girls—the sentiment was shared. I reached the compound without being stopped for an alcotest. Entering my apartment I saw a note from Cynthia, who had thankfully gone to sleep. I'd had a call from my publisher to remind me that I had to submit the manuscript of my book very soon.

Patrick waited beside the museum entrance for her to leave work. Then he followed her, glancing behind to confirm that no one was trailing them. When she turned the corner, he caught up with her and grabbed her arm. She turned, startled. 'Oh, it's you! I haven't heard from you for a month. I thought you'd forgotten me.'

Patrick made a clumsy gesture, like a child not taken seriously.

'I told you I'd come back. You're not easily forgotten.'

He looked at her. She was as beautiful as ever. He was absolutely right to come and get her.

'I've prepared everything. We're leaving on Wednesday.'

'The day after tomorrow? I must—'

'I'm here for two days. Tomorrow I'm going to a psychiatrist where some poor devil is being treated for reformist psychosis. They let me back in on condition that I would write a flattering report.'

'When shall we discuss...?'

'We'd better meet on Wednesday; we shouldn't be seen together. I'm staying at the Intercontinental with a friend who's agreed to help. She has long red hair too. We came by car through Hungary. On Wednesday we'll leave together for Austria—I have a passport ready in her name but with your photograph—one of those I took on the train.'

He perceived a certain hesitation.

'Have you changed your mind?'

'No. But it's all happening so fast. What will we do in France? What will I do?'

'We'll sort that out later. If we love each other…'
She looked at him gratefully.
'Why are you doing all this for me?'
'Because I'm in love with you. I can't live without you. What about you?'
'Well, I'm not living here anyway. I'm surviving. Right now you represent everything—love, life, freedom. Will you love me when we're in the West?'
'No. As soon as we arrive I'll sell you in a monkey parade. I provide pretty redheads to Arab sheiks.'
'Stop it! You don't understand how I feel. I'm leaving everything here. All my life, my friends, my city.'
'… The apartment with your ex-husband and his lover.'
'You can't stomach that, can you.'
'I never will. But I'm sure he'll be pleased you're going.'
'He might bend over backwards to help us.'
'Don't tell him anything. You mustn't talk to anyone, nor act unusually. Don't bring anything with you.'
'A necklace from my wedding is the only valuable thing I own.'
'Come to the Intercontinental at dusk on Wednesday. Can you leave work a little early?'
'What if they fire me?'
She had found her confidence again.
'Take the hotel elevator down to the basement garage. It's in the passage between the reception and the telephones. I'll be waiting at precisely 5 p.m. in a red Golf with French licence plates.'
'And your friend?'

'Don't worry about her. She will have left the country. With her normal passport.'

'I demand an explanation. Now!'

Cynthia had woken up and was rightly spoiling for a fight.

'Can you tell me the meaning of all of this? Since the morning of the parade, they've called a dozen times from New York looking for you. The other day a woman called and you left like a madman. The same woman called another dozen times yesterday afternoon.'

'I'm afraid I can't tell you.'

'Is there someone else?'

Her voice had a severe tone, as if willing me to say no.

'Yes. But that's not the problem.'

'Then what is?'

When your wife catches you with someone else, it's like being arrested by the police: anything you say can be used against you. I said nothing.

'Another woman,' she continued. 'That's it then. You've been taking me for a ride all this time. You haven't touched me for days.'

I kept looking at the computer screen, as if waiting for an invisible hand to write a decent answer.

'Why didn't you take Howard to the parade? Did you take her? If you carry on playing dumb, I'll pack my things and leave tomorrow morning.'

'I think that might be best. I need a little time.'

'As much as you like. We're leaving tomorrow!' she said and slammed the door in my face.

[18 November]

Lubimov was waiting for me at the entrance to Tsentralny Rynok, Moscow's central market. The place is like a foreign country within the capital, controlled by mafias from the Caucasus who give permits to sellers and fix the prices. The Soviet authorities recently tried using military-style operations to bring things into line, but they came a cropper: having bribed the local police, the mafiosi regained control of the area as soon as the Special Forces commandos left.

We entered the great covered market and climbed the stairs between old women selling plastic bags and smugglers of caviar stolen from the state storehouses. In a rectangular hall about fifty metres long were endless counters laden with fresh garden produce. A door at the back led to a muddy courtyard with outdoor stalls, tables and shoppers. Immediately beyond were two covered areas the size of cinemas. In the first were all kinds of meat and, in the second, endless milk products. At one point, when Gorbachev's popularity had hit rock bottom because the state gastronomi —Soviet-style supermarkets—and other food shops were empty, you could find whatever you wanted at the Tsentralny Rynok and half a dozen other markets in Moscow, albeit at New York prices.

I bought two plastic bags and began to fill them with meat, white cheese, caviar and bananas to remind Lubimov of the happy moments of his former service as a spy. As we walked, I told him what had happened.

'I have decided to get the child back, even though she upset me by not telling me the truth from the start.'

He smiled condescendingly, like a wise native to a naïve tourist.

'How do you know that?'

He guffawed.

'I did the same.'

'It's because you're influenced by the climate of espionage, Yuri. Didn't you talk the other day at my place about the paranoid spy who's suspicious of everyone?'

His face darkened suddenly.

'If only it were just a professional vice. But the same happened with all couples. Have you read Orwell's 1984? In 1984 they ask one thing of the protagonist: to betray the woman he loves for Big Brother. Orwell was inspired by Zamyatin's book We, published three years after the October Revolution. The protagonist betrays the woman he loves and transfers his passion to the Benefactor.

'In the era of the Great Terror, one of the worst things that could happen to you was to be judged a "relation of an enemy of the people". The penal code punished not only the enemies of the people, who were probably just people who had read a banned book, but also their close relations. Those who knew the thoughts or actions of the "enemy of the people" were punished with two to five years' imprisonment in a camp. Those who didn't know were treated better: five years' exile. To protect your spouse, they mustn't know. These things don't happen anymore, but the lack of trust has been inscribed on our chromosomes. You consider us a theatre-going people, right?'

'Everyone does.'

'Well, theatre does greatly influence our mindset. One of our most popular plays was written in 1926. Its heroine, Liuba Yarova, became legendary offstage too. The play became a movie, a film series. It was on stage until very recently. After great moral dilemmas, Yarova betrays her husband, an officer of the Whites who fought against the Bolsheviks in the Civil War, and so sends him to a firing squad.'

'I don't see where you're going.'

He looked at me hesitantly.

'I don't find Marlene's behaviour strange. You can't hold it against her that she didn't trust you.'

I sighed with relief.

'Thank you, Yuri. You know, after the kidnapping I had my doubts. Now, if you could help practically…'

I wanted him to find out, if he could, where they were keeping the child and help us get him back. I promised a healthy reward.

'That's kind, though I would do it without pay. I'm bored and hungry for some action. Aside from the fact that you, your house, your Western car, this shopping, all take me back to old times.'

'Do you think we'll find anything?'

At first he laughed, without replying. He was about

sixty, with wavy white hair, blue eyes and gentle features, of average height and with a belly that matched his age. He looked more like a writer or a successful movie director than a spy. Unless, of course, writers or successful movie directors look like spies.

Then he said, in his soft but decisive manner, 'If I asked you about a journalist in Moscow, you could find out relatively easily, because you have many journalist friends. The same goes for me. I have a few good connections in my field.'

He promised to inform me as soon as he had news, then took the two bags and made for the parking lot. I saw him putting them in an old beige Lada, before replacing the windscreen wipers he had hidden in the trunk.

'Why do you think I should be ashamed?' Masha asked, without lowering her head.

I had asked Svetlana to bring her daughter to the apartment. The consul had irritated me with his sarcasm. He hadn't said anything outright, but had used Masha's story to malign Marlene.

Masha was maintaining that prostitution was the only option for young people. She had big brown eyes, protruding lips and wore her hair up with a gold hair clip, making herself look like an innocent young girl. She had long earrings and dressed expensively by Soviet standards: a black leather jacket and jeans. Svetlana had asked her to be present for the discussion.

'But you could find honest work,' I insisted.

'Great. When I finish university I'll get a job in some institute or factory,' Masha said. 'I'll earn a hundred and fifty, maybe two hundred roubles a month. What can you do with that? Everyone is crazy for dollars, like it's our national currency.'

'It would be more honourable just to admit that it's easy money.'

'You think it's easy? It's vile work, but there's nothing else. I want to live. I can't spend my whole life working for nothing. My mother needs medicine for her heart and I have to buy it on the black market, because there's nothing in the pharmacies. I hope that you have a daughter like me if you ever need medicine.'

Masha said the last sentence between sobs. Svetlana stroked her tenderly.

'Don't worry; it's their fault,' she said, pointing upwards. 'The pimps of the Party…'

The last thing that interested me at that moment was a moral evaluation of Soviet society. I headed for my office, but Svetlana stopped me short.

She was a proud woman. She looked me in the eye and said, 'Mr Danaher, if you want me to leave…'

'No, Svetlana, there's no need. I'm very pleased with you. But we do have a problem with Masha's visa. It will be very difficult to persuade the consul that prostitution is a healthy answer to an unhealthy world.'

The great iron gate of Prague's Psychiatric Clinic No. 13 screeched open, and Patrick looked into a small, bare courtyard—no trees, and with potholes full of frozen brown mud. In one corner lay the rusty skeleton of a car, covered with snow. On the right was a two-storey red-brick building that resembled an old school. A red billboard bearing a slogan on the wonders of socialist versus capitalist psychiatry hung over its first floor. In the centre and on the left of the courtyard were two multi-storey concrete buildings. The central one had a kind of freight ramp in front of it, where an ambulance had dumped two bewildered patients like sacks of potatoes.

Patrick made for the red-brick building, the offices of the hospital's directors and doctors, with Gustav, the official guide of Patrick's earlier group, who a month before had passed his request to the ministry. Entering the lobby, they saw a nurse sitting behind a tiny wooden desk and, in one corner, two old and broken white fridges with big rusted black fans. Patrick's guide said something to the nurse, who consulted her papers and motioned them through. The two men went up the marble staircase to the first floor. On the way they encountered two nurses with white blouses, propping up a patient. He was wearing a striped prisoner's outfit, with a number embroidered on his chest in yellow thread. His head was shaven and his fat nose was covered in pussy spots. When they reached the first floor, they followed a passage painted green to an office with a small sign that read, 'Major Ztenka Kerkova'.

The psychiatrist-officer was sitting behind her desk, her head buried in papers. She looked up, made a face that might have been a smile and pointed to two wooden chairs. When Patrick and his guide sat down she asked, 'What exactly do you want to know about citizen A.K.? I am the psychiatrist observing him. I have his file here.'

Patrick had read Kerkova's article in the Journal of Criminology. He glanced at Gustav, who was sitting silently with his legs crossed.

'Reformist psychosis,' Patrick said at last. 'It must be a new illness…'

'Not really,' said Kerkova. 'Citizen A.K. had exhibited the first signs for a while, but we hadn't paid much attention. In 1976 an agent from the secret police notified Psychiatric Clinic No. 1 that A.K. should be examined, but the doctors disregarded the warning. That year he wanted to stand as an independent minister in the elections. He reappeared in 1981 and joined the Socialist Party.'

'The Socialist Party?'

'It's one of our legal parties, part of the National Front, along with the Communist Party and other smaller parties,' Gustav interrupted.

'He joined the Socialist Party to push his agenda and stand in the elections,' Kerkova continued. 'The first part of his manifesto comprised twelve points, mainly structural changes in the economic and social sector, but also changes to our socialist Constitution. The second part was more international: among other things, he suggested free movement, free trade and a common currency in Europe by 1990. No one in the Socialist Party paid any attention to this, so A.K. decided to print and distribute it himself. He printed 1,950 copies using a hectograph, like underground communists. He revealed to us that he got the idea from an old hectograph in the Klement Gottwald Museum.

'One thousand of these pamphlets he posted to addresses he found in the telephone book. Of these, forty per cent were women, ten per cent men and fifty per cent university-educated people regardless of gender. The rest he either posted or took to various public organizations, newspapers and central party organizations. He even printed a manifesto on higher-quality paper for the president of the Democracy.'

Kerkova paused in her charges to draw breath. She was a bulky brunette of about forty-five. She wore a men's watch on her left wrist.

'We discovered him after a year and he was prosecuted for criminal activities. The charge was for propaganda against basic constitutional principles of socialist power, the state and Czechoslovak society, as well as against the international interests of our democracy.'

'You mean he was a dissident,' said Patrick.

'You'll be making a grave mistake if you write that we section those who are against the regime, Mr...'

'Ventura,' completed Patrick.

'Mr Ventura,' Kerkova repeated. 'A.K. is not a dissident. In his manifesto he even criticized Charter 77, the anti-communist group. He called on it to move to creative activity, because, as he said, "it's only interested in the negative aspects of our society".'

'I am not prejudiced,' said Patrick, trying to sound

convincing, 'but I don't know what category such a person falls into.'

'Mad,' Kerkova said stiffly. 'Mentally ill. In his apartment we found tens of thousands of files, perfectly sorted. He systematically listened to various Czech radio programmes, Voice of America, Radio Free Europe and the BBC. He was particularly interested in the UN, keeping notes on the activity of its member states for ten years. During his examination, it emerged that A.K.'s mental capacities and intelligence—it is worth noting that he has a university education—were much higher than average. Do you understand?'

'Is education linked to the illness?' Patrick asked, trying to stay calm.

Kerkova looked at Gustav impatiently. He shrugged his shoulders as if to say, 'We have to explain even the blindingly obvious to this idiot.'

She took a deep breath to contain her exasperation, and said, 'I mean, he understood very well that these things were not his area of expertise. Therefore, wasting his time and money on stamps and printing manifestoes means he must be unbalanced. The specialists who examined him confirmed he is suffering from reformist psychosis, a mental illness characterized by paranoia based on a logically coherent system of paranoid ideas with social and political content. Reformist paranoia usually occurs in people aged thirty-five to fifty, among predisposed individuals.'

'Oh, so he was predisposed to it.'

'I've already explained that he had exhibited signs since 1976,' Kerkova said with satisfaction. 'The patient declares new ideas every so often, suggests ways of changing the world, as if he can make it better. Another typical feature of the illness, which we observe in A.K., is the patient's unswerving belief that his or her ideas are correct and not the product of illness. They feel completely healthy and try to persuade those around them of the soundness of their ravings. That's what A.K. did—he had a lover, whom he tried to initiate in his ideas.'

Patrick gritted his teeth. If he was to succeed in his plans with Anna, he had to show he was convinced.

'Did he succeed?' he asked with feigned interest.

'He stubbornly refused to cooperate and will not reveal her name. Even now, here in the hospital, he continues to send letters to the president of the Democracy. His therapy hasn't progressed at all.'

I hope it never does, Patrick thought of saying. He smiled and stood up, closing his notebook carefully.

'Thank you very much for the information. It was most pertinent.'

Kerkova had one more thing to say.

'The problem is serious. For if the paranoiac doesn't manage to push his agenda in official ways, he will probably try to implement it by force. The fact that we discovered him quickly means we avoided serious political mistakes. Do you see what lengths we must go to as a society to prevent and isolate such criminals —and their accomplices?'

He must be very much in love not to reveal his woman's name, Patrick reflected, as a guard heaved open the hospital gate.

[20 November]

'Where did you find that wig?'

Lubimov had kept his promise. Two days after our meeting he came to my apartment with two important pieces of information. Firstly, Erich was still in Moscow: he was being held at the East German embassy, which had a compound for diplomats and employees. Secondly, almost every afternoon a governess and two Stasi agents took him to the funfair in Gorky Park. The child played various games, finishing with shooting, a sport his grandfather had introduced him to at an early age. Lubimov hadn't found out, however, if and when they were attempting to spirit him out of the Soviet Union.

Marlene and I agreed to act as soon as possible: winter was fast approaching and the funfair would be closing any day. The day before the operation, Marlene, Lubimov and I observed the movements of the child and his escort from afar. One of the East German agents waited in the car, which was parked at the entrance to the funfair, and the other accompanied Erich and the governess. Every half hour the two men changed roles: the one in the funfair would return to the car, sending the warm one to Erich. The visit lasted about an hour and a half and at every change of shift the child remained just with his governess for three or four minutes. Throughout our observation, Marlene showed remarkable calm. At only one point did I see tears in her eyes.

Back at my apartment, we rehearsed our plan several times, using a wind-up funfair toy of Howard's, three plastic cars and some toy soldiers. We would arrive at Gorky Park with two cars, mine and Lubimov's. Marlene and I would go into the funfair and try to make Erich notice us. During the changeover we would grab him from his governess and run to the exit. At the same moment, Lubimov would ram the agents' car, distracting them for a moment. That was all we needed to get out of the gate and reach our car. So they wouldn't recognize her, Marlene had brought a blonde wig and was trying it on.

'Where did you find that wig?' I asked her, as we prepared to leave.

'In Berlin. I often wanted to see Erich, even from a distance, so I would wear it and wait outside his school.'

I tucked some protruding hair under the wig, then took her in my arms and kissed her tenderly.

'She makes a beautiful blonde, too,' said Lubimov.

I felt her trembling in my arms.

From apartment-block height, the view of Gorky Park is magnificent. We were at the highest point of the Ferris wheel and I was looking at the lights of the exhibition centre on the other side of the road. Cars, small as toys, were crossing the bridge with their headlights on. The river hadn't frozen yet and a floodlit boat was rocking on its waves. In the distance I spotted the Rock Café, a meeting point for rebellious children of the Red aristocracy, and at my feet the multi-coloured lights of the funfair kiosks flashed on and off. The governess and agent looked from above like two small grey dots who couldn't do us any harm.

It was very cold, but I was happy because everything was going to plan. We had entered the funfair without the agent in the car noticing. We followed them to the Ferris wheel and ensured that we were sitting opposite Erich. When he was at the highest point, we were at the lowest, and vice versa, but we came face to face when we were in the middle of the ride. Neither the agent nor the governess looked up much, and so we could make our presence known by signalling to Erich.

Both times we arrived opposite each other, the child seemed not to realize who we were, even though we smiled and waved subtly. At the next turn of the wheel I took off my fur hat and waved properly. My ears almost dropped off from the cold, but he noticed. I don't know if he realized who we were, but he must have seen that the couple opposite him were gesturing. His eyes were glued on us as I continued waving my hat at him. Marlene smiled and waved with a barely noticeable gesture. Then I saw out of the corner of my eye the agent moving towards the funfair exit.

When Erich reached the platform at the bottom of the ride he suddenly asked to get off. The wheel stopped and Marlene and I were stuck at the top. I saw him take the governess's hand and make for the exit. I had frozen, whether from the cold, the disappointment or both I'm not sure. We got off the wheel too and began running towards them. They had reached the exit, with us about fifty metres behind, when Marlene let out a bloodcurdling wail, making the funfair employees and customers wheel around.

'Erich! Eeeriiiiichhh!'

The child stopped, then turned towards us. For a tenth of a second he seemed to hesitate, before the governess took his hand and pulled him along as we came ever closer. I heard the collision of two cars, but when we finally exited the funfair, the car with diplomatic plates was disappearing at pace. Lubimov was lying on the pavement next to his crashed old banger, blood running from his head.

Thankfully he was not seriously hurt. The agent had struck him with the barrel of his revolver. When he had seen the governess running over with the child and a car suddenly crashing into his own, he realized that something was up. We brought Lubimov to my office on Taganka Square, which is no more than ten minutes from Gorky Park. Marlene cleaned his wound, while I returned a call to the newspaper in New York and Whitesmith tore me off a strip. What with observing the funfair and organizing the operation, I had begun to neglect even my contractual duties to the paper. Whitesmith informed me that our main competitor had just released an interview with Boris Yeltsin, Gorbachev's rival. The only thing I could promise was an interview with a member of Bauer's family, and not even in the next few days. Weber also wanted a word with me, but thankfully it wasn't urgent.

Lubimov, meanwhile, had lain down on the leather sofa and was moaning in pain. Marlene was sobbing on the chair next to him, while Natasha was looking dumfounded upon the unknown war that had broken out in her capitalist oasis. I tasked her with finding her husband or any other man to take Lubimov's crashed car to the best garage. Then I gathered together the day's wire reports for a slapdash article that I would send later: journalism that passes for research. I had to take Lubimov home.

He lived in the sticks, in an apartment-block complex between the end of Leninsky Prospekt and Yugo-Zapadnaya. By the time I handed him over to his wife he was feeling better. As Marlene and I returned in the car, I told her what had been tormenting me for hours.

'I have the feeling that Erich recognized us. As he was leaving with the governess, he turned to us and seemed to falter. He rocked from one foot to the other, like boys do when they feel awkward.'

'He couldn't have recognized us,' Marlene retorted. 'He couldn't have recognized me in a wig... and it was dark...'

'I don't understand why he suddenly got off the wheel and didn't go to the shooting as usual. It's as if he wanted to avoid us.'

Marlene looked furious. It was the second time I had seen her change.

'What do you mean? That my child prefers to be held captive?'

We didn't say anything else until we were stopped by the police for an alcotest.

'OK, OK. Tell me how much you want. A hundred roubles, five hundred, a thousand?'

I was enraged with this familiar show of the vindictive traffic police pretending to smell alcohol and summoning you for a test. In the end they always let you off for twenty or fifty roubles. Besides, the only alcohol I had been in contact with was the stuff I had put on poor Lubimov's head.

They had signalled to me to stop in the middle of nowhere, on an empty road connecting Yugo-Zapadnaya with Kutuzofsky Prospekt, the great artery of Moscow where my apartment was. Somewhere in the distance an apartment block was visible, overshadowed by three thermal power stations that looked like the Chernobyl nuclear reactor. These monsters work twenty-four hours a day, pumping out three huge grey clouds of smoke and choking various local neighbourhoods depending on the direction of the wind. Comrade Stalin's idea was for the power stations to be in the centre of inhabited neighbourhoods, so that the industrial proletariat were not cut off from the other workers and the people.

The police officer took umbrage at my manner and Marlene told me in English to calm down. He asked for my documents—driving licence and vehicle registration—and told me to follow him for a test. I wearily gave him my papers without getting out of the car and waited for that typical smile that usually precedes the backhander. But he looked at the documents and insisted I follow him. I got out of the car, fuming at the administrators of the Foreign Correspondents Club, who had assured us that the necessary steps had been taken at the Press Ministry to put an end to the syringe trick.

We headed to the patrol car, which was parked on the opposite side of the road next to some fields. I couldn't see very well: most of the lights on Soviet roads have been following the course of the Soviets themselves—they're out of service. The officer opened the front door of the vehicle. As I got in I asked to contact my embassy. Too late I realized that I had fallen into a trap. One of the two men in the back seat put a revolver to my neck and told me to sit still. I felt the driver's eyes on me. As I turned, he smiled mockingly. I had seen those pale blue eyes somewhere before: it was Müller himself.

He was everything I hate: arrogant, self-absorbed and certain that he would always be on the winning side. I wasn't planning on spending any time with him, but I was pretty sure he was a know-all too. There were hardly any curves to his face, and in the dark he looked like a robot. He motioned to his assistant in the back seat to search me. When they confirmed I had no weapon, he eased the pressure of the revolver at my neck.

Then Müller said, 'You keep getting under our feet.'

'I'm sure I've seen you somewhere. At the cinema? On television?'

'He thinks he's funny!' Müller sniggered to his henchmen.

'I mean in the video, when you're talking to Erich at the parade. Before the kidnapping.'

I was afraid, but my head was clear. If they wanted to kill me, it wouldn't be Müller coming to give me the last rites.

His face hardened.

'What you tried to do at the funfair is tantamount to a declaration of war.'

'But the kidnapping of a child is a charitable deed? Soon you'll be telling me you work with UNICEF.'

'This is an internal German affair. Keep your nose out of it... or you'll come to a bad end.'

'If you kill me your friend Yelin will get the blame. Everyone knows he can't stand me.'

'You think I give a damn about Yelin's problems?' Müller growled.

Then he added something in German, which I couldn't understand. Only then did I think how right my mother had been to push me to learn foreign languages as a child, and how foolish I had been to ignore her. Müller's cronies shoved me out of the car and began to drag me across the fields. At some point I collapsed in the mud and turned to see him standing beside his car, watching us. I was frogmarched up the outdoor iron staircase of one of the Chernobyl-style power stations and practically carried to the top. They thrust me out through the railings until I vomited from vertigo. Perhaps I was wrong to think they didn't want to kill me; I was making one wrong judgement after the other.

Eventually they pulled me in and left me in a heap on the rusty landing. Then they fled, kicking me goodbye. It took me a while to come round and return to the car. Marlene was still there. Before she could get out, I said, 'Müller. Let's go quickly.'

I asked her to drive and cranked the heater up. Kutuzofsky Prospekt wasn't far, and we met no one in the elevator up to the apartment. It was after midnight when I opened the door. I turned on the light to see someone sitting in the lounge, smoking. It was Pioneer.

It was like returning home tired, turning on the lights and seeing your friends shouting 'Surprise!' Pioneer explained himself at once.

'When I arrived your maid was still here. I begged her to let me stay. I know you've had a difficult day. I came to help.'

I asked for ten minutes to shower and change. Marlene sat silent and exhausted in an armchair. I offered Pioneer a whisky and made the introductions.

'I heard what happened in Gorky Park. It was a very amateur attempt. That's not how it's done.'

A lecture was the last thing I wanted.

'We all start like that before becoming professionals. As amateurs.'

He changed tack immediately.

'It's going to be very difficult now. They won't take the child out again.'

Marlene broke into tears and stormed out. We soon

heard her choked sobs from the next room. Pioneer was in the mood for adventure.

'I have a suggestion. That is, if you want to keep trying.'

'Do I seem like someone who gives up halfway?'

He got up, went to the window and looked outside.

'Let's talk in the courtyard.'

I glanced at my watch. The deadline to send the day's article to New York had passed. They would be furious with me.

We splashed through the mud between the parked cars. A couple of residents were walking their dogs.

'We will take on the child's release if you help us with something.'

'As I am now, I wouldn't even make it as a husband at your Society.'

'Will you go to Moscow 400?'

We had only recently heard about the forbidden cities of the Soviet Union. They are closed, artificial cities-cum-military bases, where new weapon systems, conventional and nuclear, are tested and space programmes developed. There are about twenty in the country and despite each containing more than fifty thousand inhabitants, they are never covered in the census. Moscow 400 is about six hundred miles from Moscow, and you can't find it on the map.

'I know that you have been invited with four or five other Western journalists.'

In the chaos it had slipped my mind. Professionally

speaking, it would be a very interesting trip, the first time they were opening the gates of a ghost town to Western journalists. Someone from every major Western country had been chosen, and for the USA I had exclusivity.

'Thank God you reminded me.'

'If you agree, I won't go upstairs again. I've left a black leather bag in your lounge. During your stay at Moscow 400 someone will arrange to swap it with an identical one. The only thing you have to do is bring the new one to Moscow. Forty-eight hours later you will have the child.'

'Yes, but you're not telling me what's in it.'

'There's no need. I told you last time that the area of the embassy is controlled by another family. The heads of all the families have already had a razborka. Do you know what that is?'

'A meeting to find a solution to a problem?'

'Correct. For them to collaborate I have to give them something. That something will be in the bag.'

'What if you fail?'

'I'll tell you a great secret, why I'm called Pioneer.'

'Is it serious enough to put me in danger?'

'You'll find out many things—about me, about your girl, about the child. When's the trip?'

'Day after tomorrow.'

'Good luck.'

I had turned my back when he called, 'Mention this to no one, for your own good. Absolutely no one.'

A quarter of an hour had passed since the arranged time, and Patrick began to feel nervous. He was waiting in his car in the garage of the Intercontinental, but Anna hadn't appeared. He wondered if he had taken the right course of action. All his life he had acted on impulses, been driven by obsessions. For a month his only thought had been how to get Anna out of her great prison.

He had planned everything. But was it worth the effort?

He was certainly in love with her, but was that down to all the obstacles he had faced? The fact that his passion for her could only be satisfied on the train? The sense of the forbidden and mysterious? Why couldn't he fall in love with a normal woman, one of those he met every day in Lyon? He was risking everything for someone who had charmed him, but with whom he hadn't even spent twenty-four hours.

He thought of abandoning it all. But then again, he thought, isn't it at these moments that life finds meaning? The mystery of love and its power are found precisely in the mysterious and unfathomable reasons why we fall in love with one particular woman and not just the nearest one.

He tried to order his thoughts. He was certain that it wasn't merely sexual attraction he felt for Anna; it wasn't simply that he desired her body. He liked her skin, the curls of her hair, the way she spoke, her sense of humour, the guilt she felt about her job at the police museum and the course her country had taken. He liked everything about her. She must have her faults too, but he hadn't ascertained them yet. Would he be disillusioned when the mystery had gone? He looked at his watch: twenty-five minutes had passed. He would wait another five and then set off alone. Lisa Thompson, the friend who had helped him, would be departing from Prague airport: they had planned for her to leave before Patrick and Anna arrived at the border. She, at least, was running no risk: she had obtained two visas with two different passports in her name, one in London and one in Paris, where they met before setting out for Czechoslovakia.

He heard hurried steps on the garage tarmac. She was flushed and dressed impeccably in a black hat and a brown camel-hair coat, having looked through her meagre wardrobe for the most Western outfit she possessed. Getting into the car, she looked guiltily at Patrick and apologized for being late. A group of pioneers from the provinces had unexpectedly visited the museum and she hadn't wanted to leave—she had feared arousing the suspicions of her colleagues. She began telling him how she finally got out, but Patrick stopped listening. He started the car, drove up the winding ramp to the road and opened the window to let in fresh air. They remained silent until they were out of the city and on the Prague–Bratislava motorway, from where they would enter Austria. They relaxed a bit, and Patrick patted her arm and then her legs. She leant down and kissed his neck. They had a three-hour drive; he could find out more about her life. So he asked, 'Why did you marry?'

'Yes, why did you marry?' I asked Marlene.

Marlene looked surprised. The day following the failed operation at the funfair had passed uneventfully. I was leaving the next day for Moscow 400 and was taking advantage of the quiet evening to make progress on my book. I had to finish it, and something told me that my attention would soon be elsewhere. She was sitting next to me as I wrote on the computer, reading my additions and changes. She didn't expect me to ask her Patrick's question.

'Don't tell me you're drawing on our relationship to write your novel?'

'Why not? They're both love stories.'

She scowled.

'I'm joking. But I want to know.'

'I had dreamt of it since I was about sixteen years old. My father was a party official where we lived, near Leipzig. One day Bauer visited and the party authorities organized a traditional celebration in his honour. The dictator was impressed with me, and half-jokingly said to my father that a beautiful girl like me would make an ideal wife for his son. They both forgot it, but I didn't. From the moment I got it into my head to marry Wolf, there was no way I wouldn't succeed: I always succeed if I set a goal in my life.

'When I turned nineteen I left Leipzig for Berlin. Wolf's sister was minister of culture. I got a job at the ministry and we quickly became friends. Soon after that she invited me to work on something at the palace, and at some point Wolf appeared. Two days later he proposed marriage and I accepted at once.

'Did you love him?'

'He wasn't drinking much then and he was sweet to me, but I was never in love with him. It was simply the only opportunity to escape the daily misery, to travel abroad, enjoy a free life unknown to common people. Why am I telling you this? You know it, you've written it here.'

'I like that you weren't in love with him, that you hadn't given yourself entirely to him. But the reasons you give… I expected that you, at least…'

She assumed her combative manner again.

'I'm telling you because you know my story. When I saw the rottenness and realized that Wolf was incapable of love, I didn't hesitate for a moment. And as you know, I'm still paying for it all today.'

'Since I was young I wanted to travel. I dreamt of living abroad. But you can only leave Czechoslovakia if you marry a diplomat. When I was in the last year of high school, about seventeen, I often used to hang around outside the Diplomatic Academy of Prague with some girlfriends. Our dream was to meet a future diplomat. On the day he was sworn into the Academy, the dean informed my future husband that he had been appointed to the Ministry of External Affairs in Prague. They never sent people abroad if they weren't married, as a person without family ties can easily desert. He was depressed by the news— no travel, no dollars. He asked to go outside for a minute, and approached our group. He didn't know any of us. After introducing himself, he picked me to ask to be his wife. I said yes without a second thought. Besides, he was handsome and well-mannered. He took my hand at once and presented me to the dean. "Here is my beloved fiancée. We'll be married in a few days." That's how we ended up in Argentina.'

The red Golf was approaching the Austrian border and Patrick saw from afar floodlights illuminating barbed wire and car barriers as if it were daylight. When they arrived, two armed guards signalled to him to stop. He felt his stomach tighten, while Anna nervously played with Lisa Thompson's passport and visa.

'Don't get distracted,' Patrick said yet again. 'If they talk Czech, pretend you don't understand. Only speak English and leave the rest to me.'

The building at the border was a rococo structure from the Austro-Hungarian Empire. A huge red banner hung on its fanade with a slogan on eternal Soviet–Czechoslovak friendship and collaboration. An officer stepped slowly out of the building, asked for their passports and visas and told them to get out of the car. It was snowing and cold as hell. A guard came over, with a low platform on wheels, like those used in garages to lift cars with flat tyres. A large mirror was positioned on its upper side. They looked under the car for fugitives. A German shepherd appeared, the spitting image of Brek. Anna lit a cigarette, attempting to conceal her jitters. The dog growled angrily, as if it recognized her. Patrick wanted to laugh despite the situation: the reason they met, their matchmaker, was now showing them its teeth. The dog's handler made it smell them and then put it in the car. It searched the seats and the trunk, then appeared to relax. Patrick breathed deeply. Under other circumstances he might have petted the dog—or even the guard.

The officer told them to come into the building with their baggage. He searched them thoroughly and asked if they had korunas on them. He hurriedly looked at their passports and visas, then made as if to return their papers.

Suddenly he pulled his hand back, looked at the visas again, and asked in broken English, 'You came in with three bags. Now you have two. Where is other bag?'

'Was the plot like this from the start or did you change it?' Marlene asked.

'I'm amending it a little.'

'You mean that Patrick's anxiety about whether he should get involved is like yours with us?'

I turned off the computer, took her hand and led her to the bedroom. While we were making love, I realized that we both knew the answer to that question.

[24 November]

When the aeroplane from Moscow 400 landed at Vnukovo airport in Moscow I breathed a sigh of relief. Everything had gone off without a hitch.

Even if that ghost town is opened to tourists some time I wouldn't recommend it for a vacation. It's somewhere near the Baikonur Cosmodrome, built in the desert in the middle of nowhere. Rocket launches and nuclear tests are conducted in the same region. The inhabitants we spoke to didn't reveal state secrets, but they were open about the increasing cancer cases, TB and allergic reactions, radioactive sandstorms and polluted water. The ice has started to melt, even in the desert.

The buildings in the city are military shacks and grey concrete blocks that rarely resemble apartment blocks. The workers receive a bonus of forty per cent of their salary, but they don't have the right to leave the city or have visits from relatives. Telephone calls to the outside world are very limited and strictly controlled. All those working in the city's 'letter boxes', the closed laboratories of space or nuclear research, from the director to the cleaner, have signed a podpiska, a document that prohibits them from speaking to anyone about their work. It also assigns their work a degree of confidentiality from zero to five. Those with work rated zero are punished even if they talk to members of their family.

In the past, the city's shops were considered to be better supplied than those in Moscow, but the situation has recently worsened significantly. Meat, oil and sugar are rationed. Despite being a man of the regime, the president of the workers' union openly complained that most of the scientists wanted to defect to the West and would have done so already had they not been bound by confidentiality. He added that he was even considering strike action—the first in the history of space centres.

'How are we supposed to carry out scientific research when we need to search for hours just for a little milk?' asked the president's aide, a thin young man with round glasses. 'It's not the money; it's ensuring we get some bare essentials—a sandwich, a beer, things like that.'

'How can you explain this in a country that sends people to space?' asked a British journalist.

'To go to the moon, we've put people in the basement,' he replied.

Nice headline, I thought. Whitesmith will be delighted.

I kept Pioneer's bag on me at all times. During lunch, one of the waiters came over and said, 'Did you ask for the restroom? It's free. It's at the back.'

In the restroom I found a bag identical to Pioneer's. I was anxious at the baggage check upon departure but, as he had assured me, I went through without any trouble. During the flight I fell asleep and dreamt that someone had stolen the bag. Everyone yelled at me: Pioneer and Marlene, Müller and Yelin, Lubimov, Erich, Cynthia, Patrick and Anna, even Whitesmith, who cursed me for losing the confidential documents that he would publish internationally, giving us a world exclusive. I woke up bathed in sweat and hugged the bag right until landing.

I realized that something was up when I saw two burly Soviets who looked like secret agents waiting at arrivals, right behind the metal railings separating passengers from visitors. I made to turn back, looking for Stefan from Agence France-Press. He had stayed behind to flirt with a slim air hostess. I noticed the agents looking at me and then hurrying after me. I broke into a run. When I turned around, they were running too.

I pushed open a heavy door and found myself in a long passage with dozens of doors left and right. I opened one that said 'Officials' Waiting Room'; as I would find out later, it was my day to be honoured. It was a large hall with ripped leather seats and Formica tables covered with half-open bottles of Soviet juice and cheap vodka. Thankfully at that time no other 'official' but me was flying. Through the big window, which bordered the huge departure hall of the common people, I saw thousands of people waiting to fly with Aeroflot. The average delay on its internal flights is about ten hours.

Some were sleeping on the floor, others were eating eggs and salted fish, young women were breastfeeding and groups of youngsters with roubles in their hands were squatting and playing cards. There were representatives of all the 160 ethnicities of the Soviet Union, alongside various species of the animal kingdom. Many were using their wooden rabbit or chicken cages as pillows. It looked, in short, like a refugee camp.

I heard running and voices in the passage, but luckily the window between me and the people opened at once. I entered the waiting room nonchalantly. In other circumstances I would have been floored by the stench, but it wasn't the time for sensitivities. I slipped into the crowd of this makeshift museum of Soviet ethnicities and its fauna, then came out onto the road and into the first taxi I saw. The driver wanted to bargain, but when I gave him fifty dollars he set off at once.

As we entered the city proper, near the House of the Tourist hotel, he asked, 'Where exactly are we going?'

Good question, I thought, without responding.

At that moment Pioneer was the person I most wanted to find. He had got me mixed up in something—or was it a trap?—that I had only just escaped at the last moment, if I really had escaped. I was longing to smash his face in. But I reflected that my pursuers might suspect the emotions that were coursing through me. The best I could do was to negotiate with Pioneer on the contents of the mysterious bag that I still had in my hands. I wanted to find a quiet place, break open the bag—it had a combination lock—and then call him. I would tell him one thing: 'You'll get the bag as soon as the child comes home'. Nothing more.

I had to avoid my apartment and office and the apartments of colleagues and diplomats in the compounds. My mind turned to Liuba; she might still love me. She was a painter, green-eyed and thin almost to the point of anorexia. She claimed to be madly in love with me. It was true that the last time we had made love she asked me for a hundred dollars for her little sister who wanted to buy some educational books, but I didn't take it personally: she probably did the same to all her lovers. I hadn't phoned her since meeting Marlene at the post office, but we had never sworn eternal faithfulness. Her studio was on Zubovsky Boulevard, beyond the Ministry for External Affairs. I prayed to the god of love that Liuba was there, and said decisively to the taxi driver, 'Zubovsky. Near Park Kultury station.'

I was dreaming of a warm bath at Liuba's place when I started suspecting I was being followed. We had almost arrived, leaving behind us Moscow's only open-air swimming pool, a lake-sized pool 130 metres in length, built on what was until 1931 the Cathedral of Christ the Saviour, the largest church in the capital. It had been demolished on Stalin's orders; legend has it that the church survived two attacks by Stalin before succumbing to the Bolshevik dynamite. Dedicated to the victims of Napoleon's invasion in 1812, the Cathedral was inaugurated in 1883 after forty years of work. It could hold seven thousand people and had contained the best Russia had to display, from gold and priceless precious stones to icons and paintings by famed Russian artists. No one knew where all this treasure had gone, but rumour had it that it was sold to the West in the 1930s, when the country needed a handful of dollars. In place of the church, Stalin wanted to build the Palace of the Soviets, a pharaonic construction four hundred metres high that would have a one-hundred-metre statue of Lenin on top. The plan was abandoned during the War, and in the end drowned in the waters of the people's swimming pool.

When the black Volga came up behind the taxi, I prayed to Christ the Saviour. I couldn't be certain through the darkness, but I thought I saw one of my pursuers from the airport inside. The Volga turned onto Zubovsky Boulevard when we did, and followed closely behind us, so I told the driver to make a U-turn and leave me outside the entrance to the metro. Clutching the bag tightly I opened the taxi door and ran towards the metro. The black Volga braked sharply, causing panic among those waiting at the bus stop. I ran with all my remaining strength, momentarily turning my head to see my two pals from the airport. I leapt down the stairs to the platform, where a blind musician with dark glasses was playing a Russian tune on the accordion and small vendors were selling flowers and cheese pies. By good fortune a train arrived almost immediately. I got on, but before the doors closed I saw one of the pair arrive on the platform. The doors closed loudly and the train set off, but I couldn't tell if he got into another carriage.

I needed to get off at a busy stop. Studying the route, I chose Komsomolskaya; the name, referring to the Communist Youth, was small recompense for the thousands of young people who, instead of dating, had spent years digging up Moscow so that future generations could enjoy the metro. At the next stop, my luck continued: a metro employee, just off work, entered the carriage. Pretending I had made a mistake, I asked the precise time of the train in the opposite direction. My plan was to take the same line back to Zubovsky. I had nowhere to go but Liuba's. He consulted a schedule and told me I would just make it: a train going the other way would arrive at Komsomolskaya a minute after ours. When the metro stopped I leapt out, rushed up the stairs, crossed the tracks and waited for the train coming the other way. The metro station is full of revolutionary murals and marble statues. Some—Party leaders who had fallen out of favour since the station was built—have their heads missing. A minute passed without the train appearing. Then a minute and a half.

'Come on... and they say you run on time!' I said impatiently.

Just then I saw one of my pursuers crossing the tracks towards me.

There was nothing I could do but start running again. Only then did I regret that all my time in Moscow I hadn't done any proper exercise. I was used to running from one pro-perestroika demonstration to the next, but you need normal exercise as well as revolutionary exercise. After all these days of excitement my strength was failing me and I made for the escalators. The guy who was following me was in better shape and he made ground on me, pushing aside a couple of nonchalant passengers. I had no other option: with all my might I whacked him over the head with Pioneer's bag. It opened and a metal object rolled out and bounced down the stairs. I thought I saw a skull on it but I couldn't swear to that; perhaps I was affected by the atmosphere. He seemed to go dizzy, before charging at me again. This time I hit him with my computer bag, which I had in my other hand. Luckily I had a copy of the novel on floppy disks at home. He looked at me stupidly and then fell backwards, pulling other passengers with him. I reached the top and made for the exit. From behind I heard thundering footsteps. I turned right immediately and went into the first apartment block I saw. Between the ground floor and the first floor, the architect had the bright idea of making a landing; from its window I could see what was happening in the street. My two pursuers, one of whom was clutching his head and the other the computer bag and the strange object with the skull on it, were talking to a police officer, gesturing madly. Shortly afterwards a police car arrived. I opened the window with infinite caution and heard them saying that I must be hiding in one of these buildings. So when an open garbage truck passed below I didn't hesitate: I closed my eyes and jumped. I expected a soft landing, but unfortunately I came down on a thin layer of socialist trash. Before I lost my senses, I thought that it was about time that Russia became a consumerist society.

We must have gone round and round the capital, because when I woke up I was covered in trash and dawn was breaking. I looked outside the truck. I didn't recognize the place; we were in one of those districts with identical apartment blocks that you find in all socialist countries. I was cold, my clothes were wet and my new herringbone coat, for which I had paid a fortune in Soho, was destroyed. I was hungry and simultaneously wanted to puke from the squalor around me.

We soon arrived at our destination, a landfill site on the outskirts of Moscow. The sky was brightening and the place was full of birds, which scrabbled around in the garbage alongside hundreds of scavengers of every age: retirees, veterans of the Great Patriotic War, middle-aged alcoholics looking for a drop of joy in empty vodka bottles, buxom housewives who hadn't yet decided what to cook for lunch, marginalized youngsters from the down-and-out Moscow neighbourhoods, as well as Roma, who had begun appearing recently on the streets of the city centre. I jumped out of the truck before it completely stopped, and slipped through the crowd and the rubbish. I must have looked like an unemployed Tatar, because no one paid me any attention. I put my mind to where I could go. Even Liuba's house was now out of the question, as I was afraid to return to the same area.

I put my frozen hands in my coat pocket and found a note with Masha's name and address. It had fallen out when the consul returned her passport to me on the day we argued at the auction. Mother and daughter lived together, and I decided to pay them a morning visit. Thankfully, their house was relatively near. There was no taxi rank at the landfill. I stopped a truck and, when it had unloaded, the driver agreed to make a short detour for ten roubles. He looked at me closely, knowing from my accent that I was a foreigner.

'Where are you from?'

'The United States.'

He laughed warm-heartedly.

'And there was me thinking that it was Party propaganda that the Americans are starving.'

More surprises were in store at Svetlana's house. She lived in an old building with Gothic architectural features, which in the past had probably belonged to an aristocrat. Most of these buildings were built in the early twentieth century, when, before the Revolution, Moscow had undergone major development. The high-ceilinged entrance hall hadn't been cleaned for some years. At the far end was the metal cage of an old elevator and the marble staircase to the upper floors. I asked an early-rising member of the proletariat if he knew which apartment Svetlana Filimonova lived in. He looked at me with pity, as if I were a garbage man coming for my Christmas gift. Svetlana lived on the first floor. The great surprise was the ten different names on the apartment bell next to the majestic entrance. I had stumbled upon a kommunalka, a communal apartment.

Many of the large old houses are inhabited by different families who are entitled to one room each, with a shared kitchen and toilet. Under Stalin, there was a solution to the problem of the lack of living space: you could denounce your neighbour as anti-Soviet and take over their room until the next person came. With the advent of democracy, however, things had become trickier. Of the ten million inhabitants of Moscow, around two and a half million still lived in kommunalkas.

A middle-aged woman opened the door and informed me that Svetlana's room was the last on the right at the end of the passage. In the intervening space was a small hall and, on the left, a kitchen with several fires burning, one for each family. It smelt of boiled milk and cauliflower. On the right I saw a line of five or six people waiting outside the toilet. A thirty-five-year-old with a towel slung over his shoulder was joking about the constipation of the current elderly occupant. All my dreams of a hot bath had been destroyed.

The passage was littered with piles of dusty objects and laundry nets; heavy 1950s-style bicycles were hanging on the wall. It wasn't modern decoration: they placed them there so they wouldn't be stolen from the hall. I knocked on Svetlana's door. She opened it then recoiled, as if she'd seen the Devil. She pulled me into the room, which was disproportionately high for its length and width. There was room for just two single beds, a small wooden table between them, and a cupboard behind the door. It had obviously been created by splitting one of the large old rooms in two. I must have looked ghastly, because Svetlana was staring at me goggle-eyed, as if suffering from Graves' disease. I collapsed onto the only plastic chair in the room and asked for some milk and bread, if there was any. Before Svetlana returned from the kitchen I had fallen asleep with my head on the table.

The black Moscow bread seemed tastier than ever

before. Later Svetlana led me to the second floor, to her friend Jiola's apartment—the only one in the building that was not communal. Jiola's family had lived in a substantial apartment in the building until 1917 and, despite the post-Revolution redistribution of land, they had managed to keep a two-bedroom place. The most ominous moment was when Jiola's mother died at the end of the 1950s and the local soviet declared that her room would go to an otseretnik, someone on a waiting list—and who had possibly been on it for years—seeking a room or an apartment. It was one of the worst nightmares that millions of Soviets had faced over the preceding decades: death in the family meant one room less and a stranger or, even worse, a strange family, in the house. The only way around this was for Jiola to marry, a classic method by which citizens managed to change city or move from the country to the city at times when the internal passport forbade moving to Moscow (it's still forbidden today, unless permission has been given). Svetlana had found a friend who agreed to a sham wedding with Jiola and, as a sign of her gratitude, Jiola had granted Svetlana lifelong use of her bathroom. That is the historical background to the best shower of my life. It was agreeable that Jiola didn't seem to feel the heavy bonds of marriage: I was soon trying on old-fashioned clothes that various-sized lovers had left in the apartment.

I went down to the kommunalka on the first floor dressed as a Soviet bureaucrat: grey suit, black tie and old-fashioned white shirt with a worn-out collar. It was about eight thirty in the morning and Masha was in Svetlana's apartment, just back from work. She was removing her make-up, but was still wearing a red miniskirt and black fishnet stockings.

Svetlana was ready to set out for the compound. I asked her to tell Marlene I was at her apartment and to give her a note: 'I'm fine, but being followed—by Soviets, I guess. The bag I brought from Moscow 400 contained something strange; Pioneer had probably set a trap. I'll find him and resolve the situation. Will keep you informed. I love you. Kevin.'

When Svetlana left I lay down on her bed. Masha tended to my scratched and bruised face with some creams given to her by a generous businessman. It was the first time I had understood the advantages of prostitution. I asked her if she knew a place I could stay for a couple of nights. I wanted to avoid the good hotels of Moscow, in which they could easily locate me by checking rooms and bookings. Masha didn't hesitate.

'I'm often at the Kosmos Hotel. I can get you a room there, but you'll have to fork out a couple of hundred dollars a night.'

The Kosmos is a huge twenty-five-storey hotel complex beyond the end of Mira Prospekt, about thirty-five minutes from the city centre. The pride of Soviet megalomania, it had been built for the 1980 Olympic Games. The Exhibition of Achievements of National Economy was built opposite. Shortly after the departure of the last Western fans, the hotel bars and restaurants were suddenly occupied by prostitutes, mafiosi, pimps and Westerners, permanent inhabitants of Moscow who needed their women. With two thousand four hundred rooms it's the biggest vice den in Europe, a Soviet version of Sodom and Gomorrah.

'I don't mind the money. But I don't want to give them my name.'

'I'll book it in mine. Come at eleven this evening and find me at Solaris. Do you know where it is?'

'Solaris? I'm practically an honorary member.'

Solaris, in the basement of the Kosmos, was Moscow's only functioning disco of recent years, and the only place in the city open after midnight. I often visited it with other Western correspondents suffering from insomnia.

'It would be better to pretend we don't know each other,' Masha said, 'so you'll have to make a pass at me. But go and buy some Western clothing; they won't let you in as you are.'

Just before I fell asleep, I remember her opening the door to the bedroom holding a faded towel, saying sarcastically, 'Life is hard in Moscow, don't you think?'

[25 November]

'They came to the apartment looking for you,' Svetlana said.

She woke me up in a panic around three thirty; it was already getting dark. Masha was sleeping on the next bed. I got up, my head throbbing.

'KGB', Svetlana said with a trembling voice. 'They went to your office too; Natasha called, wondering where you were. You have also been called from New York a couple of times.'

I was generally in demand.

'Marlene?'

'She sent you something to eat.'

I devoured the Georgian cheese pies, the kind we bought in great quantities on the Arbat. Then I woke Masha and asked her to go to Fabio's office and tell him what had happened. He was the only person I trusted. Vassilis Pappas was in London, invited to the house of a British journalist he had met at an event about Pontic Greeks: women would be the end of our group, I was sure; the problem was that now it was my turn. I needed Fabio to meet me that evening at Solaris—it was his second home too.

In the street I stopped an ambulance, which agreed to take me to the Rossiya Hotel for twenty-five roubles. There was some straight talking to be done with Pioneer. I sat in the back, in the place of the medic, who had obviously knocked off for his second job, or else had knocked back a few too many vodkas. The patient lying on the stretcher took my hand.

'I'm in pain,' he moaned.

'Me too,' I said. 'What are you suffering from?'

'Kidney stones. You?'

'Heart problem,' I said weakly.

'Even the health service has fallen apart,' he groaned. 'They put two patients in an ambulance without medics. Lie down—your condition is worse.'

'I'd be better off dying; I deserve it. I've had heart trouble so long and I take no precautions.'

I asked the driver to stop at the Mezhdunarodnaya Hotel, where there was a Western clothes boutique. With Jiola's lover's clothes on I must have been a dead ringer for a Soviet, because the guards at the entrance didn't let me go in until I showed them my official correspondent's card.

I bought some jeans, a brown suede jacket, a thick beige jumper and a white trench coat and put them on at once. When the patient in the ambulance saw me in my new outfit he stopped groaning and looked at me in shock. He was being admitted for a standard case of kidney stones, but he'd end up with a heart attack.

'Where did you find the money?' he just managed to ask. 'Those cost a fortune.'

'My doctors have given me a few days to live,' I croaked. 'I'm spending my savings down to the last kopeck. No, actually I'll give a little to my heirs.'

All the good guys were hanging around at the entrance to the Rossiya: KGB agents, profiteers, pimps and taxi drivers. I put on the glasses I had also bought at the Mezhdunarodnaya, slipped into a tourist group that was entering the hotel and went to the floor on which Pioneer's suite was located.

I didn't see any gorillas, a bad sign. The woman who served as a receptionist—there was one on each floor of Soviet hotels—had seen Mr Tamurian leaving. She advised me to try the restaurant on the first floor:

she had gleaned from his bodyguards' conversations that a group of girls would be meeting the American boys. The Society for the Development of Soviet–American Human Relations was having a party.

I confess that it was a sorry sight. I can't claim that we are a nation of jeunes premiers, but the specimens in the group were well below average. Most of them were middle-aged, with bald heads and paunches, and from the Midwest. All their faces were glowing with joy, obviously because there had never been another occasion on which they had received such attention from the fairer sex. With just a handful of dollars they had managed to feel like Robert Redford; plastic surgery would require much more money and more doubtful results. Some were dancing cheek to cheek on the dance floor to the sounds of a lamentable band playing 'Yesterday' by the Beatles in the wrong rhythm. The low light and the greasy yellow tablecloths made the atmosphere even more melancholic. Pioneer was nowhere to be seen, but since I saw two Soviets looking at me curiously I decided to pretend to be a prospective husband and chose the first table in front of me.

Sitting at the table was an American man with three Soviet women: two were beautiful, the third, wearing glasses, was the translator. Ron, a fifty-something from Texas, must have had a failed hair transplant, because some unruly strands were sticking out of his bald patch, like a windswept cactus in the desert of New Mexico. His short arms reached with difficulty around the shoulders of the two women he was embracing.

He looked at me warmly, apparently unfazed. From his manner of speaking I realized he was a retired army officer.

'Welcome to the sexual minefield,' he said. 'Are you one of the new conscripts? You'll need care and self-discipline here.'

It seemed that a new group of husbands had come.

'I've just arrived,' I explained to the general of sexual liberation. 'What do I need to beware of?'

'Don't let your dick catch fire from overuse! Mine's already flaming. I'm leaving tomorrow, but in the two weeks I've been here I've slept with ten women. Thankfully I've got Julia, who's accompanied me on this sexual odyssey.'

He pointed to the translator, who smiled formally before lowering her eyes in irritation. He went on, 'The ratio is ideal: twelve girls for each one of us. Three and a half thousand bucks is obviously a sizeable amount, but if you think what you'd waste in two weeks at home on fuel, food and things like that there's no real difference. If you add women to that, it's basically nothing.'

Seeing my awkwardness, he played the sentimental card.

'But it's not just the sex, captain'—he suddenly promoted me—'the Russians are the antidote to the modern American woman who puts her career above everything. The girls here like keeping the house tidy. Ours like keeping the house after the divorce.'

He leant towards me and said softly, 'If you don't want a family life, you can enjoy your sexual service for two years and then throw it in.'

'How come?' I asked with feigned interest. 'Don't we have to marry them?'

'After two years, the federal office for immigrants decides if the marriage is still going. If not, they send her home.'

I had stopped following Ron's chatter, because the two strange men had turned towards us, taken out a photograph, then whispered something to each other.

'Pick whichever bomb you want,' the general said generously. 'I'm leaving tomorrow and I can't win them both. But I don't understand—you seem young and fit. Did you have to come here to find…?'

'I'm interested in a faithful woman with a good character,' I managed to say. 'At home they all cheated on me.'

Ron looked more carefully at the grazes and plasters that Masha had put on my face.

'What happened? Did you get hurt?'

He was driving me nuts.

'No, but I was lying when I said I'm one of the new ones. I came in the group before yours. I promised one of the girls I would marry her but then tried another, so her brothers came and beat me up. They're very conservative here. Barbarians.'

As the general looked at me open-mouthed, I saw one of the two men leave at a run, while the other stared towards our table. I took the hand of one of the prospective brides as the band started playing a slow version of the lambada to facilitate physical contact. We had only just introduced ourselves when Ira cut to the chase. She didn't have a Moscow dialect.

'I have met many Americans these last months. You're all warm, polite and generous. But you... Where did you learn Russian?'

I tried to be as natural as possible.

'Alone at home using Linguaphone. I had nothing to do in the evenings. I feel very lonely under capitalism.'

Ira took this as a proposal of marriage.

'You're the most handsome in the group.'

In case of a beauty contest I certainly had 'Mr Bachelor' in the bag, but Ira didn't let me enjoy it.

'But I have to tell you that, when the time comes to choose, I'll see who has the best salary and the biggest house.'

To keep a straight face, I tried to assume the expression of an emotionally wounded ox. I held her close and then, without feeling any resistance, I pulled her into the passage at the back of the hall. In California I would already have been arrested for sexual harassment, but a legal charge was the last thing on Ira's mind. There was a sign pointing right to the toilets, and to the left I saw the waiters coming out with plates.

'You're shaking,' she said.

'How could I not be?' I replied.

I kissed her tenderly on the cheek and told her to wait. Instead of going to the toilets I went into the kitchen and walked through the indifferent waiters. As with other professions in a country in which the workers are in power, the agreeable class of waiters and cooks does not suffer from capitalist angst. Someone started telling me that I wasn't allowed to be there, but I had already made it to the other side. I opened the door and went up the service stairs to the second floor, where I crossed a huge passage with a dilapidated red rug and doors left and right. At the end of the passage I spotted a chambermaid. I pretended I was lost and wanted to find the south exit of the Rossiya, the one that looks onto the river. Initially she told me it was very difficult, but when I gave her ten dollars she took me to the fifth floor and from there into the hotel's twin building. It would be impossible for them to find me in this one-and-a-half-thousand-room leviathan. I slipped out of the other entrance and disappeared into the darkness. If Ira still loves me, she'll still be waiting.

It was after midnight, but neither Fabio nor Masha had shown up. As we had agreed, I arrived at the Kosmos for our meeting at eleven, went to the basement, paid the twenty-five-dollar entrance fee and entered Solaris. After two vodka and tonics I began to feel dizzy with tiredness. That evening I would have to sit in my room and write my report on the secret city. Ideally they would fire me, and they would be right to. But in the tussle on the metro I had employed not only Pioneer's bag but also my laptop. I would have to write by hand, which I've almost forgotten how to do; these machines have crippled us.

It was a weekday and business at the disco was slack: three Italian businessmen who had immediately found some girls and were sitting at a table trying to look like film stars; a couple making their first moves; the barman and DJ; and about thirty girls made-up and dressed to the nines, looking at the only single customer, me, like a tasty morsel. The ratio was much better than at the Rossiya; I should have brought Ron with me. The worst thing was that in this environment I wouldn't go unnoticed. A solitary man drinking at the bar with no interest in the surrounding girls happens once in a blue moon at Solaris. One of them, seeing me sad and alone, came over and asked for a cigarette. I smiled at her and asked if she wanted something to drink. She ordered a Campari. She was called Katya.

'Why are you here alone?' she asked in passable English.

She would never believe that I was suffering from heartbreak and had come to drink to forget.

'I'm waiting for a girl, a regular here. I've never seen you here before?' I said, trying to change the subject, in the manner of a bridge club member who knows all high society.

She had cropped blonde hair and large brown-green eyes. Her body was thin and muscular, like a mannequin.

'I'm new. I came from Tashkent a month ago.'

'Such a long way. Our fame is spreading throughout the whole Soviet Union!' I said, swelling with pride.

'I'm Russian and the Uzbeks don't want Russians anymore. It's impossible for a Russian woman to walk around Tashkent after six in the evening. I decided to come to Moscow but I haven't found any other work here. I don't even have a residence permit.'

I couldn't face hearing another version of the well-known story. I glanced around the empty disco.

'There's no atmosphere today.'

'Without the kosoglazi we don't get our wage.'

Kosoglazi means 'slit-eyed' in Russian. I played the dumb tourist.

'That's what we call the Japanese; they pay handsomely. Of course there are those allortsi over there,' she said, pointing to the Italians. 'But there aren't many.'

Since I had a date with another girl, she treated me like a colleague with whom she could discuss work problems.

I thought about that bastard Fabio, who was late. He would have met some girl and abandoned me. Katya was keen to continue this ethnological debate.

'They're so impatient to get us into bed that from the word go they just say allora, allora. But you see, the old ones have nabbed them,' she continued bitterly. 'They have priority.'

'Don't you choose who you want?' I asked, faithful to the principles of the free economy.

'We decide which girls are available. The privileged ones get in there first, then the rest of us.'

Another article! Something on prostitution and inequality would be right up Whitesmith's street. It would reveal that communism, despite its claims, not only hadn't abolished prostitution, but had even failed to make its prostitutes equal. I asked as nonchalantly as I could about social stratification in the oldest profession.

'Do you want a sociological analysis? I studied at the Tashkent Institute of Sociology.'

I offered her another drink. I must have been the most intellectual customer of her career.

'We have many categories. The highest-paid frequent the best hotels in Moscow, the Mezhdunarodnaya and the Savoy. They don't go below two hundred and fifty dollars a time and get more for extra services. Then there's us at the Kosmos, who get two hundred. In the third category are those who work with Western tour groups in the Belgrad and the Intourist: a hundred and fifty, but you can also get something for eighty. Do you want to know more?'

I was always interested in a people's needs.

'But aren't there prostitutes for Soviets. I mean, in roubles?'

An expression of disgust was written on her face.

'There are, but we don't consider them human beings,' Katya said. 'We don't even call them prostitutes. We have a special name for them: shalava.'

That roughly translates as 'sluts'. It's astonishing what you learn if you ask. Even the word 'prostitute' had class differentiation. Whitesmith would lap this up.

'OK, but you here—aren't you all equal?'

Katya was ready for a social critique. In another time she would have been a member of the Communist Youth.

'The old ones don't pay entrance to Solaris, but the new ones have to pay five dollars a night to get in. The police often raid the place and take all the currency we have on us. Did you know it's forbidden to have dollars or any other hard currency if you can't justify its origin? But they don't touch the old ones.'

Everything is a question of time. I looked at my watch. It was already one o'clock and Masha hadn't appeared, nor that allortsi Fabio. I glanced around; Katya seemed to read my thoughts.

'There's another difference,' she said coquettishly. 'The old ones can use the rooms of the hotel. We work from home. So if you want …'

I shrugged indifferently. Katya observed me for the first time, furrowed her eyebrows and said, 'Why are you asking me all this? Are you a journalist?'

'Not at all. A businessman.'

'Oh,' she said, furrowing her eyebrows.

For a few silent seconds I tried to catch her meaning.

'Because they told us they're looking for an American correspondent.'

'Who did?' I asked breezily.

'The KGB.'

That was when I started smoking again. I bought a packet of Marlboros from the bar, offered her one and put another in my mouth, leaning towards the barman so he could light it for me and Katya wouldn't see my hand trembling. Then I asked, apparently offhandedly, 'What's your relationship with the KGB?'

She roared with laughter, as if I'd said a great one-liner.

'Our entire existence depends on the KGB. Prostitution is illegal in the Soviet Union, but not just illegal; until recently the regime maintained that it had been eliminated. Even today, the official position of the Party hasn't changed; in reality we don't exist. If they wanted they could kick us out, send us to the gulags for anti-social behaviour, for defamation of the socialist system, for hooliganism. The KGB decides who works, where we work and when we're past it.'

She stubbed out her cigarette and took another from the packet without asking.

'They protect us too. A few days ago a group of girls from Leningrad was brought to the Kosmos by some mafioso, supposedly for three days. There was a football match between CSKA Moscow and Marseilles and therefore great demand from the French fans. The girls were pleased with the situation, because even for residents of a big city like Leningrad it's considered a great privilege to live in Moscow. When the fans left there were lots of us and a slump in business. Do you know what they did?'

She continued without waiting for my reply. As was soon revealed, I knew very little about the laws of supply and demand.

'They slashed the prices; the new ones went down to thirty dollars. A bit more and we'd have had to follow, but in the end we appealed to the KGB, who organized a great clean-up operation in the hotel. We had been informed and didn't come that evening. All the girls were arrested. And since they didn't have residence permits for Moscow—not to mention that they were carrying illegal currency—they sent them back to Leningrad the next day.'

I struggled to contain my astonishment at the KGB's assistance in conflict resolution among prostitutes. It was almost two in the morning and my mind turned to practical problems.

'Where did you say those girls work, the ones who collaborate with the KGB?'

'All the hotels. The more luxurious it is, the greater the control. In the best hotels there are usually diplomats, journalists on assignment, factory owners and arms dealers. They want to keep track of their activities. Ninety per cent of the girls in the Savoy and the Mezhdunarodnaya collaborate with the KGB. And here, many of us are in regular contact. Of course, they don't pay us like agents, but when they ask for information on someone, we have to give it. In the Oktyabrskaya though, they're all paid by the KGB.'

'The hotel of the Party Central Committee?'

'Don't be surprised. A friend who works there told me so. Many of the rooms have hidden video cameras, which the girls themselves turn on. Official party representatives from the whole world go there, you know.'

'True. What sort of comrade are you if you don't know what your guest is up to?'

My mind turned to Giuseppe: he was staying at the Oktyabrskaya as an official guest of the Party, though from the first moment he had bluntly stated that he wouldn't touch a Soviet comrade even if she were Krupskaya, Lenin's widow. I pretended to be on the lookout for gossip.

'Why are they looking for that American journalist?'

'I wish I knew. It can't be you anyway, because he doesn't wear glasses. They also said he spoke excellent Russian.'

I instinctively touched the glasses I had bought before going to the Rossiya. I had forgotten to take them off.

'Russian is all gibberish to me.'

We each looked at the time. She spoke first.

'It doesn't look as though your friend is coming. Are you going to wait any longer?'

'Do you have a better idea?'

'Come home with me. Anyway, you're pretty nice-looking.'

'On one condition. I'll pay you but we don't do anything.'

She looked me up and down. Her eyes rested for a moment on the buttons of my trousers. I felt obliged to defend myself.

'I'm in love and I can't touch another woman. I just want to sleep next to you.'

She laughed.

'I get it. You're like the Italian I met the other day. He invited two of us to his room, me and another. He gave us each two hundred and fifty dollars and didn't even want us to undress. We just sat on the bed, him in the middle. He made me touch the other girl's hand and lay them both on his dick; he didn't even want us to stroke him. He came in two minutes; we took our dollars and left. The same as you. You'll pay just to lie next to me. I don't mind, but just so you know—there's no discount.'

'Don't you have a car?'

'I'm only in Moscow a few days.'

I had fallen irredeemably in Katya's eyes. Not only

— 168 —

did I not want to sleep with her, but I didn't have a good Western car. We got into a taxi—a Volga, with exhaust fumes that would make elephants faint.

'What do your parents do?'

'Are you checking I'm from a good family?'

She had a sense of humour.

'My father is a professor at a research institute, where my mother works as a researcher.'

'Do they know what you do in Moscow?'

She looked me up and down as if to say, 'Is it worth telling you?' then asked for a cigarette.

'They found out when I was caught the first time, when I wasn't yet in the system. The police informed them. When I returned to Tashkent they didn't even want me to sit at their dinner table. My mother spoke to me on behalf of both of them and told me to pack my things and go. I left them five hundred dollars as a gift and left. What do you think they did?'

'Send it back to you?'

'You're very naïve. Two months later they came to Moscow and started sweet-talking me. They said that I wasn't wrong when I said to them during our argument that as things stood I couldn't do anything else. Then my dad asked if I wanted help managing my finances. And over the next days of their stay he borrowed a car from a friend and took me himself to Solaris every evening.'

We reached Katya's place in ten minutes. The Solaris girls had greased the right palms at the municipality to find apartments in the surrounding area. They didn't want to lose time in transport; this might be the only sector of the Soviet economy in which time is money. She lived in a ten-storey prefab in a dark, empty area. Gangs of youths frequented these places on the outskirts of Moscow and the inhabitants shut themselves in their homes from early evening. The door to the block was open and we went up to the second floor on foot as the elevator wasn't working. Katya had found a flat with one bedroom and a sitting room, which were furnished with tasteless Turkish-made furniture, the last word in fashion for socially ambitious Russians. There was a cupboard in the bedroom made of cheap wood and a double bed with a leopard-print plastic cover. On the floor were strewn Western fashion magazines and a pair of women's underwear. A Japanese radio cassette player was sitting on a suitcase along with some tapes of disco music. A Georgian folk painting hung on the wall.

When I returned from the toilet she had undressed and was lying on the bed.

'There isn't even a sofa in the sitting room. We're condemned to sleep together.'

'I told you I belong to another.'

'Here's a freak,' she said to herself, looking at the ceiling. 'He's in love, but prefers to sleep next to me. Is it my colleague, the one you were waiting for?' she asked.

'No, someone else. It's complicated.'

'So he's in love with one, has a date with another and wants to sleep with a third. How romantic! All you men are the same.'

Thankfully she was a practical woman and soon stopped complaining.

'What is it to me? Give me the two hundred.'

I'd have given five hundred to sleep peacefully for a few hours.

'Is there a telephone here?'

'Don't tell me you want to start making calls at this—'

'No, but I want to in the morning before I go.'

I hadn't decided what I would do the next day, since Masha and Fabio hadn't appeared.

'There is, but it's shared with next door. That drunkard talks all day.'

Due to the lack of telephone lines, the system of two neighbouring apartments having the same number is common. There's no problem with bills, since however many calls you make it costs peanuts. You just can't tell your secrets—and there's no chance of phone sex.

I had just lain down when there was a loud knocking on the door and the sound of shouting and swearing. Soon someone opened the door with a key and two burly men came into the room. The boorish one was carrying a club and a suitcase. He threw a few English words into his ranting. The story was that he'd returned unannounced from a trip to the country and had caught me in bed with his wife. He would beat me to a pulp and call the police. They had set up the 'cuckold' trick, waiting to pounce on an oblivious tourist who would panic when faced with two enraged Soviets. Recently there had been several unhappy stories in the press of Westerners caught at night in the back of beyond without clothes or money.

I decided to speak in Russian.

'I didn't touch the girl, nor are you her husband.'
Katya was taken aback.
'How do you know Russian?'

The cuckold took half a minute to recover his composure. He was over forty and had a fresh mark on his lower lip. After thinking it over, he shook his club and said, 'It makes no difference. Give us your money and get out.'

I took a deep breath and withdrew the money from my pocket. It was left over from my trip to Moscow 400—some twelve hundred bucks. I kept fifty and threw the rest onto the bed. As I started putting on my trousers my fears were realized.

'Leave them on the floor,' the second man said. 'Just take your coat and shoes and let's go.'

My jumper, my Levi's jeans, my leather jacket—all gone. If I told them I couldn't get other clothes they'd never believe me.

'Are you coming too?'

'No, we'll leave you to check the address and call the police,' the cuckold replied sarcastically. 'Don't worry,' he winked, 'we'll take you somewhere near a main road.'

In the passage leading to the main door I looked at myself in the mirror. I was a laughable wreck, an adulterer on the point of a nervous breakdown. The two men followed behind, and Katya after them.

There was no option left for me—I had no money, no clothes, no home and soon no job. I should already have sent the report on Moscow 400 and Weber had threatened to fire me. I would go home, and God help me.

But when Cuckold and Co. opened the door Masha was standing there with three hulks.

'Whore!' she shrieked at Katya.

Then she began to swear with a vocabulary that would have made Lenin's mummified remains blush. The cuckold and his accomplice froze on the spot: it wouldn't be an easy fight with the three new arrivals. They were as ripped as Arnold Schwarzenegger, not to mention that one had his hand on a revolver in his pocket. I returned to the bedroom, put on my clothes, took my money from Katya and winked at the cuckold: 'He who wants much, gets nothing... Oh, and look after your wife. Don't leave her alone. She's easily led astray.'

One of the three, who looked like the leader, then made a mistake.

'Come on, take your reporter and let's get out of here,' he said to Masha.

'Reporter?' Katya interrupted.

I looked daggers at her and we left the apartment. There was a new Lada parked outside the block.

'Where have you been?' I asked Masha sweetly.

'Fabio...' she said.

'What happened to Fabio?'

'He's in hospital... in a coma.'

'Porca miseria,' I spat, using one of his favourite phrases.

'He was alone at the office, waiting for me to pick him up for our 'date'. Another Italian journalist who happened to stop by found him in a pool of blood. He had brain injuries and the doctors have given him a fifty per cent chance of survival.'

'Thieves?'

'No idea. They must have been looking for a document, because they turned the office upside down. He might know something.'

'Strange.'

I knew Fabio very well. A brilliant journalist and good writer, but if he were researching something he would have told me. We didn't keep secrets from each other.

'When I arrived at the office I came across two policemen. I tried to persuade them that I had no part in it. Thankfully Fabio's secretary Elena, who had just arrived, confirmed that I was the daughter of Svetlana, who works in the apartment compound. But it took a while to extricate myself.'

'What did you say you were doing?'

'I said I had a date with Fabio.'

'Highly plausible.'

'Then I went to Solaris and the girls told me you'd gone with Katya. I realized she'd cause trouble, so I asked for some help from my friends. They're good boys.'

'How did you know?'

'She always does it. She has absolutely no honour.'

It's all relative in this life. I looked at my watch. It was past three.

'What shall we do now?'

'Solaris was closing when we left. We could go to the room.'

'Forget it. Katya told me that the KGB were looking for an American journalist.'

'The best solution is to go to my mother's. You can sleep on the floor.'

'In the kommunalka? I'll be applying for Party membership next.'

She wasn't in the mood for jokes.

'Don't you think you should tell me sometime why they're after you?'

I looked at her meaningfully.

'Do you too have some link with the KGB?'

'We all do, but don't worry, I won't denounce you.'

On the way to the kommunalka I told her what had happened.

'Will you still help?'

She didn't hesitate.

'I'll help you, because you're good to my mother. You give her a good wage so I don't have to look after her. I need a little more time to achieve my goal of saving five thousand dollars. Then I'll throw in the work and get out of here.'

'You really love your mother then.'

Despite my exhaustion I needed a drink before going to sleep. Masha and I were sitting in the kitchen of the kommunalka drinking homemade vodka, a tipple that had come into fashion when Gorbachev, shortly after his rise to power, began his famous anti-alcohol campaign. The new secretary's restrictions on sales and consumption of alcohol in public places were met with revolutionary initiatives by the Soviets. Turning every apartment into a bastion of resistance, they started brewing alcohol in their kitchens from whatever they could—potatoes, cauliflower, onions, slippers... Those who had nothing to boil just drank neat alcohol or perfume. In a few years the art of homemade spirits had significantly improved, and Masha's vodka didn't finish me off on the first glass.

There was complete silence in the kommunalka. Masha smiled at my question.

'Yes, I really do. You're surprised, yes?'

'Not at all. Why would I be?'

'Because at school they taught us not to love our parents. You know the story of Pavlik Morozov.'

Morozov is one of the most tragic stories of Stalinism: a child in the thirties who was hailed a national hero because he denounced his parents.

'I recently went to a small city outside Volgograd,' I said, lighting the last cigarette of a packet I had just bought. 'His statue is still in the main square.'

'At school we were constantly shown Eisenstein's Ivan the Terrible,' Masha continued, happy that I was following her. 'It drove us crazy. We even had a class on the script for the third part. One of Ivan's brave men shows his faithfulness to the tsar by giving a knife to his son and ordering him to kill him, his real father, as a sign of love for the tsar. Tsar, general secretary... it's all the same.'

'So how come you love your mother?'

She glanced around and pursed her lips.

'I shouldn't tell you, but you're on our side. My mother... was in the gulags.'

I should probably change career. There was an eye-witness to a concentration camp in my own home and I hadn't realized.

'Was your mother a political prisoner? A zek?'

Zek is short for zaključónnyj, Russian for 'prisoner'.

'Not exactly political, more a sexual prisoner. It all began with a typical argument here in the kommunalka, around 1950—long before I was born. My mother argued with an asshole in the next-door room, who drank and caused trouble every evening. So he went to the police and denounced my mother and father for having deviant sex. He said that he'd seen them through the keyhole.'

'What happened?'

'They were sent into exile for antisocial behaviour. Sex was acceptable only for producing members of the proletariat in order to construct socialist society.'

'Like the Church for us.'

'They do the same today for homosexuals. I have a friend who was sentenced to ten years' forced labour because he was caught in a park with another homosexual. And, despite the economic changes brought about by perestroika, the mindset hasn't changed at all. They just formed a kind of sex police, didn't they?'

'No idea.'

'What planet are you on?' she asked disapprovingly. She was right: I had been living in the world of Yelin and Müller.

'The day before yesterday the Supreme Soviet voted to create a special force to crack down on prostitution and pornography, as well as immoral behaviour. There had been protests from indignant citizens about porn magazines sold on the streets and various television programmes. Now they'll control prostitution and the porn industry. I was talking about it with the other girls. We're afraid they'll come down hard on us.'

'Do they accept volunteers? It's my dream to burst into bedrooms uninvited.'

'You would have made a good dissident,' she said, laughing. 'The morality police hate humour.'

'At first they were sent to a village outside Irkutsk in Siberia. The neighbour who denounced them took their room. It's the one I live in now with my mother. He soon lost both, because someone else denounced him for insulting Stalin when he was drunk. My parents' punishment was five years, but they settled into the village and decided to stay there after the end of their sentence. Then came de-Stalinization and they started talking openly about what had happened to them—my mother, that is. She was bolder. My father had turned to drink.

'In the early sixties my father became sick from the oppressive Siberian climate and they applied to get back their room in the kommunalka. The response was slow. In 1965 my mother was pregnant and one day she went to the local Party office to complain about the delay. The Party had her file and knew why they had been exiled. They asked my mother if she continued to "do it" differently. She was so aggravated by this point that she insulted Leonid Brezhnev, the new general secretary who had overthrown Khrushchev.

Do you know what she said? She said she liked it like that and would do it with Brezhnev himself, though he probably couldn't because he was a queen. Can you imagine what happened next?'

'Insulting the general secretary...?'

'Ten years in the gulag. In Karaganda, Kazakhstan.'

She frowned.

'I was born in the camp. My father couldn't look after me, nor himself. He disowned my mother and married another woman, but soon died. A few days after my birth they separated me from my mother, because gulag rules don't allow babies. They put me in a kind of nursery, six kilometres from the camp, but my mother had the right to come and nurse me. She made that trip for months, going twice a day along a muddy, snowy path over the steppe, and in between she had to work like the other prisoners. At that time there wasn't artificial milk for baby food; if she hadn't walked to feed me I would have died. I've no idea where she found the strength, but I owe her everything. That's why the propaganda we were fed at school against parents, and the hymns to Pavlik Morozov, never moved me in the least.'

'And then how...?'

'How did I become an interdyevouska?'

'No. How did you come back?'

'In 1973 she came out of the gulag. She collected me from the orphanage. We stayed five more years in Kazakhstan and in 1978 returned to Moscow. They gave us back the room and she began to work in a factory so I could go to school. I was very good in class, but when I was fourteen some friends of mine and I met a group of French boys at the 1980 Olympics. They were about seventeen. We became friends, nothing more. A couple of days before the end of the Games they wanted to go to the Bolshoi Ballet. We went to the theatre at seven to try and get tickets, but it was sold out—there were so many foreigners in the city. We ended up in a café and stayed there until nine. Were you here when there was a curfew of 9 p.m. for children under sixteen?'

'I was. I came to Moscow in 1985. I think the rule was abolished in 1987.'

'Exactly. When we left the bar we were arrested by the militia. They took us to the police station and interrogated us all together. They didn't keep us there long, but they informed my mother and the school. It was a serious misdemeanour—out after 9 p.m. and with foreigners. I was banned from all schools in Moscow for a year.'

'And your mother?'

'She sided with me. She said I hadn't done anything wrong, but it made her ill. Since then she's had heart trouble.'

We each downed half a glass of vodka.

'What irritates me most is their hypocrisy. Do you know a young director called Sergei Szeskin? I know him because for a while I tried to act in movies, but I had the blot on my CV so I wasn't allowed.'

She sighed.

'He recently made a movie called An Extraordinarily Significant Event on a Provincial Level based on a book of the same name by Yuri Biryukov. The extraordinary event is a Komsomol conference in the countryside: saunas, naked girls everywhere and Roman-style orgies, all shown in the movie. Such things happen all the time in the "close circle" as it's called. They pretend to be so modest, but in their circle they show they are precisely the opposite. And all this in the name of perestroika and the correction of Stalinist extremes.'

'From what I recall Gorbachev never favoured free love.'

'Stalin destroyed the family by turning children against their parents. But in the early years of the Revolution, before conservatism prevailed, they tried to destroy the family using radical measures. One of the first laws they passed was on divorce: you could divorce simply by sending a letter to ZAGS, the civil registry office. There was no compulsion even to inform your other half: ZAGS did that for you.

'They also announced that family was the first form of slavery and that, as long as it exists, bourgeois society cannot be eliminated. The liberation of women would be achieved through the destruction of the family and the end of monogamous relationships. Therefore they paved the way to free love. Alexandra Kollontai, the first woman to become a minister —a "people's commissar" for social welfare as ministers were called then—declared that fulfilling your sexual desires was like drinking a glass of water. She wrote a book entitled Love of Worker Bees about the freedom of love, urging the world to make love "like bees with flowers, like birds in the bushes and grasshoppers in the grass". Lenin, who saw that sex would slip out of the Party's control, reacted to the "glass of water" theory, calling it bourgeois. In line with the theory, Komsomol today professes to support Kollontai against "bureaucrat" Lenin and Stalin, and is even re-publishing a series of books.'

'Hang on a moment, this is hilarious.'

She went to her room and came back holding a brochure.

'They handed these out in the Komsomol gatherings.'

'I don't have the strength to read early socialist erotic literature right now.'

I put the Communist Youth brochure in my pocket.

[26 November]

The residents of the kommunalka said that my arrest reminded them of the old era of terror. There were five people: the cuckold from the night before, his accomplice and three others in plain clothes. They knocked on the door to Svetlana's room and told me not to mess around, but to dress and get out.

It was seven thirty in the morning and life in the kommunalka had already started. Some of the residents were boiling milk and tea in the kitchen and there was the usual line outside the bathroom. The cuckold said that he worked for the Committee of State Security—the KGB. Having checked there was no window through which I could escape, they let me have priority in the bathroom line: I felt myself doubly relieved with this privileged treatment.

Two black Volgas were waiting at the entrance. I got into the first with the three strangers, while the cuckold and his friend followed in the second. We took the ring road and reached Kirovskaya Street. On the way I asked a couple of times where we were going, but didn't receive a response. The cars went around Dzerzhinsky Square and stopped outside the Lubyanka building. We had arrived at the headquarters of the KGB.

I calculated that the greatest likelihood was deportation rather than prosecution, but my heart beat fast, as if in harmony with those of the hundreds of thousands who had been brought here in the past. Most hadn't come out alive. We entered the building from the side door on Dzerzhinskaya Street, walking into a large hall with grey marble columns. The walls were also grey, the marble floor emanated a sinister chill and the lighting was low. I was surprised at the deathly silence in the place. It felt like an empty church. They led me to a cubicle and only when I gave my passport to a young man did I hear a sound for the first time—my name.

We went into the elevator and one of the security officers pressed the button for the seventh floor. Now this was a scoop: the first Western journalist to enter the lair of lairs. It was a modern elevator, but it seemed very slow. The doors opened automatically and we followed an interminable passage, the sound of our footsteps absorbed by a thick yellow carpet bordered in green and red. I started counting my steps to maintain contact with my environment. At number 717 we stopped. One of my escorts knocked on the door.

'Bring him in,' came a voice from inside.

We entered a long, narrow room. In the foreground was a conference table and beside it a large wooden globe. The big window looked onto Dzerzhinsky Square and on the opposite wall was a bookcase with Lenin's Selected Works. On the back wall was a portrait of Dzerzhinsky, the founder of the Soviet secret service, labelled with the KGB slogan 'Warm heart, cool head, clean hands'. Directly underneath it was a table made of beech. In an armchair behind the desk sat Oleg Yelin.

He motioned to my escort to leave and then pointed to a chair. I preferred to stand up, irritated by now.

'Can you tell me the meaning of all these pursuits and arrests? Are you going to send me to a gulag? Didn't you hear they're closing? I want to talk to the American embassy at once.'

'Attack isn't always the best form of defence.'

'I don't understand. Do you have something to ask? Go on then, ask me!'

'It would be better for you to speak. When we start asking questions, things are already very bad.'

I raised my hands in a gesture between dissatisfaction and disapproval.

'It's unacceptable. You're acting like I'm a suspect.'

Yelin stood up from his desk, walked around me with his hands in his pockets, then went to the big window and looked outside. The usual traffic was moving around the square, watched over by the huge statue of Felix Dzerzhinsky.

'Do you see them out there?'

He pointed to the people crossing the roads, going into Detsky Mir, the largest children's shop in Moscow, and others coming out of the metro station. From above they looked like ants.

Then he looked at me and said, 'From the moment you're in here, you're guilty. Those outside are suspects.'

I too was surprised by my laughter. The world was changing, the Cold War ending, the Wall had fallen, the Soviet system collapsing and these people hadn't noticed a thing. I felt a sense of superiority, like a doctor with a patient suffering from incurable arteriosclerosis.

'That reminds me of something,' I said sarcastically. 'If I'm not mistaken, one of your predecessors used to repeat that. Beria, I think.'

He sat back at his desk, unfazed. In front of him was a matryoshka, a Russian doll. He picked it up and twirled it in his hands. Then he started opening it.

'You're right. We're like a matryoshka. You open Gorbachev and out comes Brezhnev, then Khrushchev, then Stalin, then Lenin.'

'Yet you have perestroika now.'

He looked at the ceiling for a second, calculating what to say.

'Yes, but perestroika doesn't mean that there are

no laws. You have broken Soviet laws. Thanks to perestroika, you received permission to visit the secret city of Moscow 400. As you know, this was the first time we have allowed Western journalists there. And the result? We caught you with a bag full of plutonium.'

For the first time that morning I felt the need to sit down.

'Do you know what general conclusion we as a government draw from this case?'

He was playing cat and mouse with me.

'That we were right to keep these cities closed for so long. And, more importantly, that these excesses carried out in the name of perestroika must be stopped. We will do well to rethink it—at least, that's what I will propose to the general secretary. I will mention your case to show that Western services exploit our good intentions and peaceable sentiments to steal state secrets and nuclear matter.'

I was about to protest, but couldn't articulate a word. Like in a nightmare where you're being hunted down, you want to shout for help but no sound comes out of your mouth.

'You Westerners can write what you want. Those who agree with my views are not opposed to certain necessary changes to the system. The KGB was always the best-informed service in the country, and we were first to establish that things weren't going well. But we don't want to miss the wood for the trees: the Soviet system must be maintained, even if there are changes to be made.'

I had to find a way in.

'Is it in the laws of the Soviet system to use prostitutes and tricks with cuckolds?'

'To do our job we also need to control prostitution, which is sadly a product of our times. Previously, there were very few foreigners and we knew them one by one. Now there are many, all wanting to exploit the loose morals of perestroika. They think they can buy all our girls with their dollars.'

He got up from his chair and walked around the room again. Then he stood in front of the globe and spun it around with his fingers.

'Perestroika,' he said, and was silent for a few seconds, rolling the word around his mouth as if chewing tobacco, about to spit it out. 'It means "restructuring" in Russian. Not destruction, not selling out. We didn't start perestroika to lose Hungary, Poland, Czechoslovakia, Germany. Do you know why we lost Germany?'

My face assumed a questioning expression.

'Because of some guys like Müller.'

He noticed that I shuffled in my chair.

'I know you are acquainted; we know everything here. We told them that they had to make some small changes. Every shop once in a while has to change its window to make it more attractive to customers. It's not only in the money-grubbing West that you know that trick; we know it too. But the only thing that interested the Germans was money and power. They couldn't see beyond the end of their noses. They didn't lift a finger and they were punished. In the end they'll be devoured without the least resistance.'

He glanced at the globe, which was still spinning, and

then turned and sat on the other visitor's chair in front of his desk, right next to me. Suddenly his manner became sympathetic—as much as his upbringing allowed.

'I know how you feel. But don't worry, there's a solution.'

Yelin is such a good security officer that he does what is usually done by two of his colleagues together: he plays good and bad cop simultaneously. Reaching his hand out, he pressed a button. Soon someone knocked on the door.

'I never say "Come in" when they knock,' he said to me, as if chatting to a colleague. 'I always say, "Bring him in".'

'Bring him in!' he called towards his office door.

A Russian woman dressed in KGB uniform came in carrying a tray. Yelin poured tea into a cup and offered it to me with Hungarian biscuits. I was so hungry that I couldn't resist. He also drank a glug of his tea.

'I know you aren't involved in the handling of nuclear matter. You're a victim of love. Do you want to know where you went wrong?'

I thought of asking to talk to the embassy again. In the end I remained silent.

'At heart you believe that love is a kind of resistance to our regime. You're wrong. The Party knows all about romance. It would be foolhardy to try to forbid sexual relationships as Stalin did. Even the best comrades need a little extramarital fun, just like you.

He smiled for the first time—if a jackal can smile. He took from his desk the Komsomol brochure that Masha had given me a few hours before. They had confiscated it along with all my personal possessions. He began reading: 'Dasha Cumalova is the first liberated woman in Soviet literature. In Gladkov's Cement she says to her jealous husband, "A civil war should take place inside ourselves. Nothing is more anti-revolutionary than our habits and prejudices. Jealousy, I know, simmers inside you. That is even worse than tsarism. It's the exploitation of a person by a person; it's like cannibalism."'

Yelin raised his eyes for a moment and smiled at me. Then he continued, even more bombastically, 'Most of the thousands of short stories from the revolutionary era were written by men, but the contribution of female authors is noteworthy. In one a man says, "Sex is a simple matter; there's no need to let it worry us." The girl responds, "Perhaps that's right, but what if you make me pregnant?" "What bourgeois reasoning! What bourgeois caution! How embedded you are in these bourgeois prejudices! No one could think of you as a comrade." In Moon on the Right a girl has sex with twenty-six diffcrent lovers, because this is necessitated by the attempt to build socialism. In Path of the Dog, the hero, a member of Komsomol and the secret police, says to a girl who is influenced by the old ideas, "I always thought you were a good comrade. If I came to tell you I'm hungry wouldn't you share your bread with me like a good comrade?"'

He shut the brochure and threw it onto his desk with a sneer.

'I see that you're reading erotic literature.'

'It's published by Komsomol. I don't believe that's forbidden.'

'No, but it isn't representative. These are Kollontai's theories, which Lenin crushed. If we let things run their course we would open the bags of Aeolus.'

He flattened his hair with his hands.

'There's a joke that expresses our politics better—I mean, that we allow romance, but keep it under control. Why are beds so big in the Soviet Union?'

'So three people can fit in—the couple, and Lenin. Or perhaps, the couple and the chairman of the KGB.'

Suddenly he became serious.

'What do you mean?'

Something had bothered him, but I didn't know what.

'And what if one doesn't want to have a threesome with Lenin?'

'I'm telling you all this because I know you can't write it. Rather, we should be working together.'

I felt a cold sweat. I knew that the KGB never missed an opportunity for blackmail. Many were forced to become agents because there was something that would incriminate them.

'You will publish an article in which you correct what you wrote about me—that I was on Tamurian's payroll.'

'If you give me a statement of denial, I'll publish it,' I said with relief.

'One more thing. You'll take something else out of your eulogy of me—that my comrades and I are "conservative rivals of Gorbachev".'

'And if I don't?'

'Then I'll present my own discovery: a well-known Western correspondent in Moscow is a smuggler of nuclear matter. It's quite a scoop, don't you think?'

He looked at me carefully and then said, 'You have twenty-four hours to think about it. I'll give you a good cell, one in which they used to hold party officials...'

He stopped for a moment, then added with a smile, '... before executing them. You'll have every comfort. If you agree, you'll show me a draft of your article tomorrow morning.'

'I want my computer. It was lost when I was fighting off your people. I can't write by hand.'

'No problem,' Yelin said, and pressed the button on his desk. 'Take the Komsomol brochure too. I might not agree with its contents, but it's an official document produced by our youth.'

Patrick prayed, imploring God to hide the sweat on his face. The third suitcase, which the border guards had asked for, contained Lisa's things, and she had taken it with her. A whole plan was crumbling from this blunder. Potential excuses flashed through his mind. The suitcase had been stolen in Prague—then why hadn't he informed the police? Besides, under socialism criminality doesn't exist—was he then slandering the country? He had given it to a friend in Czechoslovakia—a friend from when? Who is he? Where does he live? They forgot it in the hotel when they left—then why hadn't they said anything all this time? It disappeared from the trunk without them noticing. No, he should leave out the supernatural. There's a scientific explanation for everything.

He adopted a slightly annoyed, nonchalant expression, went over to the guard and took the papers.

'Let me see.'

He inspected the documents, pretending to try to remember what exactly happened at the border on the way into Czechoslovakia. Suddenly he had an idea.

'Your colleague made a mistake. He wrote three suitcases instead of two.'

The guard gave him a mistrustful look and shook his head as if to say 'The Czechoslovak border guards never make mistakes'. Perhaps he'd chosen the wrong excuse, but he had no choice other than to persist. He shrugged his shoulders indifferently and repeated, 'It's a mistake.'

Outside they heard the German shepherd bark. The guard looked executioner-like at Patrick.

'Is this yours?'

He pointed to Patrick's signature at the bottom of the document and then to the small print underneath. In English it read, 'Anyone signing a false declaration will be punished under Czechoslovak law.' Patrick feigned a smile.

'I didn't notice that.'

The guard inspected the visas and passports and motioned to Patrick and Anna to sit down, in a way that suggested they would be there a while. Patrick looked at Anna, who had remained entirely expressionless and still the whole time. She looked more like a wax model than a person. Through the window he saw the guard talking on the phone in the next office, holding a passport. Photographs of Lenin and Husak, the secretary of the Communist Party in Czechoslovakia, hung on the wall. Patrick realized that things were bad when four guards with automatic weapons came into the room and addressed Anna in Czech. Two of them then made him stand up, and the others took Anna away.

He rubbed his wrists, which were still hurting from the handcuffs. He had worn them from the previous evening until this morning, when they had brought him to Ivan Plita's office. This time the undersecretary was furious. He was pacing up and down, shouting and occasionally banging his fist on his desk. He remonstrated with Patrick that his comrades would put the blame on him, for he had personally intervened with the Paris embassy to get the visa. The minimum sentence, he threatened, for organizing escape from Czechoslovakia was fifteen years' forced labour. He returned to his desk, took another cigarette from a packet and lit it, still standing. Then he slumped onto his chair, next to Patrick. Abruptly lowering his voice, he hissed like a snake, 'There's only one solution.'

Patrick looked at him impatiently.

'As things have played out, both of us are coming out poorly from this affair. We need to work together,' he said wearily.

'Do you mean the article on reformist psychosis?'

Plita smiled almost warmly, as if chiding a small child.

'No, that sort of article will present you as a communist sympathizer and might damage your image. I don't want you to write anything, and I can ensure you leave the country immediately—with an assurance to my superiors that we will continue our collaboration in France.'

'You mean I'll…'

Patrick wanted to say 'spy', but didn't dare.

'Nonsense,' said Plita, waving his right hand as if warding off the evil thought. 'You will just give me pieces of information every now and then.'

Patrick felt relieved.

'I have no information to give you. I told you that I have just started working for a provincial newspaper.'

'If you don't have anything, so much the better for you. You'll remain dormant for a period. After five or six months we'll wake you up.'

'Is that all?' asked Patrick.

'More or less. In the meantime we'll ensure your career progresses, giving you various scoops—on a terrorist organization that had links with the Eastern bloc and bombed Paris; on decisions under the Warsaw Pact to do with the reduction of intercontinental missiles. You'll become famous, get a good job in a big Paris newspaper, preferably in diplomatic reportage. Then we'll be in touch again with further instructions.'

Plita went to his desk and pulled a printed document from the first drawer.

'You only have to sign this. I'll handle the rest. You'll be out of the country tomorrow.'

Patrick looked over the English text swiftly. It was addressed to the StB, the Czechoslovak secret service. It stated that he acknowledged his mistake in attempting to take a Czechoslovak citizen out of the country, and sought the forbearance and cooperation of the authorities in facing imperialist challenges.

'What will happen to Anna?'

Plita looked concerned.

'That's more difficult. But I promise I'll try to let her leave with you.'

'Without Anna I won't even consider it. In any case, without her…'

The undersecretary of internal security assumed a patriotic expression.

'I always respect idealists. Those who sacrifice themselves for an idea, whether it's social justice or love.'

'Is she OK?' Patrick asked.

'She's crying constantly, but she'll get over it.'

'Can I see her?'

'Only if you accept my proposal.'

He paused, bringing his hands to his lips.

'Excuse me a moment. This is all my own initiative—I'd better speak to my superiors. Have as many cigarettes as you want.'

Patrick confirmed that he wasn't having a nightmare, and considered what to do. He felt alone and desperately defenceless. The French embassy didn't even know he was in Czechoslovakia: he had ensured that his presence in Prague would be as low key as possible. Plita didn't mention Lisa, therefore his friend had managed to leave. She would, of course, inform the newspaper when she realized something had happened;

they had arranged a telephone appointment for the day after the escape. But even when the French diplomats found out about his arrest he doubted they would lift a finger. The second secretary had advised him to turn his attention to one of the women who, according to the socialist division of labour, was responsible for entertaining foreigners. He was possessed by an overwhelming fear—perhaps collaboration was the only solution.

Plita returned ten minutes later. He was smiling.

'I think we'll succeed. If you sign, you can take her with you. Tomorrow.'

He pushed the document towards Patrick.

'This document will follow me my whole life. I'll have to think.'

'Isn't fifteen years in prison half your life?'

The officer came into my cell swearing and forcibly took my computer. Yelin had kept his promise about a luxury cell: just the small barred window and the absence of natural light gave away that it was in the Lubyanka basements. The room was small, like those that doctors use to catch a few moments of sleep on a night shift, but tidy and clean. On one side there was a single bed against the wall, on the other a wash basin. Against the back wall, next to the bed, was a small wooden table. I had put my laptop on it and was sitting on the edge of the bed writing. The novel was the only way of killing time. Besides, it was an opportunity to finish it, along with my other obligations. I didn't even want to think about the newspaper; I couldn't remember how many days it was since I had filed a story.

At some point I tried to discern if there were other prisoners in the neighbouring cells, but I didn't hear any sound, not even a door opening. I reflected on who could have passed through this room—probably various leaders of the secret service who had fallen from grace. A wild joy filled me when I considered that Yelin too might end up here one day.

As if reading my thoughts on his boss, the officer was furious with me. I tried in vain to persuade him that Yelin himself had ordered my laptop to be brought to me. As if I didn't have enough trouble, I had now fallen upon this violent, bureaucratic cretin, who was howling that the law explicitly forbade prisoners from reading or writing. When he left, cradling my laptop gingerly like a hand grenade, I wrapped myself up in the only blanket and tried to sleep, but my nerves were taut. I glanced at the Komsomol brochure. It criticized Stalin's excesses in the realm of personal relationships, citing a novel of the time: 'I write books, I'm a writer... All this thanks to you, Stalin, our great teacher... I love a woman with a new passion; I perpetuate myself through my children, all this thanks to you... and when the woman I love gives me a child, the first word it will utter will be "Stalin".'

I was woken in the morning, brought tea and taken up to Yelin's office.

[27 November]

'I'm sorry about what happened with your computer. I just heard. I will make sure the man responsible is disciplined.'

Unwilling to meddle in internal affairs I remained silent.

'Did you write anything of what we talked about yesterday?'

'I didn't manage to. I just worked on my novel.'

'Oh, so you write literature too?'

'Not really. It's a thriller about love under socialism.'

'Interesting. You don't have trouble with the censors?'

For the first time I realized that Yelin had a sense of humour.

'I haven't yet got a deal with Novosti. For now I'll publish it in the West.'

'That's exactly what I mean.'

'There's no censorship in the US.'

He smiled knowingly.

'Come on. Can you write what you want?'

'Of course.'

'No, you can't,' Yelin said decisively. 'There's market censorship. No publisher today would publish a short story praising communism, nor a serious literary work. You have to write what's in fashion, what the majority wants, to sell your book. That's why you're writing something light, a thriller—because it sells.

You censor yourself. Only under socialism do we publish serious books, because the state funds their publication.'

'So Boris Pasternak's books weren't serious?'

'I know, sometimes we have gone too far. We want to correct that, to abolish state censorship but not go to the other extreme of market censorship.'

'I'd prefer half a dozen publishing houses to decide which book to publish, rather than an unregulated Party committee.'

Both of us realized that the discussion was going nowhere. We were silent for a moment.

'Have you decided if you'll write what I asked you?' Yelin broke the silence.

'I cannot present you and the Politburo's conservatives as right, and Gorbachev as the one making mistakes. That would be in opposition to the entire commonly held opinion in the West. Market censorship won't allow it. I'm obliged to self-censor.'

I expected him to be riled by my sarcasm, but he remained expressionless.

'Don't worry. It's immaterial now.'

I looked at him in surprise.

'The matter is becoming quite well known. It would be clear that we forced you to write the article. Besides, we've secured the word of your newspaper.'

'That ...?'

'That you'll never write about the Soviet Union again. The American embassy informed us. They promised to recall you to New York at once.'

'Bastards,' I managed to say.

'You must be jumping for joy. Soviet laws severely punish unlawful distribution of nuclear material. At most we would have swapped you for one of our spies, but only after you'd been in prison a few months.'

'Did you suddenly have a wave of kindness?'

'Not me. The American government intervened. Anyway, you're no use anymore. We've agreed you'll be out of the Soviet Union in forty-eight hours.'

I said nothing. I was thinking of Marlene and Yelin understood. He obviously knew about the relationship.

'Thinking about women again? The East German isn't coming with you. She can't, nor would she want to anymore.'

He repeated with emphasis, 'I told you, Danaher, you're no use anymore. Just remember that wherever you are, at any moment, we could bring your story out into the open. Unless…'

'Unless what?' I stammered.

'Unless you work with us.'

'Yesterday you just asked for a favourable article. What made you…?'

'I've thought more about it.'

He opened the drawer of his desk and took out a folder secured with white ties. He lifted it up with slow, sadistic movements, just enough for me to see it. The printed words read FILE, and below, COMRADE, and then, in Cyrillic script, KEVIN DANAHER.

'This is the file on your case. We know everything; we found the restaurant employee who confessed to giving you the bag. He didn't mention Tamurian—he conformed to the mafia's law of silence. Now he'll go to jail for ten years, but if he talks he'll be gobbled up by the mafia. He blamed it all on you. If you don't want me to use the file, you'll go like a good boy to the US and await orders.'

He paused a moment. Then he took a visiting card out of his pocket, wrote a number and said to me, almost charitably, 'You don't have to answer now. Call me on this number whenever you want. But think seriously about it. Either you'll work for us, or you'll find another profession—because I think you're finished as a journalist. In a few days all of New York could be talking about your adventures. You may leave now.'

He pressed the button on his desk and gestured to the guard, who came to collect me. As I was heading for the exit, he called, 'Someone has already come to give you a ticking off. They're waiting for you.'

In the hall outside the KGB chairman's office was Cynthia.

Hardman interrupted me again. His two assistants had loosened their ties. They capitalized on the break by flexing their fingers, which were aching from the writing. Weber was sprawled in an armchair, his arms folded behind his head.

'Did you consider collaborating, Mr Danaher?'
'Not for a moment, Mr Hardman.'
'Then why didn't you rule it out from the start?'
'I was taken unawares.'
'In your novel you develop precisely this version, so it clearly went through your mind.'

'Yelin obviously thought the same. Will you let me continue?'

'Carry on,' he said, without looking at me.

Cynthia and I didn't exchange a word until we were outside, in free Moscow. In the foyer of the Lubyanka building I had been given my computer and personal possessions. It was snowing softly and the city air for the first time seemed so clean to me. We walked quickly for a few hundred metres, as if wanting to escape the shadow of the KGB building, and stopped outside the Bolshoi Ballet.

Cynthia coughed and said, 'Kevin, I know everything.'

'When did you arrive?'

'Last night. I left as soon as the paper called me. Weber himself telephoned; he's furious with you. I went to your place and found that… woman.'

'It's better that way,' I managed to say.

'They told me you have to leave Moscow within forty-eight hours.'

'Who told you?' I asked angrily.

'Weber.'

'He's wrong. I can't leave here before I clear my name.'

'Kevin, I came to pick you up to go back to New York. I have two tickets for four o'clock this afternoon. Let's try again. It's all in the past now. I'm ready to forgive you. Howard and I love you.'

'And I love you too. But, Cynthia…'

I took her arm and turned her around, back towards Dzerzhinsky Square. She looked at me in surprise.

'Don't worry,' I smiled, 'we're not returning to the KGB. I want to buy him a present from Detsky Mir.'

We entered the children's shop and took the escalators to the second floor. From the big windows I saw the Lubyanka building again. In the misty morning, covered in snow, it looked like a children's castle made of wood. Sometime I'll get a Guinness World Record for the shortest amount of time spent in that building.

Cynthia was in tears. I bought a drum-playing monkey and gave it to her. She looked at me and said, 'Kevin, this is your last chance.'

I held her by the shoulders.

'Thank you for everything. For coming, for your patience and generosity. I've regretted this mess I'm in a thousand times, but I can't go back now. Because of me, a child like our own is in danger; I can't leave him like that.'

'Do you mean that you're not in love with her anymore?'

I hesitated, but finally reflected that since I hadn't made any agreement with Yelin there was no reason to lie to Cynthia.

'No, I don't mean that.'

We went into the street. I wiped away her tears and stroked her hair.

'It would be better for you to leave Moscow at once; you shouldn't put your own life at risk. Things have gotten pretty bad here. They're after me, and Fabio's in hospital in a terrible condition and I don't know why. Someone needs to look after our child. Where did you stay last night?'

'With the consul. He's waiting at the embassy for news.'

'Let me take you there. It's on my way—I'm going to the office.'

'Don't worry; I know the way,' she said abruptly, and turned around.

I watched her walk away and then took a taxi to Taganka Square. I had to explain to the paper what had happened. We got stuck in traffic and I turned on the laptop to check if it was still working. Someone had opened the file containing the novel. They were never particularly good with new technology.

'Artistically inclined informants,' I murmured.

I realized something bad had happened from the look on Natasha's face: she lowered her eyes as if admitting some wrongdoing. I stormed into my office to make a call, only to find John Holby, an ambitious young man from the foreign desk, sitting comfortably in my chair, reading the latest wire reports. I knew that he had long ago put himself forward to replace me when I decided to leave Moscow. He didn't move from his seat.

'What the hell is going on?'

'I'm sorry, Kevin,' he squawked.

He handed me a fax from New York without a word. Weber informed me that after everything that had happened he was obliged to discontinue my employment. He was sending an aeroplane ticket for New York with

Cynthia, and the paper would handle all my removal expenses to America. The apartment, which the UPDK —the Soviet ministry that manages compounds—had provided for the paper, must be emptied as soon as possible for the new correspondent. I also needed to hand in the car, which was the property of the newspaper.

Holby, a redhead with a pointed nose and the indelible marks of acne on his face, looked at me triumphantly.

To bring him down a peg, I said, 'Right. Well, can you vacate this corner for a little while? I want to call New York.'

He looked at his watch.

'I'm the new correspondent and as of yesterday the office belongs to me. You can call from the telephone in Natasha's office, but you won't find anyone awake.'

'Congratulations on your new post. You deserve it, but the truth is that the KGB also had a hand in it. May I at least gather my personal possessions from the desk, or did you inherit them too?'

He stood up, annoyed, and went to the kitchen. I was longing to punch him in the face, but I settled for filling a plastic bag with whatever I thought was valuable at that moment: a photograph of Cynthia and Howard, the telephone directory, a few floppy disks and a couple of files with Russian newspaper clippings and wire reports. I took my shaving equipment from the toilet, and two ties I had for emergencies.

I went to the other room and kissed Natasha, who looked at me as though I was about to die. She managed to tell me that she had been in touch with Elena and Marina, the two secretaries at the Corriere della Sera.

Fabio was a little better but needed absolute quiet. He still couldn't speak, nor give testimony to the police.

I had almost reached the elevator when Natasha caught up with me, holding the passports belonging to Marlene and little Erich. I had given them to the consul for their visas, so they could leave as soon as the boy was released. There was a note from the consul that read, 'I think these visa applications are no longer valid.'

While waiting for the elevator, I looked absent-mindedly at the passports and thought of my next move. I could get a couple of jobs as a freelancer in Moscow until we found out what would happen to Erich and I had clarified my own position, but that pathetic Yelin had given me just forty-eight hours' notice. I had no house or car. I looked first at Marlene's smiling face in her passport photograph, then opened the child's passport. I read 'Erich Bauer, date of birth: 9 November 1980'.

The elevator door opened in front of me, but I let it close again, to the surprise of the Japanese correspondent who was taking down an ugly black bulldog for a walk. I went into the office and asked Natasha, 'Do you remember the date the Wall fell?'

She consulted a couple of papers briefly, while the ugly muzzle of the new correspondent poked out questioningly.

'The ninth of November,' Natasha replied.

'A strange coincidence,' I said, and left at once.

PART THREE

'Juliet'

In the flames of feverish kisses
    Karl Marx's ideal of equality, in all its beauty
    Emerges from me and falls upon the sheet.
    For a moment, the intoxication of caresses brushes it aside
    But look how it rises up again before me like a conquering hero.

NINA SERPINSKAYA, 1923

I had no desire to see him, but there he was in front of me in the courtyard of the compound. He looked at me with a smile, as if nothing had come between us, and paused. I was obliged to do the same.

'All well at the American embassy?'

I put as much sarcasm into my voice as I could. The consul's gaze cut through me.

'Kevin, you will have learnt we did all we could for you.'

'I can't complain. You even ensured on my behalf that I would never write anything against the KGB.'

'Your newspaper did that. It's true we intervened. But what did you want? To go to jail?'

'So am I free now?'

'That's not our fault. You got mixed up in Moscow 400 by yourself. I warned you to abandon it.'

'Abandon a boy into the hands of the Stasi?'

He continued, ignoring my comment.

'I took Cynthia to the airport.'

'Thanks.'

'What are you thinking of doing now?'

'I think I'll party for a few more hours. Sex, drink,

drugs… then I'll abandon the women and orphans and go.'

I observed that he tolerated my sarcasm.

'It's the best you can do. Things are getting tough here.'

'They can't get worse for me.'

'I mean the political situation. Gorbachev has made a conservative swing and, according to our intelligence, it's he who is instructing the Russian General Staff to renege on the treaty limiting nuclear weapons. The hawks in Washington are pressuring us too. In the next few days, the president will give Gorbachev an ultimatum: if the American–Soviet agreement isn't applied, we'll activate our plan for Star Wars. All this is off the record, top secret and I'm just telling you so you can plan your movements. I wouldn't mention the slightest thing—though I consider you a friend—if I knew you still worked at the newspaper.'

'The trust you show in an unemployed man does me great honour.'

I had no wish to look at him any longer. I turned around and left, waving goodbye.

As soon as Marlene saw me she got up and kissed me. But when you're in love, your senses are sharpened. I discerned a coolness in her embrace. Her arms hesitated to wrap around me and her lips weren't as warm as before. It was as though she was embracing a political prisoner whose release pleased her, not her lover. Svetlana was standing discreetly behind her. She told me at once that it wasn't her who had turned me into the secret police when I was staying with her.

I patted her on the back: 'I know, Svetlana. Don't worry. You did all you could. And Masha saved me from the cuckold in the first place.'

I needed a warm bath, but was impatient to talk to Marlene. Alone at last in the bedroom, we fell into each other's arms on the bed. I sat up next to her; all these days I had wanted us to be alone more than anything, but now I was gnawed with curiosity to find out about the date.

I took a deep breath and said, 'I can't believe it's a coincidence.'

Her face transformed, like it had that night by the lake. She got up from the bed and curled into the armchair like an angry cat.

'I don't understand where you're going with this. Since it's Erich's birthday, I know well that the ninth of November is a historic day for Germany. On that day in 1918 the Empire collapsed and democracy was announced. On the same day in 1923 Hitler's Munich putsch failed, and in 1938 we had the notorious Kristallnacht. On the ninth of November 1967 students took to the streets in Hamburg. Do you want more?'

'And in 1989 the Wall fell.'

'Perhaps those who planned to overthrow the 'old man' wanted to link it with other dates.'

'So he was overthrown.'

'Why? Did I claim anything to the contrary?'

Her voice had gathered intensity. I tried to keep my cool.

'No, but I'm amazed that you never mentioned the coincidence of Bauer's fall with Erich's birthday. The dictator had taken your child and you took him back on such a fateful day. It's the perfect revenge.'

She laughed irritably.

'What are you trying to say? Do you think I asked Bauer's enemies to ensure I was happy when blowing out the candles on Erich's birthday?'

It was true I had gone too far. I don't know how I'd got stuck on this idea since I'd seen the passports. They used to say that no one comes out of the Lubyanka building sane, but I was heading in the wrong direction after just twenty-four hours there and with no torture. Marlene was riled.

'There is such a thing as divine justice. I don't know where or how, but it's true. I grew up in a Marxist environment, but it seems to me it's actually you who believes in historical materialism. I truly wanted to have revenge, because I suffered a lot, but at the same time I wanted to have my child back. Around those two desires a huge energy had built up. Don't ask me what kind like some physics teacher at school would do, because I don't know.'

'Sorry, I'm probably not thinking straight. What with splitting up with Cynthia, being fired from my job and having to leave the Soviet Union in forty-eight hours, I'm risking losing trust even in you. And the worst thing is that I can't help get Erich back anymore. The only thing I can do is to give you some money to get you through for a bit.'

'Why do you have to leave?' she asked, rather coldly.

I explained to her the whole fiasco.

Instead of commenting she simply stroked my hair—more as one would soothe a hurt child than a lover.

'Kevin, you're the most wonderful person I have met. But you're not to blame for what happened. You got involved in something against your will. There's no need for you to break up your family. Cynthia still loves you... I bear you no ill will. I understand you.'

'You don't understand, Marlene.'

'No, you haven't understood how I feel. I love you; I don't want you to be destroyed. You've gone through enough for me.'

'I spoke to Cynthia. Our relationship is over for good. I told her I love you. I want us to live together. I'll wait for you in New York. As soon as you have Erich back...'

She hardened.

'But I want us to split up—for your own good.'

I felt the world spinning around me; my hands shook and I wanted to throw up—like an abandoned provincial girl in some cheap sentimental novella.

'You're leaving, but I have to stay,' she continued.

Talk of her own problem brought me back into the conversation.

'The situation is getting worse. What'll you do here alone? I just met the consul: the American embassy believes that Gorbachev has made a conservative swing; the president is going to give him an ultimatum. It'll be another Cold War.'

She shrugged her shoulders, as if saying, 'The only thing that concerns me is my child.'

'In my cell at Lubyanka I had a lot of time to think. The only solution is for you to speak openly about what happened. You'll tell your story, that Orwellian saga, with them forbidding you to see your child, and erasing the word "mother" from the school books, and then the abduction here in Moscow. You'll give an interview to the Soviet and foreign press—I can secure you an interview with whichever TV channel you want. Global public opinion will be moved, and rightly so. The Soviet government will force Müller to free the child.'

'Impossible,' she said decisively.

I was bewildered.

'All these years their slanders drove him to hate his mother. I don't want him to hate his father and grandfather too.'

'Then what will you do?'

'I don't know yet. They said they would bring the old man to Moscow.'

I leapt up from the bed.

'Bauer?'

'Haven't you read the papers?'

With everything that had happened I was worse-informed than the correspondents of the Mongolian Democratic Union.

'It seems that the old man is losing his grip. He's taken refuge in a Red Army military hospital just outside Dresden, claiming to be very sick. Television reporters are saying that he'll be brought here for treatment, probably today. It's clear that this solution benefits all sides. The West German government wants to avoid putting on trial someone with whom they had dealings all these years. The old man knows a lot and is threatening to open his mouth. He's capable of doing so because he's stubborn; he can reveal spy exchanges, or secret loans given by West German banks when he didn't want to take any more from Moscow—deals that not even the Americans know of. Meanwhile, discussions have already begun on the unification of the two German states, essentially the annexation of the East by the West. The old man won't want to stay in Germany; he's afraid that he might be prosecuted for economic irregularities, or for executing those who tried to get over the Wall.'

'I don't understand how you're going to get the child.'

'If he's lost his grip entirely he might just let Erich go. He intended him as his successor but, if the communist world has truly fallen apart, there's no position even for a prince. I'll wait for developments.'

'If only we'd known all this a few days ago.'

'It was all decided in the last few days. Bauer's successors don't seem capable of maintaining East Germany as an independent state.'

'So in the end it seems only the old man and I will come out as losers. He loses his authority; I lose you.'

'You'll find someone else, Kevin. You're the ideal man.'

'No, Yelin was right: I'm no use anymore.'

'Don't be a child.'

'I want you to think it over. You had sworn me eternal fidelity.'

'OK, I'll think it over,' she said conciliatorily.

Fabio had fortunately been taken up by the Fourth Directorate of the Ministry of Health of the Union of Soviet Socialist Republics. It was the directorate that dealt with the two or three thousand select members of the Red aristocracy and had access to fancy hospitals, Western drugs and machines, the best Soviet doctors and nurses who don't act like pneumatic drill operators on a kolkhoz. He had been taken to the hospital near the Ministry of Foreign Affairs, opposite the Belgrad hotel. At that time the democratic newspapers were asking for the health privileges of the nomenklatura to be removed and special hospitals to be opened for all. For the first time I wasn't in favour of the radical reforms, at least not until Fabio had recovered.

The waiting room looked like the lobby of a first-rate hotel. On the way in I met a couple of girls to whom Fabio had introduced me some time before. They were now waiting patiently to see him—no arguments or hair-pulling. If he didn't recover, half the female population of Moscow would fall into a depression. From the end of the passage I saw Giuseppe walking wearily towards me. Unshaven and red-eyed from lack of sleep, he looked as though he had aged by a decade.

'He's a little better, but the doctors say he's not out of the woods yet.'

We were both thinking the same thing. Giuseppe vocalized it first: 'Who the hell were they? Do you think it's about a woman?'

From the get-go I had suspected that the whole affair had to do with women. Before Fabio initiated Miss

KGB into romance ũ la Italia he was going out with Zana, a huge Russian-Kazakh woman with a Russian body and an Asian face. Zana was one of the best catches in Moscow, but she had a weakness: she was the mistress of Scarface, a deputy commander in the mafia, who made his men watch a video of Brian de Palma's film Scarface almost every evening. The cuckolded Scarface had beaten Zana black and blue for her infidelities and, via a common friend—the director of a modelling school—had warned Fabio that if he continued dating his mistress, he should expect 'a punishment to make even the Sicilian mafiosi jealous'.

'But something doesn't quite fit,' said Giuseppe. 'Fabio broke up with Zana when he met Larissa, so Scarface had no reason to do this. Anyway, vendettas are a Sicilian, not Soviet, custom.'

'Larissa?'

'She hasn't left his pillow all these days. She's crying constantly. Just this morning I persuaded her to go home to rest a little. She says she loves him.'

It was the first time that Giuseppe had doubted the sincerity of a member of the honoured KGB.

The nurse interrupted our conversation.

'You can see him, but only for two minutes.'

At first I didn't recognize him. His head had been shaved and two large circles had replaced his eyes. His whole face was purple and deformed. Thankfully he couldn't get up, because if he saw himself in the mirror he would suffer narcissistic mortification. One of his hands was in plaster, wired up with tubes and machines.

I tried to smile, but he didn't respond. Sitting beside

him on the bed, I took his good hand. Giuseppe was only just holding back tears. The nurse had followed us into the room to check we were following her strict commands: he must not talk or be moved—emotionally or physically.

'Allora', I managed to say.

He withdrew his hand from mine and tried to remove the tubes from his nose. Then he whispered, 'They were looking…'

'Looking for what?'

The nurse prodded me in the back.

'About the Wall…' Fabio managed to stutter.

'Who?' I asked.

He closed his eyes, as if trying to gather the strength to talk. A minute passed without him opening them again, so the nurse took me by the hand and led me outside with Giuseppe.

In the meantime Larissa had arrived at the hospital. She came running over when she saw us and we sat together on a couch.

'How is he?'

'Like socialism. Almost comatose.'

Giuseppe looked at me less angrily than I expected. I looked her over.

'Did he ever have contact with East Germans?'

'Never heard that before. Why do you ask?'

'Because if he didn't, you certainly do.'

'Kevin, I swear that what happened has nothing to do with me.'

It was the first time I'd seen a KGB woman welling up. Unless they gave acting lessons at the agency she was telling the truth.

'Why don't you believe me? I love him too much to do him wrong. You don't understand what Fabio means to me—you don't know what Soviet men are like.'

'I admit it's not my area of expertise.'

'In Fabio I discovered that a man can be kind and gentle. Do you realize what it meant to me when he asked me if I was feeling alright before we made love? That he kissed me again after we made love? That he asked my opinion on where we would go in the evening? That he wasn't violent towards me or drunk all the time?'

'It sounds like a Harlequin novel, Larissa.'

'Remind me what a Harlequin novel is?'

'Sentimental novels about Western women full of mushy romance.'

'I don't know why you're laughing at me, but there are no such romance novels here. I've never read one in my life.'

'Come on, Larissa, you have so much literature here,' replied Giuseppe after an awkward silence.

'At school they read us texts where the heroes swoon over the working class. A classic novel was Gladkov's Energy. I know it by heart. "The young worker Ivan grabbed his drill. As soon as he touched the surface of the metal he felt moved. A shudder passed through his body. The deafening sound thrust Sonia away from him. He put his hand on her shoulder and touched the hair behind her ear... At the same time the two young people felt an electrical charge shoot through them. Ivan groaned and clutched his tool more tightly."'

'Don't tell me he means the drill...'

It was the first time I had laughed in days. Larissa sighed.

'Soviet women don't have time to read, or fall in love. In the name of equality we were given the right to work, and the result is that we do all the heavy lifting. We work the same hours as men and then have to queue for shopping, cook, take care of the house and bring up the children. We're victims of gender equality.'

Giuseppe didn't have the strength to respond.

'So, a feminist.'

I said it to rile her, as if talking to a friend in New York. She looked annoyed.

'You want to call a KGB woman a feminist? Well, thanks to perestroika and the KGB I went to the West last year for the first time. We went to Spain as part of a secret service exchange programme. Most of us were enraptured by the supermarkets abroad. But what made the biggest impression wasn't wealth or consumer goods, but that the Spanish women were more feminine than us.'

'Even in your personal relationships you and my brother are spinning anti-Communist propaganda,' Giuseppe said, looking at Larissa with disappointment. 'You know why the Party chose me for the legal delegation? Because ninety per cent of comrades who come here and stay longer than the tourists return with their minds changed. Some leave the Party; others ask us to take even greater distance from the Soviet Union. They chose me because I'm solid as a rock. You won't break my ideology, you and my brother, with your damned love affairs.'

Ignoring Giuseppe's tirade I turned to Larissa.

'I've had problems with your agency. They set a trap for me and I spent a night in Lubyanka.'

'In Lubyanka…' Larissa repeated with terror, as if she didn't go there every day. 'Why? Who arrested you?'

'The cuckold. He was furious that I was going to sleep with his wife.'

'Good on him,' interjected Giuseppe.

'He played the cuckold in the evening, and in the morning arrested me. He was a KGB officer.'

'Impossible,' said Giuseppe.

'Vaffanculo,' I swore at him in Italian. 'Do you even know about Russian cuckolds?'

I turned to Larissa.

'I have the address of the apartment where they set the trap. It's obviously their headquarters. Can you find out anything?'

I gave her the address and described the appearance of the cuckold and of Katya.

Before I left, Larissa took out a piece of paper from her pocket and wrote something.

'My home address. If you need me, come right away, but telephone first since we're followed too. With everything that's happened I'm so disillusioned that I might even quit the KGB.'

'Why leave such an excellent post?' asked Giuseppe. 'Thousands of girls would envy your position.'

Larissa ignored him.

'I'll do anything for you and Fabio. I just want one favour.'

'I'm not going to Lubyanka again.'

'Can you bring me a Harlequin?'

'It's one of the first things a spy learns,' said Lubimov. 'The choice of meeting place often determines the success or failure of a mission.'

We met in the line outside Lenin's Mausoleum. It's true that I was numb with cold, but few could suspect two men in fur hats waiting with the hundreds of other believers to worship the mummy. The line before us was more than a hundred metres long; we were still on the sidewalk before Red Square and had all the time in the world. Lubimov had recovered from his injuries, and had gleefully accepted the two thousand dollars that I had sent him via Natasha for a repair that cost him a tenth of that at the state-owned Lada garage. He was in good spirits.

'I've been remembering old times.'

He paused, as if not knowing how to begin.

'Do you know the joke the Poles tell about the good and bad news? The good news is that Lenin has died; the bad news is that his mother is pregnant. Which do you want first?'

'I can't face more bad news at the moment. Start with the good news.'

'I found out about the Bauer family. Marlene was very closely connected to and patronized by Eva Bauer, the first-born daughter of the dictator. She was second in the regime after her father, and destined to be his successor in the Party, instead of her drunkard brother. She had close contacts with the Soviets, particularly with the KGB and its chief, Yuri Andropov, who later became general secretary. Andropov was in favour of reforms, but before he could begin them he died—in 1983, not two years after he took power. The KGB was the first to set out the need for some changes.'

'Yelin told me the same thing.'

'Even the KGB sometimes tell the truth. Before he died Andropov managed to propel his protégé Mikhail Gorbachev into the Party hierarchy, as well as like-minded people, such as Bauer, in other countries. In 1982 Eva died suddenly, shortly before Marlene divorced. The true cause of death remains unknown: officially it was a heart attack, but many believe she was poisoned by a substance that was never found. The East German secret services—the Stasi—were specialists in producing such poisons. It's possible that Andropov and Gorbachev's opponents did her in, with Bauer's consent.'

'Don't say that you even suspect her own father?'

He looked at me condescendingly, as though at a child who is too innocent to understand.

'I explained already—the family didn't flourish under communism. Particularly in the higher echelons, every human emotion was crushed under political games. Anyway, you know that from the West too.

In the halls of power there's no room for family relationships. Have you heard of Kalinin, president of the Soviet Union in the thirties when Stalin was general secretary?'

'I walk along Kalinina Prospekt every day to my house.'

'Good. To keep him under his thumb, Stalin put Kalinin's wife in jail when he was president. He did the same with Molotov, his right hand, who was minister of foreign affairs for thirteen years and made the secret deals with Hitler before the war. At the same time Molotov's wife was in a gulag. And these unbelievable people not only didn't resist, I'm certain they would have patted Stalin on the back. The gulags are certainly an effective way of getting rid of your wife, but still…'

We had already entered the Mausoleum. The faithful were walking around Lenin's mummified body with religious piety, one or two crossing themselves. I fumed inwardly at the Bolshevik leader—if it weren't for him I might have been writing beautiful reportage from Paris about the renovation of the Champs-Élysées. He seemed unruffled, utterly convinced he had been right in everything he did.

'If that's the good news,' I whispered to Lubimov, 'I can guess what the bad news is.'

He hesitated again.

'Do you know the joke we tell here? Lenin, resurrected, asks to read the back issues of Pravda in order to inform himself of the progress of the Revolution. After a short while he looks up and says, "I'm afraid we'll have to go back to square one."'

I elbowed him impatiently.

'Marlene didn't come into conflict with Bauer because she wanted to divorce his son. She was involved in some power play, and when Eva died she fell out of favour. Later she had the problems that we know about. She divorced and they forbade her from seeing the child. Everything she's told you after that is true.'

The Mausoleum was cold as a grave. Specialized air-conditioning units kept the temperature down to preserve the mummy. In this country not even Lenin could escape Siberia.

'If Eva collaborated with the KGB, do you think that Marlene could have done the same?'

He looked at me squarely as if gauging my mental health—as you do when wanting to announce someone's death, but wondering if the person you're talking to will be able to bear the news.

'I can't rule it out, but I have no proof. What happened in Moscow 400 worries me. Someone shopped it to the KGB.'

'Pioneer. He confessed to me that he maintained contact with the KGB. He was even bankrolling Yelin. Marlene had no reason to do it as she was going to get her child back.'

'Pioneer had nothing to gain from sabotaging the plan. The mafia is extending its activities in the trafficking of nuclear matter. You must have been carrying a sample for some prospective buyer.'

'But he might have been double bluffing. I need to find out.'

'Won't you give up? Sometimes the less you know, the better.'

'I want to be sure about Marlene. I still love her. And I have responsibility for the child.'

'Are you in a hurry?'

I looked at my watch. It was seven in the evening and I had to leave the day after next. I had less than forty-eight hours.

He remained thoughtful, as if something was bothering him. We walked around Lenin once more. Soon we'd be taken for fanatical communists or necrophiliacs. I looked more closely at the Bolshevik leader's face: it was becoming deformed and they had covered it with a thick layer of make-up.

'I shouldn't really tell you this,' he said in a low voice.

He looked around and whispered in my ear, 'Have you heard about the OibE? That's the German abbreviation for "officers on special duty".'

I shrugged, still looking at Lenin. He also looked ignorant.

'It's paranoia. The Stasi has around a hundred thousand paid agents, not counting occasional workers. Half of the East Germans inform on the other half. In making such a huge army of agents, Bauer felt like the creator of Frankenstein: he was terrified that he would lose control of this monstrous power, and it would turn against him. So he made another super-Stasi to spy on the Stasi.

'They're the OibE, the super-agents. There are about a thousand of them, and they must have shown in practice their absolute loyalty to the Party and the working class. As Bauer himself once said, they must display "capacity for mental and physical resilience above the norm". They have gone through special training and exhaustive trials to test their endurance—something akin to James Bond. Their families know nothing about their position, and they're not paid by the Stasi like normal agents, but by the job that they hold as an official cover. They have key roles in the ministries, the press, universities, theatres, embassies and missions abroad, in the Party and in the Stasi itself. It's a kind of internal party, a super-government. I calculate that there are around four or five such people in Moscow. They must know everything about Marlene and Müller.'

I thought about money. Lubimov read my mind.

'Money is good bait. But it must be enough for them to bend their capacity for mental resilience above the norm. I guess you don't have a hundred thousand dollars spare.'

All I had earned those years in Moscow was just enough to rent and furnish an apartment in New York.

'I served in East Berlin right after the 1953 uprising,' he continued. 'I discovered that a young man, a rather fanatical Stasi agent, had been an SS agent in the War. He swore to me that he had become an anti-fascist, and that's why he was working for the East German agency. He seemed sincere and I left him to continue with his new life. Besides, those with a burdened past become the best. Now he's an "officer on special duty" in Moscow. I hope he'll repay the old debt.'

Lubimov took his freezing hands out of his pockets and blew on them. We had emerged into Red Square, where it was warmer than it had been in Lenin's Mausoleum.

'There's another source that we should investigate, but you'll have to do that in your capacity as a journalist. Vera Berger is here at the moment. Have you heard of her?'

'Not the dissident who was deported from East Germany in 1988?'

'Precisely. The day after the Wall fell she returned and began investigating the Stasi's files. Her research brought her to Moscow, because she's trying to find out about the links between the Stasi and the KGB. She's staying at the Savoy. Go and meet her today if you can, then let's meet tomorrow on the little boat that goes around Moscow. It stops at the pier below the Hotel Ukraina at ten past ten. I'll already be on it. Just try not to let anyone see you. Will you manage?'

'It's bothering me less and less that I was expelled from the paper. I'll become a private detective specializing in political romances. But I'm confused about something: who checks those thousands of OibE so they themselves don't break off?'

Lubimov looked surprised.

'Do you know about the "submarines"?'

'Nuclear or normal? I'm only a detective; I'll become a submarine specialist when I grow up.'

'And yet you hit the bullseye. To control the OibE,

Bauer created the so-called submarine agents. They're called that because they can be anybody: the director of Pravda, the leader of the Red Army or the French ambassador. There are no more than fifty and they're scattered around the world. To become a submarine, it's not enough to have the qualities of the OibE: you must owe gratitude to Bauer himself. He must know you personally. The Nazis had arrested Bauer in the thirties: he was head of the illegal network of the Communist Party. Bauer didn't talk, despite torture from the Gestapo. All of those people owe him their lives. They're ready to die for him. That's who the submarines are. There will only be one, if any, in Moscow. If only I knew who... Bauer alone knows, and maybe Mielke, the head of the Stasi.'

'Forget it. We'll find the submarine on another mission.'

By good fortune, Vera Berger was at the Savoy and had no objection to meeting me immediately. She was around forty-five, with big green eyes that immediately inspired trust. I had seen her before in East Berlin, during some semi-illegal gathering in a church, before she was expelled for dissident activity. She seemed happy enough, but her eyes were red as if she'd been crying for days. I cut to the chase.

'I'm looking for what was behind the fall of Bauer and the Wall.'

She sighed. I couldn't tell whether from relief or disappointment.

'Oh, I thought you had come to ask me about the scandal associated with me.'

Again, my ignorance had been shown up.

'You know, here in the Soviet Union our information is very limited about the outside world.'

She sighed again.

'Perhaps it's better you don't know. I would prefer not to know too.'

She paused briefly, looking at the window.

'It's the talk of the town. Do you want something to drink?'

'Thanks, but I'm very tired.'

She stood up, filled a glass with whisky and ice from the mini-fridge and took a long drag on her cigarette.

'I played a leading role in the opening of files, because I was asked very personal questions in interrogations. From back then I suspected that some close friend of ours was working with the Stasi. I was one of the first lucky people who were given the chance to see their file: they had eleven hefty folders about me, a few thousand pages. At first I said I wouldn't read anything since I would have to spend the rest of my life reading about what I did in the first half. But, when I started to flick through the files, I saw that they had noted even the most insignificant details: what detergent I used, the little things I had in my room, where I shopped, what my children ate at school, even when I said good morning to a neighbour. An agent code-named Donald had signed most of the memos. For me they used two code names: Virus and Hypocrite. Virus because I was poisoning the country with my ideas, and Hypocrite because, while it was suspected that I didn't love the country since I was against the regime, I refused all the Stasi's invitations to leave for the West, using the argument that I loved my homeland.'

She lit another cigarette from the butt of the last.

'When I read conversations that had occurred in bed I had no more doubt: Donald was my husband.'

'You mean your ex-husband?'

'My husband with whom I had two children, with whom I was expelled from East Germany. He was a Stasi agent.'

'May I have a drink?'

She nodded, served me a glass, then lit another cigarette and took a drag almost to the middle of it.

'I had studied mathematics, but I never thought I would need to apply the law of probabilities in my own home. In a population of twelve million, around one in twenty worked for the Stasi. The Gestapo were much harsher, but in 1944 they only had forty thousand agents. Their goal was to follow the Jews and Communists, whereas Bauer wanted to follow the whole population. Unlike the Nazis, he didn't have the support of the people.'

'Then why did so many collaborate?'

'That is what people are currently trying to explain. They talk of the unbearable pressures—psychological and social—that the Stasi exerted on those lined up for recruitment. They got some of them gently, making them believe that it wasn't too serious to give a little bit of information. Others were terrified of saying no. Then there is the German mentality: we fall in with power and the state, regardless of who is in charge. Many were proud that the Stasi asked them to collaborate: it gave them a sense of self-worth.'

She downed the whisky like a Russian drinking vodka, like we drink Coca Cola.

'And yet, for anyone who wanted, there was a simple way of rejecting the proposal.'

'Which was?'

'They could tell members of their family, or friends or colleagues. The Stasi immediately backed off from a garrulous candidate who violated the supreme rule of collusion.'

'I still don't understand. You had children, a family. Was it the money?'

'I don't know if you'll ever be able to understand. The vast majority of collaborators were not paid. If they got anything, it was a pittance. But East German society was harsh, a society with few sentiments. Even within the family, relationships had been poisoned by lack of trust or the daily problems of survival. It's telling that they recruited so many orphans. My husband was born in Leipzig in 1944, during the bombings. His parents were buried beneath the ruins a few days after he was born. The Stasi were a second family for many.

'The mystery of romance was replaced by the conspiratorial, secret relationship with the secret services. Many turned in others to give some meaning to their life, to escape their tedious, miserable daily grind. Relationships between officers and the Stasi were stronger than family or romantic ones.'

It ended up as the most difficult interview of my life.

'Had you not suspected anything?'

'Of course not. Otherwise I wouldn't have married him. I loved him. He was the father of my children.'

She sighed.

'Even recently I felt in love. But...'

She weighed up exactly what she wanted to say.

'I don't know how to put it. Power and politics corrupt emotions. Absolute power perverts them entirely.'

She lit another cigarette, observing me closely.

'But you said that you hadn't come to talk about me.'

'I'm interested in Marlene Bauer, Bauer's former daughter-in-law. I'm wondering if you've found anything in the files of the Stasi, or of the KGB here in Moscow...'

There was a pause of a few seconds. I felt my heart beating hard.

'I've known about her from old times, since it was well known that she divorced and they took away her child. Do you know her?'

'I'm in love with her.'

She took a few notes out of a bag and glanced at them.

'The KGB refuses to give any information. But in Berlin I found the list with all the Stasi agents who worked in Bauer's palace and its environs. I never encountered her name.'

It was my turn to sigh—from relief. I had finished my second whisky and felt so at home with this lady that I stood up and poured myself another.

'All of these stories have made you suspicious, yes?' she asked sadly. 'The only solution is to trust your emotions.'

'You, of all people, are telling me that?'

'There is no other way. Otherwise we'd have to suspect our own shadow.'

'You're a very brave woman. Did you tell your children about all this?'

Her face darkened.

'I had to explain to them why I divorced their father. But I think they'll have significant problems in the future, like everyone. The Stasi's poison will remain in all of us for many years.'

I had to leave, but a question was running through my mind continuously.

'Can you forgive someone after that kind of betrayal?'

She had thought about this a lot, for she answered immediately.

'Forgiveness requires that there has been a specific level of regret. At least, an acceptance of wrongdoing.'

'And your husband?'

She looked at the ceiling while her face hardened, as though she was having a nightmare.

'After a quarter of an hour he confessed everything. I continued to ask him questions as calmly as I could, even though I could hardly breathe from the frog in my throat. The explanations given by informers are always the same: everyone claims that they wanted to avoid something worse. He told me that he had protected me from greater persecution by what he did.'

I don't know why, but instead of saying goodbye to her I embraced her silently and kissed her tenderly on the cheek. Then I made to leave.

'One moment, Mr Danaher. I want to say something else.'

She came closer.

'I would prefer to have been in prison for years, rather than to experience what happened to me. In prison you know why you are there, but I will never know why my husband did all that. I'll never understand it.'

I turned around and looked at her before closing the door. She was wiping a tear from her cheek.

At his suite in the Rossiya Hotel, Pioneer had left a message for me. If I called, he was at a wedding reception at the Olympus restaurant and I should go there.

The Olympus, a modern glass-and-brick structure near the Luzhinki Stadium, is the mafia's restaurant. Outside were parked fifty or so Mercedes and BMWs —armoured, of course. Traffic police were in operation around the restaurant, while men from the anti-terror team of the Ministry of Internal Affairs were pacing around with their walkie-talkies. They were armed with automatic weapons and wearing bulletproof vests, fearful of another bloody clash between rival gangs.

The jurisdiction of the prosecuting authorities ended at the sidewalk: the entrance was guarded by bouncers in their finest jogging outfits and sneakers. The name Sergei Tamurian was a kind of password, and it let me through the checks relatively smoothly. The main hall was full of mafiosi, women and lobster buffets. In the centre a huge white cake—an imitation of Stalin's Seven Sisters—was waiting patiently. A band was playing jazz.

Pioneer was surrounded by long legs topped with miniskirts. He was ever generous: 'Come join our group. The girls are old comrades from the Communist Youth. They were responsible for entertaining the senior members of the organization and the official foreign representatives. Isn't that right, girls?'

They laughed coquettishly. It seemed that Pioneer had wanted to be a history teacher from a young age.

'Do you like jazz?' he asked, pointing at the band. 'Previously they practically forbade it, because in 1928 that idiot Maxim Gorky came out and said that it was imperialist music for well-fed capitalists. Thankfully, an American communist a few years later announced that it was the music of black people and all the wretched of the earth. So they stopped persecuting the musicians and started inviting them to musical evenings at the Kremlin. Only once did the trombonist Vasia mess up: before a private performance that Stalin was going to attend, he joked that he had a bomb in his trombone. It took eight months to get him out of prison, and he hasn't played well since then. He's the old man in the band, with the out-of-tune trombone.'

'Your musical review is flawless. And you're not too bad at betrayal, too.'

He grimaced.

'Is that why you wanted to see me urgently the other day? Don't be a fool. I wanted the mission to succeed as much as you did.'

He turned towards the girls and told them to leave us alone.

'Fine. Let's speak rationally. Why would I set a trap for you?'

'That's exactly what I want to find out.'

'I had warned you not to tell anyone anything about the mission.'

'The only person who knew was Marlene. But she had absolutely no reason to turn me in.'

'You're very naïve, Kevin.'

'What do you mean?'

'You trust women.'

I had no desire for macho chat.

'Oh, get lost, you jerk.'

Pioneer was irked.

'So you lost the material, and now you want your money back?'

I got up angrily to leave.

'Hold on. Did you tell her in your apartment?'

I tried to remember how it had happened. After the discussion with Pioneer in the courtyard of the compound, I had returned to the apartment and Marlene asked what had been said between us. At first I simply promised that she would soon have Erich back, but she insisted that she deserved to know. In the end I told her.

'Which room were you in? Can you remember?' asked Pioneer.

'The bedroom.'

'Well, then they might have heard.'
Suddenly I had an idea.
'There might be a way of finding out. See you later.'
I turned to go, but Pioneer grabbed me by the shoulder.
'Wait five minutes, I have something else to tell you.'

'I made a promise to you last time and I usually keep my promises.'
'What promise?'
'To explain why they call me Pioneer.'
My ears pricked up.
'In reality I'm not called Sergei Tamurian. I'm called Pavlik Morozov.'
'What, the child—'
'... who turned in his parents,' Pioneer continued.
He filled his glass with whisky and drank it in one. What an evening this was! I felt as though I was reporting on the alcoholism brought on by politics and history.
'They executed them both, my mother and father. It wasn't my fault.'
'I know.'
'I was eight years old. It's easy to fanaticize a child of that age. It was 1934; I was at a good primary school in Stalingrad. Maxim Gorky came to speak. For us children he wasn't simply our national writer; he was a demigod. We knew his novels by heart; his portrait hung in every classroom next to Lenin and Stalin.
'It was when the Party had begun spreading the

slogan, "Destroying family bonds gives the final blow to the bourgeois regime". He spoke to us of the new Soviet person we were building under communism. I remember him saying, word for word, "If one of your parents turns out to be an enemy of the people, the fact that they are a member of your family is of no relevance whatsoever. They are an enemy you have no reason to pity." He informed us that he had prepared a decree with comrade Stalin under which "any parent who neglected their children" could be taken to court. We just had to protest to our teacher and she would be obliged to refer the matter to the courts. He also announced that we could send to court teachers who didn't treat us well. They belonged, he said, to the previous generation and were steeped in the old ideas.'

He took a long draft from a glass abandoned by one of the girls.

'Then he asked us if we had any questions, urging us to speak freely. I put up my hand and asked what we should do if we realize that our parents are anti-revolutionaries. "Spiritual kinship is far higher than blood relations," Gorky replied, before finishing with, "Children, be careful of what's around you. You'll see that there are a lot of relics of the old society. It's good to make a note of them and inform us." When I got home, they asked me what we had learnt in school that day. I told them what had happened. "Just listen to what they tell children!" my father fumed. I recall my mother motioning him to be silent. That was the last time I saw them.'

I hadn't imagined that Pioneer could cry. He held the tears in with difficulty and lit a cigarette.

'The next day I mentioned my father's comment to the headmaster. I went back to class, but when the day's lessons were over they told me I couldn't go home, because my parents had been arrested. They accused them of being part of a counter-revolutionary group planning to sabotage the railways, one of the usual accusations against those they wanted to get rid of. They took me out of school and put me in an orphanage, where they gave me another name, supposedly because the counter-revolutionaries might have taken revenge and killed me. There they called me Sergei Tamurian. To cover my tracks, they wrote in the press that my grandfather had killed me for revenge, along with my brother Fyodor. So I turned into myth: they put up statues of me, wrote poems extolling my achievement. In every school there were special gatherings and the children were called to follow my example. Stalin himself used me in his speeches to show the pluck of the new Soviet person and how unscrupulous the old person was. I wasn't allowed to tell anyone who I really was, because then I really would be in danger. Not from the fanatical counter-revolutionary friends of my parents, but from the regime that had to preserve its mythical hero. No one knew who I was apart from the director of the orphanage. He called me "Pioneer".'

'I'm wondering why you're telling me all this.'

'To explain that I really did want to help you get the child back, and why it wasn't me who turned you in. Beyond that, draw your own conclusions.'

On the return home, I tried to put my thoughts in order. Now everything was in doubt. I didn't know if Marlene was telling the truth, or if it was she who had shopped me. The fact that, according to Berger, she didn't work for the Stasi had eased my mind, but only temporarily. What if she worked for the KGB? I wasn't sure if Erich wanted to return to his mother or if he had already been set against her by Bauer's slanders. On that day at the theme park had he realized from the start who we were and preferred to return to Müller? Did Lubimov know things that he didn't want to say, or couldn't? And Pioneer? How much faith can you have in someone who turned in his own parents?

My friend was bedridden in hospital and had tried to tell me about some guys who were looking for information about the Wall. My son was far away in America with Cynthia. On one matter I was certain: I had to leave the Soviet Union and its depraved climate as soon as I settled the matter and restored my name. I had been tainted by the lack of faith and the constant threat of imminent betrayal. I had to trust someone and decided to start with Marlene.

Turning off the ring road I arrived at Stockmann, the first supermarket to open in Moscow. It is essentially a temple to consumerism. The first days that it was open, all Soviets who had a few dollars visited it and bought something small to pay their respects—like lighting a candle in church: a toothbrush, detergent, a banana. Because of the crush of people, the management were forced to abandon cash purchases: only those with credit cards—in other words, foreigners—can shop there now. From one perspective, therefore, Stockmann put a Soviet ideal into practice: the abolition of money. The vision of the founders of Marxism–Leninism was not much different: we would shop with credit cards without being obliged to pay them off. We would buy whatever we wanted—each according to their needs.

With my American Express card I bought a crate of vodka, put it in the car and headed to the Kutuzovsky compound. Keeping to protocol, the KGB guards at the entrance enquired if I had anything to offer them. I asked for their boss, who arrived swiftly, smiling. He was about forty, with rosy cheeks, small blue eyes and a huge blond moustache. His name was Volodya. I gave him the crate.

'I need just one favour.'

'Anything you like.'

'I want to hear the recordings from my apartment.'

He sized me up for a few seconds, looking me in the eye. Then he said, 'No one must find out a thing.'

We went into the apartment block where the KGB officers lived. On the ground floor, inside Volodya's office, there was a staircase that led to the basement. We went down, then along a corridor that looked like a mine shaft and smelt of mould. Suddenly we found ourselves in a vast underground space with many pillars, which must have had the same footprint as the courtyard of the compound. It was the size of about ten basketball courts, and divided by chipboard and glass into cubicles. Hundreds of people were sitting behind long wooden counters, which had rows of reel-to-reel tape recorders on them, many of which were in operation. Most of the people sitting at the counters were wearing earphones. I had before me a huge bugging workshop.

Volodya asked me which block I lived in and my entrance number. Without much difficulty he found the cubicle that corresponded to my place. We went inside. An ugly figure came towards us, a questioning look in his eyes, but my friend gave him two bottles of vodka and said, 'Let him listen. It's his home.'

The ugly man asked the number of my apartment, and only then did I realize that there were three microphones assigned just for me. They each had a label attached: living room, bedroom, kitchen. I asked to see if they had recorded my conversation with Marlene the day before my journey to Moscow 400. He bent down to the shelves under the counter: dozens of reels were ordered by place and date.

'We have automatic microphones sensitive to the human voice,' he said, swelling with pride, 'but there's still a lot of material. Do you want something to drink?'

My throat was dry from sleeplessness. I asked for a cup of tea.

'Tea,' he repeated disdainfully. He summoned a young man and gave him the order.

Then he asked which room I wanted to hear the conversation from. When I said the bedroom he nodded his head in understanding: evidently he took me for a cuckold. He picked out a reel, plugged a spare cassette player into a socket and gave me the earphones, saying mischievously, 'Here you are. If only I had such facilities I would leave my wife alone at home without worrying.'

I thought of saying that, with a face like his, he had reason to be suspicious of his wife. But, in the position I was in, I had to be kind to the eavesdroppers. I soon realized that everything had been recorded: conversations, sweet-talking, moans from the bed. It's very strange to listen again to your whole life a few days later: it's as if it's not you. So much seems insignificant or superfluous. Erotic talk sounds ridiculous, like pornos without a picture.

That ugly face interrupted me. He was holding a cup of tea, which he gave me with a Russian joke: 'Careful, this isn't vodka, you know. It's not to be drunk all day long.'

At last I reached the critical point. The comrades had used advanced technology, since the whole softly spoken conversation had been clearly recorded. Initially I refused to reveal my agreement with Pioneer, but Marlene was as insistent as ever.

'You have to tell me; it concerns me.'

I went on to tell her about Pioneer's proposal of collaboration in exchange for Erich's release.

'And what do you have to do?'
'Transfer a bag that they'll give me.'
'What does it have in it? Do you know?'
'No. I don't think I want to.'

I motioned the ugly man to turn off the tape player. My suspicions were unjustified, and now I was happy. I was almost flying. I got up from my seat and said to Volodya that we could leave. The ugly man had already drunk half a bottle and he stammered another gag: 'Does vodka hinder work? Then let's stop working!'

I clapped him heartily on the back, pointing at the underground installations, 'Don't let's destroy the only thing left standing in this country.'

I entered my apartment like a bull in a china shop. In the small storeroom by the kitchen I found a hammer and a big steel screwdriver. I set about tearing down the walls one by one: kitchen, living room, bedroom. In the living room I uncovered a microphone in the lamp, but I wasn't planning on losing time with the ends of the system: the whole network had to be destroyed. Wires, microphones and plaster started to fall on the floor on all sides. Marlene looked without expression at the ruined carpets and the bedroom before trying to stop me. But I have never been so out of my mind. From the bedcover to the antiques, everything was covered in a thick layer of white dust. After about an hour of crazed destruction, the three bugged rooms looked bombed out: the bricks had been left bare on the walls, with cables and microphones hanging from them. I sat in an armchair, exhausted.

'Now we can talk freely. I apologize.'

Marlene shrugged.

'It's your home. Do what you like.'

'It's not that. I doubted you once more.'

'Three strikes and you're out. The first was Erich's birthday. What is it this time?'

I was too embarrassed to tell her about my discussions with Berger and Pioneer.

'I don't even really know. I found out you were a close friend of Eva Bauer.'

'I had told you that. That's how I met my husband.'

'Had you told me that you worked closely with her at her ministry?'

'What is this? An interrogation?'

'No, I'm just saying that in a way your fates were linked.'

'What do you mean?'

'I mean that her death weakened your own position.'

'Who's been telling you this nonsense? That fool Lubimov?'

She was livid by now.

'I'll tell you for the last time. If I hadn't divorced I wouldn't be going through all this—and, most importantly, I would have my child. You can believe whatever you like: that I wanted to become general secretary of the Party in place of Bauer, that I overthrew him. Yes, it was me who toppled the Wall! Go on, interview me!'

There were a few moments of silence. She softened a bit and changed the subject. 'Giuseppe called from hospital. Fabio is doing better.'

'That's another mystery,' I sighed. 'What the hell were they looking for about the Wall in the Corriere della Sera offices?'

'What a mystery,' she replied sarcastically. 'What goes "meow" on the roof? Larissa. I would bet that she works for the department of the KGB in charge of socialist countries. The night we met she spoke to me constantly about her trips to East Berlin. She was involved in some plot, and she dragged in Fabio, too.'

Patrick was woken by searing pains through his whole body. His chest and head were on fire —he must have had a high fever. The previous evening a police car had taken him to Prague's Psychiatric Clinic No. 13. A nurse had given him drugs, telling him that they would help him calm down. He was indeed very angry and afraid. After his categorical refusal to collaborate with the Czechoslovak spy service, the undersecretary of internal affairs said he would be sent to the clinic to be with the other crazy people. The term he had used was 'psychopaths'.

When he had confirmed that the whole affair beginning with his arrest at the border wasn't just a bad dream, he looked around him. They had put him in a ward smelling of formalin and with walls painted yellow. There were a dozen tall iron-framed beds, each with a white wooden bedside table next to it. Patrick became aware that he had company: other men were lying on the beds near him, their eyes closed.

When he tried to check the time he remembered that they had taken his watch as they lifted him onto the ramp of the clinic's central building. There were no windows in the ward, just a large lamp that emitted dim blue light. A few of his fellow inmates were uncovered and he noticed that they were wearing striped uniforms that looked like prisoners' outfits. On their chests each had a number embroidered with yellow thread. Only then did he realize that he was wearing the same uniform. He tried to read his number, but his eyes couldn't focus on near objects.

Suddenly the ward door opened and a person in an inmate's outfit came in, dragging his feet. His head was shaved, he had a long white beard and in his hands he held a towel with a yellow number embroidered onto it. He couldn't have noticed Patrick, because the moment he saw him look up from the bed, he stopped in his tracks. He was wearing brown sandals, again numbered with bright yellow thread. The strange man came towards Patrick. He couldn't have been more than forty-five years old. He asked Patrick something in Czech.

'I'm hurting,' Patrick said in English.

'Where are you from?' the man asked, also in English.

'From France,' Patrick replied, hesitantly.

'Good. Let's talk French then,' the stranger said, smiling.

Patrick reflected that he hadn't seen a smiling person in several days.

'I haven't spoken French in a while,' the man continued. 'You're the first foreigner I've seen here. Have they drugged you?'

'Yesterday evening.'

'That's why you're hurting.'

The bearded man went to his bed, searched in his mattress and came back holding a white pill and a glass of water.

'Take it. It's a painkiller.'

Patrick sat up in bed, put the pillow behind him and drank the pill. He saw that his hands were trembling.

'Don't get up yet; you'll feel dizzy. What's your name?'

'Patrick Ventura.'

'Arnold Khrushko,' he said, extending his hand. It was skeletal.

'Don't take the pills they give you, and try to eat as little as possible. They put sedatives in it.'

'How do you know all this?' Patrick managed to ask.

'I'm a biologist.'

'And why are you here?'

'It's hard to explain. Reformist psychosis.'

Patrick's eyes widened.

'Are you... Are you citizen A.K.?'

'I knew they had written about me in the Journal of Criminology, but I didn't know I was famous.'

'Essentially, I was sent here because I didn't betray my love,' A.K. said.

Half an hour had passed and Patrick was feeling better. A.K. had informed him that it was six in the morning. The contact with time helped him regain his composure. His new friend gave him a couple of dried rusks, which he ate hungrily.

'She wasn't an accomplice; she had no role at all,' continued A.K. 'But if they had been able to make me betray her I would have become their tool, like most Czechoslovaks.'

He stopped to crunch a rusk on his canines. Patrick saw that his front teeth were missing. A.K. loudly swallowed the unchewed rusk.

'I was working for years at the Institute of Psychological Stimuli. It was a very well-paid position because we were developing a secret plan on behalf of the government. We were studying the behaviour of rabbits to draw conclusions about humans—looking at what human emotions we could control and in turn replace with the emotions that the new socialist man had to possess: group mentality, blind enthusiasm and obedience.

'Human activity is defined by four emotions: fear, hate, hunger and love. It's not a new discovery; we knew that this was the case both for humans and animals. But the experiments on rabbits showed that by provoking or inactivating these emotions we could change their behaviour.'

His face darkened.

'In socialist countries they already control three of the four: hunger, because they give us food whenever they want and in the quantities they choose; hate, because they've made us hate capitalists, and also each other—those who take our place in the queue, those who manage to procure a piece of meat in the neighbourhood state shop. We would put two rabbits in two cages next to each other and give food just to one. The one without food changed behaviour, becoming more aggressive. The moment we opened the hatch between them, it leapt onto the other one's food, or attacked the rabbit itself. The next day we swapped the roles and the previously well-fed rabbit attacked the other.

'Then fear, which hugely influenced the rabbits—they were terrified of the noises and the electric shocks. When they realized, from a light that turned on or a particular smell, that they would hear the terrifying noise, they would cower in a corner and become obedient. The same has happened with us: they have made us afraid even of our own shadows. We live in the era of great fear, without knowing exactly what our mistake is. Only in our romantic relationships are things more complicated among us. Have I bored you yet?'

Patrick looked at him gratefully.

'I'm just happy I can talk to someone.'

'Man is the only being that does not possess automated sexual behaviour. Most animals go through entirely defined periods of sexual excitement and periods of indifference, and they always make love in the same way. The ritual differs from animal to animal, but only in humans does sex arouse the imagination, because we have developed the history and discoveries of eroticism. Unlike animals, for whom sex is used for reproduction, we have stepped up the sexual instinct. Our research reached a dead end eventually, because, as far as you manage to make a society uniform, it's still impossible to forbid humans their fantasies.'

A.K. stopped for a moment, as if something was bothering him.

At last he said, 'Then there's romantic love. Love which is devoted to a specific person.'

'With everything that's happened to me here I've been wondering if such love can survive in a totalitarian regime.'

A.K. smiled.

'That's a huge topic and we don't have time for it now. They tried to do that to me: if I had betrayed the woman I loved, they would have stolen from me the only emotion they hadn't managed to control.'

He put a little of the second rusk that he was holding into his mouth and chewed it like a sweet. Then he asked Patrick, 'So, why are you here? This wing is only for political prisoners.'

'I tried to get a Czechoslovak woman I loved out of the country.'

'And did she want to go with you?'

Patrick looked at him in confusion.

'Yes, because she loved me.'

'Strange,' said A.K.

'Let me continue! I want to see what happens,' said Marlene. 'It's getting interesting.'

'You can read it on your own.'

'I told you I don't know how to work these machines.'

I looked at her quizzically. I was almost certain that whenever I left the apartment someone was opening the novel on my computer. I hadn't thought more of it, believing that like everything else those days, my computer was also experiencing strange times.

'This morning you told me you found it odd that the woman I love wanted to leave.'

Patrick had managed to get A.K. on his own during

lunch. The two of them were left in the clinic's grubby restaurant, sitting around a kidney-shaped table. The other patients had gone out into the courtyard: it was time for the afternoon walk. Despite the noise in the ward and the voices of the nurses, Patrick, pretending that the drugs were working on him, had fallen asleep again until midday, and now he felt better. A.K.'s presence had greatly heartened him. This was someone he could even talk French to, and he was in the clinic for the same reason as Patrick: love for a woman. Patrick was hungry, but A.K. advised him again to eat as little as possible. It didn't need much effort, as lunch in Clinic No. 13 didn't quite follow the recipes of the famed Bohemian cuisine to the letter. A.K. dubbed the usual lunch dish a safari, a watery soup through which the inmates had to hunt for the scarce meat. A.K. only ate bread: the inmates had concluded that it was the only food that didn't contain drugs.

Now he looked squarely at Patrick, 'Because everyone wants to leave, but no one wants to leave the country.'

'Strange,' said Patrick. 'I had quite the opposite impression.'

'In the West you have a false impression of the communist regimes. You think they're big prisons, but that's only half the truth. In reality communism is something between a prison and a children's playground.'

He paused momentarily, as if searching for the words.

'They have systematically infantilized the population. Everything is organized, from what you eat and drink to what time you go to sleep. If you accept the system you can get through life without anxiety and trouble. You can sing a song if you like, as long as it's a socialist one. Then there's the fear of punishment. Like the children who eat their food so the bad wolf doesn't come, we're obedient so that we don't hear those three terrifying letters at our door: the KGB in Russia, the StB in Czechoslovakia, the Stasi in Germany. The secret services have achieved mythical dimensions, like the wolf in the fairy tale. I was surprised that your girlfriend tried to leave, because we all suffer from a fear of freedom. Think of a child who doesn't like the playground: he's unhappy but he's also afraid to go out, because he doesn't know where he will go and what he will discover out there.'

The patients who had chosen the occupational therapy programme were lazily collecting the trays with the leftovers from the tables. Some were nibbling the bits of bread like hungry sparrows.

'Anna had me,' Patrick said stubbornly. 'She loved me.'

A.K. patted me genially on the shoulder.

'Let's make the most of the afternoon walk. We'll go stir-crazy in here!'

'I can't understand why you sent out those pamphlets with your manifesto,' Patrick said to A.K as they walked along the corridor to the courtyard. 'It was like you wanted them to arrest you.'

'That wasn't my goal,' A.K. replied with a smile, 'I

was simply playing a joke on them. To put my candidacy forward I invoked the laws that they themselves had made. I wanted to do something that they hadn't foreseen, to panic them. And I succeeded.'

Patrick glanced around at the strange sight: about thirty people, men and women, walking in two separate circles around the snowy courtyard. They were wearing their striped prisoner uniforms with long, dark blue overcoats on top. Addled by the drugs, some of them were leaning on the skeleton of the abandoned car. Patrick and A.K. joined the men's circle. All of their heads were shaved, as if in a concentration camp. Most of them were walking silently, looking dazed.

'Here are the political patients,' A.K. said, pointing. 'Reformist psychosis, democratic paranoia, hooliganism, disobedience. We are separated from the rest.'

In the other circle, Patrick noticed a woman with cropped white hair talking to herself with her head turned towards the sky. Following was another woman, with short red hair and dark circles under eyes that looked familiar to Patrick. When their eyes met, the woman stopped and looked more closely at him. 'Oh God, it's Lisa Thompson. They arrested her too,' he thought, before the woman cried, 'Patrick!'

They fell into each other's arms. Lisa started to cry pitifully.

'How did you end up here? When did they catch you?'

'At the airport.'

'They said nothing to me about you. I thought you had left.'

'They didn't let me get on the plane. I was left to wait and a few hours later they arrested me. They interrogated me and brought me here.'

Lisa let go of him and looked him in the eyes. Her gaze hardened like a mad woman's.

'She turned us in.'

He bit his lip, until he tasted blood in his mouth.

'Impossible. How did you come to that conclusion?' he asked.

'No one else knew about the plan.'

'She wanted to leave.'

'I know it was her,' Lisa said determinedly. 'It was like they were expecting me. They pretended that they discovered me by chance, so as not to reveal her part.'

'You're insane!' Patrick retorted. 'The surroundings have got to you.'

'Then why didn't they tell you that I had been arrested? So that you wouldn't realize they knew the plan from the start!'

Patrick was overcome by something like madness. He grabbed Lisa by the collar of her uniform and began to shake her.

'She loved me, understand? She loves me!'

His cries echoed around the courtyard, so loudly that two male nurses in white shirts took Patrick's arms and dragged him into the emergency ward.

'Darling, I knew that you trusted me—that this depraved climate we live in wouldn't affect you,' Marlene said to me, lifting her eyes from the screen.

She unbuttoned her skirt and took off her clothes with slow movements until she was completely naked. Then she began to undress me violently, kissing my whole body.

When we finished making love, I asked her, 'Have you thought whether you will live with me?'

She bent down to my ear, as if afraid they were still listening to us. Her big eyes were full of tears. Before she started kissing me again, she whispered, 'I will never leave you. As soon as I have Erich, we'll come and find you.'

[28th November]

I don't know if I was being followed, but I still took all precautions. Leaving the compound by car I headed as usual onto Kutuzovsky Prospekt in the direction of the White House, the building of the Supreme Soviet. On Radio Moscow I managed to hear only the first headline: Erich Bauer, the former general secretary of the communist German Democratic Republic, had arrived in the capital that morning. A wing of the Oktyabrskaya Hotel had been made up suitably for the communist leader, who was gravely ill.

Two hundred metres down the road I stopped, got out of the car without locking it, took the underpass and crossed to the opposite side of the road. If someone were following me, they would have to follow the same route. At ten in the morning it's unthinkable to cross the main road on foot—it's wider than a motorway. I looked behind me—no one was there. Back on the road, I came to the Ukraina Hotel and reached the pier on time. I had no idea that the Moscow boat tour was so popular: a hundred or so people were waiting with me. It wasn't snowing, but the weather was dingy and there was a heavy atmosphere. It was one of those Moscow mornings when you wouldn't really mind if you died.

Lubimov was on the deck, inspecting the passengers and the surrounding area. Just before the boat moored he went and sat on the last of the two-seat benches on the deck. I boarded and sat next to him. We remained silent, looking at the river until the boat set off again. Then he whispered, 'It turns out that it's a really juicy story.'

'You don't say. I was almost dying of boredom.'

'Since the conservatives were making war on him, Gorbachev wanted perestroika to be extended to the satellite countries as well. If the whole socialist camp began reforms, the Soviet Union's position would be reinforced. Of the leaders of the brother countries, the one who was most averse to the idea of change was Bauer: the old man belonged to the old generation of Stalinists and kept obstructing Gorby, to the point that he forbade the circulation of Soviet newspapers and magazines with perestroika propaganda. He had placed all his hopes in an overthrow of Gorbachev by some conservative coup in the Politburo. In turn the Soviet leader reached the conclusion that there was no other solution to the East German problem than to replace Bauer. Essentially, in the years before the fall of the Wall the two leaders were playing at who would be overthrown first.

'Of course, in a reckoning like that, boneheaded Bauer was lost from the start: the German Democratic Republic was a satellite of Moscow. Soviet forces are even stationed there. And, most importantly, the KGB is the past master in conspiracies. When the protests began in the summer in German cities, Gorbachev ordered the KGB to organize the overthrow of Bauer. Not even Yelin liked the East German leader—he was far too old-fashioned. Yes, Yelin disagreed with Gorbachev because he saw the situation was getting out of hand, but still he wanted some changes. So they appointed a KGB agent to organize Bauer's demise—a woman who knew people in Berlin. Her code name was "Juliet". Do you know where it comes from?'

'If you say Shakespeare I won't believe you.'

'In the Stasi, the young men they chose based on looks and physical characteristics were called "Romeos". They were sent to West Germany under false identities and their main targets were women who worked in government offices as secretaries of high-powered people. The Stasi exploited the loneliness of West German women working in a capital like Bonn, which, as my former colleague John le Carré wrote, is "half as big as a Chicago cemetery and twice as dead".

'The irony is that the Stasi's Romeos were inspired by the KGB's Juliets—an old trick whereby they used beautiful women to entice back men who were inclined towards Western societies. One such Juliet infiltrated the East German leadership and organized the coup against Bauer.'

We had left the Rossiya behind us on our right, and now the coloured Kremlin was coming into view. When we passed under the Bolshoy Moskvoretsky Bridge, Lubimov halted his narrative.

'The bridge was built by Alexey Shchusev, the architect of the Mausoleum. Isn't it beautiful?'

Despite his complaints about daily life, Lubimov couldn't hide his love for Russia. Besides, right after the bridge the view was magnificent: from the river we could see the white Ivan the Great Bell Tower, the tallest bell tower of the Kremlin, and the yellow-white Grand Kremlin Palace. To our left was the coloured building of the British embassy and the old church of St Sophia. A little further along the left bank, near the Bolshoy Kamenny Bridge, appeared the House on the Embankment, one of the first apartment blocks in Moscow. It had been built opposite the Kremlin for Party aristocracy. They never really enjoyed the view: so many of the building's inhabitants were arrested during Stalin's rule that the ground floor has recently been turned into a museum for the victims of the purge. Next to the House on the Embankment was the white and red building of the Science Museum and, right after that, Red October.

'Red October was the first chocolate factory in Moscow,' Lubimov said. 'It was founded in 1867.' Then he became serious, 'They were looking for Juliet in the Corriere della Sera offices.'

'Bastards! That's why Fabio stammered something about the Wall to me in the hospital.'

'Bauer is desperate to find out who organized his overthrow. He's manically searching to find the identity of this Juliet. He has even ordered her execution—he's evidently very vindictive.'

'Marlene says the same.'

'Those who beat up your friend Fabio are his people.'

'Still, there are a few grey areas. First, what's Fabio's link to all of this? And second—'

'I've no idea on the first,' Lubimov interrupted. 'You'll know better. Second?'

'Since Juliet belongs to the KGB, why aren't they guarding her?'

'Because Juliet made a mess of things. They gave her instructions to organize Bauer's downfall, but also to replace him with some Party leader, a fresh face to govern the country. She chose some guys who let the Wall fall. And if I tell you that it wasn't supposed to fall…'

I looked at him with incredulity.

'Soon you'll be telling me there was no Cold War.'

Lubimov stroked the bump on his head, a souvenir from the funfair.

'On the morning of the ninth of November the Politburo met in Berlin. Most of its members had come to an understanding beforehand under the guidance of the KGB. The majority decided to remove Bauer from his duties so, up until this point, Juliet had done a good job. But Bauer's replacement was a spineless nobody with no sway in the Party. He panicked, like the whole leadership: they had lost the man who had led them for years. The old man was a sly dog, the only one who knew how to govern, while the others were used simply to approving his decisions with revolutionary zeal.

'Meanwhile, since the summer, thousands of East Germans pretending to be tourists had entered the West German embassies in Prague and Budapest, seeking political asylum. The sister governments persuaded the East Germans to do something, as did the West German government, whose embassies had been flooded by refugees, rubbish and shit.'

The riverboat reached Lenin Stadium, one of the largest in the world: the Soviets boasted that the whole population of the state of Monaco could fit into its stands. Directly opposite were the Lenin Hills, with their small ski slopes for the Muscovites. In the background we could see the Novodevichy Convent, the old castle of Ivan the Terrible. We were approaching the end of the route.

Lubimov continued. 'Having unseated Bauer, the Politburo addressed the hot topic of the tourist fugitives, whose numbers were continually growing. It was clear that they couldn't stem the tide, so they decided to allow East Germans to travel to the West. Their goal was to defuse the tension and then see what to do next. It hadn't crossed their minds that the Wall would fall in just a few hours. So they assigned a bureaucrat in the Ministry of Internal Affairs the task of amending the existing law to allow travel for personal purposes only.'

'Here it is still forbidden,' I said. 'For a Soviet to travel to the West, they must either be on official duty or have an invitation from abroad.'

'Quite,' said Lubimov, pleased that I was following. 'Of course, every citizen had to apply, and the state authorities had the last word. In the afternoon the Central Committee met again. The topic that monopolized discussion was Bauer's dismissal. Towards the end of the meeting a plan on the law regarding travel abroad was read out. The members of the Committee took it for one of the tedious decisions on solidarity in Nicaragua or traffic control on the weekend, and they passed it orally, in general indifference. Then they gave a piece of paper with the law to the Party's press attaché. Until he began reading it in front of the television cameras in the live press conference, which was principally about Bauer, he hadn't even glanced at it. Well, he announced that travel to the West was allowed, without going into the details of the law. Then some journalist asked when the law would be applied. He replied nonchalantly, "I think from now". The moment they heard this the East German citizens rushed to the Wall and began pouring into West Berlin. The border guards had heard the announcement on the television too and none of the new leadership could give them orders on how to respond. So they let everyone through. Soon they began to drink champagne on the Wall and to tear it down.'

'Yuri, that's marvellous reporting. Do you want to work with me at the newspaper when this ghastly business is over?'

I still hadn't taken it in that I was fired.

'There's another lovely thing I found out. Do you know what the press attaché did next?'

'Hara-kiri?'

'He went home to sleep, certain that this new law had defused the tense situation. Only when he saw from his window the crowds thronging to cross the Wall did he realize what he had announced. He simply said, "The German Democratic Republic is emptying."'

My guffawing laughter made me afraid that the other passengers were watching us. I looked around and suddenly felt a cold sweat running down my back: there was no one on deck; they had all vanished, like in a horror or science fiction movie.

Now it was Lubimov's turn to laugh. 'Don't worry; we're on the love boat. Where do you think everyone is going at ten in the morning? No one in Moscow goes to work by riverboat. Anyway, the river is frozen for six months of the year. All the people you saw are now in the cabins for their romantic assignations. These boats on the Moscow River are among the few places where you can find a bed without having to show your internal passport.'

Smiling, he lit a cigar.

'There is even literary production on the subject. A satirical short story describes the journey of a lone traveller, just like us. He thinks he is alone, until the boat arrives and he sees hundreds of people coming out of the cabins, their faces happy but tired, their hair messy and many of their clothes unbuttoned. Andrei Voznesensky, one of our best poets, has written a poem on the subject. It ends like this:

*A love boat is never met by people bearing flowers
but is only ever met by relatives bearing batons.*

'The Wall couldn't hold; sometime it would fall,' Lubimov continued, moving effortlessly from literature to politics. 'But none of the great powers wanted it to be toppled by uncontrolled protestors without any idea of what would happen next. They were faced with serious conundrums: the likely unification of Germany and its incorporation into NATO, the Red Army forces stationed in East Germany, a united Germany's new borders with Poland, the unforeseen political developments in the rest of the Eastern bloc... Gorbachev's entire plan for establishing socialism with a human face throughout Eastern Europe, maintaining Soviet influence, is collapsing.

'Mitterrand is beside himself because, if East and West Germany unite, France will lose its leading position in the EEC. I imagine you know the French saying, "I love Germany so much I want there to be two." Everyone wanted to open doors, but not tear them down. That's why the KGB and the Stasi have their knives out. The Germans accuse the Soviets of conspiring behind their backs and making a mess of everything. The KGB respond that they should have changed by themselves before chaos took over. The only point on which they concur is Juliet: the Germans accuse her of conspiracy, the Russians of leaving the job unfinished. This is the unwritten rule of the secret services: if you fail, you pay.'

'I reckon I know who Juliet is: Larissa. She was

recently in Berlin, is beautiful, a member of the KGB and frequently in Fabio's office.'

Lubimov furrowed his brow.

'The day I met her she didn't seem so capable.'

'Surely a capable agent must seem harmless.'

'To others perhaps, but not to us agents. If they assigned her such a difficult mission they must be colossal fools.'

'They might have hired her just because, as you say, she isn't so capable—so that she would mess things up. Yes—yesterday she told me that she is fed up with the KGB and wants to quit.'

'I'm not persuaded,' he said after some thought.

We had reached the end of the route: the pier near Dorogomilovsky Street, beside the Kiev railway station. The couples emerged from the cabins, and the deck came to life again, as if the god of love had tapped it with his magic cane. In front of the plank connecting the boat to the pier Lubimov lost his balance and fell forward. I momentarily saw someone in a grey trench coat striding along the plank and making off swiftly, slipping through those waiting to board the boat. I will never forget that long black umbrella in his hand, with which he pierced Lubimov's leg. It was the poisoned umbrella, a contribution of the Bulgarian secret service to the spy wars. By the same method a Bulgarian seditionist had been killed in London a few years earlier. Lubimov had lost his senses and I was holding him by the neck so he wouldn't fall into the freezing river. I dragged him onto land with the help of a member of the crew. His face had turned white.

'I'm dying,' he stammered.

'No, Yuri, we'll make it. I'll do everything—'

'All those years I was acquainted with death. But when I retired, I thought I would die naturally.'

His voice was fading. He hadn't managed to tell me everything he knew. Again I was in the difficult position of the journalist who wants to ask something just as his interview subject has other things on his mind—this time, he was dying. He lifted up his head as if wanting to speak.

'The child,' he croaked.

I bent down to listen.

'The child... the key...'

He rolled onto his back and half closed his eyes.

'Remember me as a good human being who did an inhuman job. I'm dying from a baton, just like in Voznesensky's poem...'

Those were his last words. He was left with his eyes open, staring at the cloudy sky of his city. I walked away, pretending I was looking for an ambulance. To be caught up in the murder of a former spy in the centre of Moscow was the last thing I needed.

I practically ran to the hospital where Fabio was being treated. Even at a normal walking pace it's barely ten minutes from the Kiev station. It had started to drizzle and Moscow was ugly. The nurse told me that his condition was stable. Finally there was some news that wasn't terrible. I asked to see him but he was sleeping. Giuseppe had gone into the corridor to smoke and appeared shortly. His face was calmer and he had shaved. It was time for me to bring him down to earth once and for all about the harsh Soviet reality.

'They got Lubimov.'

He was speechless, as if I had told him that the thirteenth five-year plan hadn't achieved its goals.

'Just near here, in the centre of Moscow. I'm certain that the Stasi killed him, and I reckon I know who got your brother involved: Larissa.'

'What are you basing this on?' he asked suspiciously. I was ruining his image of the only relationship of Fabio's that he wholeheartedly approved of, even if Miss KGB was inclining towards capitalism.

I explained to him what the Stasi were looking for in the Corriere's offices.

'Do you remember that, at my dinner, Larissa said she often went to Berlin? She had even been there over the days the Wall came down.'

'And?' Giuseppe retorted. 'Marlene was also in Berlin those days. She also knows people there. You suspect everyone apart from the one who's been pulling the wool over your eyes all this time.'

The blood rose to my head.

'Come on, Giuseppe. I know everyone in New York, but that doesn't mean that I work as a Romeo in the service of the Kremlin. We've been unjust to Marlene. She was there to get her child. You're completely pig-headed. We're looking for a Juliet who is a Soviet agent—and we have the Soviet version of Juliet in Miss KGB. She obviously works in the First Directorate, dealing with socialist countries, because she regularly visits

Berlin. She uses her charms to get together with a Western journalist, and the next thing we know they're beating him to death, asking about the Wall. And you suspect some other hapless girl whose child has been abducted? If she's a KGB agent why did they take her child? Why didn't they give him back to her?'

He shrugged.

'There is more evidence,' I ploughed on. 'Yelin seemed furious with Müller, and one of the reasons must have been that the Stasi agents beat up Fabio, Miss KGB's lover, so badly. They clearly ruined some job that they were going to involve Fabio in. I should go to the Corriere offices to ask the girls if they know anything.'

'I asked them myself when my brother told me that they were after information about the Wall. The girls have no idea and insist that Fabio never had anything to do with the fall of the Wall. He was only interested in Miss KGB falling into his arms.'

'Exactly my point. Marlene had never set foot in Fabio's offices, unlike Larissa, who was always there.'

His eyes turned in their sockets, looking for arguments.

'Non è vero, cazzo,' he swore, professing his disbelief.

'Since you consider KGB agents to be little angels who walk the blind from one side of the street to the other, let's ask her ourselves.'

Larissa lived just beyond Sheremetyevo 2, Moscow's international airport. The Germans had come closer to the centre in World War II. The taxi driver grunted happily about the ride: when he left us, he would go to the airport to hunt naïve, rich tourists.

We took Barikate Street without a word from Giuseppe, crossed Leningradsky Prospekt and then left Moscow behind as we headed for the airport. Giuseppe was silent throughout the ride, the first time I had seen him so thoughtful. When we reached the neighbourhood that Larissa had written on a piece of paper for me, the taxi driver stopped at the side of the road, took out a tourist map from the Volga's dirty glove compartment and started searching. After some time he swore in Russian.

'Shosse Entusiastov. This road doesn't exist here.'

'Enthusiasm Street. What a lovely name,' Giuseppe gushed.

'It must,' I insisted. 'If we find it you'll get fifty roubles more.'

'I'll ask. Many street names have recently changed. Even I can't get to grips with the centre of Moscow. They've changed Gorky Street to Tverskaya, Kropotkinskaya to Prechistenka, Kalinina to Novi Arbat and so on. The same with the metro stations. I can't serve my customers anymore. It's a mess. In the past at least we knew where we were going.'

Giuseppe turned to me and scowled like a child whose toy has been taken away. Despite the gravity of the situation, I couldn't hold back my laughter.

'Giuseppe, you can't blame me for the change of names.'

With difficulty I stopped my sides from splitting, until the taxi driver returned. He shook his head.

'In this area, the local soviet is of the old school —they haven't changed any names. And on this map there isn't a road of that name.'

'I told you—she's fooled us. She is Juliet.'

An entire world crumbled in Giuseppe's eyes.

'Puttana,' he swore in Italian. 'She doesn't live on Enthusiasm Street, but on Betrayal Avenue.'

'How are you, sweetheart?'

I had stolen five minutes from the search for Larissa to see Marlene.

'You need to be careful,' I said.

I described to her the scene on the pier and Lubimov's murder.

'He managed to tell me that some female KGB agent code-named Juliet organized Bauer's fall. He also found out that the East Germans were looking in Fabio's office for the traces of this Juliet—clearly Larissa. You were right to suspect her.'

She brought out her greatest weapon, her charming smile.

'I told you to trust me.'

'The funny thing is that Giuseppe even suspected you, because, he said, you know people in Berlin. But we went to find Larissa at home and she'd given us a false address.'

'Don't tell me that you denied me a third time.'

'Not for a moment. The bad thing is that Lubimov didn't manage to reveal to me what he had found out

— 271 —

about Erich. He only said that Erich is the key to the mystery—something like that.'

She sat up in her chair. Her mind must have been spinning a million times a minute.

'Key to the mystery? Is that exactly what he said? Why didn't you persist? And I thought you were a decent journalist,' she said, almost scornfully.

'I'm not so hot on interviews with the dead.'

'Come on, I'm joking,' she said. 'What do you think you're going to do with Larissa?'

'What can I do with an arch-agent of the KGB? I'll tell her to stay away from Fabio and then I'll come to see you. Anyway, I need to pack.'

Giuseppe and I lay in wait outside the compound. Larissa didn't take long to arrive in her small East German Trabant, which she parked on Kutuzovsky Street. We called her into the car and I cut to the chase.

'Hello, Juliet.'

She looked bewildered. Giuseppe shrieked, 'Don't pretend you don't understand! The sad thing is that Romeo has lost his tongue. That's not what happened in the real story.'

'It seems you've both gone crazy.'

'We're reading a lot of Shakespeare,' I said.

'It's not just us who have gone crazy,' Giuseppe continued, 'but a taxi driver too, who spent two hours looking for a road that doesn't exist.'

'Oh, God. Did you come looking for me at home?'

We looked at each other, smiling sardonically.

'I forgot to tell you. My road, like some others, isn't on the tourist map of Moscow. The KGB changed the maps to confuse foreign spies.'

'She's got the lie at the tip of her tongue,' said Giuseppe, somewhere between anger and admiration. Then he rounded on her, 'That's how you told me all your tales about your great love for Fabio. Did they give you acting lessons too?'

She started sobbing.

'It's the truth. In the last half century all the maps have been changed by order of the KGB. Almost everything has changed place: roads and rivers have been moved, neighbourhoods erased. On the tourist map of Moscow only the centre is mapped correctly; the suburb where I live has been altered too.'

'Yes, and I'm Rasputin.'

'And I'm Don Corleone,' Giuseppe added.

'I'll write the whole story of how Juliet—Miss KGB—organized the conspiracy to topple Bauer.'

She assumed an expression of desperation.

'I overthrew Bauer?'

'You never told us what department of the KGB you work in.'

'It's a secret.'

'Might you work in the directorate that deals with sister countries?'

'Where did you get that idea?'

'That evening at my apartment you told us you had visited East Berlin many times. Was that tourism?'

'I'm afraid I'm not at liberty to say.'

I looked at her sarcastically.

'Let's go there and I'll show you the road really does exist,' she continued.

'What do you take us for? Stupid Americans?' said Giuseppe, before realizing his gaffe and quietening.

I let it go. Larissa made a final attempt.

'Kevin, I've found out a lot of information about those cuckolds. I should tell you.'

'The only thing I want you to tell us is what you tried to get Fabio mixed up in. What were the Stasi looking for in his office?'

'The Stasi? I've no idea.'

We had run out of patience.

'We're wasting our time with you. Get out of here!'

'And hands off my brother!' added Giuseppe, as if shouting a slogan on the union rights of Italian workers.

We got out of the car, went into the compound and up the stairs to Fabio's office.

In the Corriere's offices, Marina and Elena were still teary eyed and melancholic. Andrea, the previous Moscow correspondent for the paper, had come urgently from Milan to fill the gap. He was a timid northern Italian, completely at odds with Fabio's explosive Sicilian temperament. His presence limited my movements: I had it in mind to turn the office upside down, to find what Müller's people were looking for. I maintained the hope that they hadn't taken it with them that fateful evening. Andrea invited me to a game of chess, like in the good old days. I politely declined: soon I would be checkmated by the Stasi and the KGB. I decided to speak to the girls since they knew Fabio's movements well.

'Did you ever hear Fabio talking to Larissa about some East German matters?'

Elena smiled sadly. She was a thin young woman from the Ukraine, with dark circles around her big eyes.

'Kevin, are you now a detective as well?'

'Yes. As soon as Fabio is better we'll open an office in Moscow. It seems it would do rather well.'

The thought of Fabio getting better gave us all hope. I knew that we were all remembering the same thing: those happy moments with Fabio's jokes and jibes.

'Over the last months he hardly had anything to do with Eastern Europe. He was dealing with the Baltics.'

They both smiled. Fabio kept a close eye on the emancipation attempts of the Baltic states—and particularly those of the female population.

'We've turned his office upside down but haven't found anything. We looked through all his personal possessions, both here and at his apartment,' Elena said.

While I was talking to the girls I dialled my newspaper's number in New York. I got through to Whitesmith and asked to speak directly to the big boss. Weber came onto the line. His voice was more formal than ever.

'I'm listening...'

'I know what has happened between us, but I'm gradually realizing that I've been the victim of a setup.

For now I want to suggest a one-off collaboration, because I've found out what went on backstage when the Wall fell. It's going to be a fantastic article with everything you could want—intrigue, mystery, spies, even women. It'll suffice to tell you that the Wall essentially fell by mistake. The KGB was behind the operation, or rather, a KGB agent code-named Juliet was. She is, in fact, Miss KGB. You know how usually I prefer others to judge my reporting rather than advertising it myself? Well, this time I'm breaking the rules, as it really is something special.'

The telephone connection to New York is via satellite, so you can hear the echo of the other person's voice. For several more hours, I had Weber's voice ringing in my ear.

'I'm ashamed for you, Kevin.'

'About what?'

'I shouldn't really tell you but to hell with state secrets now—I'm thinking of Cynthia and the child. They tested you and you fell like a mutt into their trap. You took the consul's bait.'

'What bait? It seems you've all gone crazy too.'

'He gave you false information about the new Cold War and some supposed plans of the president to reactivate Star Wars. They wanted to see if you could keep your mouth closed or if you'd spill to the KGB. A few hours later the Soviet ambassador in Washington made an informal complaint. The State Department disproved it, of course, but only you knew this false information. It would be better not to come back to the US. The FBI are waiting to interrogate you.'

My mouth must have frozen, because Elena got up and brought me a glass of water without my asking. I drank it in one, and then said to Weber, 'They were following me; my apartment had more bugs than the Watergate building.'

'Did you talk to the consul in your apartment?'

I hesitated. I had to explain that I had told Marlene, but the game was lost anyway. Whatever I said worked against me.

'No, in the courtyard.'

'Well… get your ass outta here.'

Hardman interrupted me again with a gesture. He turned to Weber.

'Did you really tell him about the bait, Mr Weber?'

The big boss looked at me. A few seconds passed of complete silence. Weber folded his arms.

'Everything happened exactly as he is describing.'

'You broke American law,' Hardman said.

Weber looked at him condescendingly and eventually replied with the manner of someone who could not be fazed. 'Nonsense. The bait you used wasn't a legal method either.'

Hardman turned back to me. 'This is a friendly conversation. Do continue, Mr Danaher.'

I had to leave the Soviet Union the next day, but had nowhere to go. The only thing left was to seek political asylum in Albania.

Elena stopped me as I was leaving the office. 'Should we give you what Marlene asked us for?'

'What did she ask you for? I've no idea.'

'She was here five minutes before you came. She was looking for the original of the fax that we sent to Berlin from here. I think it was the day you met. Remember?'

She spoke with venom, but I was in no mood for jealousy.

'Marina put it in the folder with the sent faxes. But I didn't know that, and I told her that we must have thrown it out. She said that if we hadn't kept it, no matter.'

I took it to put in my pocket, but luckily Elena—who is Miss Gossip in Moscow—asked, laughing, 'Why does Marlene sign with a J?'

'Won't you read us the whole thing?' Giuseppe and I said at once, pouncing on the fax.

'It says nothing interesting,' Elena, who knew German, replied. Then she began to read:

> Everything is ready for the movie. Just the lead role is missing—we await your suggestions. Sensibly, the producers here don't want to destroy the old stage set and make a new one. They say that it's better we use the existing one.
>
> Suggested date to begin shooting: 9 November.
>
> J.

I looked at Giuseppe. He had a triumphant look, as if they had just taken power in El Salvador against the odds. At once he asked me, 'Did you tell her we had found out about Juliet?'

'Just now, at the apartment.'

'Has she completely bewitched you?' Giuseppe erupted. 'Can't you keep your mouth shut for five minutes? What the hell! You spew everything the moment you see her? Not even if you were Italian and she was your mother... Porca Madonna... What if they had given this to her?'

I hadn't blushed so much since being scolded by my teacher in primary school. I just managed to stammer, 'If Marlene asks you again, don't say that you found it. I want to surprise her.'

We walked down the stairs, because I was afraid I would vomit in the elevator. I took a few deep breaths of the polluted Moscow air.

'We must find Larissa at once!' I cried to Giuseppe. 'She might be in danger. The Corriere's telephone must be tapped—and I, idiot that I am, told Weber that she is Juliet. The worst thing is that I told Marlene the same story earlier. If they do away with Larissa everything can be blamed on her.'

'Why would they do that?'

'Because Marlene doesn't want the old man to find out that she herself overthrew him. He would never give her back the child.'

'Where the hell will we find Larissa now?' Giuseppe asked.

'If she really loves him she'll have gone to the hospital,' I said. We made for the car at a run.

Giuseppe swore in Italian the whole journey. Atheist that he is, his repertoire included Christ, the Virgin Mary, the KGB and the Stasi—and of course Fabio and, above all, me.

'Stronzo, che cazzo. You're stronzi, you and my brother. I thought you were better than him, but in the end you're worse.'

It was past ten in the evening when we arrived at the hospital and visiting hours were over. We ran through the entrance like doped-up East German sprinters. The fat porter didn't even manage to invoke the Soviet laws. The elevator was engaged and we heard the porter shouting as we climbed the stairs two by two to the fifth floor. A deathly silence reigned throughout the hospital. We made for the nurses' room, and fell panting upon the nurse who was looking after Fabio.

'Have you seen that woman who comes here every day to visit him?'

'The crybaby?' she asked with a nurse's severity. 'She was here until two minutes ago. She asked to see your friend, but I told her he was sleeping and she left. What's the matter with you all?'

'All of us?'

'Some others asked for her too. They looked like—'

'Like what?' Giuseppe and I said in unison.

She hesitated, casting her gaze over us.

'Like mafiosi.'

'Where did they go? Did they speak to her?'

'I didn't think so. If you run, you'll catch up with her. Did you come by the elevator?'

'No, the stairs.'

'Then she would have been going down in the elevator at the same time.'

We tore down the stairs, sped past the surprised

porter again and spied the figure of Larissa in the distance, walking towards the car park. We reached her five metres before her car. She was still crying when I grabbed her arm.

'Larissa, it's okay; we made a mistake.'

'Sorry, comrade,' Giuseppe said with communist humility.

She released her arm with an abrupt movement, went to the Trabant and unlocked the door. In the darkness and absolute silence we heard loud sobs.

I went over and decisively shut the door.

'Let's go to the hospital and talk it over calmly.'

She followed us, crying now with pleasure—an unjustly accused girl who has been proved right. The bomb in the car exploded when we were about fifty metres away. We heard a terrifying din, then the smashing of windows, then saw Larissa's car in flames.

'It's the new bomb technology,' she said, unflustered. 'They blow up one minute after the door has been opened and closed once. With the old ones, which were activated by turning the engine on, you were able to check if someone had messed with the wires.'

She looked at her car sadly.

'A shame. Even for us in the KGB there's a two-year waiting list to get a car. If I resign it'll be five years.'

'Don't worry; Fabio will buy you a new one,' Giuseppe joked, putting his arm around her.

Then he turned angrily to me. 'Murders, booby-trapped cars... You've managed to turn Moscow into Hollywood.'

I went into counter-attack. 'Tonight you should sleep with Larissa.'

He looked at me as if I were Oedipus Rex.

'Take her with you to the Oktyabrskaya,' I continued. 'She mustn't be seen anywhere. It's better for them to think they've got her. Now go before the police come!'

We could already hear sirens in the distance.

'What the hell will you do? You have to leave tomorrow evening,' Giuseppe said.

'I think I know how to extend it,' I replied enigmatically. 'I'll have to make some changes to my novel.'

Before they disappeared into the darkness I saw them looking back at me as though I were a madman.

'I can't take these madmen anymore,' Patrick said to the director of Psychiatric Clinic No. 13. 'I want you to notify Ivan Plita, the undersecretary of internal affairs.'

The director cast an eye over Patrick. He was a tall man, around fifty-five, with a big pointed nose.

'You understand that I cannot disturb the undersecretary without good reason.'

'Call him now and tell him that I accept his offer. He'll understand.'

The director consulted an address book, dialled a number and began talking in Czech. Then he handed the receiver to Patrick.

'It's the undersecretary. He wants to speak to you.'

'I accept your offer,' Kevin said. 'I'm prepared to collaborate, but on one condition.'

'You're not in a position to dictate conditions,' he said coldly.

'Let Lisa Thompson go. She's not to blame for anything.'

Plita seemed to think it over.

'OK. A car will come to collect you both.'

'At once,' Patrick said.

'In an hour,' the undersecretary replied and put down the phone.

I turned off the computer, went to the bedroom and lay down on the bed. From the office I heard Marlene's voice, complaining: 'It's our last evening together. And you're spending it writing and sleeping.'

I was so exhausted that I didn't even have to act much. As naturally as I could, I said, 'Sorry darling, but I'm so tired. Let's talk in the morning. Can you turn off the light?'

I closed my eyes and then dug my nails into my palms to stop myself sleeping. I felt them bleeding. She was quick to look over what I had written: after just ten minutes I heard the sound of the computer being turned on. When I heard her making a phone call and speaking in a whisper, I fell asleep in peace.

PART FOUR

The Red Sketch Pad

All of this is very far away today. How strange that secret fear sounds now—of accusations and knocks on the door. And the fear of talking to a foreigner! What do I mean, a foreigner? Even to your own wife.

YEVGENY YEVTUSHENKO
Kater Zviazi, 1966

[29 November]

Sleep is the most soothing thing for anger. When I woke in the morning and felt her naked body next to mine I wanted to stroke her and make love to her. I desired her despite everything she had done to me. She had even betrayed my thoughts. I was angry at myself for loving her still. The only thing that made me get up was the thought of the long catalogue of tasks that I had to accomplish in very few hours. I left her sleeping there; it took some effort not to wake her and simply ask, 'Why?'

I made coffee and dialled Yelin's personal telephone number. As I had envisaged, he was expecting me. He didn't even go to the trouble of feigning surprise.

'Good morning.'

'I think we need to talk.'

'It's Friday today and I'm not usually in the office long. I will go to the sauna at Peredelkino, in the old Communist Youth sanatorium. Do you know where it is?'

'I'll be there at noon.'

I needed half an hour to reach Peredelkino, the beautiful riverside resort of the Soviet elite. It's in the same direction as Vnukovo, the domestic airport from where I had escaped three days earlier carrying top-grade nuclear material. I turned right before the airport onto a road with tall trees and wooden dachas.

Yelin was having his treatment in the luxurious villa that used to belong to the Communist Youth. It had recently been given over to a joint venture between an Italian company and some Komsomol officers, who had transformed themselves from firebrands of the new generation to pioneers of arbitrary privatization. The new contract let the high-ranking officers of the regime enjoy for free the services that they had been entitled to before. It's an ugly concrete building with grand halls and neo-Baroque decoration. The reception hall is decorated with flags of capitalist countries that have hard currency. Only a slogan is missing: 'Currency exchangers unite!' For Russians, the prices are prohibitive: around a hundred and eighty dollars a night, with breakfast and sauna.

Yelin had just come out of the swimming pool. Wearing a long white dressing gown with his initials embroidered on the chest, he was lounging in a wicker chair drinking orange juice. He looked at me silently, faithful to his principles: don't ask questions; listen to answers.

'I want to talk, but I would prefer us to take a walk.'

He looked around, laughing.

'You don't think I bug myself, do you?'

'I don't know. Here everyone is following everyone else.'

He must have thought me a first-class sucker,

because he immediately agreed to do me this favour. Getting wearily to his feet, he went into a cubicle and returned a couple of minutes later wearing a green tracksuit and trainers. He threw a brown leather jacket over the top and nodded to me that he was ready to go outside. We took a path heading down to the river.

'You'll make me catch cold.'

He had lost his icy gaze and was playing good cop. I hadn't time to lose.

'This proposal of yours... What does the collaboration involve?'

He threw his hands up as if to say, 'You've brought me into the cold for this insignificant matter?' Then, as though he was talking about a routine job, he said, 'Nothing dangerous. You'll tell us anything you find interesting—an exchange with a diplomat, some piece of information you think we don't know. What field will you be working in when you return to the US?'

'That's exactly what I wanted to discuss. I've been here so long and I know the language, the politics. I have good contacts at my embassy. I'm hoping to string for a couple of American or Australian newspapers. If I go back there's no way I'll find work. Unless you want me to tell you what activities are going on in the movement of the unemployed.'

'Not a chance. You're leaving for the United States at once.'

We had reached the banks of the Moscow River. Despite the low temperatures, the river hadn't frozen yet and a couple of boys were playing soccer on the sand. A fisherman in tall green boots had waded up to his knees into the water. Yelin thought for a little, but it seemed he was searching for a reason to send me away.

'If you stay here they might suspect we're working together. We'll have to cut all contact for a while. We'll find you in New York when we judge that the moment is right.'

He wanted to get rid of me, but I couldn't understand why. Surely he knew that I had taken the consul's bait and that the FBI already suspected me: I was no use in the USA.

In the end I asked him for what I wanted more than anything: 'Can I at least stay a little longer? With all this fuss I haven't even managed to pack my bags.'

He bent down, picked up a stone and flung it irritably into the water.

'You have another forty-eight hours… and…'

I had already turned my back.

'Your codename is Eros.'

'What you did, Mr Danaher, is very serious.'

Hardman had loosened his tie. The table in the newspaper's meeting room was covered in Coca Cola Light cans and empty plastic coffee cups. Weber looked at his watch every so often.

'As you will have realized, I had absolutely no intention of collaborating. I did it to gain time to prove that I was innocent.'

'How do we know that?' said Hardman.

'I followed the instructions of Mrs Berger. She told

me that when a secret service proposes collaboration and you're in a difficult position, you must publicize it. That's exactly what I did.'

'Who did you tell?' asked Hardman impatiently.

'I wrote it in my novel. When Patrick accepts the proposal of the Czechoslovak secret service in the passage I just read to you, he's not called Patrick but Kevin. Perhaps you didn't notice, nor did Marlene. The novel suggested that I was prepared to collaborate, and she informed Yelin. On Friday morning, before meeting Yelin, I sent the half-finished chapter to New York with Kevin instead of Patrick.'

He eyed me suspiciously.

'Who is your publisher?'

I wrote him a note with the name and telephone number. As Hardman gave it to his assistant, Weber smiled and winked at me. I had regained his confidence.

Hardman persisted. 'Despite that, collaboration crossed your mind.'

This time Weber was strict. 'Let's not be like the communists, who punish thoughts.'

When I returned home, Marlene had slipped out. A note said that she had left urgently because a friend of hers had fallen ill and she needed to bring medicine to her. She would telephone at about one o'clock to accompany me to the airport. I had half an hour to put my thoughts in order. I was worried about Giuseppe and Larissa and thought of calling the Corriere's offices, but the cordless phone in the apartment wasn't working. I had forgotten to charge it the previous evening. Looking for a normal device, I found the two telephones with the number-recognition display, which I had purchased at the exhibition of Soviet technology the day after the Wall came down. It took me twenty minutes to read the instructions and connect this innovation. The moment I had finished, the telephone rang. Before picking up the receiver I noted the number on the display. Marlene was on the line.

'Are you there? I'm coming in about half an hour.'

I explained that I had an extension and that it would be better for us to meet in the afternoon as I had some errands to run. In that case, she said, she would do some urgent shopping. I hung up and dialled the number she had called me from. A woman's voice answered.

'Oktyabrskaya Hotel.'

'Thank you, that information was very important.'

I hung up before she could swear at me. The telephone rang again. This time I knew the number: Fabio's office. It was Giuseppe.

'How are you all? And Larissa?'

'She's here with me. We talked all night.'

Under other circumstances I would have given anything to listen in on their conversation.

'Fabio?'

His voice softened.

'He's doing better.'

'Great. Come over here. I'll make coffee.'

I asked Svetlana if she knew where Masha was. It turned out that she was asleep in their room at the kommunalka, but I asked Svetlana to call her and tell her to come quickly—it was an absolute necessity. About ten minutes later Giuseppe and Larissa arrived. When they came in I kissed her and apologized again. They glanced around in surprise at the cables dangling out of the walls. Svetlana had cleaned up the plaster and the apartment looked post-modern.

Larissa pointed at the walls. 'Don't worry; I understand. We've reached the point of trusting absolutely no one. I'll hand in my resignation.'

She was ready to cry, but she righted her voice a little and said, 'Yesterday I didn't manage to explain, but I found out many things about the cuckold affair. It's a network of KGB agents.'

Giuseppe looked at her guardedly. I indicated for her to continue.

'Like everyone else, the KGB agents are looking for hard currency, so they have made a parallel racket doing the cuckold trick on tourists. About thirteen thousand girls aged between sixteen and thirty work in this ring. The script is always the same: the girls meet a foreigner and get him drunk. Then comes the moment they go somewhere together. The girl refuses point blank to go to a hotel room or the victim's apartment, and she takes him to her place. The fee is always two hundred dollars, and there is never a discount. Five minutes later the "deceived husband" comes in with his friend. If five hundred of the thirteen thousand find a victim every night, that's a hundred thousand dollars in a night, shared between them all. Whatever extra they get from the terrified prospective stud is shared on the spot.'

'One hundred thousand dollars a night! That's not a racket; that's an industry. Do you know anything more?'

'The girls are chosen based on their physical qualities. Some are already prostitutes; the others want to be. They are then led through a quick education: they are taught a little English before being sent to the big hotels. The education is done in a special KGB centre in south Moscow.'

'So the KGB leadership knows all about this?'

'Some of the high-ranking ones, but I don't think Yelin is directly involved. He believes that the fraud is happening on a limited scale and the aim is entrapping rivals, not profit. It's not the end of the world if the boys get something out of it for themselves; it gives them an extra incentive.'

Larissa stopped for a moment.

'You can see why I'm sick of it. I'll resign.'

'Not yet. You might be useful.'

I called Ellen Forsythe, the American TV correspondent who was a guest at that dinner party at my apartment.

'Do you still have those contacts with the police? I want to follow a night-time operation with the new force against pornography and immoral behaviour.'

'I can arrange it, but they'll need money. When do you want to go?'

'Tonight. And I agree to whatever amount they ask for. I'll be with a colleague.'

When Masha arrived, rudely awoken, I explained to the group the day's plan. Marlene had telephoned from the Oktyabrskaya, so most likely she had met with Bauer. If possible, we had to find out what words had been exchanged between them.

Giuseppe had questions.

'And how will we find that out?'

'The rooms are tapped.'

'There's no way so many rooms could be tapped,' Giuseppe said. 'They would need an entire floor.'

Giuseppe had made huge progress. Four months ago he would have insisted that it was unthinkable that comrades were following each other.

'I know what goes on,' Masha interrupted, 'from a friend of mine who works there. They operate from a large suite on the fifth floor. There are six permanent staff working three eight-hour shifts. They often invite her to keep them company. If she refuses they will deny her entry to the hotel.'

She took a deep breath.

'But they don't tap all of the rooms.'

Giuseppe breathed a sigh of relief.

'What are you sighing for, Giuseppe? Even if they were watching your room, what would they see? At the very most—'

'Enough!'

I liked teasing Giuseppe. Communists are good people; it's only when they're in power that they go rotten.

'They've put cameras and microphones in the bars and restaurants of the hotel, in the corridors and in thirty or so specially chosen rooms and suites,' Masha continued.

'They'll definitely be watching Bauer,' I said.

'Probably, because he'll be in a two-pocket suite. The protocol is very strict: for high-ranking guests, secretaries and members of all the Politburos of foreign communist parties, they have silk pyjamas with two pockets. The other rooms get normal cotton pyjamas with one pocket. My friend has told me that when two-pocket pyjamas are supplied for some foreign official she knows that whatever happens in the room is recorded on video.'

'Mine are cotton,' Giuseppe said.

'I don't know why you're so afraid they're following you.'

Giuseppe became enigmatic. 'I'll tell you another time.'

Under other circumstances, I would be opening a bottle of champagne with Fabio now to celebrate his brother's dawning enlightenment. I turned to Masha. 'Can you find this friend of yours?'

'We just need the number of the suite they use for tapping. I'll take it from there,' Larissa continued.

'They won't let you into the suite,' Masha said. 'I don't think anyone can go in, not even KGB agents.'

'You've missed certain episodes,' Larissa replied, laughing. 'I specialize in East Germany for the directorate for sister countries, so I'm entitled to ask for information. These boys almost concluded that I was Juliet and had brought down the Wall.'

'Entrance to the hotel is usually forbidden,' I continued, explaining the plan. 'We'll say that we're going to Giuseppe's room.

We went out into the courtyard of the compound. Into my car stepped the most motley crew for dangerous missions in history: a fired and betrayed journalist, whom the FBI suspected was an agent of the Soviets; Miss KGB, who had grown sick of the service because she was in love; a currency whore who was born in a gulag because her parents had violated the sexual rules of the Party; and a stiff-necked Western communist who had begun to suspect that something was rotten in the state of Denmark. I was wounded by Marlene's betrayal, but the composition of the group made me smile.

Lenin's statue in Oktyabrskaya Square is the size of a small apartment block. The chief of the Revolution is wearing his famous suit with its waistcoat and open jacket billowing in the winds of history. He's holding his cap in his left hand and with his right he's showing the masses the way to the Winter Palace and socialism.

The couples from the weekend's weddings had arrived in the square. Soviet custom decrees that newlyweds, after their civil ceremony at the Town Hall, deposit a bouquet of flowers at the Mausoleum or one of Lenin's statues. It's like in the West, where some couples have a religious wedding after a civil one. I felt an unbridled jealousy for all those young people being photographed in each other's arms in front of Lenin. I longed to be one of those obscure, poor but enamoured

Soviet citizens, who had the privilege of being able to swear eternal faith and devotion to their beloved, to feel happy even for a few moments. I yearned more than anything else in the world to dream that I could share something similar with Marlene. Suddenly I felt hatred for her: she had taken away my right to dream.

Masha interrupted my thoughts.

'When will they tear all this down too?'

We had watched the statues being torn down in East Germany.

'The Soviet Union isn't Germany,' Giuseppe protested.

'Some years ago we confiscated the thesis of a philosophy student,' Larissa said happily. He had studied the style and presentation of statues of Lenin according to the periods of Soviet history.'

Giuseppe frowned at her, but she ignored him.

'What we have before us is from the first period, right after his death. It's Lenin the revolutionary, just returned from exile and leading the proletariat to power. During Stalin's rule, Lenin loses the image of political leader; those duties belonged to Stalin. The statues of this period present Lenin as a man of theory, whether sitting at his desk, writing or deep in the study of an article. After Stalin's death, he changes again.

'Does he become leader again?' Giuseppe asked, a note of hope in his voice.

'No, he becomes relaxed, seemingly happy to be free of Stalin. He walks in a garden with his hands in his pockets; he takes on a human persona. In the fourth period, the era of stagnancy, he is grave and motionless. It's no coincidence that Bauer chose such a statue to erect in East Berlin.'

'Right, we're here. No more art. Time for some action.'

Comrade Giuseppe showed his special card with his room number, and we walked past the four policemen guarding the entrance to the hotel of the Central Committee without trouble. It was a five star hotel. The reception desk was made of heavy dark wood and the furniture was all impeccable nineteenth-century antiques. Gold-fringed lampshades were placed on heavy statues from the 1930s. A thick red carpet covered the floor and on the walls hung paintings from the mature period of socialist realism without the extremes of the first period. In one picture a group of working women were walking in the background, each with a rake in her hand, while in the foreground young women were swimming and sunbathing by the river with full-body swimsuits on. The colours and style were reminiscent of Toulouse-Lautrec, with the workers as a proletarian cover. When they want to, comrades have good taste.

Masha went to find her friend and colleague, while the rest of us went straight to Giuseppe's room to keep a low profile. It was decorated stylishly: an old bed with a mosquito net and, on the walls, authentic engravings of pre-Revolution Moscow showing carriages and Red Square full of stalls and vendors. Back then it was called Beautiful Square; in old Russian, 'red' meant beautiful. Just to be sure I glanced around for hidden microphones or cameras. I didn't spot anything suspicious.

'Soon I'll become a journalist specializing in bugs.'

'I don't understand why you don't throw in the towel,' Giuseppe said.

'In my country they suspect me of collaboration with the KGB, who they believe now have me in the palm of their hand. I need to prove that I'm not an agent but simply the victim of a setup. Then I want to find out if Marlene betrayed me from the start.'

'Do you still love her?'

I bowed my head.

'I think I do.'

Giuseppe almost jumped out of his skin.

'Have you lost your mind completely? She even reads your novel and gives the plot away to Yelin. What more does she need to do?'

'I want to know if she betrayed me from the start or if she began collaborating with Yelin when she saw that she couldn't get the child back with my help. I have to find out if it was her that snitched about the bag in Moscow 400.'

It was too painful a subject to discuss further. I turned to Larissa. 'You say that you'll resign from the KGB. What will you do next?'

'If, as they claim, private publications will be allowed, then I'll open a publishing house for women. I'll translate Harlequin novels into Russian. I think Fabio will help.'

The first thing Giuseppe had done when we entered his room was to look at his pyjamas. They were cotton, but he wanted to confirm that they really did have only one pocket.

Something was tormenting him. Eventually he couldn't contain himself. 'A few days ago a female comrade visited me.'

'With a comrade, I see,' I teased him.

'With who else? Some counter-revolutionary?!'

'It's lucky they don't watch the one-pocket rooms, otherwise you'd be a porn star. Soon they'll be selling tapes on the free market.'

He was blushing like a little child.

'She works at the Central Committee's Department of International Relations. Her office is in the Party headquarters in Old Square. She told me that the Party doesn't trust the KGB absolutely, nor vice versa.'

'What are you talking about? Do such things happen in the country of revolutionary trust?'

'I'm not joking. In the headquarters of the Central Committee there is a whole section with all the equipment for disguise and forgery of documents. This comrade didn't even know anything—'

A knock on the door interrupted our conversation.

Masha came in, saying, 'The suite used for tapping is on the fifth floor: number 51/01 to 51/03.'

'I'll take it from here,' Larissa said decisively.

'One more thing,' Masha added. 'Bauer is staying in a suite with silk pyjamas and two pockets.'

We remained silent for five minutes looking at the antique clock hanging on the wall. Giuseppe was looking for an excuse to continue his narrative, but I had no desire to hear the sad story of the comrade who discovered that the Central Committee would even cross-dress if the needs of the international revolutionary movement demanded it. Larissa returned quickly, but seemed disappointed.

'I got into the suite without trouble. They're watching and videotaping Bauer's every move, but the chief told me that no woman matching Marlene's description had visited him.'

'Shit!' I cried. 'Do you believe him?'

'I have no reason not to. He told me that, since Bauer came to Moscow, he had been visited by an envoy of the Central Committee as a formality, and a blonde woman. He didn't listen to their conversation, because he was preoccupied with a woman from the hotel.'

'Let's leave,' I said. 'I still have a couple of good ideas. If we catch the cuckold ring red-handed, Yelin will find himself in a difficult position.'

We all headed towards the door of the bedroom, when a deus ex machina knocked on the door of my tired brain.

'Wig,' I said, stopping.

All three of them looked at me sympathetically.

'The woman who met Bauer was Marlene. She has a blonde wig and she obviously used it to avoid recognition. It's the one she used at the funfair when we tried to take back her child.'

'I'll go and see,' said Larissa. 'Do you have a hundred dollars?'

Another five interminable minutes passed. When

Larissa returned she had a triumphant look and a video camera in her hand. She shook it at us as if it were the flag of the Revolution.

'It certainly is Marlene. I saw a little of the film and recognized her. Come on, we don't have much time; I just borrowed it for an hour. It's lucky that the major is always preoccupied with one of the girls. Miss KGB's reputation helped, of course.'

We left the hotel almost at a run. When we reached the car, I thought aloud: 'We need a place near here with two video players. Then we can watch it and make a copy. Let's go to my old office on Taganka Square.'

'And the new correspondent?' asked Larissa.

'Screw him. I imagine you know good German.'

She nodded. We took the ring road at vertiginous speed. When we arrived at the office, out of breath, Natasha looked at me as if she had seen a ghost, and Holby emerged uneasily from the next office.

'What's happening? What do you want here?'

'Haven't they informed you from New York? I'm in charge of the bureau again. From now on I'll tell you what you're reporting on. I'm thinking probably armed conflicts: Azerbaijan, Tajikistan, Ossetia. For the present we want four coffees and no one to disturb us.'

He must have had a kind of allergic reaction, because the marks of his acne reddened at once. He turned around and headed to his office. It was two in the afternoon, so six in the morning in New York. He would have to wait a few hours before protesting to Whitesmith about my appointment.

Out of the corner of my eye I saw Weber trying to hold in his laughter. Eventually he burst out: 'He woke up poor old Whitesmith at seven in the morning!'

Hardman didn't really understand journalistic rivalries.

'Let's see this tape then. You can explain to us what happened.'

Old man Bauer was wearing printed silk pyjamas and sitting next to the bed, behind a small traditional escritoire with carved, rounded legs on which various papers and notes were scattered. As far as I could tell from the video image he looked exhausted and very thin. His white hair was uncombed and his voice emerged with difficulty. In front of him stood a woman with her back to the camera. She had blonde hair, but from her stature and trench coat I had no doubt: it was Marlene.

Bauer was speaking sharply, and Larissa translated for me: 'What do you want with me?'

'To... talk about Erich. Are you writing something?'

'I would consider it ignoble to leave the stage of history without setting down my views on the extraordinary developments. In the same way that I didn't let the fascist Gestapo shut my mouth, I am determined not to let today's victors muzzle me. I'm writing to condemn the counter-revolution.'

'The counter-revolution...' Marlene repeated mechanically.

'Just recently they sent someone from the Central Committee. They're sad, they say, about the turn things have taken in the GDR; if they had known there would be such developments, they would have acted differently. I told Gorbachev in our last meeting that bringing socialism towards capitalism is like marrying fire with water. He pressured me over so many years to make changes, but communism is like an egg: if you try to change its shape it will crack.'

'He's further to the left than me!' Giuseppe interrupted.

'Shh. Let's listen.'

'Do you know what's to blame?' Bauer continued.

Marlene was standing marble-still, not speaking. Like a person in the face of power.

'Soviet jealousy. We organized a giant operation to make the grandeur of the first socialist state on earth accessible to the Germans. A whole people were educated to forget their enmity with the Soviet Union and become friends with it. But, because they're lazy alcoholics, the Soviets couldn't accept that our citizens lived well. Do you know what Brezhnev once told me when he asked for a loan and consumer goods? "The Soviets would also like to live on the third floor like the East Germans."'

'We're finding out things first-hand!' cried Giuseppe, impressed. 'And I thought it was the Soviet Union that helped the other countries.'

All three of us looked disapprovingly at him. The old man stood up from his chair with effort and walked around the suite, approaching the hidden camera. His face was contorted. In the corner of his mouth was dry white spittle. He still hadn't told Marlene to sit down.

'Now they accuse me of everything under the sun, but soon they'll see what capitalism and unemployment mean. We secured work for everyone without discriminating on age or gender. Everyone had the right to education and everyone was granted a house. They say that we fell behind West Germany, but what is forty years in the whole passage of history? Capitalism had hundreds of years to develop. We made sacrifices to secure a better future for everyone, particularly young people and children.'

'I wanted to talk about my child,' said Marlene, seizing the opportunity.

As if he had only just become aware of her presence he interrupted his political delirium for a moment and said softly, 'We haven't seen each other for a long time.'

Marlene nodded, without saying a word.

'Erich was a lucky child. He had everything,' the old man continued.

'How can a child be happy without his mother?'

'His mother betrayed her country for the Soviet Union. She wasn't worthy of bringing up my grandson.'

'They accused Eva and me unjustly. We weren't working for the KGB. I told you.'

Bauer looked at her grimly and retreated towards his bed. He sat on the edge, leaning forward.

'They blamed me for the Stasi, too,' he said, but you can't have a revolution with clean hands.'

He got up again and pointed accusingly at Marlene. 'I sent you here to work with my friends in the Soviet party. I told you that if you really were loyal, as you said you were, I would let you see the child. But you betrayed me again. I can't help but think that you are the Juliet who overthrew me.'

'That's a lie. I am not Juliet. She is from the First Directorate of the KGB. Her name is Larissa. They even made her Miss KGB to muddy the waters.'

'Puttana!' Giuseppe burst out.

While I looked at Marlene accusingly, Larissa remained expressionless and continued translating.

'They told me something about her. We found out where the fax was sent from, the one that made the KGB give the final go-ahead to overthrow me,' the old man said. 'It had some codes about a movie, that cultural stuff of yours.'

He said 'cultural' with disdain. Obviously he was of Goebbels' persuasion. 'When I hear the word "culture" that's when I reach for my revolver.' He added, 'It was sent from the office of a Western correspondent. And they tell me that you're going around with an American.'

'Not with an Italian. The fax was sent from the office of an Italian newspaper, the Corriere della Sera. Their correspondent has shacked up with the KGB girl I mentioned.'

'Anyway, what are you doing with an American reporter? They're all agents of the CIA.'

Giuseppe looked quizzically at me. I shot him an angry glance and he made an apologetic gesture.

— 307 —

'Mine is a mutt; he doesn't understand any of that. Never mind that; we're not together anymore.'

Bauer remained silent for a little and then said, 'Everyone betrayed me. The moment they saw the ship was sinking they fled like rats.'

'I didn't betray you,' Marlene retorted. 'I could have spoken to journalists about my personal tragedy. They even urged me to, but I didn't agree to do it. We'll have to see what will happen with Müller; he's holding Erich hostage.'

'Müller,' Bauer repeated, laughing testily. 'He's jumped ship as well. You should have monitored him. I knew back then that their interrogation to make you talk wasn't harsh enough. They were affected by the fact you were my daughter-in-law.'

'Anyone would have talked after an interrogation like that. I had nothing to say.'

'That's why I made you an officer on special duty,' Bauer continued, ignoring Marlene. 'Because you were tough. But it's your fault Müller ran off to do his own thing. You were his boss.'

'What does officer on special duty mean?' Giuseppe whispered.

'Super-agent. I'll explain later.'

Marlene brought the conversation back to Erich.

'Müller might harm the child. He killed a former Soviet spy who got under his toes.'

'Lubimov,' we all said together.

'He's unscrupulous, only interested in money,' she continued.

Bauer paced the room with his hands behind his

back. Then he stood in front of the mirror and looked at himself for a while without talking. Marlene was still standing, her head bowed.

'I've aged a lot, but lessons must be learnt by the next generation of communists. I made mistakes in the education of my Party; that's why they're still interested in money. That was my mistake. We didn't manage to create the new person. We lost the battle of hearts and minds.'

The old man looked exhausted.

'Sit down,' he said, pointing at a chair. Marlene obeyed, while Bauer sat at the escritoire again.

'How much does he want?'

'Five hundred thousand dollars.'

The old man opened the drawer, took out a pill and drank it with a little water.

'Don't believe what's written in the press. There's no red suitcase, just as there's no special elevator in the Central Committee headquarters to a treasure house. What I did, I did for Erich.'

He indicated to her to come over to the escritoire, glancing furtively around the room as if afraid to talk. The old wolf suspected he was being observed. Marlene came and stood beside him, her back hiding the greater part of the camera's visual field. Bauer wrote something that we couldn't see on a piece of paper. When she had read it the old man took it to the toilet. We heard the noise of the cistern and soon he appeared in the room again.

'Go and get him back,' he said in a flat voice. 'Some others are trying too—those who have remained loyal.'

'Perhaps I should meet them?' asked Marlene. 'If we combine our strength, we might succeed faster.'

'I have no trust in you whatsoever,' Bauer responded curtly. 'Now leave.'

Marlene turned and opened the door. The tape finished.

Hardman stopped the video with the remote. He turned around and said, 'We'll need this tape.'

'There's original historical material in it,' I replied. 'I'll give it to you in a few days when I've written it up for the paper.'

'OK, we'll see about that later,' said Hardman, having confirmed that Weber agreed with me. 'Continue.'

'Are you still not happy?' Giuseppe asked. 'We have found out so much: the mutt's beloved was a super-agent of the Stasi. I hope you love her even more now.'

'I saw that she can lie with great ease, as she did with the identity of Juliet. But I didn't find out if it was her who betrayed me to the KGB.'

'What patience!' said Giuseppe sarcastically. 'And you maintain that there is no romantic love under socialism.'

I looked daggers at him, but Larissa interjected.

'We also found out that Müller works only for himself now and wants a ransom before he returns the child. But then, who was looking for Juliet in Fabio's office? Who is trying to get rid of me?'

'It must be someone who wanted to take revenge on Juliet. It's the same person who is trying to release the child on behalf of the old man. Probably a Moscow submarine.'

'Does Moscow have submarines too?' asked Giuseppe, astounded.

I tried to focus.

'Someone who is completely loyal to him. We didn't find out much about the child's secret. Before Lubimov died he told me that the child was the key.'

I paused.

'Or did he mean that the child has some key? That's it! The child has something on him. Bauer asked Marlene how much Müller wants. Therefore... put the video on again!'

'We have to give it back,' said Larissa nervily. 'Time is short.'

I quickly found the scene in question. The old man was saying, 'Don't believe what's written in the press. There's no red suitcase, just as there's no special elevator in the Central Committee headquarters to a treasure house. What I did, I did for Erich.'

Then he wrote the note that we couldn't see.

'The child must have a bank-account book or something similar on him,' I concluded. 'Maybe that's what Lubimov wanted to tell me before he died.'

Masha added, with the ingenious female mind, 'An account with at least half a million dollars.'

'We need to get Erich back,' I said decisively. 'He's the key to the mystery.'

Giuseppe's situation reminded me of a Soviet saying: in America everything is possible; here, nothing is impossible. Since even that puritanical Sicilian communist had shacked up with a comrade from the Central Committee's Department of International Relations everything seemed possible in the Soviet Union.

After the successful conclusion of operation Oktyabrskaya the girls went to rest. We had a big night ahead of us: operation cuckolds. We were worried about Larissa, so I suggested to her a relatively safe place to spend the rest of the day: her office in the Lubyanka building, the KGB headquarters.

Evening was drawing in. I had parked a few hundred metres away in a side street off Old Square. I was waiting for Giuseppe, who had gone into the Central Committee to see his beloved.

The reason for the visit wasn't purely sentimental. The comrade had discovered an entire workshop of disguise and forgery on the first floor of the department. Some of the equipment would be necessary for us. The locked steel door opened with a special combination. Until recently, only a very few department employees had known the secret. The others had thought that it was where top-secret documents belonging to the international communist party were stored and only that Methuselah, Boris Ponomarev, head of the Internal Affairs Department of the Politburo, and his cronies had access. Comrade Alla, as Giuseppe's darling was called, had discovered the secret department by chance when she found a forgotten piece of paper with the door's combination on it. The party mechanisms were showing signs of crumbling.

We chose to visit the headquarters of the Central Committee around six, because at that time on a Friday the employees and their managers have left for their dachas. Giuseppe took a passport photograph of mine to forge an identity card showing I was an employee of the UPDK, which deals with foreigners, as well as the maintenance of buildings belonging to the diplomatic corps. I would try to use it the next day to go into the Embassy of the German Democratic Republic and get Erich.

I saw Giuseppe approaching from afar, but, since optimism is permanently etched on his face, I couldn't tell if he had succeeded or if it was simply his usual ideological health. He got into his car and we set off at once.

'I did it. We made the identity card. But if you saw what was going on in there…'

'I can't believe you made love in the headquarters of the Central Committee!'

'That's always where you mind goes and then we never get anything done. They have everything: stamps for all the airports in the world, passports from most states, fake identities, outfits, moustaches, male and female wigs.'

'Did you get a wig for Larissa?'

'Of course. But do you know what else I discovered? In one filing cabinet there are photographs of leading members of all the communist parties in "relaxed situations". You wouldn't believe what I saw…

Raul Castro, Fidel's brother… You just wouldn't believe your eyes.'

'The future of the Party is secured, Giuseppe. With all those pictures and video recordings you could open the best porno shop on the planet. Throw in some handcuffs for orgies, a few chains…'

'I haven't seen chains anywhere.'

'There are lots. Everywhere.'

He had seen so much in the last few days that he hadn't the strength to react.

I stole a little time before the nocturnal operation began to solve the final question about my life. Having left Giuseppe at the hospital I visited Beriozka, the foreign currency supermarket on Bolshaya Dorogomilovskaya, and then greeted the compound guards with two crates of vodka, like an alcoholic's Santa. This time I didn't even need to explain what I wanted. They received the goods with a smile and led me straight down to the observation room in the bowels of the earth. The ugly man was still there. When he saw me he inclined his head in understanding. He looked just over my head, perhaps imagining that he could already see the horns.

I asked to listen to the recordings of the days that the KGB was after me. Something told me that Marlene must have spoken to Yelin—and I wasn't wrong. It was just before Yelin let me go.

I heard Marlene's irate voice saying, 'We had agreed you would leave him alone.'

'But Eros was carrying nuclear material.'

He had already given me the nickname back then.

'What did you think he was going to bring back from a military city? Kites? You promised me that if I told you what he was doing in Moscow 400 you wouldn't bother him. If you want, take Pioneer.'

'Do you think I care about Pioneer? Danaher annoys me because he's sleeping with you. I told you after that night that I saw you together at the lake that you should leave him.'

Marlene said nothing.

'You still want him, don't you?'

'But Oleg, we're over.'

'After all those years we can't be over just like that. We're made for each other, Marlene.'

Her voice was sad and ironic: 'We're made to spy. That's all we know how to do. I've told you before—the job in Berlin was my last operation.'

'But you made a mess of it. You only dealt with the child. You took him and went, leaving the Wall to fall.'

'Is it my fault that the generation educated by Bauer turned out to be incompetent? I recommended they make a decision on travel abroad, not pull down the Wall. But anyway, it's better that it fell. It would have happened anyway some day.'

'But it fell on my watch and I had no idea it was going to happen. If my people at the Politburo weren't supporting me Gorbachev would have kicked me out.'

He paused.

'I want to see you.'

Marlene seemed to hesitate.

'I can't even touch you. I hate you. I hate myself. I want to live a normal life.'

'With Eros? His wife has come to see him. She's here, outside my office. I helped you overthrow the old man and get Erich back. We'll all live together.'

'They took Erich away again.'

'Why did you entrust him to that jerk?'

Instead of defending me Marlene remained silent. Then she said, 'Get my child back and we'll see.'

'There's that gangster Müller. You know that he's not kept in check by anyone. He only looks out for himself. Like everyone else, he's started a private initiative.'

'Give his ransom money.'

'Half a million dollars? Are you mad?'

'Then organize a kidnapping. What kind of a KGB chief are you?'

'I'll try, if you leave Eros.'

There were a few moments of silence. Then Yelin added, 'At most you can stay a couple of days more with him. I've suggested that we collaborate and I want you to find out what he's thinking.'

'If I ask he'll realize.'

'You know how; you told me the method yourself. Read his novel. I'm amazed he's got the energy for literature in all this mess, but it's simple: what happens in life, the idiot puts into his novel. I gave him his computer to see what he would write and took it back later. He hasn't ruled out collaboration.'

'You'll put him into the madness that we've been in all these years?'

'If he comes under my command I'll force him not to see you. I also don't want you to see him.'

'I accept on one condition: let him leave.'

'I'll let him go, and when he comes crawling home you'll tell him you're breaking up, so that he'll pack and leave Moscow as quickly as possible. Leave him; he's finished!'

'OK, but I want Erich back.'

'I'll see what I can do. Send me a kiss.'

The ugly man deep down was tender-hearted. He saw me sitting there stunned and patted me on the back.

'Don't worry, comrade. It happens to the best families.'

It took us longer than usual to persuade an Italian to play the role of the Latin lover. In the end Giuseppe agreed to wear a modern pinstripe suit, shave and go out as an authentic allortsi to Solaris, in search of Katya from Tashkent. He would recognize her when Masha asked her for a cigarette at eleven thirty.

Things went according to plan. Giuseppe approached her and initiated conversation. Around 1 a.m., Katya suggested they go to her apartment and Giuseppe gladly accepted. The price was, as always, two hundred dollars.

We were waiting outside the disco from half past midnight in two cars with private licence plates. There were eight of us in total: Larissa, the mutt—in other words, me—and six policemen from the Ministry against Immoral Behaviour. This was the new ministry founded after repeated complaints by deputies to the Supreme Soviet that the whole country was falling into sin. At a congress Gorbachev himself made a speech announcing the founding of the new force, alongside an anti-pornography panel that would introduce 'urgent measures against pornography, erotic videos and pseudo-medical information'. According to the general secretary of the Party, the panel itself would have to draw the line between pornography and art.

With a whole history of prohibition behind it, the panel had a difficult task. Nabokov's Lolita had just been published after years of censorship, while Viktor Yerofeyev's latest novel, Russian Beauty, began with an analytical description of the female sexual organs and continues by describing the life of a prostitute who spends all her time in bed with men and women. All the latest movies include at least one sex scene, a trend heralded two years earlier by Little Vera. The movie caused an uproar in the country, though it wasn't pornographic, nor even daring by Western standards. It simply demolished a taboo. Rumour had it that Gorbachev himself left halfway through, sickened, even though its message was one of rejuvenation. Perhaps the Soviet leaders had better material at home: recordings of their comrades' relaxed moments from hundreds of cameras hidden in hotels and resorts throughout the country.

The task of the men in the Ministry against Immoral Behaviour was even more difficult. Among their duties was 'locating people knowingly spreading STDs and

AIDS'. The head of the team that accompanied us that evening, a pockmarked officer with a contorted face, was completely incapable of explaining to me how his men would locate the suspects. He admitted that what he was doing was entirely new, adding that all members of the team felt awkward, despite the special seminars they had attended on sexually transmitted diseases and the use of contraception. Contrary to the content of their work, which remained unclear, the new force did have extensive power: without evidence or warrants it could arrest officers of the regime or members of the special security forces engaging in immoral activities, or even KGB agents. The Soviet establishment was making a final attempt at controlling a phenomenon that had gradually got out of hand and now appeared utterly unchecked.

So as not to arouse suspicion that our only goal was the ring of KGB cuckolds, we had asked the officer if we could begin at eight in the evening with a Ministry-organized tour of the depraved quarters of the city. I kept careful notes and Larissa posed as my translator, wearing the wig she had pillaged from the disguise department of the Central Committee. At first we observed the Ministry confiscating a number of cheap books and magazines and few packs of cards depicting naked women that were sold by vendors in the Arbat underpass. In the West, most of these items would go unnoticed at kiosks, but in Moscow the passers-by gathered to gawp at them. Each magazine deployed an artistic or scientific premise: Baltia had instructions on body painting and tattoos in sensitive places; Sex Press displayed twenty-nine different sex positions, which were beneficial for exercise and weight loss. If you could lose weight easily from sex, humanity would never get out of bed and Fabio— how was Fabio, poor thing?—would have become a skeleton. Some of the magazines published poorly printed photographs stolen from Playboy, while others were just photocopies of Penthouse. They were like the samizdat— the makeshift dissident newspapers of the old days— but on sexual matters.

The illegal movie theatre that we visited immediately afterwards was more advanced. We entered a typical courtyard with a wooden see-saw in the middle for the apartment block's children. In a corner there was a small shop with a rusty Kodak sign. The line that had formed outside initially made me think they were selling alcohol and that the guys from the Ministry had decided to confiscate a bottle or two of vodka to make the night pass more easily. The shop was a small room with a dilapidated ceiling. One side was covered with wooden chairs and on the other was a standard-sized television set connected to a video player. When we entered, pretending to be sexually famished, it was playing Juliet, a German soft porn movie from the seventies. It was set in a large country house, and showed a group of people eating continuously before screwing each other.

In foreign movies or imported videos shown in Russia there is no subtitling or dubbing of the actors. One lone male can be heard reading the translation of the script in a bland voice. In the case of Juliet, we heard two women talking dirty during lesbian sex with this male voice-over. With difficulty I stopped myself from bursting out laughing. It was cold in the room, but most of the viewers had taken their coats off and put them over their legs. All the time that the Ministry men let the movie go on—clearly just to confirm that there was something reprehensible in it—I didn't hear any strange sounds. Only at one moment did a soldier in the back row groan when he saw the main character's Mercedes.

'Who wants to have an orgasm?'

'Me! Me!' cried a hundred or so women ecstatically.

The Ministry tour included a seminar with Boris Zolotov, a man who had recently bewitched the Soviets. We were near the Central Dynamo Stadium in a large warehouse that was used as a primitive disco for members of the Communist Youth. On the walls there remained the red velvet banners with Lenin's portrait and a half-torn Komsomol flag. The floor of the space, which was larger than a basketball court, was covered in white mattresses and blankets that formed the biggest bed in world history. A sea of women's bodies, wearing skirts and short-sleeved shirts of all colours, was swaying to the sounds of American soul music. The place reeked of female sweat mingled with dust.

'Now dance with me! Focus on me!' shouted the great guru of Soviet sex, a tall, thin man with a dancer's figure, blond hair and blue eyes. He was standing on a small wooden podium, like a speaker at a formal event, and was wearing jeans, a white short-sleeved shirt and braces. He then began waving his arms around like a conductor, his face screwed up in concentration.

Most newspapers had devoted tonnes of ink to the Zolotov phenomenon. Mr Gold—zolotov means gold in Russian—had divided Soviet society. His fanatical supporters had fits of hysteria over him. Many followed him on his tours to the four corners of the Soviet Union. But the more conservative Soviet contingent wanted his head on a plate. The polls showed that half the population wanted him hanged in Red Square and the other half that he continue his mass production of orgasms unimpeded. Pravda accused him of being a sex maniac, an attack to which many attributed the sharp decline in the newspaper's circulation. The Communist Party considered Zolotov the extreme example of the flourishing of eroticism and the degeneracy of morals. The state trade unions and official women's organizations wanted his followers arrested, along with those who circulated his pamphlets. A mother from Leningrad complained in a letter to Izvestia that one of Zolotov's interviews on the television had led her fifteen-year-old son to masturbation. At first the Russian Orthodox Church accused him of being an accomplice of the Devil and responsible for the sharp rise in the number of divorces, but the strong protests of many believers compelled it ultimately to adopt a neutral stance. Since early times priests have shown that they know how to adapt to situations.

'Men learn from me!' cried Zolotov to the crowd. 'My knowledge passes from man to man. There is just one secret: men must understand that their mission is to make women happy.'

Suddenly the music became louder, the women held hands and formed a big circle and began jumping in evident ecstasy. Zolotov stepped off the podium and started dancing with them, stroking and kissing them.

I looked sideways at Larissa. She seemed impressed. When she realized I was looking at her, she said, 'They say a lot about Zolotov, but his success is founded on the care and tenderness he shows to women. Don't forget that there are more of us than there are men. With the civil war and Stalin's purges, they found around 1930 there were five million more women. After World War II there were twenty million more women. But even today, women live twelve years longer than men, who die young, drowned in alcohol. That's how we ended up chasing men.'

'Every man's dream.'

'Not a dream of Soviet men. They're emasculated. They're under the most pressure to conform, to be obedient, to go into the Party, to have a career.'

She turned and looked around, as if wanting to see if anyone was listening.

'Recently I was assigned a job in the ministry where we keep the confiscated samizdat, the illegal newspapers from the seventies. Do you know what I discovered?'

'With all that's happened over the last days my imagination has run dry.'

'The illegal women's magazines that talk of the tragic state of women in the country. Every Soviet woman has an average of six to eight abortions in her life. They write of group abortions with no anaesthetic, of nurseries where people steal the children's food, of the five-rouble subsidy the state gives for illegitimate children. One article explained that, thanks to communist education, men remain children their entire lives. How could, it said, a man who never received anything other than discipline have internal freedom? At home we say "Careful, don't touch that! Don't do that!" At the nursery, "Wake up! Hold your partner's hand! Why are you slower than the other children?" At school, "Leave your imagination at home!" In class, "Listen to what your elders tell you!" At the Institute, "Do you think you're cleverer than the rest? Don't ask stupid questions!" In life, "Don't do that! It's forbidden." And so they take revenge on us for all the humiliations they have suffered. Do you see now why I love Fabio?'

The spotty officer dealt the fatal blow just as fifty or so women were lying on the 'bed', their legs open and their eyes shut. Some of them were moaning, as if they had reached an orgasm after intercourse with the spectre. The officer walked between women, who paid him no attention, then across the bed, risking losing his balance, before finally reaching the podium. He stood on it and clapped his hands for silence. The moans and the music stopped and the hall fell silent.

He shouted, 'Ministry against Immoral Behaviour! This is an illegal gathering. Comrade Zolotov is arrested.'

It was perhaps the second most significant rebellion in Russian history after that on the battleship Potemkin. The women who were lying down leapt up and, along with the others, who were more aggressive —probably because they hadn't yet been satisfied— moved threateningly towards him. They began shouting all together, creating pandemonium. We were sitting at the edge of the hall but the incensed wave of women swept us towards the podium and I too found myself walking on the bed of pleasure. Some of the women were crying and others were shouting in the direction of the officer, 'I'm having multiple orgasms and I'm in love with him. If you arrest him I'll kill myself.' 'I never had orgasms before, but for the last eight weeks that I've been attending the seminars I'm better every day.' 'He gets out all my creative energy. I paint and write poetry now.' 'It's better with him than it is with my husband.' 'My husband and I have been cured. We used to be incapable.'

The women crowded threateningly around the podium and I saw that the officer had taken fright. He waved his arms to calm everyone down and called, 'OK, OK. You can carry on.'

Some women stopped screaming, but others continued gesturing and shouting. Those whom he had interrupted just before they finished were beating their hands on the wooden podium, and at some point one of them threw a shoe towards him. Within a minute the unfortunate upholder of morals was showered with shoes and clogs. The other men from the Ministry were left dumbfounded; in the special seminars they had never imagined that they would need to know how to face women having multiple orgasms. Thankfully, Zolotov himself moved onto the podium and the shower of shoes stopped. The final one, somewhat delayed, landed by mistake on the head of a plump fifty-year-old wearing a yellow bow tie and standing beside him. Zolotov raised his hands for silence.

'Let's not pay any more attention to this episode than we need to. The golden road seminars will continue. Now please welcome the best Soviet sexologist, Professor Igor Kant.'

Some women clapped uncertainly. The plump man straightened his glasses and bow tie.

'What just happened here is no coincidence. We have the unfortunate privilege of being the most backward country in the world in terms of sex. Since the early 1920s, the Party has tried to destroy our sexual instinct. They put us in small houses and deprived us of the possibility of being alone. They forbade us from kissing and walking down the road hand in hand. The vigilant eye of the Party watched us everywhere. You'll remember the lyrics from the song "Tovarisch Paramonova" by our famous poet Alexander Galich. Two mature people working in the same place fall in love, and for that reason they are called to defend themselves at the Party organization where the lover's wife is a secretary. How many lovers were forced to abandon the partner they loved after a Party decision? We were never allowed to read George Orwell's 1984, because it talks of a totalitarian society in which romantic love is forbidden; because, as in Orwell's society, here there was also a Ministry of Love in every Party organization and in every workplace. The trajectory of the Revolution is reflected in the trajectory of love affairs.'

'Booo!' shouted the women, 'Down with the Revolution!'

'It wasn't like that in the first years after the Revolution. There was sexual liberation then; men and women bathed naked near here, in the river, within Moscow itself. But with Stalinism everything changed. They almost made premarital and extramarital relationships illegal. Do you know why? Because puritanism is a fundamental part of Communist ideology; it's part of the system of prisons and gulags. If you have freedom in love, you have freedom in everything. You have a place you can feel free: your bed.'

'Yes, yes!' cried the women together, jumping up and down. 'Your bed!'

'But in a totalitarian system, everything is a state matter: work, home, art, philosophy, sex and love. And so they created Homo sovieticus. In our country a young man cannot go with his girlfriend to a good restaurant or on a trip; he doesn't even have money for a taxi to go to her house. He has learnt that sex is the fruit of the corrupt West. Those of us whom they let travel abroad were forced to visit specific places. In Paris we had to go to the cemetery where the heroes of the Commune were buried, to Lenin's apartment on Rue Marie-Rose and to Place Pigalle with all the prostitutes to witness the corruption of the old world with our own eyes.

'You can spot a Soviet citizen travelling abroad from a mile off: from his manner, his dress, the way he walks. Homo sovieticus is a miserable and submissive being, but his fundamental characteristic is that he is sexually backward. Don't be angry with your husbands; first of all you should be angry with the system. A few months ago I was in the USA for a congress and I was talking to a sexologist who has many Russian émigrés as clients. He told me that they were so ignorant about sex that at first he thought they were mocking him. In our country we know everything about the American military bases, but nothing about our sexuality. Until a couple of years ago, even Freud was forbidden. I was the first person to speak about the G-spot in my new book, and I explain with diagrams where it is to be found.'

'Tell us how to find it!' cried the women.

'What's the G-spot?' asked Larissa.

'I can't show you right now. Wait until Fabio gets better.'

The professor cleared his throat.

'Under Gorbachev, things eased at first. In 1985, when he became general secretary, the country tried 301 cases of infringement of the Penal Code's article 228 on pornography. In 1989 only 30 cases were tried. But today the Kremlin is being influenced more and more by the conservatives, who are trying to reinstate the old values. The right uses pornography to weaken perestroika. This new police force, which interrupted today's beautiful mingling, is Gorbachev's trick to win allies among the conservatives.'

'Take the unloved ones and let's go,' I said to Larissa. 'Another gaffe this evening and we won't be able to do our job.'

'Comrades, the Liberation Movement and the Union of Homosexuals and Lesbians stand in solidarity with your cause.'

We had almost reached the exit of the first orgasm-workshop I had seen in my life when we heard a loud, almost shrill, voice followed by enthusiastic applause. A young man, around twenty-five, was on the podium. He was dressed like a heavy metal singer, with a black T-shirt and tight jeans. An earring dangled from his right ear—a very rare phenomenon in the Soviet Union—and he spoke while gesticulating with his long bony arms.

'Who's that?' I asked Larissa.

'Kalinin. Don't you know him?'

I had read about Roman Kalinin. Not long before, Pravda had made him famous with a piece of libel entitled, "The pinks and political orgasm". Kalinin dared to present himself as leader of homosexuals, stating that if there were free elections, he would put himself forward for president of the Soviet Union. Other communist papers wrote that he wanted to take power in order to sack all the members of the Communist Party and legalise necrophilia.

'In a gathering last week in a forest in Moscow, two hundred representatives from across the Soviet Union decided to fight for the abolition of discrimination against gays, lesbians and women,' Kalinin declaimed. 'The punishment for homosexuality today is five years in prison or forced labour. Many of our comrades are rotting in jail. And when we talk of Soviet jails, we mean daily brutality.

'TASS recently talked of hundreds of thousands of homosexuals in the USSR, but that's a joke. Studies show that ten per cent of the population is homosexual. Therefore we are about twenty-eight million. Between five and ten million have been persecuted for homosexuality. Thankfully, they didn't find all of us.'

The women in the auditorium applauded enthusiastically.

'We have the most anti-erotic male politicians of all countries. When I see Yelin on the television I lose all erotic feeling. Yeltsin and Pavlov are completely unsatisfied. And Pavlov has already imposed his repressed sexuality onto Soviet society: he screwed us all and particularly women with the increase in prices. I think that if Gorbachev was more liberated things would be going better. I recently stated that I would never make love to him—and I even learnt that Gorbachev heard this himself and was pretty offended. I can't think why.'

Some of the women in the auditorium laughed and others jeered.

'Our law is worse even than backward Islamic countries,' Kalinin continued. His rhetorical skill was infinitely better than those Politburo members with their wooden language. 'In schools there is absolutely no sex education. No one deals with the problem of AIDS, because no one in our country wants to talk about sex, even safe sex. We have recently begun a campaign with the slogan "Give out condoms! They protect against all diseases: AIDS, syphilis or communism." I invite you next week to distribute condoms outside Red Square, with the slogan "A submarine costs as much as five billion condoms."

'For those who don't know, I was a professional engineer. I worked as a coal miner in Siberia, but they fired me because I'm gay. They accused me of drug use and necrophilia. After those articles, my telephone was inundated by necrophiliacs expressing their solidarity.'

He stopped for a moment to gauge the crowd's reaction.

'But, after gays and lesbians, the greatest injustices of Soviet society are against women. Women are supposedly equal to men, but no woman has ever become general secretary of the Party. In capitalist Great Britain, Margaret Thatcher has been prime minister for years.'

Maggie had always had many followers in the Soviet Union; at the mention of her name, the women started cheering.

'Our model is Ancient Greece, where homosexuality was recognized and women had rights for the first time in history. Since they had democracy in Ancient Greece, women left their homes and began dealing with society. Romantic love—eros—was discovered in Athens, showing that it is impossible for love or democracy to exist without the liberation of women.'

'Bravo! Bravo!' cried the women, while Larissa looked at me, trying to read my thoughts. Kalinin waited contentedly until the cries of the crowd had died down.

'We have one slogan: Russia must finally be governed by a woman. The future female Soviet president should have charming bodyguards instead of those gorillas surrounding Gorbachev, and half of the cabinet should be women. Onwards to a government suitable for the land of madmen, the land of the naïve! Do you remember Gulliver in the land of the idiots, who planted golden coins to grow a golden tree? We've been doing the same thing for years, planting golden coins and waiting. I promise you that the moment I am elected I will have gender surgery and become a woman.'

The cries were so loud that I had to shout for Larissa to hear me: 'Will you vote for Kalinin if there are elections?'

I felt a shiver down my spine as we passed the KGB headquarters, heading three blocks further to the U Kamina restaurant. The indefatigable chief of the anti-pornography brigade had assured us that at By the Fireside (which is what U Kamina means) we could witness the most brazen display in Moscow. In the main hall of the restaurant were a couple of large tables facing a dance floor, but at the back there were a few partitions. The director of The Godfather Part IV would not have been able to find a better clientele gathered together.

I sat at a table with Larissa, the head of the Ministry

and a few of his men. The bare-chested waitress, from whom I ordered champagne for the others, responded with the phrase 'I love you, baby'. She said it so often while she served us that I began to wonder whether she had fallen madly in love with me or if she thought it meant bon appétit.

The show started with a conjuror coming over to our table. I would have laughed if he managed to remove the boss's underwear without him realizing, but he limited himself to producing a rabbit out of a hat. The atmosphere warmed up when two dancers appeared on the floor without underwear. Then a girl began her number, wearing just a G-string and shaking her behind in the face of the head of the anti-pornography group, who in the half-light was looking more and more like the Marquis de Sade. I thought of showing Larissa roughly where the G-spot was, but she seemed annoyed. The two girls who had come out at the start returned dressed as nuns and, having undressed, made homoerotic love. Then the G-string girl came out without her G-string and began masturbating to the sounds of Sinéad O'Connor's 'Nothing Compares 2U'. The boss looked dazed; it didn't even cross his mind to arrest the masturbating girl. Besides, he had a lot of arrests to make that evening.

Giuseppe got into a taxi with Katya, followed by a strange convoy: the cuckolds in their car, and us with the moral brigade in two others. As we had foreseen, they made for the apartment used by Katya, where they had caught me in flagrante committing adultery. Soon the cuckold, brandishing an empty suitcase, and his accomplice walked towards the apartment block. We approached soundlessly—Larissa, followed by the head of the group with his assistant, and me carrying my beloved video camera. The rest followed behind. We waited a minute before going up to the apartment. From inside we heard shouting.

Already overexcited by the sights they had witnessed, three men from the Ministry flung themselves at the door. It gave way at once and six of us entered the apartment, with the other two guarding outside against any eventuality. The Ministry men drew their revolvers and shouted 'Hands up! Ministry against Immoral Behaviour!' With his hands on his head, the cuckold really did look as though he had horns. Katya was shaking, while Giuseppe, who at first hid his nudity behind a women's magazine, put his clothes on quickly. The cuckold reacted when the built-in camera light shone in his face.

'Stop this nonsense. We're from the State Security Service.'

'And I'm Richard the Lionheart,' replied the boss.

'You'll regret this!' the cuckold threatened. 'Tell that jerk to stop recording me. Can I lower my hands? I'll show you my ID.'

The boss hesitated, but Larissa intervened at just the right moment. Only then did I realize that she was armed. She drew a revolver with one hand and with the other an ID card from her pocket, shouting, 'He's lying! I'm KGB!'

She put the card in her pocket and took off her wig.

'Miss KGB,' said the boss, impressed.

'I'm from the KGB too,' the cuckold insisted.

'Yes, but you're not Miss KGB, are you,' interjected Giuseppe, who had dressed and wanted to uphold the reputation of his future sister-in-law.

'What an idiot, to repeat it like that,' I whispered, without taking my eye from the camera.

'Is the young lady from the KGB too?' asked the boss.

'No. She's my cousin.'

'And what are you doing here?'

'We're on a mission.'

'You take your cousins with you on your missions?' asked Larissa. 'You should know it's strictly forbidden under the regulations.'

'She helps me locate anti-socialist elements.'

It was the worst thing he could have said, infuriating Giuseppe.

'I am an anti-socialist element?' Giuseppe protested in broken Russian. 'I'm an official guest of the Central Committee! You bring socialism into disrepute with what you're doing.'

'OK, Giuseppe, leave the re-education for later.' I turned towards Katya.

'Give him the two hundred dollars.'

She took it from her bra and gave it to Giuseppe. I felt a wild joy flooding me as I recorded this moment.

Larissa acted flawlessly. She proceeded towards the cuckold with her gun outstretched and took an ID out of his pocket. She did the same to his friend.

'Let's see. Are they criminal members of the KGB? I've heard that there's an organized racket.'

'I've done nothing wrong,' sobbed Katya. 'I'm not his cousin. I have nothing to do with him.'

'What are you then?'

'I work evenings at Solaris.'

'And what were you doing at the KGB seminars?' Larissa bluffed.

'This KGB man forced me to attend so we could steal from tourists together,' Katya stammered.

'You're right; it's a racket,' said the boss. His chest puffed out, ready to receive his medal.

Larissa put the KGB badges on the table for me to record them using the camera zoom. Then she said, 'They're violating the oath of the KGB. Take them in.'

'You are arrested,' echoed the boss.

His men handcuffed them, while the cuckold continued cursing, threatening fire and fury. I followed him to the car and before he got in I called, 'Aren't you ashamed, being cuckolded every night?'

I gave Larissa a smacking kiss on the cheek. 'Now I've really got Yelin by the horns. Don't worry about your job, sweetie, I'll make you the representative of Harlequin novels for the whole Soviet state.'

When I returned home at three in the morning, Marlene was asleep. I was dead from exhaustion, but I had to write the end of the novel. She would read it the next day, just as the final act of my own drama was being played out.

[30 November]

'This must be Müller's house. Most likely they have Erich there,' Larissa said, stooping over the map of the East German embassy that she had stolen from her office. 'It's at the back of the embassy and to reach it you must in theory pass two checkpoints. The first, the most difficult, is in the main entrance. There are not only the usual embassy guards there—my colleagues—but also well-trained Stasi agents. The second checkpoint is in the backyard, at the point that leads from the main area of the embassy to the diplomats' houses. It's guarded only by KGB people, and they're not particularly careful, since anyone who has got there has passed through the main entrance. I know a way of avoiding the first checkpoint.'

Giuseppe and I bent over the maps that Miss KGB had laid out on a desk in the Corriere's offices.

'We're very lucky that today is Saturday, as most people will have left for their dachas. You should go between two and three in the afternoon, the time of pereriv. At pereriv on a Saturday you could probably make it to Gorbachev's bedroom.'

'Let's leave that for another time. I'm concerned about how we will get to the back avoiding the stricter checkpoint.'

'From the secret city,' Larissa said.

Giuseppe and I looked at each other, he puckering his lips and giving his moustache the shape of Stalin's.

'There is an entire city in the bowls of Moscow, one

hundred metres deep,' Larissa explained, pushing aside the plan of the embassy and replacing it with another. 'It was built under the city to protect the Party leadership in case of nuclear war, and spans two hundred hectares. It's a proper city, with buildings, gyms, recreation areas, cinemas, even roads for cars. There is a special metro line going to Vnukovo airport. It can house thirty thousand people and has enough supplies for twenty years, meaning no need for contact with the outside world.'

'I've heard of the bunker in Virginia, which can house the members of the American Congress—slightly over five hundred people.'

'Here we're talking of a city about ten times the size of Wembley Stadium,' Larissa said, not hiding a certain satisfaction on the superiority of the bunkers of socialism as opposed to those of capitalism. 'They built it over sixteen years, during the Cold War, from 1960 to 1975. Our specialists estimated that the whole population of Denver could fit inside.'

Giuseppe swelled like a socialist turkey. He was gradually reclaiming his confidence.

'I didn't realize the Kremlin were such underground guys,' I teased.

'There was a plan for diplomats from the sister countries too,' Larissa continued. 'In every embassy of a socialist country there is a secret entrance leading to the city. There is a well in the courtyard of the East German embassy, which supposedly can be used to draw unpolluted water from the ground in case of war. That's a myth: the well is the entrance to the secret city. It is usually guarded by a KGB man, but now security has slackened. I am certain that during pereriv they'll have slouched off. But you need to get the job done in an hour. Will you manage it?'

'I hope so. How do we enter the secret city?'

'There are entrances from all government buildings and ministries, and the homes of Party and KGB leaders. But they are guarded.'

'Not to mention it's difficult for me psychologically to go back into KGB buildings. I feel a kind of sadness…'

'Will you let the comrade explain?' said Giuseppe, frustrated.

'The construction of the city was founded on an older underground system from tsarist Russia,' Larissa continued. 'The first galleries in Moscow were built by monks during the reign of Ivan the Terrible, so they could slip away when barbarians were besieging their monasteries. There is an unguarded entrance in Novodevichy Convent. We can enter there.'

'Oh, don't take me to a church now!' Giuseppe protested. 'That's the only thing I didn't come to Moscow for. Besides, I need to go to the hospital.'

'Leave off that, Giuseppe. You went this morning and Fabio's health is improving steadily. You have a date with the comrade from the Central Committee.'

'She's very sweet,' he said, blushing. 'But I would like to come with you.'

Giuseppe couldn't hide his jealousy when I put on a worker's outfit as we left the Corriere offices with Larissa. We had bought it that morning from the market at Izmaylovo Park. If he knew decent enough Russian not to risk the guards catching wind of us, he too could have worn the honoured clothes of the Soviet working class—even if it was for an operation to infiltrate the embassy of another socialist state.

'We have to be careful,' Larissa said to me, while I was parking the car outside the Novodevichy Convent. 'The majority of church leaders collaborate with the Fifth Directorate of the KGB, responsible for church affairs.

'You lot have done an excellent job. In all fields…'

I had recently written an article about this matter, following publications in the progressive Soviet newspapers that ironically called the members of the Orthodox Church hierarchy the Metropolitburo. They had uncovered the code names of several big personalities working with the KGB: Adamantios was the code name of Metropolitan Juvenal of Moscow, Abat was Metropolitan Pitirim, head of foreign relations at the patriarchate and Antonov was Metropolitan Filaret of Kiev.

Saturday is a visiting day at the convent, and we slipped into a group of Austrian tourists without much difficulty. It was a very mild day for the time of year; it wasn't cold and, even rarer, the sun appeared now and then, making the river waters shimmer. According to the plan we had in our hands, access to the secret city was from the sanctuary of the side chapel of St Nicholas. We left the tourist group and reached the empty chapel. Entering the sanctuary we discerned at the back a small wooden trapdoor that opened easily. We descended about a hundred narrow stone steps before reaching a landing, from which a second set of mossy spiral steps started. I began counting, but at around three hundred I lost count. Suddenly the mouldy-smelling walls lost their dampness: we must have descended beneath the river level. We found ourselves in front of a large half-rusted gate that screeched open. When we shut it behind us, the landscape suddenly changed: we were in a long, narrow space, like a metro station.

'Here we are,' whispered Larissa. 'Now we need to walk along the metro tracks for about a kilometre.'

It was the city of absolute silence. We could only hear our own steps and the sounds of droves of rats that took to their heels at our footsteps.

'The underground city has five floors,' Larissa explained, 'and we are now on the fifth. Here there are apartments for government officials, members of the Central Committee and foreign diplomats. There used to be guards, but under Gorbachev they were withdrawn and sent to fight crime. The houses of Politburo members are on the floor below for greater protection, and on the third there are conference halls, cinemas, theatres and swimming pools. The first and second floors are huge storehouses for food.'

The platform above the metro lines narrowed in various places, where huge two-metre-wide cylinders blocked the way. As Larissa explained, they were gas pipes. Suddenly the absolute silence was broken by voices and steps coming towards us.

'Bad luck!' Larissa whispered. 'We've met a patrol. Since many homeless people find refuge here, they clean it up every so often.'

She took me by the hand and pulled me down a corridor to the right, which led to a huge storeroom lit by yellow bulbs. It was full of big plaster busts of Lenin. They had evidently wanted to decorate the place, but the plan had been abandoned. The busts had been placed in a row, like a small white army of Leninists who had lost the war without fighting one battle. We ran to the back of the storeroom and hid behind the busts, almost flat on the ground. The voices came closer and we heard the boss giving orders for the whole area to be searched. I felt a fear pierce my stomach and swore that if I wasn't caught I would reread all of Lenin's Selected Works. Displaying unprecedented disrespect for the founder of the first socialist country in the world, a mouse scuttled out from under a bust, making Larissa jerk. Thankfully the sound was lost under the footsteps of the patrol. I clutched her arm tightly and when they moved away took a deep breath. Since Lenin was protecting us, we had nothing to fear. We waited for a little, hidden, before leaving the storeroom and returning to the path beside the tracks. It took a fair while to reach the cylindrical stone structure that looked like a chimney and had a wooden door at its base. Having consulted the map, Larissa put her head inside the door and looked up. An iron ladder was attached to the wall, climbing as high as I could see.

'We're here,' she said, giving me the map in her hand. 'This is the well that emerges in the embassy courtyard. I'll wait for you, and I hope for Erich too, outside the convent. Do you think you'll manage to find the way back?'

'If I get lost I'll go down to the floor with the swimming pools and food.'

Larissa glanced at her watch.

'You must hurry; we're late. It's two twenty.'

It took me five minutes to get up the ladder. At the top I peeked over the edge of the well. There was no one in the embassy courtyard. I put on the glasses that had been useful to me the other day and the moustache we had stolen from the Central Committee department, then lowered my cap to cover my forehead. I jumped out and headed with swift, worker-like footsteps towards the gate that joined the main embassy area to the diplomats' housing complex. If Whitesmith could see me, he would have died of shame: I was now a member of the Soviet working class.

The guards at the entrance paid very little attention to the UPDK identity card that I showed them. The only thing that surprised them was that I was working on Saturday—and at pereriv. I told them that it wasn't right to leave one of our sister countries with a leaking sewage pipe. Since they dealt with foreign embassies, the UPDK employees were considered special, justifying a slight deviation from the proletariat's triumphs in their work rights. Only one of them noticed that I had a strange accent, and asked where I was from.

I had prepared myself: 'From Georgia.'

'Ah! Great wine!' he said in admiration, lifting up the metal barrier.

'Do you know where the apartment of comrade Müller is?'

He consulted a map pinned on the wall.

'Behind the main building, last on the right.'

Apart from a Trabant, two Golfs and one black Mercedes with dark windows in the courtyard, the embassy complex was empty. Everyone had left for the weekend to the dachas that the Soviet government gives for free to diplomats of socialist countries. Müller's house was a two-storey building made of grey concrete. As I knocked on the door I thought my heart would explode. Pioneer had told us that every Saturday morning Müller left the embassy early, without the child, for his dacha in Peredelkino, but I was afraid that for some reason the Stasi stationmaster and first secretary had changed his plans. The governess opened the door. She was around sixty-five, ugly and with a long, wrinkled face, the kind that made children eat their food.

'Is comrade Müller here?'

'He's out at the moment. What do you need him for?'

I breathed deeply.

'From the UPDK. They told us that there was a gas leak. It must be in the kitchen.'

She didn't seem surprised by another piece of Soviet damage, but opened the door for me and led me to the kitchen along a dark and narrow corridor. On the right there was a closed glass door that must have opened onto the living room, and at the end was the kitchen with a wooden spiral staircase to the first floor.

When we reached the cooker, I pretended to examine the gas pipe. I swore in a way that would have made the leader of the Komsomol blush with shame, and opened the metal toolbox I had with me. The governess walked away. I heard her go down the corridor and open the door to the living room. With my ear to the corridor wall I discerned a child's voice: Erich.

I took the hammer from the toolbox—the drill was waiting for my assault on the Winter Palace—and went into the living room, brandishing the tool threateningly at the governess.

'Don't move! I usually struggle to hammer even a nail into the wall, thanks to the capitalist problem of the opposition between manual and mental labour, but I can hit a human head with one try.'

Erich was kneeling in front of a low coffee table laid with an old-fashioned white tablecloth. The living room was fitted with furniture from the 1960s, apart from an old wooden desk at the back and a shapeless couch with a cheap beige leather throw on it, wrinkled like the governess' face. On the floor was a rug from Dagestan. The child was drawing in the sketch pad with the thick red cover. I saw he had drawn a funfair like the one in Gorky Park. On the big wheel was a child and, opposite the child, a woman and a man. I was now certain that Erich had realized it was us but preferred to return to the embassy. For him to have drawn that scene he must have been going over it again in his mind, wondering if he had done the right thing. He barely reacted when he saw me: he seemed distracted, as if something was tormenting him.

I took off my moustache and the glasses and said, 'Erich, it's me, Kevin. I've come to get you.'

He thought for a moment before shutting his pad and gathering his paints.

'Where is my mother?'

'She's here, in Moscow, waiting for you.'

Just as he stood up, Müller walked into the room.

'The boy is going nowhere,' he commanded. 'We're soon going back to Germany, to his grandfather.'

He was wearing a grey coat and holding a plastic bag of food in his hand.

'Erich, everything he's telling you is a lie. Your grandfather has lost the game. He's here in Moscow, ill and alone.'

Müller laughed maliciously and pointed at me.

'This person has a great imagination.'

He went on to try and stroke Erich's hair, but the boy pushed him away. I was clutching the hammer tightly, but had frozen still as a statue depicting the international proletariat. The governess retreated to the back of the room and stood in front of the desk. I didn't pay her much attention, as all my senses were focussed on Müller and the child.

At last I said, 'You're a fraud, a common kidnapper and an extortionist.'

He only took issue with 'kidnapper'.

'I didn't kidnap anyone. We met at the parade and Erich came of his own volition. And that day that you saw us at the funfair, again he preferred to come here. Isn't that right, Erich?' The boy lowered his head without saying anything.

'He came because you lied to him about his grandfather.'

'Mama lies, too,' Erich replied. 'She told me not to tell you who we are.'

'Your mom loves you, Erich.'

'It's Mama's fault that they sent away Grandpa and put Papa in prison. And before that she wanted to come and take me away in a helicopter.'

'No, Erich, don't believe what they tell you about your mom. In all the countries like yours, the friends of your grandpa have lost what they had. It's not your mom's fault. Don't let them make you hate her.'

The boy was in a state of shock. He seemed to be faltering.

'Is Grandpa here?'

'Yes, they've got him in the Oktyabrskaya Hotel.'

'He's crazy,' Müller said.

'I'll show you. Call the hotel and ask. 2439700.'

I couldn't forget the number of the hotel from the moment I saw it on the telephone screen.

The boy seemed shattered.

'I want to go to the cinema. And to a big supermarket,' he said eventually.

'We can go today! As soon as we leave here.'

When the child took the pad and his paints and began coming towards me, the governess opened the desk drawer, took out a revolver and pointed it at Erich.

'You're going nowhere!' she screeched.

Müller smiled nastily, took the revolver from her hands and pointed it at me.

'If I don't get the money from the old man, the boy won't leave. I haven't played daddy all these days for nothing. I want five hundred thousand dollars, no less. You've got under my feet quite enough, Danaher. You seemed as soft as all the other Westerners of your ilk, but in the end you're dangerous. I'll send you to find your friend Lubimov.'

As he was preparing to fire, my knees started shaking and my life passed before my eyes like a silent video clip: my mother breastfeeding me, my father shaving, the first time I made love as a college student, my reporting in Nicaragua, my marriage to Cynthia, the first time I saw Howard in the hospital. I'm not ashamed to say this, since it must be a common reaction for those about to die: I felt liquid running under my trouser leg. Then in the video clip of my life I saw the first day I met Marlene. All for a damned fax, I thought.

Suddenly Erich leapt between us. He was shaking all over and managed to say, 'Don't kill him!'

He turned to Müller and gave him the red sketch pad.

'There's a key inside,' he added, through chattering teeth.

Still pointing his gun at me, Müller took the pad and went to the desk. He picked up a paper knife and split the thick red cover.

'The key and the number of a safe,' he said triumphantly. 'Anonymous Bank of Switzerland, Geneva.'

He turned to Erich.

'Well, this is the first time your mother has told you the truth. She didn't have that money.'

Then he turned to the governess who was hanging on his words like a lover. She was perhaps the first woman who could have fallen in love with Müller.

'The old man had told the secret to his grandson, who played possum all this time.'

'Brat!' she said to Erich, who ran to me and clasped me tight.

'Sorry,' he stuttered. 'I thought you wanted to take me to my grandpa.'

Müller turned to me. 'Do you remember that evening when you took the bait with the traffic policemen? While my people were showing you the view from the chimneys, I spoke to your lover. She swore she had no money, but I didn't believe her.'

She had hidden yet another incident from me. Even that evening she had behaved as though she knew nothing—and I had swallowed her acting like a sucker. The others, from Weber to Marlene, were right: I was a mutt.

Müller pulled me out of my thoughts.

'I could have extracted myself days ago: the mafia promised me the ransom. But you screwed up at Moscow 400 and the deal was off.'

My self-esteem had now reached zero, but Müller took a different view.

'Danaher, you're marvellous. If you hadn't come here today, I would still be playing the good stepfather to this spoilt brat who thinks we're all here to serve him. Until a short while ago I was cursing myself for not doing you in that evening, but now I see that magnanimity pays off.'

The governess smiled, showing misshapen teeth. Müller was in high spirits. He valued money more than even the most barefaced capitalist.

'Get out at once, Danaher! This crisis of generosity may be over quickly. I will keep his royal highness until I know that the account contains at least five hundred thousand dollars. I'm not sure that the damned old man has saved enough: he thought he would be in power for life.'

The governess came over to take Erich, who clung to me. Now I had to go, leaving the child who had just saved my life. I had made a mess of everything, not to mention my trousers. It crossed my mind to rush Müller, but I had no chance.

'Kevin, take me with you!' Erich wailed.

'Scram!' shouted Müller, pointing the pistol at me.

I cursed my bad luck. If I hadn't done that interview with Pioneer, I thought, I wouldn't have gone to the post office.

Just then the door opened and two men barged in. The first held a pistol with a silencer and the other a big automatic weapon. It was Pioneer and one of his Afghanis.

'It's all over, Müller,' Pioneer said. 'Put the gun down.'

He must have been one of the few five-minute millionaires in history. He laid his gun on the desk.

'Pioneer,' Müller growled. 'What business does the mafia have in the Embassy of the German Democratic Republic?'

'I'm ashamed on your behalf,' Pioneer replied.

Müller was cynical even in his most difficult moments: 'You're ashamed? Is there anyone left in this country who feels shame?'

'Embassy secretaries shouldn't be asking for ransom. Nor the stationmasters of the Stasi.'

'Look who's talking!' Müller retorted. 'You can't go anywhere; the embassy is blockaded. Soon half the Stasi will be here.'

'You're very amusing,' Pioneer replied.

I looked at my watch: it was ten to three. Müller tried to win time.

'Let's make an agreement. If you leave me, you'll have half a million dollars.'

'I have more,' Pioneer said.

'First time I've seen a millionaire waving a pistol.'

'You were a millionaire with a pistol too, but you lost it immediately,' I jibed. 'We'll put you in the Guinness book of world records.'

'Shut up, Danaher. A million dollars,' he proposed to Pioneer.

'Let's go, Pioneer,' I said. 'The pereriv will be over.'

'Don't worry about that,' Pioneer said.

I remember what happened next as though it was a movie. Müller took the revolver he had put down and tried to turn it against the two new arrivals. Pioneer buried three bullets in him, one after another, and he fell onto the desk, making a horrid sound, before sliding onto the floor. There was a hole in his forehead—the door through which he left this world to the one above. Erich was glued onto me like a barnacle. I had put my hand over his eyes. The governess had probably had a heart attack, an occurrence that didn't sadden me much. It was five to three.

'You came at just the right moment,' I said to Pioneer as I picked up Erich's pad and the key to the safe. 'Come on, let's go.'

'I'm afraid that you've misunderstood something,' he replied. 'The boy isn't going with you. He'll go to the Oktyabrskaya, to his grandfather who is waiting for us. I promised him and, as you know, I always keep my promises. Particularly to Bauer, to whom I owe so much.'

'Are you... Bauer's submarine in Moscow?'

'You were slow, but you got there in the end.'

'I didn't tell you my whole story,' Pioneer said. 'After the orphanage in Moscow they sent me to an institute in west Ukraine. Any trace of Pavlik Morozov had to disappear, you see. The Germans occupied the area in June 1941, the second day of the attack against the Soviet Union. I was arrested with the other young men and the women who were in good physical shape and sent to Germany for forced labour. Many German anti-fascists had been brought to the concentration camp, among them Erich Bauer, who was the head of the group of imprisoned communists. Back then he had huge respect for anything that came from the great homeland of socialism. He took me under his wing, ensuring I was fed and given light work. Thanks to him I didn't die of hunger and hardship. I hid my past from him, because I didn't know how he would react.

'We lost touch for a few years, because the communists were moved to another camp. When the Red Army freed us in 1945 I made for Berlin on foot. I had learnt German in the camp and so became translator for the Soviet divisions, earning a plate of food every day and a bed to sleep in. But I couldn't return to the Soviet Union; I was worried that they would find me and then I wouldn't have anyone at all on my side.'

We had left the embassy like chiefs in Pioneer's BMW, first passing the guards of the residences and then those at the main entrance, who greeted Pioneer like an old friend. I was sitting beside him in the back seat, while the Afghani was driving and Erich was in the passenger seat, inspecting the dashboard with awe. When we were near my apartment, at the bridge opposite the Supreme Soviet, Pioneer ordered the driver to stop, in order to finish telling me the most tragic life story I had heard over all those years.

'From 1945 to 1949 I remained in the Soviet sector of Berlin, getting by on menial work. After the founding of the GDR in 1949 I went to find Bauer. He wasn't yet general secretary, but he was very powerful. To explain why I hadn't returned to the Soviet Union I was forced to tell him my real identity. He was moved by my story, because he believed the Soviet authorities hadn't behaved correctly towards me. The Germans were reorganizing their secret services and he found me a paid position: my mission was to spy on the movements of Russian émigrés in West Berlin. When

Nikita Khrushchev began the deposition of Stalin in the Soviet Union in 1956, Bauer spoke to him about me. Khrushchev allowed me to return to the Soviet Union as Sergei Tamurian, but he didn't want my story ever to see the light of day. De-Stalinization had its limits, you see. I continued to travel to East Germany and met Bauer often, but the Stasi then had little to do in the Soviet Union. For many years I was dormant. In 1970 the Cold War was at its height and he asked me to work as a submarine, overseeing the officers on special duty acting in Moscow.'

'So you must also have been the boss of...'

'I knew about your relationship from the start. I was waiting to see if you would manage to get the child back without my direct intervention. Submarines reveal their real identity only when they run out of other means. I was forced to do so today in order to get into the embassy, when they informed me that Müller had returned home. I reckoned you'd get into a tight spot. Luckily the Stasi agents at the Moscow embassy are still loyal to Bauer... with the exception of our late friend.'

'So did you know that Marlene had a relationship with Yelin?' I voiced my sorrow.

'She wanted to escape him, but she was trapped.'

I pointed at the boy.

'You said that Bauer didn't approve of Stalin's behaviour to you. The astonishing thing is that he did almost the same thing with Erich. He took him from his mother and tried to make him hate her.'

He raised his arms in a gesture of disappointment.

'It's like asking how communists ended up as they

did. In Germany I knew them well before they took power, and most of them had the best intentions.'

There were a few seconds of silence. Then he said, 'You can get out now. We're going to the Oktyabrskaya.'

Erich started crying again.

'I can't stay in a hotel anymore. I want to go to my mother.'

Pioneer looked thoughtful.

'I want a mother like other children,' Erich repeated.

I saw Pioneer crying for the second time in two days.

'Damn it all,' he said. 'I'll never forget—I'm very old now. But a young child can. I freed the only being that he loves. I owe him nothing.'

'Kevin, you'll keep your promise, won't you? You promised to take me to a supermarket and to the cinema,' Erich cried with relief.

The car turned back onto Kalinina Prospekt. We stopped in front of the big Irish supermarket that had just opened.

'Leave us here,' I said to Pioneer, shaking his hand.

'I realized from the start that you were a good guy, Danaher. I hear you're leaving.'

'I've gotten mixed up in things, but I think I've found my way out.'

'If you need anything, you know where to find me.'

'I hope I won't. And you? What will you do?'

'Business. Everyone has started copying my foreign husband scheme; international matchmaking offices have sprung up everywhere. Today everyone is stealing from the crumbling state and soon there will be thousands of Soviet nouveaux riche. I'll found a company for the development of Soviet–Soviet relationships on a human level.'

'With rich Soviet husbands?'

'Are you crazy? I'd go bankrupt. Soviet men won't give a dime for women and it'll be like that for many years to come. What do the laws of supply and demand say? There are many women in the Soviet Union and few men. I'll start a company through which wealthy women can find a husband. Sex isn't power. Money is.'

I made to open the door, but Pioneer took my hand.

'One more thing. Apologize to your friend Fabio. Some barbarians among my people messed him up, but I hear he survived.'

'Are you still looking for Juliet?'

'We found her.'

'Ah! That's where you're wrong, Pioneer. The girl you believe you killed the other day is alive. And she isn't Juliet.'

'Impossible. We were told for sure by…'

He hesitated before adding, '… by your girl, Marlene.'

'I thought the same, but Juliet isn't who we thought she was. Are you still looking for the real Juliet?'

'That matter is over. Now I'm quits with Bauer, I told you. I was in Berlin in 1961, when they built the Wall. I knew that someday it would fall. I'm not hunting anyone anymore. But who is she?'

I looked at Erich. He had already got out of the car and was waiting impatiently on the sidewalk.

'You can speak to her if you telephone my apartment. Do me a favour while you're at it. Tell her that I have her child and I'll go there once we've had a little trip. And that she should read the end of my novel if she hasn't done so already.'

He looked at me for a moment, bewildered.

'Spying on thoughts, Pioneer. Not even you could imagine that.'

'I reckon you know more on that subject than me,' he said, leaning over to open the door. Then he retracted his hand, remembering something.

'What will you do with the key to the safe? Why not give it to her, so she can begin a new life with the boy?'

'That money will tie them to the past forever. Here there's an East German from the new government, Vera Berger. I'll give her the key and the safe number so the money can go back where it belongs: the East German state. If you want, you can help Marlene yourself.'

'Any idea how?'

'Find her a rich American husband; she likes them. As of yesterday she knew that Erich had the key, because Bauer told her. But she preferred not to bargain with Müller until she saw whether you would manage to free him without ransom, so the money in the safe wouldn't be wasted.'

'I screwed up like an amateur,' Pioneer said.

'She is very capable. I fell victim to love, which is

blind. But even you, who was keeping tabs on her, didn't realize that she was Juliet. She fooled us both.'

The newly built church of Moscow's capitalism is on Kalinina Street, on the first floor of a big shopping mall. To reach this Western oasis, you need first to go through the desert of the ground-floor gastronom, which sells in roubles from its near-empty shelves whatever it can get. The scenery changes immediately with the Irish department store on the first floor, where there is one section for electrical goods and clothes and one for food. There wasn't a single cabinet in the electronic section that Erich didn't look into. I saw him staring at a Walkman, before looking meaningfully at me, not saying a word. After all he had been through, he deserved a gift. For my part, I took the opportunity to buy a political version of the traditional matryoshka from a market stall outside. The matryoshkas were a new discovery of Soviet traders and were sold to Western tourists obsessed with perestroika. Yeltsin was on the outside, then Gorbachev, Brezhnev, Khrushchev, Stalin and, smallest of all, Lenin.

'What do you want that for?' Erich asked with a smile.

'I'm going to send it with a note to a bitter enemy of mine. I was in his office the other day and he showed me a matryoshka.'

We went to the food section and I bought the boy a huge bar of Swiss chocolate and a Coca Cola. He looked thoughtful, then asked, 'Why don't we have these kinds of shops in East Germany?'

'You should probably ask your grandfather.'

When, in November 1989, Patrick Ventura saw Havel and Dubček speaking to a million people in Wenceslas Square in Prague, he felt an overwhelming wave of elation passing through him. The people beside him were crying with joy and he cried with them. There wasn't a single person that evening in the square in Prague without a tear in their eye. It was as though the crowd had been overcome by an oceanic emotion that flooded the whole of humanity and made them feel, for a moment, beautiful, superhuman. It was the same feeling you got crying naked in the arms of a woman you love, having just made love, or when you cry alone coming out of jail and fall into the arms of your waiting relatives. That emotion that you feel only when you are deeply happy or finally free.

He had made sure to come to Prague. Everything suggested that the regime was breathing its last, otherwise they might have stopped him at the border for that affair of 1983 when, after his trial and sentence, he was deported from Czechoslovakia. He didn't regret that adventure and, more importantly, he now saw that the stance he had taken when they arrested him and Anna was the right one. Anyway, Patrick had never seriously considered collaborating with the Czechoslovak secret service. He had pretended he wanted to discuss it just to win time.

The next morning, hardly thinking about it, he let his steps lead him to the police museum. It was freezing and empty. There were no longer those candidates for party membership, who had to visit the museum as part of the recruitment process. Nor were there the rowdy pioneers, who would loiter noisily in its halls to get out of a few hours of class. Even on heroic Brek's stunted face Patrick saw the lines of fallen grandeur. He continued into the desolate museum, hearing only his own steps on the marble floor. In the room with the failed escape attempts, a new desk had been brought in. Behind it sat Anna.

Or rather, the ghost of the old Anna. The six years that had passed had aged her. There were streaks of white in her hair and her face was pale and gaunt. In her eyes was a sad and vacant look, as if something terrible had happened to her. She recognized him at once. Her hands jerked up and remained limp in front of her eyes, as if she had finally seen something that she had been afraid of for some time, but had convinced herself would never actually materialize.

She remained still as a pillar of salt, until Patrick approached her and asked, 'Why did you betray me?'

She seemed not to have the strength to speak, but in the end managed to say, 'I betrayed you, did I?'

'Let's not waste time. I know everything. What I'm asking is why you betrayed me.'

She bowed her head.

'For six years I have tried to find an answer to that question,' Patrick continued. 'I know you were afraid. A.K. explained to me in the psychiatric clinic that most people preferred the certainty of jail to the unknown element of freedom. I know that you did not trust me, because you were taught not to trust one another. I understand that, too. You aren't to blame. But I can't stomach the fact you didn't love me.'

'I didn't love you?' the woman behind the desk said mechanically.

'You didn't love me, because love presupposes freedom. It is a condition of free people. You weren't free. I know that you worked for the secret services. At some point you found yourself in a difficult position and decided to collaborate with them, but you went much too far and I can't forgive you for that. You make me sick, because you were sleeping with the head of the secret service.'

'With the head of the secret service? Where did you dream that up?'

'Don't try to deny it; I know everything. A member of the secret service can't fall in love, because love is subversive. I've told you before. A state of lovesick people would be ungovernable. You could have fallen in love with me, stopped spying on me, if you had staged a little revolution as Larissa did. She really is in love with Fabio.'

'Fabio, Larissa? Have you lost your mind? I don't know a Larissa.'

Patrick smiled.

'You know her: Miss KGB, who you tried to claim was Juliet.'

'Miss KGB? Juliet?' she repeated like a robot.

'I know you'll tell me that you did it for the child.'

'The child,' she said faintly. 'I don't have children.'

'You didn't do it for the child. You did it because you didn't believe that we could free the child. You don't believe in people and in love. You believe in power.'

Anna tried to speak, but Patrick had been waiting for years to say this.

'I know, I know. You'll tell me that you betrayed me to protect me, that it was the best you could have done. You all say the same thing, because you don't believe in people but in mechanisms. You executed me in the name of love.'

He felt relieved, saying what had tormented him for so long.

'I would have forgiven you everything, had you not stolen the thing that was most valuable to me.

'I stole…'

'My thoughts. You read my thoughts and turned them in.'

'But I didn't read your thoughts, Patrick.'

'You read them on the computer. And you know it, Marlene.'

'Marlene? I'm not called—'

'Yes, you're called Marlene. And you know that I'm not called Patrick. I'm called Kevin. Good luck,' he said, leaving.

He had reached the end of the room in the police museum when he turned and called, 'But you didn't succeed. You didn't manage to make me hate people or hate love.'

When we returned home, Marlene avoided looking me in the eye. Before she hid her face, falling to her knees and clutching Erich in her arms, I saw that her eyes were red. I glanced at the computer on my desk and saw that it was on. She had read the end of the novel.

I heard Erich asking her, 'Mama, I'm going to the cinema with Kevin. Do you want to come too?'

'We'll have to ask him.'

'Kevin, can we take Mama with us?'

At first I thought of suggesting she went to a Stasi or KGB special screening, but when I saw the boy's face alight with joy, I realized that it wouldn't be right to deprive him of his mother once more.

It was an evening premiere and you could hear a pin drop in the House of Cinema, near Mayakovskaya Square. The crème de la crème of Soviet intellectuals were there, as well as some of the bright minds of the Soviet leadership. Based on the phenomenon of criminality, the movie gave a tragic view of life in the Soviet Union. The title was taken from the legendary phrase of Gorbachev: 'We can't go on like this anymore.' The famous Soviet poet Yevgeny Yevtushenko, who had written a poem with the same title, was himself present.

Before the movie started, a well-known Soviet scriptwriter made a short but passionate introduction: 'This movie speaks about criminality. Not the usual criminality, but that special form of criminality that was born in our society and which we are all obliged to carry inside us. We felt proud when one of our brothers killed another; we were accustomed to the sight of the strong killing the weak. We were pleased that our culture and spirituality were destroyed, that the true workers and possessors of goods disappeared from the face of the earth. We sang happy songs when the so-called enemies of the people were put in front of firing squads. We felt joy when the sword of the new cold-blooded power decapitated one of us. In time, this behaviour produced an astonishing phenomenon: a hereditary criminality within each of us. We are victims of the pride, joy and pleasure we felt, of our coexistence with criminality. We are captives of the criminality that we ourselves created.'

A deathly silence reigned in the room. The speaker faltered, as if about to cry, took a deep breath and continued.

'The crime of the old power was their creation of a new type of person who learnt to hate instead of to love, who is afraid to love. Now we see that we cannot go on like this anymore, without loving humanity, but we realized this when we found ourselves in inhumanity. This movie is a study of the disfigurement of our country.'

An endless round of applause interrupted the speech. Many viewers around me were crying. I glanced at Marlene, sitting on the other side of Erich. She was watching the speech like a statue, as if she wasn't there. Larissa was in tears, and Giuseppe showed signs of annoyance.

'There is no love in the Soviet Union; we must accept that,' continued the man on the stage. 'We learnt to show solidarity with the Sandinistas and to love only the liberation movement in Africa. But now the ice is melting again. A couple of days ago I witnessed a scene that made me believe that the cherry trees will soon blossom again. It was a young couple on the escalators of the metro. Around them, hundreds of grey faces loaded with empty bags were running with coupons in their hands to make it to a state shop that they heard had some products left—all apart from the couple, who were exhibiting unusual, antisocial behaviour. The man was one stair below, taking advantage of the ease of the escalator. And what do you think he was doing for the entire ride? He was kissing his beloved, his eyes closed. They stopped kissing only when they reached land, and I saw their eyes shining. Where there are people kissing, everything is possible.

'Here lies hope. I don't believe that in one week, one month, six months or a year, three hundred and sixty kinds of cheese will appear, as in France, nor sixty kinds of German beer. But already from today, even though we have to continue working for a handful of roubles and struggling to survive, let's begin loving and falling in love. Let's concentrate on those age-old human activities. Let's agree that it isn't the worst side of our life, and that we don't have to feel guilt or shame for it. Besides, this sphere doesn't require emergency economic support from the West. Our women are beautiful and, as perestroika shows, our men still have great reserves of strength. It doesn't matter if we produce better missiles or how far we are off the per capita income of the states in the West. Let's compete with developed countries in the number of people whose eyes shine in the morning.'

Erich's behaviour during the movie made me smile: every time he particularly liked a scene he jumped up and cheered loudly. He reacted like that because he was used to watching movies in private viewings with friends of his age.

I stroked his head and whispered, 'Erich, you need to become a normal child.'

He turned and looked at me, surprised.

'Why, Kevin? Won't you be with us anymore?'

I smiled at him again.

'I need to leave tomorrow and I might not return to the Soviet Union. You must stay with your mother and begin a new life without, I'm afraid, private cinemas and all the grand stuff.'

Giuseppe had his objections when, in the interval, we went to the bar for a juice.

'I agree that many mistakes were made,' he admitted for the first time in his life. 'But what infinitely annoys me is this idealization of the West. They think Westerners live in paradise.'

We stopped our conversation, because the bell informed us that the second half was starting. Then Marlene spoke to me for the first time.

'Will you forgive me?'

I looked around. Erich had gone ahead with Larissa. I gave her a slap that she would never forget.

[1 December]

When I telephoned Yelin at ten in the morning he was in his office. He must have been expecting the call and, as it turned out, I had ruined his weekend.

'The day before yesterday I observed the activities of the KGB forces. It seems that your men continue working tirelessly through the night. I wonder if you pay them overtime.'

'You must know that I had no idea.'

'I'm afraid I don't care. You are a believer in the system that leads to these phenomena with mathematical precision.'

'Look where we've ended up: you're even giving us lessons.'

'When a whole society is brought up on the principle "the end justifies the means", the result is the same. Yesterday it was the Revolution, today it's the dollar. But I didn't call to moralize. I have a gift for you.'

'The video tape from that evening?'

'No, a political matryoshka. You keep on opening and you reach Lenin. The tape with your cuckold subordinates isn't a gift. It can only be exchanged.'

'For what?'

'For the file of Comrade Kevin Danaher. With all the details and evidence, as well as official confirmation from the KGB and the Soviet Ministry of Justice that everything that happened at Moscow 400 was a trap and that absolutely no accusation against me is pending. The goods will be exchanged in person.'

'OK. Where shall we meet?'

'The two of us don't need to meet again. Send one of your minions to the American embassy in an hour.'

'The embassy?' he asked, perplexed.

'Yes, I'll be there. I need to rectify something.'

He remained silent, as if wondering how to put his question.

'What will you do, Mr Danaher? Will you leave Moscow?'

It was the first time he had spoken formally to me.

'Perhaps, but not because you want me to. What will you do? I see the KGB collapsing. Half your agents are playing cuckold by night. As things are going, you'll be a general without an army.'

He cackled.

'Don't worry. It'll be born again, like a phoenix from the ashes.'

Half an hour later I was with Masha outside the embassy. I had begged the consul to come in for an emergency, but Masha was the last person he expected to see with me.

'My dear Mr Consul.'

'Why the formalities, Kevin?'

'Because, as it turned out, our relationship was always merely formal.'

He tried to laugh, without success, before bowing his head.

'Anyway,' I broke the silence, 'I want a visa for my fiancée.'

He looked as though he was about to lose any remaining hair.

'Your what?'

'My fiancée. Isn't that the only way for Soviets to get a visa for the United States? When the evil empire didn't let them travel, we were ready to receive them for reasons of propaganda. Now the crumbling Soviet Union lets them go, but the good empire won't accept them. The new wall is being built by us.'

I was speaking philosophically, but he insisted on getting involved in my family affairs.

'But, to her?'

'Come on, dear consul. Let's not deceive ourselves; she does the most honourable profession in the land. Besides, you've told me before that all labour is prostitution. Mine, yours…'

Vexed, he stamped Masha's passport. I gave it to her with a kiss on the cheek.

'Good luck. Earn the money you want then get out of there.'

Masha hadn't even left when, before the astonished eyes of the consul, I exchanged gifts with the man from the Ministry of Internal Affairs. I gave him the matryoshka and the tape, and he gave me the file and confirmations.

'Can you convey a message to Mr Yelin?' I asked him before he left.

'Gladly.'

'I want you to tell him that Eros has wings. He always escapes.'

I turned back to Hardman. After five hours of special briefing we were all exhausted.

'That's all of it. Yesterday afternoon I caught the aeroplane to New York.'

Hardman pointed to the sizeable grey file I had in front of me. He opened it and flicked through the official documents in Cyrillic script.

'That's fine, Mr Danaher. I will return the file in a couple of days. We need to perform a small check as a formality. I confess that my Russian is no better than my Greek. Thank you for your time. And you, Mr Weber.'

The big boss stood up and clasped my shoulders. I was dead from exhaustion but content.

'Kevin, if you want you can return to Moscow. You'll be bureau chief. But if you want to stay here, I've got another good proposition for you. We have time to discuss everything, but for the moment I want a series of articles on this story.'

'One moment, Mr Weber,' Hardman said. 'I'm afraid that many of these subjects cannot be presented as Mr Danaher has told them. They concern state secrets. Our relations with the Soviet Union are still fragile, and the situation is unstable. It might be necessary to wait some years before the story is published.'

Weber looked ready for a fight.

'But our Constitution—'

'Don't worry, Mr Weber,' I said. 'I need time to digest everything; it all happened so quickly. I'll write what we here don't consider to be state secrets, and the rest I'll write later.'

'Have you decided where you want to go?' Weber asked.

'I don't think I'll return to the Soviet Union. I experienced everything there. It was like a love affair—all that passionate love mingled with hatred, destined to end.'

EPILOGUE

> Love is the great discovery
> of our civilisation
>
> Octavio Paz

[A few years later]

I saw her four years later in an airport in New York. To be precise, I saw Ron first, that genial general-in-command of sex whom I had met in the Rossiya Hotel in Moscow. After him came Erich, and then her. It was July 1993 and a devilish, humid heat was baking New York City. Erich was now an adolescent, cultivating a wispy moustache, like a dissident of the Soviet Union, which had now collapsed. He was wearing a baseball cap, a Queen T-shirt and trainers of the kind advertised by basketball stars on the television. Ron looked contented. She was beautiful as ever.

She recognized me immediately and came over.

'Kevin, you look great. You haven't changed at all.'

'People don't change, Marlene. Ever.'

'Do you have news from Moscow?'

'From whom? Yelin?'

Her face cooled at once. The former head of the KGB was still in jail after the failed coup against Gorbachev.

'I'm joking. Everyone is fine. Fabio is still there, living with Larissa. She left the KGB and now represents Harlequin novels in Moscow. She's made a mint and they're soon getting married. Giuseppe is in Italy.

He jumped ship to the Democratic Party of the Left, established by former communists. To be precise, he became leader of the party. Pioneer is doing a roaring trade.'

'Pioneer,' she said, turning impulsively to Ron.

'I went to Moscow this spring. He's opened a club only for nouveaux riche women; entrance is forbidden to men. He has male strippers, organizes beauty contests for men and every Saturday morning an auction.'

'An auction?'

'Women compete on who will pay the most for the available men. He invited me along, and I laughed my ass off. Prices start at two hundred dollars for an evening, and beyond that the final price depends on the competition and the product. There are dozens of them: failed models, students, movie directors, former members of the Communist Youth. Every time a potential man is secured for a woman, Pioneer takes a ten per cent cut.'

'Isn't that ridiculous?'

'It's the revenge of Soviet women.'

'Are you still with Cynthia?'

'We split up. I had to stay consistent with what I had said and done back then. And you? Are you living here in New York?'

'Texas.'

'Are you in love?'

Ron was loading the bags onto the scales of the check-in desk.

'I'm calm and contented. Whether I'm in love... You know, I've thought a lot about our relationship. I think you were right in what you said about love being destroyed under communism. But here, too, I don't see many people in love.'

'Well, that's something we agree on. In your country, love was a slave of the state, but here it's a slave to profit. Love is everywhere, apart from in people's hearts. The more couples we see in love on the television, the fewer there are in real life. We live in a society that's opposed to love, where naked bodies only meet on screens. The object of our desire is a car, a pot of yoghurt, a vacuum cleaner. Yesterday evening I saw an advert in which a man telephones the owner of a car; he had stolen the car and wouldn't give it back, because he says he has fallen in love with it!

'Now we don't fall in love with people, but objects. People, real people, don't exist anywhere. And the worst thing is that we are used to this situation; we take our poison every day in small doses. It becomes necessary and we don't revolt. Our only reaction is to change channel with the remote, looking for another advert we can love. The last rebellion I saw was back then in Moscow, with Zolotov. I'm afraid your father-in-law—'

'What father-in-law?'

'I mean your former father-in-law. I'm afraid that he was right when he said that what matters is the battle for the conquest of the soul. The mistake he made was that the soul isn't conquered by secret police. What a relief that we have finished with those regimes! They preoccupied us for the entire twentieth century. They swept us into a fruitless debate about whether the future of humanity is communism. They threw us into the eddies of the Cold War, in which each side made its own situation look beautiful. The highest criterion was who had the weapons and the money, not which system places human beings at its centre. We're living in the wrong age, Marlene. We're living in an age in which they steal love, not cars.'

She remained silent for a moment. Then she noticed the bulletproof vest I was carrying.

'I'm leaving shortly. Final destination Sarajevo.'

'Bosnia? What are you doing there? Aren't you afraid?'

'Everyone is afraid of death.'

'I suppose you've been sent there for work.'

'No one is forced to go to Sarajevo. The last few years I've been covering the war in former Yugoslavia, so I want to go. Anyway, it's the most love-filled city in the world.'

'What? Sarajevo? They're killing each other.'

'Precisely because they're killing each other. Love is the only antidote to death: you become immortal, if only for a few moments.'

'You're still looking for ideal love, but you're in the wrong place. Where is humanity in Sarajevo? They're murdering one another.'

'Because there, too, politics—national objectives, preservation of power by every means, cultivation of hate against others—prevailed over love. Humanity and its emotions were ignored. But Sarajevo isn't only that ghastly public face that we see on the television. There is solidarity among people. The criterion for good or bad is not the make of your car, but your humanity. I don't support war, nor suggest it as a solution. War brings out the worst elements in humanity, but I think I've said that before?'

'What?'

'No, sorry, Patrick said that to Anna. Just as there is hatred in love, so in hatred born of war there is also passionate love. Whoever goes to the front or returns from it has one person in mind whom they want to meet more than anyone else: the person they love. Even in that multi-ethnic city, love exists because... Do you remember the first conversation we had on this subject?'

'At your apartment?'

'Yes, when we said that love was always subversive. Just as Larissa and Doctor Zhivago overcame the civil war in Russia, in the same way love between two people of different ethnicities in Sarajevo subverts the entire logic of war. The only antidote to war is love.'

'Come on, Mom.'

Erich interrupted our conversation. When he saw me he ran into my arms.

'Kevin, we've missed you. When will you come and see us? Oh, about that: Mom, you said that you wanted us to go to JFK airport... to meet...'

'What do you mean, Erich?' I asked. All of our adventures in Moscow flashed through my mind.

'We had tickets for this evening from the other airport, Newark. But Mom insisted we change to leave from here. Come on, Mom, let's go. It's the final call.'

Marlene looked as though she wanted to ask something.

'What happened with the novel? Did you publish it?'

'In the end I changed my mind. I decided to incorporate it into a new novel I'm writing about our own story.'

'I've got a title for you,' she said slyly. 'Never go to the post office alone.'

She made to leave, but I caught her arm. It was burning hot.

'I just want to clear up one point before I finish: was it a coincidence that we met at the post office or had Yelin told you to meet me?'

She wrapped her arms around Erich and, as they were leaving, turned to me. She had her usual mysterious and charming smile.

'As much a coincidence as our meeting here.'

READ THE MODERN GREEK CLASSICS

The Modern Greek Classics series highlights
the most significant writers, poets,
and works of literature of the nineteenth
and twentieth centuries in English translation.
A tour of Greece
through its literary history.

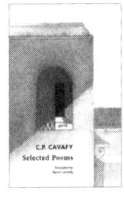

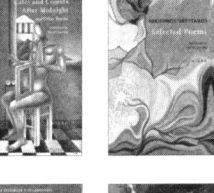

www.aiorabooks.com